By Salman Rushdie

FICTION

Grimus
Midnight's Children
Shame
The Satanic Verses
Haroun and the Sea of Stories
East, West
The Moor's Last Sigh
The Ground Beneath Her Feet
Fury
Shalimar the Clown
The Enchantress of Florence
Luka and the Fire of Life
Two Years Eight Months and Twenty-Eight Nights
The Golden House
Quichotte
Victory City

NONFICTION

Joseph Anton: A Memoir
The Jaguar Smile: A Nicaraguan Journey
Imaginary Homelands: Essays and Criticism 1981–1991
Step Across This Line: Collected Nonfiction 1992–2002
Languages of Truth: Essays 2003–2020

SCREENPLAY

Midnight's Children

ANTHOLOGIES

Mirrorwork: 50 Years of Indian Writing, 1947–1997 (co-editor)
Best American Short Stories 2008 (co-editor)

VICTORY CITY

SALMAN RUSHDIE

VICTORY CITY

A Novel

RANDOM HOUSE
NEW YORK

Published in the United States by Random House, an imprint and division of Penguin Random House LLC, New York.

Random House and the House colophon are registered trademarks of Penguin Random House LLC.

Published in the United Kingdom by Jonathan Cape, an imprint of Vintage, part of the Penguin Random House group of companies, and in Canada by Knopf Canada, an imprint of Penguin Random House Canada.

Library of Congress Cataloging-in-Publication Data

Names: Rushdie, Salman, author.
Title: Victory city: a novel / Salman Rushdie.
Description: First Edition. | New York: Random House, [2023]
Identifiers: LCCN 2022022929 (print) | LCCN 2022022930 (ebook) |
ISBN 9780593243398 (hardcover) | ISBN 9780593243404 (ebook)
Subjects: LCGFT: Novels.
Classification: LCC PR6068.U757 V53 2023 (print) |
LCC PR6068.U757 (ebook) | DDC 823/.914—dc23
LC record available at https://lccn.loc.gov/2022022929
LC ebook record available at https://lccn.loc.gov/2022022930

International edition ISBN 9780593597217

Printed in the United States of America on acid-free paper

randomhousebooks.com

2 4 6 8 9 7 5 3 1

First U.S. Edition

For Hanan

CONTENTS

PART ONE

| *Birth* |

1

On the last day of her life, when she was two hundred and forty-seven years old, the blind poet, miracle worker, and prophetess Pampa Kampana completed her immense narrative poem about Bisnaga and buried it in a clay pot sealed with wax in the heart of the ruined Royal Enclosure, as a message to the future. Four and a half centuries later we found that pot and read for the first time the immortal masterpiece named the *Jayaparajaya,* meaning "Victory and Defeat," written in the Sanskrit language, as long as the *Ramayana,* made up of twenty-four thousand verses, and we learned the secrets of the empire she had concealed from history for more than one hundred and sixty thousand days. We knew only the ruins that remained, and our memory of its history was ruined as well, by the passage of time, the imperfections of memory, and the falsehoods of those who came after. As we read Pampa Kampana's book the past was regained, the Bisnaga Empire was reborn as it truly had been, its women warriors, its mountains of gold, its generosity of spirit and its times of mean-spiritedness, its weaknesses and its strengths. We heard for the first time the full account of the kingdom that began and ended with a burning and a severed head. This is that story, retold in plainer language by the present author, who is neither a scholar nor a poet but merely a spinner of yarns, and who offers this version for the simple entertainment and possible edification of today's readers, the old and the young, the educated and the not so educated, those in search of wisdom and those amused by folly, northerners and southerners, followers of different gods and of no gods, the broad-minded and the narrow-minded, men and women and members of the genders beyond and in between, scions of the nobility and rank commoners, good people and rogues, charlatans and foreigners, humble sages, and egotistical fools.

The story of Bisnaga began in the fourteenth century of the Common Era, in the south of what we now call India, Bharat, Hindustan. The old king whose rolling head got everything going wasn't much of a monarch, just the type of ersatz ruler who crops up between the decline of one great kingdom and the rise of another. His name was Kampila of the tiny principality of Kampili, "Kampila Raya," *raya* being the regional version of *raja*, king. This second-rate *raya* had just about enough time on his third-rate throne to build a fourth-rate fortress on the banks of the Pampa river, to put a fifth-rate temple inside it, and to carve a few grandiose inscriptions into the side of a rocky hill, but then the army of the north came south to deal with him. The battle that followed was a one-sided affair, so unimportant that nobody bothered to give it a name. After the people from the north had routed Kampila Raya's forces and killed most of his army they grabbed hold of the phony king and chopped off his crownless head. Then they filled it with straw and sent it north for the pleasure of the Delhi sultan. There was nothing particularly special about the battle without a name, or about the head. In those days battles were commonplace affairs and naming them was a thing a lot of people didn't bother with; and severed heads were traveling across our great land all the time for the pleasure of this prince or that one. The sultan in his northern capital city had built up quite a collection.

After the insignificant battle, surprisingly, there was an event of the kind that changes history. The story goes that the women of the tiny, defeated kingdom, most of them recently widowed as a result of the no-name battle, left the fourth-rate fortress, after making final offerings at the fifth-rate temple, crossed the river in small boats, improbably defying the turbulence of the water, walked some distance to the west along the southern bank, and then lit a great bonfire and committed mass suicide in the flames. Gravely, without making any complaint, they said farewell to one another and walked forward without flinching. Nor were there any screams when their flesh caught fire and the stink of death filled the air. They burned in silence; only the crackling of the fire itself could be heard. Pampa Kampana saw it all happen. It was as if the universe itself was sending her a message, saying, open your ears, breathe in, and learn. She was nine years old and stood watching with tears in her eyes, holding her dry-eyed mother's hand as tightly as she could, while all the women she knew entered the fire and sat or stood or lay in the heart of the furnace spouting flames from their ears and mouths: the old woman who had seen everything and the young woman just starting out in life and the girl who hated her father the dead soldier and the wife who was ashamed of her husband because he hadn't given up his life on the battlefield and the woman with the beautiful singing voice and the woman with the frightening laugh and the woman as skinny as a stick and the woman as fat as a melon. Into the fire they marched and the stench of their death made Pampa feel like retching and then to her horror her own mother Radha Kampana gently detached her hand and very slowly but with absolute conviction walked forward to join the bonfire of the dead, without even saying goodbye.

For the rest of her life Pampa Kampana, who shared a name with the river on whose banks all this happened, would carry the scent of her mother's burning flesh in her nostrils. The pyre was made of perfumed sandalwood, and an abundance of cloves and garlic and cumin seeds and sticks of cinnamon had been added to it as if the burning ladies were being prepared as a well-spiced dish to set before the sultan's victorious generals for their gastronomic delight, but those fragrances—the turmeric, the big cardamoms, and the little cardamoms too—failed to mask the unique, cannibal pungency of women being cooked alive, and made their odor, if anything, even harder to bear. Pampa Kampana never ate meat again, and could not bring herself to remain in any kitchen in which it was being prepared. All such dishes exuded the memory of her mother and when other people ate dead animals Pampa Kampana had to avert her gaze.

Pampa's own father had died young, long before the nameless battle, so her mother was not one of the newly widowed. Arjuna Kampana had died so long ago that Pampa had no memory of his face. All she knew about him was what Radha Kampana had told her, that he had been a kind man, the well-loved potter of the town of Kampili, and that he had encouraged his wife to learn the potter's art as well, so after he died she took over his trade and proved to be more than his equal. Radha, in turn, had guided little Pampa's hands at the potter's wheel and the child was already a skilled thrower of pots and bowls and had learned an important lesson, which was that there was no such thing as men's work. Pampa Kampana had believed that this would be her life, making beautiful things with her mother, side by side at the wheel. But that dream was over now. Her mother had let go of her hand and abandoned her to her fate.

For a long moment Pampa tried to convince herself that her mother was just being sociable and going along with the crowd, because she had always been a woman for whom the friendship of women was of paramount importance. She told herself that the undulating wall of fire was a curtain behind which the ladies had gathered to gossip, and soon they would all walk out of the flames, unharmed, maybe a little scorched, smelling a little of kitchen perfumes, perhaps, but that would pass soon enough. And then Pampa and her mother would go home.

Only when she saw the last slabs of roasted flesh fall away from Radha Kampana's bones to reveal the naked skull did she understand that her childhood was over and from now on she must conduct herself as an adult and never commit her mother's last mistake. She would laugh at death and turn her face toward life. She would not sacrifice her body merely to follow dead men into the afterworld. She would refuse to die young and live, instead, to be impossibly, defiantly old. It was at this point that she received the celestial blessing that would change everything, because this was the moment when the goddess Pampa's voice, as old as Time, started coming out of her nine-year-old mouth.

It was an enormous voice, like the thunder of a high waterfall booming in a valley of sweet echoes. It possessed a music she had never heard before, a melody to which she later gave the name of *kindness.* She was terrified, of course, but also reassured. This was not a possession by a demon. There was goodness in the voice, and majesty. Radha Kampana had once told her that two of the highest deities of the pantheon had spent the earliest days of their courtship near here, by the angry waters of the rushing river. Perhaps this was the queen of the gods herself, returning in a time of death to the place where her own love had been born. Like the river, Pampa Kampana had been named after the deity—"Pampa" was one of the goddess Parvati's local names, and her lover Shiva, the mighty Lord of the Dance himself, had appeared to her here in his local, three-eyed incarnation—so it all began to make sense. With a feeling of serene detachment Pampa, the human being, began to listen to the words of Pampa, the goddess, coming out of her mouth. She had no more control over them than a member of the audience has over the monologue of the star, and her career as a prophet and miracle worker began.

Physically, she didn't feel any different. There were no unpleasant side effects. She didn't tremble, or feel faint, or experience a hot flush, or a cold sweat. She didn't froth at the mouth or fall down in an epileptic fit, as she had been led to believe could happen, and had happened to other people, in such cases. If anything, there was a great calm surrounding her like a soft cloak, reassuring her that the world was still a good place and things would work out well.

"From blood and fire," the goddess said, "life and power will be born. In this exact place a great city will rise, the wonder of the world, and its empire will last for more than two centuries. And you," the goddess addressed Pampa Kampana directly, giving the young girl the unique experience of being personally spoken to by a supernatural stranger speaking through her own mouth, "you will fight to make sure that no more women are ever burned in this fashion, and that men start considering women in new ways, and you will live just long enough to witness both your success and your failure, to see it all and tell its story, even though once you have finished telling it you will die immediately and nobody will remember you for four hundred and fifty years." In this way Pampa Kampana learned that a deity's bounty was always a two-edged sword.

She began to walk without knowing where she was going. If she had lived in our time she might have said that the landscape looked like the surface of the moon, the pockmarked plains, the valleys of dirt, the rock piles, the emptiness, the sense of a melancholy void where burgeoning life should have been. But she had no sense of the moon as a place. To her it was just a shining god in the sky. On and on she walked until she began to see miracles. She saw a cobra using its hood to shield a pregnant frog from the heat of the sun. She saw a rabbit turn and face a dog that was hunting it, and bite the dog on its nose and make it run away. These wonders made her feel that something marvelous was at hand. Soon after these visions, which might have been sent as signs by the gods, she arrived at the little *mutt* at Mandana.

A *mutt* could also be called a *peetham* but to avoid confusion let us simply say: it was a monk's dwelling. Later, as the empire grew, the Mandana *mutt* became a grand place extending all the way to the banks of the rushing river, an enormous complex employing thousands of priests, servitors, tradesmen, craftsmen, janitors, elephant keepers, monkey handlers, stable hands, and workers in the *mutt*'s extensive paddy fields, and it was revered as the sacred place where emperors came for advice, but in this early time before the beginning began it was humble, little more than an ascetic's cave and a vegetable patch, and the resident ascetic, still a young man at that time, a twenty-five-year-old scholar with long curly locks flowing down his back all the way to his waist, went by the name of Vidyasagar, which meant that there was a knowledge-ocean, a *vidya-sagara,* inside his large head. When he saw the girl approaching with hunger on her tongue and madness in her eyes he understood at once that she had witnessed terrible things and gave her water to drink and what little food he had.

After that, at least in Vidyasagar's version of events, they lived together easily enough, sleeping on opposite corners of the floor of the cave, and they got along fine, in part because the monk had sworn a solemn vow of abstinence from the things of the flesh, so that even when Pampa Kampana blossomed into the grandeur of her beauty he never laid a finger on her although the cave wasn't very big and they were alone in the dark. For the rest of his life that was what he said to anyone who asked—and there were people who asked, because the world is a cynical and suspicious place and, being full of liars, thinks of everything as a lie. Which is what Vidyasagar's story was.

Pampa Kampana, when asked, did not reply. From an early age she acquired the ability of shutting away from her consciousness many of the evils that life handed out. She had not yet understood or harnessed the power of the goddess within her, so she had not been able to protect herself when the supposedly abstinent scholar crossed the invisible line between them and did what he did. He did not do it often, because scholarship usually left him too tired to do much about his lusts, but he did it often enough, and every time he did it she erased his deed from her memory by an act of will. She also erased her mother, whose self-sacrifice had sacrificed her daughter upon the altar of the ascetic's desires, and for a long time she tried to tell herself that what happened in the cave was an illusion, and that she had never had a mother at all.

In this way she was able to accept her fate in silence; but an angry power began to grow in her, a force from which the future would be born. In time. All in good time.

She did not say a single word for the next nine years, which meant that Vidyasagar, who knew many things, didn't even know her name. He decided to call her Gangadevi, and she accepted the name without complaint, and helped him gather berries and roots to eat, to sweep out their poor residence, and to haul water from the well. Her silence suited him perfectly, because on most days he was lost in meditation, considering the meanings of the sacred texts which he had learned by heart, and seeking answers to two great questions: whether wisdom existed or there was only folly, and the related question of whether there was such a thing as *vidya*, true knowledge, or only many different kinds of ignorance, and true knowledge, after which he was named, was possessed only by the gods. In addition, he thought about peace, and asked himself how to ensure the triumph of nonviolence in a violent age.

This was how men were, Pampa Kampana thought. A man philosophized about peace but in his treatment of the helpless girl sleeping in his cave his deeds were not in alignment with his philosophy.

Although the girl was silent as she grew into a young woman, she wrote copiously in a strong flowing hand, which astonished the sage, who had expected her to be illiterate. After she began to speak she admitted that she didn't know she could write either, and put the miracle of her literacy down to the benevolent intervention of the goddess. She wrote almost every day, and allowed Vidyasagar to read her scribblings, so that during those nine years the awestruck sage became the first witness of the flowering of her poetic genius. This was the period in which she composed what became the Prelude to her *Victory and Defeat*. The subject of the main part of the poem would be the history of Bisnaga from its creation to its destruction, but those things still lay in the future. The Prelude dealt with antiquity, telling the story of the monkey kingdom of Kishkindha, which had flourished in that region long ago in the Time of Fable, and it contained a vivid account of the life and deeds of Lord Hanuman the monkey king, who could grow as big as a mountain and leap across the sea. It is generally agreed by scholars and ordinary readers alike that the quality of Pampa Kampana's verse rivals, and perhaps even improves upon, the language of the *Ramayana* itself.

After the nine years were over, the two Sangama brothers came to call: the tall, gray-haired, good-looking one who stood very still and looked deep into your eyes as if he could see your thoughts, and his much younger sibling, the small rotund one who buzzed around him, and everyone else, like a bee. They were cowherds from the hill town of Gooty who had gone to war, war being one of the growth industries of the time; they had joined up with a local princeling's army, and because they were amateurs in the arts of killing they had been captured by the Delhi sultan's forces and sent into the north, where to save their skins they pretended to be converted to the religion of their captors and then escaped soon afterward, shedding their adopted faith like an unwanted shawl, getting away before they could be circumcised according to the requirements of the religion in which they didn't really believe. They were local boys, they now explained, and they had heard of the wisdom of the sage Vidyasagar and, to be honest, they had also heard of the beauty of the mute young woman who lived with him, and so here they were in search of some good advice.

They did not come empty-handed. They brought baskets of fresh fruits and a sack of nuts and an urn filled with milk from their favorite cow, and also a sack of seeds, which turned out to be the thing that changed their lives. Their names, they said, were Hukka and Bukka Sangama—Hukka the handsome oldster and Bukka the young bee—and after their escape from the north they were looking for a new direction in life. The care of cows had ceased to be enough for them after their military escapade, they said, their horizons were wider now and their ambitions were greater, so they would appreciate any guidance, any ripples flowing from the amplitude of the Ocean of Knowledge, any whispers from the deeps of wisdom that the sage might be willing to offer, anything at all that might show them the way. "We know of you as the great apostle of peace," Hukka Sangama said. "We're not so keen on soldiering ourselves, after our recent experiences. Show us the fruits that nonviolence can grow."

To everyone's surprise it was not the monk but his eighteen-year-old companion who replied, in an ordinary, conversational voice, strong and low, a voice that gave no hint that it hadn't been used for nine years. It was a voice by which both brothers were instantly seduced. "Suppose you had a sackful of seeds," she said. "Then suppose you could plant them and grow a city, and grow its inhabitants too, as if people were plants, budding and flowering in the spring, only to wither in the autumn. Suppose now that these seeds could grow generations, and bring forth a history, a new reality, an empire. Suppose they could make you kings, and your children too, and your children's children."

"Sounds good," said young Bukka, the more outspoken of the brothers, "but where are we supposed to find seeds like that? We are only cowherds, but we know better than to believe in fairy tales."

"Your name, Sangama, is a sign," she said. "A *sangam* is a confluence, such as the creation of the river Pampa by the joining of the Tunga and Bhadra rivers, which were created by the sweat pouring down the two sides of the head of Lord Vishnu, and so it also means the flowing together of different parts to make a new kind of whole. This is your destiny. Go to the place of the women's sacrifice, the sacred place where my mother died, which is also the place where in ancient times Lord Ram and his brother Lakshman joined forces with the mighty Lord Hanuman of Kishkindha and went forth to battle many-headed Ravana of Lanka, who had abducted the lady Sita. You two are brothers just as Ram and Lakshman were. Build your city there."

Now the sage spoke up. "It's not such a bad start, being cowherds," he said. "The sultanate of Golconda was started by shepherds, you know—in fact its name means 'the shepherds' hill'—but those shepherds lucked out because they discovered that the place was rich in diamonds, and now they are diamond princes, owners of the Twenty-Three Mines, discoverers of most of the world's pink diamonds, and possessors of the Great Table Diamond, which they keep in the deepest dungeon of their mountaintop fortress, the most impregnable castle in the land, even harder to take than Mehrangarh, up in Jodhpur, or Udayagiri, right down the road."

"And your seeds are better than diamonds," the young woman said, handing back the sack that the brothers had brought with them.

"What, these seeds?" Bukka asked, very surprised. "But these are just an ordinary assortment we brought along as a gift for your vegetable patch—they are for okra, beans, and snake gourds, all mixed up together."

The prophetess shook her head. "Not anymore," she said. "Now these are the seeds of the future. Your city will grow from them."

The two brothers realized at that moment that they were both truly, deeply, and forever in love with this strange beauty who was clearly a great sorceress, or at the very least a person touched by a god and granted exceptional powers. "They say Vidyasagar gave you the name of Gangadevi," Hukka said. "But what is your real name? I would very much like to know that, so that I can remember you in the manner your parents intended."

"Go and make your city," she said. "Come back and ask me my name again when it has sprouted up out of rocks and dust. Maybe I'll tell you then."

2

After they had come to the designated place and scattered the seeds, their hearts filled with great perplexity and just a little hope, the two Sangama brothers climbed to the top of a hill of large boulders and thornbushes that tore at their peasant clothes, and sat down in the late afternoon to wait and watch. After no more than an hour, they saw the air begin to shimmer as it does during the hottest hours of the hottest days, and then the miracle city started growing before their astonished eyes, the stone edifices of the central zone pushing up from the rocky ground, and the majesty of the royal palace, and the first great temple too. (This was forever afterward known as the Underground Temple, because it had emerged from a place beneath the earth's surface, and also as the Monkey Temple, because from the moment of its rising it swarmed with long-tailed gray temple monkeys of the breed known as Hanuman langurs, chattering among themselves and ringing the temple's many bells, and because of the gigantic sculpture of Lord Hanuman himself that rose up with it, to stand by its gates.) All these and more arose in old-fashioned splendor and stared down toward the palace and the Royal Enclosure spreading out at the far end of the long market street. The mud, wood and cowshit hovels of the common people also made their humble way into the air at the city's periphery.

• • •

(A note on monkeys. It may be useful to observe here that monkeys will play a significant role in Pampa Kampana's narrative. In these early verses the benevolent shadow of mighty Lord Hanuman falls across her pages, and his power and courage become characteristics of Bisnaga, the real-life successor to his mythical Kishkindha. Later, however, there will be other, malevolent monkeys to confront. There is no need to anticipate those events any further. We merely point out the dualist, binary nature of the monkey motif in the work.)

In those first moments the city was not yet fully alive. Spreading out from the shadow of the barren bouldered hills, it looked like a shining cosmopolis whose inhabitants had all abandoned it. The villas of the rich stood unoccupied, villas with stone foundations upon which stood graceful, pillared structures of brick and wood; the canopied market stalls were empty, awaiting the arrival of florists, butchers, tailors, wine merchants, and dentists; in the red-light district there were brothels, but, as yet, no whores. The river rushed along and the banks where washerwomen and washermen would do their work seemed to wait expectantly for some action, some movement that would give meaning to the place. In the Royal Enclosure the great Elephant House with its eleven arches anticipated the coming of the tuskers and their dung.

Then life began, and hundreds—no, thousands—of men and women were born full-grown from the brown earth, shaking the dirt off their garments, and thronging the streets in the evening breeze. Stray dogs and bony cows walked in the streets, trees burst into blossom and leaf, and the sky swarmed with parrots, yes, and crows. There was laundry upon the riverbank, and royal elephants trumpeting in their mansion, and armed guards—women!—at the Royal Enclosure's gates. An army camp could be seen beyond the city's boundary, a substantial cantonment in which stood an awesome force of thousands more newborn human beings, equipped with clattering armor and weapons, as well as ranks of elephants, camels, and horses, and siege weaponry—battering rams, trebuchets, and the like.

"This is what it must feel like to be a god," Bukka Sangama said to his brother in a trembling voice. "To perform the act of creation, a thing only the gods can do."

"We must become gods now," Hukka said, "to make sure the people worship us." He looked up into the sky. "There, you see," he pointed. "There is our father, the Moon."

"No," Bukka shook his head. "We'll never get away with that."

"The great Moon God, our ancestor," said Hukka, making it up as he went along, "he had a son, whose name was Budha. And then after a number of generations the family line arrived at the Moon King of the mythological era. Pururavas. That was his name. He had two sons, Yadu and Turvasu. Some say there were five, but I say two is plenty. And we are the sons of the sons of Yadu. Thus we are a part of the illustrious Lunar Lineage, like the great warrior Arjuna in the *Mahabharata*, and even Lord Krishna himself."

"There are five of us too," Bukka said. "Five Sangamas, like the five sons of the Moon King. Hukka, Bukka, Pukka, Chukka, and Dev."

"That may be so," Hukka said. "But I say two is plenty. Our brothers are not noble characters. They are disreputable. They are unworthy. But yes, we will have to work out what to do with them."

"Let's go down and take a look at the palace," Bukka suggested. "I hope there are plenty of servants and cooks and not just a bunch of empty chambers of state. I hope there are beds as soft as clouds and maybe a women's wing of ready-made wives of unimaginable beauty as well. We should celebrate, right? We aren't cowherds anymore."

"But cows will remain important to us," Hukka proposed.

"Metaphorically, you mean," Bukka asked. "I'm not planning to do any more milking."

"Yes," Hukka Sangama said. "Metaphorically, of course."

They were both silent for a while, awed by what they had brought into being. "If something can come out of nothing like this," Bukka finally said, "maybe anything is possible in this world, and we can really be great men, although we will need to have great thoughts as well, and we don't have any seeds for those."

Hukka was thinking along different lines. "If we can grow people like tapioca plants," he mused, "then it doesn't matter how many soldiers we lose in battle, because there will be plenty more where they came from, and therefore we will be invincible and will be able to conquer the world. These thousands are just a beginning. We will grow hundreds of thousands of citizens, maybe a million, and a million soldiers as well. There are plenty of seeds left. We barely used half the sack."

Bukka was thinking about Pampa Kampana. "She talked a lot about peace but if that's what she wants why did she grow us this army?" he wondered. "Is it peace she really wants, or revenge? For her mother's death, I mean."

"It's up to us now," Hukka told him. "An army can be a force for peace as well as war."

"And another thing I'm wondering," Bukka said. "Those people down there, our new citizens—the men, I mean—do you think they are circumcised or not circumcised?"

Hukka pondered this question. "What do you want to do?" he asked finally. "Do you want to go down there and ask them all to open their lungis, pull down their pajamas, unwrap their sarongs? You think that's a good way to begin?"

"The truth is," Bukka replied, "I don't really care. It's probably a mixture, and so what."

"Exactly," Hukka said. "So what."

"So I don't care if you don't care," Bukka said.

"I don't care," Hukka replied.

"Then so what," Bukka confirmed.

They were silent again, staring down at the miracle, trying to accept its incomprehensibility, its beauty, its consequences. "We should go and introduce ourselves," Bukka said after a while. "They need to know who's in charge."

"There's no rush," Hukka replied. "I think we're both a little crazy right now, because we are in the middle of a great craziness, and we both need a minute to absorb it, and to get a grip on our sanity again. And in the second place . . ." And here he paused.

"Yes?" Bukka urged him on. "What's in the second place?"

"In the second place," Hukka said slowly, "we have to decide which one of the two of us is going to be king first, and who will be in the second place."

"Well," Bukka said, hopefully, "I'm the smartest."

"That's debatable," Hukka said. "However, I'm the oldest."

"And I'm the most likable."

"Again, debatable. But I repeat: I'm the oldest."

"Yes, you're old. But I'm the most dynamic."

"Dynamic isn't the same thing as regal," Hukka said. "And I'm still the oldest."

"You say that as if it's some sort of commandment," Bukka protested. "Oldest goes first. Where does it say that? Where's that written down?"

Hukka's hand moved to the hilt of his sword. "Here," he said.

A bird flew across the sun. The earth itself took a deep breath. The gods, if there were any gods, stopped doing what they were doing and paid attention.

Bukka gave in. "Okay, okay," he said, raising his hands in surrender. "You're my older brother and I love you and you go first."

"Thank you," said Hukka. "I love you too."

"But," Bukka added, "I get to decide the next thing."

"Agreed," said Hukka Sangama, who was now King Hukka—Hukka Raya I. "You get first pick of bedrooms in the palace."

"And concubines," Bukka insisted.

"Yes, yes," Hukka Raya I said, waving an irritated hand. "And concubines as well."

After another moment's silence, Bukka attempted a great thought. "What is a human being?" he wondered. "I mean, what makes us what we are? Did we all start out as seeds, are all our ancestors vegetables, if we go back far enough? Or did we grow out of fishes, are we fishes who learned to breathe air? Or maybe we are cows who lost our udders and two of our legs. Somehow I'm finding the vegetable possibility the most upsetting. I don't want to discover that my great-grandfather was a brinjal, or a pea."

"And yet it is from seeds that our subjects have been born," Hukka said, shaking his head. "So the vegetable possibility is the most probable."

"Things are simpler for vegetables," mused Bukka. "You have your roots, so you know your place. You grow, and you serve your purpose by propagating and then being consumed. But we are rootless and we don't want to be eaten. So how are we supposed to live? What is a human life? What's a good life and what isn't? Who and what are these thousands we have just brought into being?"

"The question of origins," Hukka said gravely, "we must leave to the gods. The question we must answer is this one: now that we find ourselves here—and they, our seed people, are down there—how shall we live?"

"If we were philosophers," Bukka said, "we could answer such questions philosophically. But we are poor cowherds only, who became unsuccessful soldiers, and have suddenly somehow risen above our station, so we had better just get down there and begin, and find out the answers by being there and seeing how things work out. An army is a question, and the answer to the question of the army is to fight. A cow is a question too, and the answer to the question of the cow is to milk it. Down there is a city that appeared out of nowhere, and that's a bigger question than we have ever been asked. And so maybe the answer to the question of the city is to live in it."

"Also," Hukka said, "we should get on with that before our brothers arrive and try to steal a march on us."

But still, as if dazed, the two brothers remained on the hill, immobile, watching the movement of the new people in the streets of the new city below them, and often shaking their heads in disbelief. It was as if they feared going down into those streets, afraid that the whole thing was some sort of hallucination, and that if they entered it the deception would be revealed, the vision would dissolve, and they would return to the previous nothingness of their lives. Perhaps their stunned condition explained why they did not notice that the people in the new streets, and in the army camp beyond, were behaving peculiarly, as if they, too, had been driven a little crazy by their incomprehension of their own sudden existence, and were incapable of dealing with the fact of having been brought into being out of nowhere. There was a good deal of shouting, and of crying, and some of the people were rolling on the ground and kicking their legs in the air, punching the air as if to say, *Where am I, let me out of here.* In the fruit and vegetable market people were throwing produce at one another, and it was unclear if they were playing or expressing their inarticulate rage. In fact they seemed incapable of expressing what they truly wanted, food, or shelter, or someone to explain the world to them and make them feel safe in it, someone whose soft words could grant them the happy illusion of understanding what they could not understand. The fights in the army camp, where the new people carried weapons, were more dangerous, and there were injuries.

The sun was already diving toward the horizon when Hukka and Bukka finally made their way down the rocky hill. As evening shadows crawled across the many enigmatic boulders that crowded around their path it seemed to them both that the stones were acquiring human faces, with hollow eyes which were examining them closely, as if to ask, *What, are these unimpressive individuals the ones who brought a whole city to life?* Hukka, who was already putting on royal airs like a boy trying on the new birthday clothes his parents had left at the foot of his bed while he slept, chose to ignore the staring stones, but Bukka grew afraid, because the stones didn't seem to be their friends, and could easily start an avalanche that would bury the two brothers forever before they were able to step into their glorious future. The new city was surrounded by rocky hillsides of this sort, except along the riverbank, and all the boulders on all the hills now seemed to have become giant heads, whose faces wore hostile frowns, and whose mouths were on the verge of speech. They never spoke, but Bukka made a note. "We are surrounded by enemies," he told himself, "and if we are not quick to defend ourselves against them they will thunder down upon us and crush us to bits." Aloud he said to his brother the king, "You know what this city doesn't have, and needs as soon as possible? Walls. High, thick walls, strong enough to withstand any attack."

Hukka nodded his assent. "Build them," he said.

Then they entered the city and, as night fell, found themselves at the dawn of time, and in the midst of the chaos which is the first condition of all new universes. By now many of their new progeny had fallen asleep, in the street, on the doorstep of the palace, in the shadow of the temple, everywhere. There was also a rank odor in the air, because hundreds of the citizens had fouled their garments. Those who were not asleep were like sleepwalkers, empty people with empty eyes, walking the streets like automata, buying fruit at the fruit stalls without knowing what they were putting in their baskets, or selling the fruits without knowing what they were called, or, at the stalls offering religious paraphernalia, buying and selling enamel eyes, pink and white with black irises, selling and buying these and many other trinkets to be used in the temple's daily devotions, without knowing which deities liked to receive what offerings, or why. It was night now, but even in the darkness the sleepwalkers continued buying, selling, roaming the confused streets, and their glazed presences were even more alarming than the stinking sleepers.

The new king, Hukka, was dismayed at the condition of his subjects. "It looks like that witch has given us a kingdom of subhumans," he cried. "These people are as brainless as cows, and they don't even have udders to give us milk."

Bukka, the more imaginative of the two brothers, put a consoling hand on Hukka's shoulder. "Calm down," he said. "Even human babies take some time to emerge from their mothers and start breathing air. And when they emerge they have no idea what to do, and so they cry, they laugh, they piss and shit, and they wait for their parents to take care of everything. I think what's happening here is that our city is still in the process of being born, and all these people, including all the grown-ups, are babies right now, and we just have to hope that they grow up fast, because we don't have mothers to care for them."

"And if you're right, what are we supposed to do with this half-born crowd?" Hukka wanted to know.

"We wait," Bukka told him, having no better idea to offer. "This is the first lesson of your new kingship: patience. We must allow our new citizens—our new subjects—to become real, to grow into their newly created selves. Do they even know their names? Where do they think they came from? It's a problem. Maybe they will change quickly. Maybe by the morning they will have become men and women, and we can talk about everything. Until then, there's nothing to be done."

The full moon burst out of the sky like a descending angel and bathed the new world in milky light. And on that moon-blessed night at the beginning of the beginning the Sangama brothers understood that the act of creation was only the first of many necessary acts, that even the powerful magic of the seeds could not provide everything that was needed. They themselves were exhausted, worn out by everything they had wrought, and so they made their way into the palace.

Here different rules seemed to apply. As they approached the arched gate into the first courtyard they saw a full complement of servitors standing before them like statues, equerries and grooms frozen beside their immobile horses, musicians on a stage leaning into their silent instruments, and any number of household servants and aides, dressed in such finery as was appropriate for those who served a king—cockaded turbans, brocaded coats, shoes that curled up at their pointed toes, necklaces, and rings. No sooner had Hukka and Bukka passed through the gate than the scene sprang to life, and all was bustle and hum. Courtiers rushed forward to escort them, and these were not the big babies of the city streets, but grown men and women, well-spoken and knowledgeable, and fully competent to carry out their duties. A flunky approached Hukka carrying a crown on a red velvet cushion, and Hukka set it happily on his head, noting that it was a perfect fit. He received the service of the palace staff as if it was his right and his due, but Bukka, walking a step or two behind him, had other thoughts. *Looks like even the magic seeds have one rule for the rulers and another for the ruled,* he reflected. *But if the ruled continue to be unruly it won't be easy to rule them.*

The bedroom suites were so lavishly appointed that the question of who slept where was resolved without much discussion, and there were lords of the bedchamber to bring them their nightgowns and show them the wardrobes filled with royal garments appropriate to their stature. But they were too tired to take in much about their new home, or to be interested in concubines, and within moments they were both fast asleep.

In the morning things were different. "How is the city today?" Hukka asked the courtier who came into his bedroom to draw back the curtains. This individual turned and bowed deeply. "Perfect, as always, sire," he replied. "The city thrives under Your Majesty's rule, today and every day."

Hukka and Bukka summoned horses and rode out to see the state of things for themselves. They were astonished to find a metropolis bustling about its business, thronged with adults behaving like grown-ups and children running around their feet as children should. It was as if everyone had lived here for years, as if the adults had been children there, and grown to adulthood, and married, and raised children of their own; as if they possessed memories and histories, and formed a long-established community, a city of love and death, tears and laughter, loyalty and betrayal, and everything else that human nature contains, everything that, when added together, adds up to the meaning of life, all conjured up out of nothing by the magic seeds. The noises of the city—street vendors, horses' hooves, the clatter of carts, songs and arguments—filled the air. In the military cantonment a formidable army stood at the ready, awaiting its lords' commands.

"How did this happen?" Hukka asked his brother in wonderment.

"There's your answer," said Bukka, pointing.

Coming toward them through the crowd, dressed in an ascetic's simple saffron wrap, and carrying a wooden staff, was Pampa Kampana, with whom they were both in love. There was a fire blazing in her eyes, which would not be extinguished for more than two hundred years.

"We built the city," Hukka said to her. "You said when we had done that we could ask you for your real name."

So Pampa Kampana told them her name, and congratulated them as well. "You've done well," she said. "They just needed someone to whisper their dreams into their ears."

"The people needed a mother," Bukka said. "Now they have one, and everything works."

"The city needs a queen," said Hukka Raya I. "Pampa is a good name for a queen."

"I can't be the queen of a town without a name," said Pampa Kampana. "What's it called, this city of yours?"

"I'll name it Pampanagar," Hukka said. "Because you built it, not us."

"That would be vanity," said Pampa Kampana. "Choose another name."

"Vidyanagar, then," said Hukka. "After the great sage. The city of wisdom."

"He would refuse that too," Pampa Kampana said. "I refuse it for him."

"Then I don't know," said Hukka Raya I. "Maybe Vijaya."

"Victory," Pampa Kampana said. "The city is a victory, that's true. But I don't know if such boastfulness is wise."

The question of the name would remain unresolved until the stammering foreigner came to town.

3

The Portuguese visitor arrived on Easter Sunday. His name was Sunday as well—Domingo Nunes—and he was as handsome as the daylight, his eyes the green of the grass at dawn, his hair the red of the sun as it set, and he had a speech impediment that only made him more charming to the people of the new city, because it allowed him to avoid the arrogance of white men when confronted with darker skins. His business was horses, but in truth that was just a pretext, because his real love was travel. He had seen the world from Alpha to Omega, from up to down, from give to take, from win to lose, and he had learned that wherever he went the world was illusion, and that that was beautiful. He had been in floods and fires and other hairbreadth escapes, and had seen deserts, quarries, rocks, and hills whose heads touched heaven. Or so he said. He had been sold into slavery, and afterward redeemed, and after that he had gone on journeying, telling the stories of his travels to all who would listen, and those tales were not of the humdrum quotidian variety, not accounts of the everydayness of the world, but of its wonders; or, rather, they were stories that insisted that human life was not banal, but extraordinary. And when he arrived in the new city he understood immediately that it was one of the greatest of miracles, a marvel to be compared to the Egyptian Pyramids, the Hanging Gardens of Babylon, or the Colossus of Rhodes. Accordingly, after he had sold the string of horses he had brought from the port of Goa to the head groom at the army cantonment, he went immediately to observe the golden city wall with disbelieving eyes—as he afterward wrote in the journal of his visit, sections of which were quoted by Pampa Kampana in her book. The wall was rising from the ground as he watched, higher every hour, smoothly dressed stones appearing out of nowhere and placing themselves alongside and on top of one another in immaculate alignment without any visible sign of stonemasons or other workers; which was possible only if some great occultist was nearby, conjuring the fortifications into being with a wave of his imperious wand.

"Foreigner! Come here!" Domingo Nunes had learned enough of the local language to understand that he was being addressed, peremptorily, with little attempt at courtesy. In the shadow of the barbican gate that stood between the city and the cantonment, its twin towers rising higher and higher into the sky as he watched, a small man was leaning out between the curtains of a lordly palanquin. "You! Foreigner! Here!"

The man was either a rude buffoon, or a prince, or both, thought Domingo Nunes. He decided to be on the safe side, and answer discourtesy with courtesy. "At your sir sir service sir," he declared with a deep bow, which impressed Crown Prince Bukka, who was still getting used to being a person before whom strangers bowed deeply.

"Are you the horse guy?" Bukka asked, no less rudely. "I was told a horse-trader who couldn't talk properly was in town."

Domingo Nunes gave an intriguing reply. "I pay my way with whore whore horses," he said, "but in seek secret I am one of those whose tata task it is to travel the whir whir world and tell its tales, so that others may no no know what it's like."

"I don't know how you tell stories," Bukka said, "when you have such trouble finishing sentences. But this is interesting. Come sit beside me. My brother the king and I myself would like to hear these tales."

"Before that," Domingo Nunes dared to say, "I muss muss must know the secret of this magic war war wall, the greatest won wonder I have ever seen. Who is the mum magician who is doodoo doing this? I must shay shay shake his hand."

"Get in," Bukka said, moving over to make room for the foreigner in the palanquin. The men tasked with carrying the palanquin tried not to show their feelings about the increased load. "I'll present you to her. The city whisperer and the giver of seeds. Hers is a story that should be told far and wide. You'll see that she is a storyteller too."

It was a small room, unlike any other room in the palace, not in the least ornate, with plain whitewashed walls, and unfurnished except for a bare wooden plinth. A small high window allowed a single ray of sunlight to descend at a steep angle toward the young woman below, like a shaft of angelic grace. In this austere setting, struck by that thunderbolt of startling light, sitting cross-legged, with her eyes closed, her arms outstretched and resting on her knees, her hands with the thumbs and index fingers joined at their tips, her lips slightly parted, there she was: Pampa Kampana, lost in the ecstasy of the act of creation. She was silent, but it seemed to Domingo Nunes, as he was ushered into her presence by Bukka Sangama, that a great throng of whispered words was flowing from her, from her parted lips, down her chin and neck, along her arms and out across the floor, escaping from her as a river escapes from its source, and heading out into the world. The whispers were so soft that they were barely audible, and for a moment Domingo Nunes told himself he was imagining them, that he was telling himself some sort of occult tale to make sense of the impossible things he was seeing.

Then Bukka Sangama whispered in his ear. "You hear it, yes?"

Domingo Nunes nodded.

"This is how she is for twenty hours a day," Bukka said. "Then she opens her eyes and eats a little and drinks something also. Then she closes her eyes and lies down for three hours to rest. Then she sits up and starts again."

"But wha wha what is she ack ack actually doing?" Domingo Nunes asked.

"You can ask her," said Bukka softly. "This is the hour when her eyes open."

Pampa Kampana opened her eyes and saw the beautiful young man staring at her with the glow of adoration on his face and at that moment the question of her proposed marriage to Hukka Raya I, and perhaps to Crown Prince Bukka after his death (depending on who survived whom), developed new complications. He didn't have to ask her anything. "Yes," she said in reply to his unspoken question, "I'll tell you everything."

She had finally opened the door to the locked room that contained the memory of her mother and her early childhood, and it had all flooded out and filled her with strength. She told Domingo Nunes about Radha Kampana the potter, who taught her that women could be as good at pottery as men were, as good at everything as men were, and about her mother's departure, which had left a void in her that she was now trying to fill. She described the fire and the goddess who spoke through her mouth. She told him about the seeds that built the city on the site of her personal calamity. Any new place where people decide to live takes time to feel real, she said, it can take a generation or more. The first people arrive with pictures of the world in their luggage, with things from elsewhere filling their heads, but the new place feels strange, it's hard for them to believe in it, even though they have nowhere else to go, and nobody else to be. They make the best of it, and then they begin forgetting, they tell the next generation some of it, they forget the rest, and the children forget more and change things in their heads, but they were born here, that's the difference, they are of the place, they are the place and the place is them, and their spreading roots give the place the nourishment it needs, it flowers, it blossoms, it lives, so that by the time the first people depart they can leave happy in the knowledge that they began something that will continue.

Little Bukka was astonished by her volubility. "She never talks like this," he said, perplexed. "When she was younger, she didn't talk at all for nine years. Pampa Kampana, why are you all of a sudden talking so much?"

"We have a guest," she said, gazing into Domingo Nunes's green eyes, "and we must make him feel at home."

Everyone came from a seed, she told him. Men planted seeds in women and so forth. But this was different. A whole city, people of all kinds and ages, blooming from the earth on the same day, such flowers have no souls, they don't know who they are, because the truth is they are nothing. But such truth is unacceptable. It was necessary, she said, to do something to cure the multitude of its unreality. Her solution was fiction. She was making up their lives, their castes, their faiths, how many brothers and sisters they had, and what childhood games they had played, and sending the stories whispering through the streets into the ears that needed to hear them, writing the grand narrative of the city, creating its story now that she had created its life. Some of her stories came from her memories of lost Kampili, the slaughtered fathers and the burned mothers, she was trying to bring that place back to life in this place, bringing back the old dead in the newly living; but memory wasn't enough, there were too many lives to enliven, and so imagination had to take over from the point at which memory failed.

"My mother abandoned me," she said, "but I will be the mother of them all."

Domingo Nunes didn't understand much of what he was being told. Then all of a sudden he heard a whisper, heard it not through his ears but somehow through his brain, a whisper winding itself around his throat, untying the knots inside him, clearing what was tangled, and setting his tongue free. It was simultaneously exhilarating and terrifying, and he found himself clutching at his throat and crying out. *Stop. Go on. Stop.*

"The whispers know what you need," said Pampa Kampana. "The new people need stories to tell them what kind of people they are, honest, dishonest, or something in between. Soon the whole city will have stories, memories, friendships, rivalries. We can't wait a generation for the city to become a real place. We have to do it now, so that there can be a new empire; so that the city of victory can rule the land, and make sure the slaughter never happens again, and, above all, that no more women ever have to walk into walls of flame, and that all women are treated better than orphans at men's mercy in the dark. But you," she added, making it sound like an afterthought although in fact it was what she really wanted to say, "you had other needs."

"Today is the day of the resurrection," Domingo Nunes said without faltering. "*Ele ressuscitou,* we say in my language. He is risen. But I see that the one you are trying to resurrect is someone else, someone you loved who walked into a fire. You are using your sorcery to bring a whole city to life in the hope that she will return."

"Your speech impediment," Bukka Sangama said. "Where did that go?"

"She whispered in my ear," Domingo Nunes said.

"Welcome to Vijayanagar," Pampa Kampana said. She pronounced the *v* almost like a *b,* which was a thing that sometimes happened.

"Bizana . . . ?" repeated Domingo Nunes. "I'm sorry. What did you call it?"

"First say *vij-aya,* victory," Pampa Kampana said. "Then say *nagar,* city. It's not so difficult. Nag-gar. Vijayanagar: Victory City."

"My tongue can't make those sounds," Domingo Nunes confessed. "Not because of any speech impediment. It just won't come out of my mouth the way you say it."

"What does your tongue want to call it?" Pampa Kampana asked.

"Bij . . . Biz . . . so, in the first place, Bis . . . and in the second place . . . nagá," said Domingo Nunes. "Adding up—and here I make my best effort—to *Bisnaga*."

Pampa Kampana and Crown Prince Bukka both laughed. Pampa clapped her hands, and Bukka, looking hard at her, saw that she had fallen in love.

"Then Bisnaga it is," she said, clapping her hands. "You have given us our name."

"What are you saying?" Bukka cried. "Are you going to let this foreigner label our city with the noises of his twisted tongue?"

"Yes," she said. "This is not an ancient city with an ancient name. The city just arrived and so has he. They are the same. I accept his name. From now on this is and will be Bisnaga."

"The day will come," Bukka said mutinously, "when we will no longer allow foreigners to tell us who we are."

(Thanks to Pampa Kampana's amused delight in Domingo Nunes and his garbled mispronunciation, she chose to refer to both the city and the empire as "Bisnaga" throughout her epic poem, intending, perhaps, to remind us that while her work is based on real events, there is an inevitable distance between the imagined world and the actual. "Bisnaga" belongs not to history but to her. After all, a poem is not an essay or a news report. The reality of poetry and the imagination follows its own rules. We have elected to follow Pampa Kampana's lead, so it is her dream-city of "Bisnaga" that is so named and portrayed here. To do otherwise would be to betray the artist and her work.)

Even though Pampa Kampana was still deep in her whispering trance for twenty hours a day, her evident new feelings for the foreigner—her eyes searching for him during the one hour in which they were open—were the cause of much royal displeasure. News of Pampa's infatuation reached King Hukka Raya I's ears before Nunes was presented to him for the first time, and caused much irritation. The Portuguese, who hadn't been informed of this, introduced himself to the king with ornate courtesy, and mentioned his gift for traveler's tales. "If you permit," he said, "I could entertain you with a few?"

Hukka grunted noncommittally. "It may be," he said, "that the traveler is of greater interest to us than the tales."

Domingo Nunes didn't know what to make of this, so in some confusion he began to speak of his journeyings among the cannibals—the Anthropophagi—and men whose heads grew beneath their shoulders. Hukka raised a hand to stop him. "Tell us instead," he said, "of the unnaturally pale-faced peoples, the white Europeans, the pink English, of their unreliability and treacheries." Nunes was unnerved. "Sire," he said, "among Europeans, the savagery of the French is exceeded only by the cruelty of the Dutch. The English are at present a backward race, but it is my guess, though many of my countrymen would disagree with me, that they may end up being the worst of the whole bunch, and the map of half the world may be colored pink. We Portuguese, however, are reliable and honorable. Genoese merchants and Arab traders alike will speak to you of our fairness. But we are dreamers too. We imagine, for example, that the world is round, and we dream of circumnavigating it. We think of the cape of Africa and we suspect the existence of unknown continents to the west of the Ocean Sea. We are the earth's prime adventurers, but unlike lesser tribes, we hold to our contracts, and we pay our bills on time."

Like his newborn subjects, Hukka Raya I was still getting used to his new incarnation. He had already experienced several metamorphoses in his eventful life. The slow easy ways of the cowherd had given way to the regimented discipline of the soldier, and then as a captured soldier there had been the forced change of religion and therefore also of name, and after that escape, the shedding of the false skin of his conversion, and of the garb and habits of soldiering as well, and the transition back into something like his original cowherd self, or at least into a peasant in search of some new destiny. As a child his one wish had been that the world would never change, that he would always be nine years old and his mother and father would always be moving toward him with loving arms outstretched, but life had taught him its great lesson, which was mutability. Now, given a throne to sit upon, he found that the childhood dream of changelessness had returned. He wanted this scene, the throne room, the guardian women, the lavish furnishings, to be removed from the mutable world and become eternal, but before that happened he needed to marry his queen, he needed Pampa Kampana to accept him and sit garlanded by his side while the citizenry applauded their nuptials, and once that great day was over, then time could stop, Hukka himself might be able to stop it by raising his royal scepter, and Pampa Kampana could very probably stop it, because if she could bring a world into being with nothing more than a bunch of seeds and a few days of whispering then she could probably encircle it with a magic garland that was more powerful than the calendar, and then they would live happily ever after.

From this dream the arrival of the foreigner and the news of Pampa Kampana's interest in him had rudely awakened the new king. Hukka began to imagine the foreigner's head detached from his shoulders and stuffed with straw, and the only thing that deterred him from decapitating the newcomer at once was the probability that Pampa Kampana would strongly disapprove of such a course of action. However, he continued to look at Domingo Nunes's elegant long neck with a kind of lethal desire.

"We are lucky then," he said, with heavy sarcasm, "that it is a sophisticated and handsome Portuguese gentleman, a silver-tongued charmer, who comes to us today, and not a representative of the barbarian French or Dutch, or the primitive, rosy English." And before Domingo Nunes could say another word, the king waved him away, and he was led by two armed women out of the monarch's sight. As he left the throne room, Domingo Nunes guessed that his life might be in danger, understood that it probably had something to do with his encounter with the whispering woman, and immediately began to think about his escape. However, as things turned out, he would stay for twenty years.

When Pampa Kampana finally emerged from her nine long days and nights of magic she wasn't sure if the red-haired, green-eyed young god she had seen truly existed, or if he had just been some sort of vision. When nobody in the palace would answer her questions her puzzlement grew. However, it was necessary to put aside her confusion for a moment to deliver the message for which Hukka and Bukka had been waiting since the moment they came down from the mountain into the city of empty-eyed people. She found the two princes trying to forget their boredom by playing chess, a game neither of them had fully mastered, so that they overestimated the importance of knights and castles and, being men, severely underestimated the queen.

"It's done," Pampa Kampana said, interrupting their amateurish moves without standing on ceremony. "Everyone has been told their story. The city is fully alive."

Outside in the great market street it was easy to see the proof of her assertion. Women were greeting one another like old friends, lovers were buying one another their favorite sweetmeats, blacksmiths were shoeing horses for riders they believed they had served for years, grandmothers were telling grandchildren their family stories, stories which went back three generations at least, and men with old quarrels were coming to blows over long-remembered slights. The character of this new city was shaped, in important ways, by Pampa Kampana's memories—no longer suppressed—of what her mother had taught her. All over the city women were doing what, elsewhere in the country, was thought of as work unsuitable for them. Here was a lawyer's office staffed by women advocates and women clerks, there you could see strong women laborers unloading goods from barges tethered at the dock on the riverbank. There were women policing the streets, and working as scribes, and pulling teeth, and beating *mridangam* drums while men danced to the rhythm in a square. None of this struck anyone as odd. The city thrived in the richness of its fictions, the tales whispered in their ears by Pampa Kampana, stories whose fictionality was drowned out and forever lost beneath the clamorous rhythm of the new day, and the walls around the citizens had risen to their final, impregnable height, and above the arch of the great barbican gate, engraved in stone, was the city's name, which all its inhabitants knew for certain, and would insist on the knowledge if you had asked them, to be a name from the remote past, handed down through the centuries from the time of legend, when the Monkey God Hanuman was alive and living in Kishkindha nearby:

Bisnaga.

News of a nine-day festival of celebration arrived and ran rapidly through the city. Gods would be worshipped in the temples and there would be dancing in the streets. Domingo Nunes, who had found lodgings in the hayloft of the family of the head groom to whom he had sold his horses, heard about the party, and had the idea that would keep him safe from the vengeance of a jealous monarch and his brother too. As he was preparing to go to the palace gates and request an audience, the head groom's wife called up to him to tell him he had a visitor. He clambered down his wooden ladder and there was Pampa Kampana, who had given the whole city dreams to believe in and now wanted to see if she could believe in her own dream. When she saw Domingo Nunes she clapped her hands in delight.

"Good," she said.

Once their eyes had met and what could not be spoken had been said without words, Domingo understood that he had better move quickly to get onto safer ground. "On my travels in the kingdom of Cathay," he said, perspiring a little, "I learned the secret of what their alchemists originally called the devil's distillate."

"Your first words to me today are about the devil," she said. "Those are not appropriate terms of endearment."

"It's not really anything to do with the devil," he said. "The alchemists discovered it by accident and got scared. They were trying to make gold, unsuccessfully of course, but they ended up making something more powerful. It's just saltpeter, sulfur, and charcoal, powdered and mixed up. You add a spark to it, and boom! It's something to see."

"In spite of all your travels," she replied, "you haven't learned how to talk to a woman."

"What I'm trying to tell you," he said, "is that, in the first place, this can make the city's celebrations more exciting. We can make what are called 'fireworks.' Wheels that spin with fire, rockets that zoom into the sky."

"What you mean to tell me," she said, "is that your heart is spinning like a wheel on fire, and your love is like a rocket flying up to the gods."

"Also, in the second place," he said, perspiring more freely, "they learned in Cathay that this substance could be used in weapons. They stopped calling it by the devil's name, and they invented new words for new things. They invented the word 'bomb' for a thing that could blow up a house, or knock down a fortress wall. They began to call the distillate 'gunpowder.' That was after they invented the word 'gun.'"

"What's a gun?" Pampa Kampana asked.

"It's a weapon that will change the world," Domingo Nunes said. "And I can build it for you if you want."

"They make love differently in Portugal," said Pampa Kampana. "I see that now."

That night, when the city was full of music and crowds, Pampa Kampana brought Hukka and Bukka to a small square in which Domingo Nunes was waiting for them, surrounded by a series of bottles with sticks protruding from their necks. Hukka was extremely annoyed by the sight of his Portuguese rival, and Bukka, who was next in line for the throne and, he believed, for Pampa Kampana's hand, had his own irritations as well.

"Why have you brought us before this man?" Hukka demanded.

"Watch," Pampa told him. "Watch and learn."

Domingo Nunes sent his fireworks soaring into the sky. The Sangama brothers, open-mouthed, watched them fly, and understood that the future was being born, and that Domingo Nunes would be its midwife.

"Teach us," said Hukka Raya I.

4

Hukka and Bukka's three disreputable brothers had arrived some time earlier, riding into town together, side by side down the main street, bandits trying to look like aristocrats. With their thick, unkempt hair and their wild beards and handlebar mustachios they looked, and smelled, more like hoodlums than princes, however many airs they tried to put on, and people reacted to them with fear, not respect. They had cast-iron shields strapped to their backs. Pukka Sangama's shield featured a portrait of a snarling tiger, Chukka Sangama's shield was decorated with butterflies and moths, and Dev's boasted a floral design. Swords and daggers hung from their waistbands and in dirty leather sheaths worn beneath the shields, the hilts of the swords protruding for easy access. In short, Pukka, Chukka, and Dev were as terrifying a sight as could be imagined as they rode up to the palace gates, and the citizenry scattered before them as they advanced.

The news of Hukka and Bukka establishing their rule over a miraculously newborn city had spread fast, along with rumors of a treasury overflowing with golden coins called *pagodas,* and also, people said, golden *varahas* of different weights. Pukka, Chukka, and Dev were determined not to be cut out of history if there was easy wealth to be had. At the palace gates they remained mounted and demanded admission.

"Where are those rascally brothers of ours?" bellowed Chukka Sangama. "Did they think they could keep all these riches to themselves?"

But he and his brothers were faced with a sight so unfamiliar in their experience that it punctured the balloon of their belligerence and made them scratch their heads. What stood before them was a phalanx of spear-carrying palace guards wearing golden breastplates, shin guards, and forearm cuffs, with swords in golden scabbards at their waists and long hair braided beautifully on top of their heads. They wore golden shields and grim expressions. And they were women. All of them. Tall, muscular women soldiers who meant business. Chukka, Pukka, and Dev had never seen such a thing.

"Is this what those fools are doing now?" Chukka demanded. "Sending ladies out to do unladylike business?"

"This is nothing new," said the captain of the guard, a giant with a ferocious face and large, heavy-lidded eyes. Her name was Ulupi, and she was named after the daughter of the Serpent King. "In this city, women have guarded the Imperial Palace for generations."

"That's interesting," said Pukka Sangama, "because I'm sure this city wasn't here the last time we passed through the neighborhood."

"You must be blind," Captain Ulupi answered him. "For the power of the empire and the grandeur of its capital city have been known to all for longer than it is necessary to say."

"And so Hukka and Bukka are in there, taking part in this phantom delirium?" Dev demanded. "Whatever this delusion is, they are happy to go along with it? And with you?"

"The king and the crown prince are fully supportive of the highly trained and fully professional officers of the palace guard," said the captain. "And you'll find, if you defy us, that we are not so ladylike at all."

Now the truth was that the three younger Sangama brothers had been earning a dishonest living for some time as highway robbers and cattle thieves, and had recently added horse-thievery to their repertoire on account of the establishment of an international horse-trading enterprise at the port of Goa. Portuguese entrepreneurs had begun importing Arab stallions by sea to sell to several regional princes. Ambushing the horse convoys and reselling the beautiful animals on the black market was proving to be lucrative business, but it was also becoming dangerous, because the ruthless Tamil gangs of Maravar and Kallar thieves had moved into the area and brought along their murderous reputations, and the Sangama brothers, fearing for their lives, and being less than heroic, were looking for something less life-threatening to do. Their brothers' new golden city glistened with exactly the kind of opportunities they sought.

"Take us to our brothers at once," Chukka Sangama said in his most commanding tones. "We need to explain to them why there is no difference between thieves and kings."

In the throne room, Hukka Raya I and Crown Prince Bukka were getting used to their large seats, their *gaddis,* so jewel-encrusted that they would have been uncomfortable if there hadn't been thick cushions covered in brocaded silk to sit upon. Hukka soon found that if he sat upright on the *gaddi* then his feet didn't touch the ground, and he looked like a child. Therefore, it was better to lounge, and if sitting up was absolutely necessary, then footstools would be required. All these things were being worked out, to ensure the princeliness of the crown prince and the kingliness of the king. Chukka, Pukka, and Dev entered the royal presence to see the royal personage, their brother, experimenting with footstools of different heights. Bukka's *gaddi* was a little lower. He, too, was learning how to lounge regally, and if he sat up his feet touched the floor, so he did not have to deal with the problem of dangling.

"So this is what it means to be a king," Chukka Sangama taunted his brother. "It's a matter of getting the furniture right."

"We are disappointed in our siblings," said Hukka Raya I, using, for the first time, the royal plural, and speaking to the throne room in general, as if it were a person. "Our siblings are unable to live up to the role for which history has chosen us. They are dark princes, shadow lords, phantoms of the blood. They are stale bread. They are rotting fruit. They are moons in eclipse."

"As they are our brothers," Bukka said, also addressing the empty air, "our choices are straightforward, but limited. Either we have them executed immediately, as potential traitors, would-be usurpers, or else we give them a job."

"It's too early in the morning to spill family blood," said Hukka Raya I. "Let's think of something for them to do."

"Let's give them a job far away," Bukka suggested.

"Very far away," Hukka Raya I agreed.

"Nellore," Bukka proposed. That was on the eastern seacoast, approximately three hundred miles distant. "It needs conquering," Bukka added, "and these three won't be much trouble to us there."

Hukka had a grander vision. "First Nellore to the east," he said, "then Mulbagal to the south, and then Chandragutti to the west. Once you capture Nellore, Brother Chukka, you can stay back there and take charge. And Brother Pukka, you can have Mulbagal when it falls, and Brother Dev, you'll go alone to handle the conquest of Chandragutti, and then stay put there. So each of you ends up with a *kursi*, a throne, and I hope you'll be very happy. And in the meanwhile Bukka and I will conquer everything in between."

The three disreputable brothers shifted their feet and frowned. Was this a good deal or a poisoned cup? They weren't certain. "You get the treasury overflowing with *pagodas*," Chukka objected. "That doesn't seem right."

"Let me be clear," said Hukka Raya I. "I will provide each of you with a formidable army. An undefeatable force. On one condition: my generals will be in charge of the soldiering. You can sit back on your horses under the imperial flag, and after the battles my generals will put you on the throne, but in combat you'll do exactly what they tell you to do. And after it's done you'll each have a province to rule, which is a much better option than stealing horses and worrying about being killed by the Kallar and Maravar gangs. Brother Chukka, you'll have the privilege of worshipping in the Jagannath Temple at Puri. Pukka my brother, the great hero Arjuna's temple will be yours. And Dev, your temple's in a cave, that's true, but to compensate for that, you'll get the best of the three forts, an awesome hilltop fortress, with pleasing views on all sides. In addition I will provide each of you with a personal guard detachment, drawn from the women of the Imperial Defense Force. You'll be safe with them, but if you attempt any kind of treasonous insurrection against the empire—against *us*—they have orders to kill you on the spot."

"That sounds like a bad offer," Pukka said. "We'll just be your puppets. This is what you're really saying. Maybe we should just refuse your proposal and take our chances."

"You're free to refuse, by all means," said Hukka Raya I, not unkindly, "but then you won't leave this room alive. You understand why. It's nothing personal. Just family business."

"Take it or leave it," Bukka told his brothers.

"I'll take it," said Dev Sangama immediately, and the other two slowly, thoughtfully, nodded their heads.

"Be off with you then," said Hukka Raya I. "There's an empire to be conquered, and history to be made."

The captain of the guard, Ulupi, as serpentine as her name, hissed at Chukka, Pukka, and Dev that the audience was at an end. Her tongue flickered between her teeth before and after she spoke.

"One more thing," Hukka Raya I called after them. "I don't know when we will see each other again, if ever, so there's something you should know."

"What's that?" growled Chukka, the most discontented of the exiting three.

"We love you," Hukka said. "You are our brothers, and we will love you until you die."

• • •

It wasn't possible for the three departing Sangama brothers to leave immediately. An army took time to move. There were the traveling palanquins of the military grandees to plump and burnish so that those gentlemen could journey to their destination in comfort, and canopied howdahs had to be mounted on the backs of battle elephants so that these same high-ranking officers could ride to war while reclining on cushions and pillows, and there were thousands of elephants to feed, pack elephants and battle elephants, because elephants ate constantly, and had to be loaded with their own fodder as well as all the goods needed by the regiments, for example the massive moving parts that would later be assembled as siege engines that hurled boulders at the walls of the fortresses of the enemy. And tents had to be collapsed and loaded onto bullock-carts, along with benches, stools, straw for camp mattresses, and latrines; there was an entire armaments division to transport, so that the army's weapons could be kept in good order, swords could be sharpened, arrows balanced and bowstrings kept taut, javelin-points checked daily to ensure that they were as sharp as daggers, and shields repaired after hard days on the battlefield; and there was a whole kitchen-city to mobilize, ovens as well as cooks, and great cartloads of vegetables, rice and beans, and caged chickens and tethered goats, too, because there were many chicken- and goat-eaters among the ranks, in spite of what their religion formally decreed; and there had to be wood for fires, and cauldrons to be filled with soups and stews; and there were other camp followers to marshal, including courtesans who would attend nightly to the needs of the most desperate soldiers. The medical equipment, the surgeons and nurses, the fearsome saws used for cutting off limbs, the canisters of salve for blinded eyes, the leeches, the healing herbs, would all be placed at the rear of the column. No soldier going to war wanted to see such things. It was necessary for them to feel immortal, or, at least, to persuade themselves that crippling injury, agonizing wounds, and death were things that happened to other people. It was important that each individual foot soldier and cavalryman was allowed to believe that they personally would emerge from combat unscathed.

And this was no ordinary army. It was a fighting force that was gradually being born. Like everyone else in the new city the soldiers woke up each day with whispers in their ears, each soldier hearing—for the first time, but as if the information had always been there—the story of his life. (Or her life. The women soldiers were fewer, but they were there. They had whispered memories too.) In that mysterious moment between sleeping and waking they each heard the imaginary narrative of their family's fictional generations, and discovered how long ago they had decided to join the new empire's forces, and how far they had traveled, what rivers they had crossed, what friends they had made along the way, what obstacles and foes they had had to overcome. They learned their own names, and the names of their parents and villages and tribes, and the names of love given to them by their wives—their wives, who were waiting for them in their villages, nursing their children!—and their personalities, too, dripped into their ears, they found out if they were funny or bad-tempered, and how they spoke; some were voluble, others were people of few words, and some used foul language, as soldiers often did, while others disliked it; some of them were open about their feelings while others concealed them. In this they, like the civilian population of the city, became human beings, even if the stories in their heads were fictions. Fictions could be as powerful as histories, revealing the new people to themselves, allowing them to understand their own natures and the natures of those around them, and making them real. This was the paradox of the whispered stories: they were no more than make-believe but they created the truth, and brought into being a city and an army with all the rich diversity of nonfictional people with deep roots in the actually existing world.

The one thing the soldiers all had in common, the whispers told them, was their courage and skill on the battlefield. They were a brotherhood (and sisterhood) of overpowering warriors, and they could never be defeated. Each day as they awoke this knowledge of their invincibility deepened. Soon they would be ready to follow orders unquestioningly and obliterate their enemies and march relentlessly to victory.

In the shadow of the city's golden walls, which grew higher and more imposing every day, stood the carpeted tent assigned to the three ostensible leaders of the coming expedition. Inside these palatial quarters scattered with brocaded cushions and illuminated by filigreed brass lanterns, Chukka, Pukka, and Dev Sangama—the titular though not the actual commanders of the grand venture—could be found trying to make sense of their new world. It was plain to all three brothers that some powerful sorcery was at hand, and fear battled with ambition in their breasts.

"I have the feeling," Chukka Sangama said, "that even though our Hukka and Bukka have put on royal airs, they are in the grip of some wizard who can make the unliving live." He was the most confident and aggressive of the three, but at that moment he sounded shaken and uncertain.

His brother Pukka, always less brutal and more calculating, weighed up the odds. "So we can be kings," he said, "if we're okay with leading an army of ghosts."

Dev, the youngest, was the least heroic and most romantic one. "Ghosts or no ghosts," he said, "our guardian angels are ladies of the highest quality. If we can win them over to be our consorts, I don't give a damn if they are human beings or specters of the night. Before death comes to claim me, I want to know what it's like to be in love."

"And before death comes for me," Chukka said, "I want to rule the kingdom of Nellore. Or at least to take command of that, as a beginning."

"If death comes for us," Pukka Sangama reasoned, "it will be sent in our direction by our brothers Bukka and Hukka. I'd like to send the exterminating angel in their direction before they send him in ours. After that we can worry about ghosts."

• • •

Commander Shakti, Commander Adi, and Commander Gauri, the three intrepid palace officers assigned to guard but also to spy on the three departing Sangamas, were known as the Sisters of the Mountains (although they were not really sisters), because their names were also those of three of the many forms of the goddess Parvati, daughter of Himalaya, the King of the Mountains—and their air of authority was so irresistible that it was inevitable that the recently reformed bandits should fall in love with them.

In their dreams each brother saw his personal Sister beckoning to him, issuing erotic challenges and making sweet promises of rewards. Chukka Sangama, the most extroverted, even aggressive, of the three brothers, met his match in Commander Shakti, in whose name the dynamic energy of the cosmos was contained. "Chukka, Chukka," Shakti whispered to him in his dreams, "I am lightning. Catch me if you can. I am the thunder and the avalanche, the transformation and the flow, the destruction and the renewal. I may be too much for you. Chukka, Chukka, come to me." He was possessed by the thrill of her, but when he woke up she was standing spear in hand, stone-faced and impassive, at the door of the tent, not looking as if she had had the same dream.

Meanwhile Pukka Sangama, the cautious and rational one, dreamed of Commander Adi, who revealed herself to him as the eternal truth of the universe. "Pukka, Pukka," she sighed, "I see that you are a seeker, and want always to know the meaning of things. I am the answer to all your questions. I am the how and why, the what and the when and the where. I am the only explanation that you need. Pukka, Pukka. Find me and you will know." He awoke bright-eyed and eager, but there she was, beside her fellow Sister, spear in hand, impassive, at the door of the tent with a face that could have been carved in the hardest granite.

And Dev Sangama, the most beautiful brother and the least

courageous, was visited by Commander Gauri, the most beautiful of all beings, and her dream-incarnation was four-armed, holding a tambourine and a trident, and her dream-skin was as white as snow, an analogy which came to Dev Sangama in his dream even though he had never once seen snow in his whole hot life. "Dev, Dev," murmured Gauri, dripping her words like sweet poison into his sleeping ear, and shaking her tambourine, "your beauty makes you a worthy companion for me, but no mortal man can survive the devastating force of making love to a goddess. Dev, Dev, will you give up your life for a single night of celestial bliss?" And he awoke with the words of assent on his lips, *yes, yes I will, yes,* but there she was standing granite-faced beside her stony co-Sisters, as impassive as they were, with only two arms, no tambourine, and a spear, not a trident, in her hand.

When the Sisters of the Mountains were discussing matters they leaned in toward one another so that their heads touched, and they spoke in a private language. Some of the words were the everyday words the Sangama brothers could understand, like *food* and *sword* and *river* and *kill.* But there were many other words that were a complete mystery. Dev Sangama, the fearful one, became convinced that this was some sort of demon-language. In that army cantonment in which soldiers were listening to secret whispers whose source was unknown, acquiring individuality, memory, and history, and gradually turning into fully realized human beings, it was easy to believe that a kingdom of demons was being born, and that their elder siblings Hukka and Bukka had fallen under their spell. In the bright light of day he tried to convince Chukka and Pukka that they were in danger of losing their eternal souls and that the risks of a life on the highway stealing horses were smaller than the dangers of being the figurehead commanders of this occult military force. But at night when Sister Gauri visited him his fears were quelled and he longed only for her love. So he was torn, and as a result incapable of making any sort of radical decision, but did not abandon the plan.

Finally he asked Gauri about the unknown words and was told that this was the hidden language of security, the coded tongue which defeated the best efforts of any spying ears. In the language of security there were ordinary words for extraordinary things, a *running stream* might indicate a certain kind of cavalry advance, and a *feast* might be a slaughter; so even the words Dev could understand might have meanings he could not know. And at a higher level of safety there were new words, words that looked at individuals in battlefield terms, for example, so that the word for a man on the front line was not the same as the word for a man on the flanks, and there were chronology words too, describing people as beings moving in time, words that could make the difference, in war, between life and death. "Don't worry about words," Gauri told Dev. "Words are for word people. You are not a person of that type. Concern yourself only with deeds." Dev was not sure whether or not this advice was a kind of insult. He suspected that it was, but he took no offense, being in the grip of love.

In the evenings the three Sangamas took their meals in the royal tent with the three Sisters. The brothers, coarsened by their outlaw lives, devoured heaped platters of roasted goat meat without any concern for religious niceties, goats slathered in chilies that made the men's eyes water and their heads sweat and their copious hair stand on end. The women, by contrast, with grace and care ate delicately flavored vegetables, with the air of people who barely needed to eat. And yet it was plain to all six of them that these well-mannered angels were by far the more dangerous, and the men gazed upon them with an unfamiliar mixture of fear and desire, unable to express the desire because of the fear; and, so unmanned, tore into their goat legs with ever more barbaric ferocity, hoping that this would give them at least the appearance of masculinity. It was not clear to them if this gastronomic performance made any kind of favorable impression on the ladies, whose expressions remained enigmatic, even obscure.

Pukka Sangama, the one who wanted answers, asked questions. "When the three of you lean your heads together like that," he wanted to know, "is that an even more secret form of communication, a wordless form? Are you talking to one another brain-to-brain? Or is that a comfortable way for you to rest while standing up?"

"Pukka, Pukka," Commander Adi reproved him, "do not ask questions whose answers you do not have the capacity to understand."

Chukka Sangama lost his temper. "What is going on around here?" he demanded. "We've been sitting in this tent for so long that the days have become blurry and I can't remember what time it is. Somebody needs to tell us what we are supposed to do and when we are supposed to do it. We are not men accustomed to sitting on our behinds like pet dogs waiting for a treat."

"Thank you for your patience," Sister Gauri replied. "In fact we were planning to tell you this evening that the army is ready to march. We will set out at dawn." It was the exact moment at which Pampa Kampana was informing Hukka Raya I and Crown Prince Bukka that the city too had been told its stories and its creation was finally complete. Soldiers as well as civilians were ready for whatever history had in store.

Chukka jumped to his feet. "Thank god," he cried. "Finally something that makes sense. Let's go to war and bring peace to the land."

"Do as you're told," Gauri said, "and everything should go well."

Music burst out from the city, and the three Sangama brothers in their cantonment tent could hear the celebrations clearly even through the thick city walls. They heard, too, the shrieks and cries that greeted the sight of the first fireworks in the history of the land soaring up above the gathered masses. But they were unable to join the party. "Sleep," Sister Gauri commanded them. "Dancing doesn't matter. It's tomorrow that the empire will begin to be born."

5

Domingo Nunes would remain in Bisnaga, the city he had named, until Pampa Kampana broke his heart. In the early years, when he was still unsure of his status, and feared that one or other of the royal brothers might send a knife looking for his ribs on a moonless night, he was absent for long periods, traveling west across the sea to buy horses from the Arabs, and bringing them back through the port of Goa to sell them to the head groom of the city, whose cavalry—which featured large numbers of elephants and camels as well as horses—grew larger every year as the empire's reach spread ever wider. When in Bisnaga he tried not to draw attention to himself, continuing to find lodgings in the head groom's humble hayloft. Pampa Kampana visited him there more often than was wise, but everyone in the groom's family pretended not to notice; they, too, were afraid of drawing royal wrath down upon their complicit heads. However, in the end Domingo Nunes's skill with explosives, his value to the empire as a specialist in munitions, won him favor. He was given the title of Trusted Foreigner in Charge of Explosions, paid a generous salary, and encouraged to give up horse-trading and devote himself to the cause of Bisnaga. And when Pampa Kampana and Hukka Raya I got married, this now-eminent foreigner was considered important enough to be invited to the wedding celebrations; which he did, in spite of his own emotions, and after a considerable internal struggle, attend.

The marriage of Hukka Raya I and Pampa Kampana was not a love match, at least not for the bride. The king had desired her since the moment he first saw her, and had waited—longer than any king was comfortable with waiting—for her to accept his proposal. He was not blind, and his eyes and ears were everywhere in the city's streets, so he knew perfectly well that his beloved paid regular nocturnal visits to a certain hayloft, and on the day she finally surrendered to his blandishments he confronted her with what he knew. He invited her to walk with him in the palace gardens, where they could speak more privately than was possible in the eavesdropper-filled interior chambers, and asked her why she had finally made up her mind.

"There are things that must be done that are important for the general good, things larger than ourselves," she said. "Things we do in the service of the future."

"I had hoped for some more personal reason," Hukka told her.

"As to the personal," she responded, with a shrug, "you know where my heart lies, and let me tell you that I will not abandon the interests of my heart even though I will accept your hand to establish the bloodline of the empire."

"You expect me to put up with that?" Hukka asked, and he was angry now. "I should have the bastard's head cut off this very afternoon."

"You won't do that," she replied, "because you too are bound to act in the service of the future, and you need his Chinese artistry. Also, to speak more personally, if you harm him, you will never lay a finger on me."

Hukka's frustrations boiled over. "Very few men, let alone a monarch, would be prepared to consider marrying—excuse my frankness—a loose woman—some would say a slattern—at the very least a hussy—who freely—some would say shamelessly—let me say, *sports*—with a person who is not even a member of her race or religion—and who informs her husband-to-be of her intention to continue with her intolerable activity—I could say her debauched activity—after they are wed," he cried, not caring if he was being overheard; but he was knocked out of his stride by her unexpected response, which was to unleash a loud peal of laughter, as if he had just said the funniest thing in the world.

"I fail to see the humor," Hukka huffily said, but Pampa Kampana was weeping as she pointed a hilarious finger in his direction. "Your face," she said, "it's covered in spots. Suppurating zits, good gracious. Every time you used one of those unkind words, another one burst out of your skin. I think you had better clean up your tongue or your whole face might just become one big boil."

Hukka brought his hands up to his face in alarm and felt his forehead, cheeks, nose, and chin, and there they were, the pustules. It was clear that Pampa Kampana's magic extended far beyond the enchantment of seeds. He realized that he was scared of her, and a moment later understood, additionally, that his fear of her magic was sexually arousing.

"Let's get married right away," he said.

"As long as you're clear about my terms," she insisted.

"Whatever you want," he cried. "Yes, I accept. You are so unbelievably dangerous. I must have you."

After the wedding, and for the first twenty years of the Bisnaga Empire, Queen Pampa Kampana openly maintained two lovers, the king and the foreigner, and even though both men were unhappy about the setup, and often said as much, Pampa moved between the two of them with a serenity that suggested she had no difficulty with the arrangement, which only increased their displeasure. Consequently, they both found ways of being absent for long periods from the source of their discontents. Domingo Nunes, having provided the empire with a large storehouse full of powerful explosives, flung himself back into horse-trading, finding in the love of horses some consolation for having only half the love of the woman of his dreams. As for Hukka Raya I, he embarked on the great business of empire-building, establishing formidable fortresses at Barkuru, Badami, and Udayagiri, conquering all the lands around the Pampa river, and earning the right to be named the monarch of the whole country between the eastern and western seas. None of it made him happy. "It doesn't matter how much land you have," he complained to Pampa Kampana, "or how many seas you can wash your feet in, if your wife has beds in two different houses, and you're only in one of them."

In Hukka's absence Bukka tried to intercede on his brother's behalf. He took Pampa Kampana for a walk along the bank of the river whose name she bore to encourage her to give up her liaison with the foreigner. "Think of the empire," he implored her. "We all bow down before you as the enchantress who brought all this into being, but we expect you to remain in a high place and avoid slipping into the gutter."

The harshness of that squalid noun, *gutter,* stirred Pampa to reply. "I'll tell you a secret," she said. "I'm going to have a child, and I'm not sure which one of them is the father."

Bukka stopped walking. "The child is Hukka's," he said. "Be in no doubt about that, or the city you have built will crack and break and the walls will tumble down around our ears."

In the next three years Pampa Kampana gave birth to three daughters and after that the foreigner's name could never be spoken within the palace walls or anywhere that her husband was present, and nobody, on pain of death, was allowed to notice the young princesses' Iberian good looks, their fair skin, their reddish hair, their green eyes, and so on. In the future these attributes would create dissension in the kingdom, but for the moment their right to be members of the royal lineage was beyond dispute. But Hukka himself noticed what there was to notice, and his demeanor grew dark and withdrawn, also because Pampa Kampana had proved incapable of bearing him a son. As the years passed, his sadness grew, and in spite of all his military triumphs he became known as a monarch of gloomy disposition. When he was out fighting and conquering he felt better, because killing his adversaries on the battlefield was preferable to not being able to kill his romantic adversary back home. Every man he killed had the face of Domingo Nunes; but the satisfaction didn't last long, because the real Domingo was back in Bisnaga fucking the queen. Hukka came back to his palace soaked in blood and dissatisfaction, and his feeling of unrequited love turned him toward God.

On a hot dry day in the last year of his reign he summoned all his brothers to a meeting at the Mandana *mutt,* to dedicate the new temple being built there. By this time Chukka Sangama was established as the regent of Nellore, Pukka was the unquestioned strongman of Mulbagal, and Dev was firmly seated on the *kursi* of Chandragutti. They arrived at Mandana surrounded by the splendor of their mounted knights and many flags, and they had made wives and princesses of their guardian warriors, the Sisters of the Mountains, Shakti, Adi, and Gauri. Hukka watched his married brothers arrive with some envy—their women were not sleeping with bastard foreigners, were they?—but then he remembered that the Sisters were under orders to slit the throats of their husbands if they ever so much as thought of rising up against the king in Bisnaga, which was to say, himself. And he was the one who had given those orders, and the loyalty of the Sisters was beyond question.

"I guess it's better to have an unfaithful spouse," he told himself, "than one who is more loyal to your brother than to you, and whose knife, therefore, is always very close to your treacherous throat."

Chukka, the loudmouth brother, professed himself amazed by what he saw at Mandana. "What happened here?" he cried. "Did some god show up and decide to turn the monk's cave into a palace?" For Mandana was in the process of becoming a majestic religious destination, thronging with pilgrims and priests, boasting architecture-in-progress that promised to become as ornate as the old, ascetic refuge of the sage Vidyasagar, the Ocean of Knowledge, had been plain.

Vidyasagar himself stepped forward to reply. "The gods have better things to do than build temples," he said. "But for men there is no higher duty they can perform."

"Be careful," Hukka warned his brother. "You are on the edge of blasphemy, and if you fall into the pit that lies beyond, no amount of prayers will save your wretched soul."

"So you've changed as well as this place," Chukka retorted. "Now that you're turning Mandana into a palace-temple maybe you think you're the king in here as well."

"Second warning," said Hukka Raya, and Chukka's consort Shakti moved her hand to the hilt of the dagger in the sash around her waist.

"But the temple isn't finished," Chukka went on. "All you have so far is half of the entrance tower, the *gopuram*, the Imperishable Gateway. So I'm thinking you aren't finished either—not divine or imperishable yourself, or not yet, anyway."

"We are gathered to dedicate the temple to Lord Virupaksha, who is also Shiva, the mighty consort of the river goddess Pampa, who is also Parvati," Hukka said angrily, "and so I will not spill your blood today. Today there's a higher purpose. And as well as the temple, we must speak of the Diamond King of Golconda to the north, who is becoming too powerful for his own good, and follows an alien faith, and must therefore be declared our deadly foe. Not to mention all those diamond mines of his."

Now Pukka the reasonable Sangama brother spoke up. "I understand about the diamond mines, naturally," he said. "But for the rest of it, the alien-faith business, don't be silly. Bukka always said that neither of you cared about foreskins, on or off, and suddenly you're a hater of the circumcised? That sort of talk isn't even sensible. At least a third of the armies of Bisnaga, and maybe half of the merchants and shopkeepers trading in the streets, are followers of that alien faith. Are they our enemies too, all of a sudden? Does Bukka now agree with your new extremism? And where is the crown prince, by the way?"

"Never mind," said Hukka Raya I. "Enough discussion. Vidyasagar, please proceed with the dedication. We must ask the god to look kindly upon us, even upon those among us who are weak in their belief."

"You're really different now that you're older," Dev Sangama said, speaking up for the first time. "I think I liked you better before. And if I may ask—if this whole city of Bisnaga rose up overnight, people included, and if the wall climbed up around it the next day, and if that was all on account of a bag of seeds, why isn't that happening here and now with the temple complex? Why can't we just sit back and watch the magic show as the temple grows before our eyes?"

Queen Pampa answered for the king. "The supply of magic is not endless," she said. "Divine enchantment is sometimes available to human beings when they first set out in the world. After that initial period the time comes when they must learn to stand on their own feet, achieve their own achievements, and win their own battles. I could say, you begin as children, but finally you have to grow up and live in the adult world."

"You are the mother of the empire," Dev Sangama said. "But today your message of love sounds a little harsh."

In a dirty backstreet of Bisnaga City, in the unglamorous tavern known as the Cashew, Bukka Sangama at the precise moment of the temple's consecration was drinking the afternoon away with his comrade in debauchery, a grizzled old soldier named Haleya Kote, who had introduced the crown prince to the pleasures of cashew feni, the new liquor in town. Feni could be distilled from many sources, most notably the coconut toddy palm, but this new drink was something else, tastier, in the opinion of many tipplers, and—at least in the version offered for sale in this tavern—significantly more potent. The cashew plant was the other great gift brought across the seas by the Portuguese along with the Arab horses, and in fact the tavern was secretly owned by Domingo Nunes, although he preferred to keep the fact hidden behind a screen of proxy day- and night-managers, because he rightly feared that Pampa Kampana would disapprove. In this long, dark, and narrow place, the drinkers sat on simple three-legged stools around the plain wooden tables nearest the door, sipping the potent feni, each man slipping toward happiness or melancholy according to his nature, while toward the rear of the inn there were things going on over which it would be advisable to draw a veil. After a few jars of liquor, however, the alcohol blurred the perceptions of the drinkers sufficiently for the activities in the rear to continue without drawing any comment.

Haleya Kote was not one of the citizens of Bisnaga created by the magic seeds. He had seen combat with Hukka and Bukka during their soldiering days, was over a decade older than the brothers and more experienced in the ways of war, but had been captured just the same along with them by the armies of the sultan of the north, and, like them, had managed to escape his servitude far away in Delhi, some years after their own flight. He arrived in Bisnaga grayer and thinner than the Sangamas remembered, but his fondness for drink soon began to fatten him up. By the time he reached Bisnaga, Hukka was already lost in the golden labyrinths of kingship and had little time for friends from the old days, but Bukka was delighted to see a familiar face with whom he shared real memories which were not the creations of Pampa Kampana's whisperings. As the years passed and Hukka was pushed by his private resentments into the embrace of religion, a gulf had grown between the brothers, Bukka remaining cheerfully casual in the matter of faith while his older brother grew ever more austere. Also, the younger brother began to be concerned about the question of succession. Would the agreement he had made with Hukka that he, Bukka, would follow his brother onto the throne continue to hold, or would one of the king's Portuguese bastards try to make a grab for the empire? He took Pampa Kampana for another walk along the riverbank to discuss this and received a surprisingly positive reply.

"For sure you will be king after your brother," Pampa Kampana told him, "and to be perfectly frank, I can't wait until I'm your queen."

Bukka felt a shiver of fear run down his spine. He knew the king his brother was already finding it difficult to tolerate the continued attachment of Domingo Nunes's handsome head to his long and elegant neck, but now another neck and head—his own—were in danger of being separated as well. If Hukka Raya received even a hint that his wife, the promiscuous beauty whom neither time nor motherhood could age or tame, was prepared to enter his brother's bed once he himself was dead—was actually looking forward to entering it and was, by her own admission, eager for the day of Hukka's death to arrive!—then the tide of blood would surely become a flood, and the empire would be lost in a dreadful civil war.

"You and I must never speak again," he told Pampa Kampana, "until that day arrives."

After that he began to drink. Haleya Kote arrived in the city with perfect timing, just when the crown prince needed a drinking buddy, and the two became inseparable. Hukka, knowing nothing of Bukka's conversations with Pampa Kampana, deplored his younger brother's slide into his cups, and first threatened him with removal from the royal council, which was the government of the city and oversight body of the empire, unless he cleaned up his way of life, and then, when Bukka showed no sign of changing his ways, actually did remove the crown prince from that august body, thus making a public fact of what had long been privately whispered: namely, that the two most senior figures in the empire, the founders of Bisnaga, had fallen out. Now there was factionalism at court. Those who admired Hukka's reign, with its efficient administration and its many triumphs on the battlefield, stepped away from boozy Bukka, while those who noted that the king's health was beginning to be poor, that he was prone to headaches, fevers, and chills, thought that their best interests demanded a greater loyalty to the heir to the throne than to the king. Meanwhile, the crown prince spent his days at the Cashew tavern, wrapped in the fogs that feni so readily induced.

Bukka was popular in the city for the good-humored buffoonery of these years, and his lack of royal grandeur. When compared to the increasingly severe and melancholy king, he came across as a figure to whom it was much easier for the citizens to relate. Afterward, when he had become an impressive monarch, people wondered if Bukka had just been playacting in those drunken days, or if he had really been a dissolute fool. Bukka himself only ever gave a cryptic answer to this question. "I made myself look foolish," he said, "so that I might look better by contrast when I put aside my folly and put on the imperial crown."

Nobody asked such questions about Haleya Kote, who was dismissed by everyone as an overweight and washed-up old soak. However, the truth was that Kote was a member, perhaps even the leader, of an extremist underground sect known as the Remonstrance, whose leaflets detailing the so-called Five Remonstrances accused the "structural elements" of their religion—which was to say, the priesthood—of rank corruption, and demanded radical reforms. In the First Remonstrance they asserted that the world of faith had grown altogether too close to the temporal power, following the bad example set by the sage Vidyasagar himself; and that persons in high positions in the empire's temples should not take up posts in the city's ruling body. In the Second Remonstrance they criticized the new ceremonies of mass collective worship surrounding the recent dedication of the new temple, which, they asserted, had no basis in theology or scripture. In the Third Remonstrance they proposed that asceticism in general, and the celibacy of holy men in particular, had promoted the practice of sodomy. In the Fourth Remonstrance they said that true believers should refrain from all acts of war. And in the Fifth Remonstrance they denounced the arts, stating that too much attention was being paid to beauty in architecture, poetry, and music, and that such attention should immediately and forever be diverted from frivolities toward the worship of the gods.

It was perhaps an indication of the rapidly increasing maturity of the city and the empire that was spreading outward from it, that it had already acquired dissidents. However, the Remonstrance had gained few followers in Bisnaga, whose citizens loved everything beautiful, took pride in the glorious architecture rising up all around them, and rejoiced in poetry and song; and who enthusiastically enjoyed the practice of sodomy as well as heterosexuality, many Bisnagans seeing no need to love only members of the opposite sex, and taking equal pleasure in enjoying the companionship of their own gender as well. In the evenings at the time of the sunset promenade it was possible to see couples of all sorts taking the air and holding hands without embarrassment: men and men, women and women, and yes, men and women too. These were not people who were likely to feel that the Remonstrance's sexual condemnations were justified. Also, people were afraid of agreeing with the Remonstrance's political assertions. The assault on the probity of the revered Vidyasagar—and the pacifist rejection of war, when the armies of Bisnaga had proved themselves near-invincible—and the broad accusations of public corruption—to proclaim such beliefs openly was to invite slaughter. So the Remonstrance had so far failed to grow larger than a tiny cult, and Haleya Kote drank his woes away.

All of this was known to the crown prince, but he gave no indication of knowing, either on that afternoon at the Cashew on which a temple was being consecrated elsewhere in the city, or indeed on any other afternoon. Had some spy come up to tell him that he was getting drunk with the empire's most notorious underground rebel, its leading would-be revolutionary, he would have feigned shock and told the spy he could no longer down his feni in peace. And if Haleya Kote had suspected that a great and determined king was slowly hatching beneath the surface of the prince's rollicking exterior, a king with detailed plans for how he would treat the Remonstrance cult, he might have worried about the safety of his own head. As it was, however, they passed their afternoons happily, without an apparent care in the world. The future was left to arrive in its own good time.

• • •

Domingo Nunes, being a Christian heathen, had of course not been present at the dedication of the temple. But that night Pampa Kampana came to him. After many years in the hayloft he had finally acquired a small house in an anonymous quarter of the city, which he was filling with sheaves of paper on which he was writing his account of his time in Bisnaga. *It is a windy place,* he wrote, *a flat country, except for the mountains; but to the west the wind blows less fiercely, because of the many groves of trees where the mangoes and the jackfruit grow.* It seemed interesting to him to list banalities, to enumerate all the livestock and produce of the region, the cows, buffaloes, sheep, and birds, the barley and the wheat, as if he were a farmer, though he had never spent a single day working on any kind of farm. *On the way here from the port at Goa I found a tree under which three hundred and twenty horses could be kept safe from the sun and rain.* And so on. He spoke of the droughts in summer and the floods in the rainy season. He mentioned a temple with an elephant-headed god and the women who belonged to the temple and danced for the god. *These are women of loose character,* he wrote, *but they live in the best streets of the city, and they can visit the concubines of the king, and chew betel with them. They also eat pork and beef.* He wrote a great deal on a variety of subjects, such as the oiling of the king each day with quantities of sesame oil, and the feast days of the year, and other matters of no interest to local people, who knew all this already. The writing was clearly intended for foreign consumption. When Pampa Kampana saw the writing, in a language she could not read, she guessed its purpose and asked him if he was planning to leave Bisnaga, not just to buy horses and return, but for good. Domingo Nunes denied any such intention. "I am merely making a record for my own interest," he said, "because the place is so marvelous, it deserves a proper chronicle."

Pampa Kampana didn't believe him. "I think you are scared of the king and getting ready to run," she said, "even though I have told you many times that with my protection it is impossible for you to be harmed."

"It isn't that," said Domingo Nunes, "because I love you more fiercely than I have loved anyone in my life. But it's become clear to me that you love me less—and not only because I have to share you with the king!—but yes, partly because of that!—and not even because you have obliged me to deny!—never to see!—the three lovely girls about whom nobody can so much as whisper that they look exactly like me!—but yes, partly because of that too!—and I have agreed to all of it—all of it!—because of my love for you!—but still I sense this every day: that I am the one who loves more strongly than he is loved."

Pampa Kampana heard him out without interruption. Then she kissed him, which did not placate him, and was not intended to. "You are so handsome, and I have always loved your body as it moves against mine," she said. "But you're right. It's hard for me to love anyone with my whole heart, because I know that they are going to die."

"What kind of excuse is that?" Domingo Nunes demanded, anger rising in him. "Everybody in the entire human race faces that fate. You do, too."

"No," she said. "I will live for nearly two hundred and fifty years, and look forever young, or almost young. You, on the other hand, have already aged, you have developed a round-shouldered stoop, and the end . . ."

Domingo Nunes put his hands over his ears. "No!" he shrieked. "Don't tell me! I don't want to know!" He was aware that he was aging badly, that his health was no longer robust as it had formerly been, and he already feared that he would not make old bones. Sometimes he thought that his end would be violent, that it might very well come on the horse road between Goa and Bisnaga, where the marauding Kallar and Maravar gangs were still dangerous. He even suspected that the reason Hukka Raya I did nothing about the horse thieves was that he privately hoped they would waylay Domingo Nunes and do the king a service by ripping out the foreigner's treacherous heart. But Pampa Kampana had a different ending in mind for him.

". . . and the end is near," she said. "You will die the day after tomorrow, because your heart will explode, and perhaps it will be my fault. I'm sorry."

"You are a heartless bitch," Domingo Nunes said. "Leave me alone."

"Yes, that's best," Pampa Kampana said. "I don't want to watch the finale."

The truth behind Pampa's hard words was that her refusal to grow older was almost as much of a conundrum to her as it was to everyone else. From the age of nine, after the goddess spoke out of her mouth, she had grown up like any other girl until she reached eighteen, but things had been different ever since the day she gave the sack of magic seeds to Hukka and Bukka Sangama. Twenty years had passed since then and when she looked carefully at herself in the polished shield hanging on the wall of her bedchamber in the palace, she estimated that she might have aged two years at most in those two decades. If that was correct then by the end of the more-than-two-centuries-long span of life the goddess had allotted her she would have the appearance of a woman in her early- to middle-forties. This was a surprise. She had expected that by her third century of life she would have become a stooped and wizened old crone but it seemed that this was not to be. Her lovers would die, her children (who already looked more like her sisters than her offspring) would look older than their mother and fade away, the generations would flow past her, but her beauty would not fade. The knowledge brought her very little pleasure. "The story of a life," she told herself, "has a beginning, a middle, and an end. But if the middle is unnaturally prolonged then the story is no longer a pleasure. It's a curse."

She understood that it was her destiny to lose everyone she cared for and to be left standing at the end surrounded by their burning corpses just as her nine-year-old self had stood alone watching her mother and the women burn. She would relive, in slow motion, over eons, the catastrophe of the lethal pyre of her childhood. Everyone would die just as before, but this second immolation would take almost two hundred and fifty years instead of a couple of hours.

6

Domingo Nunes, unable to disbelieve Pampa Kampana's prophecy, spent that night and the whole of the next twenty-four hours getting drunk at the Cashew in the company of Bukka Sangama and Haleya Kote and crying out against Azrael the exterminating angel and Pampa's prediction of his imminent arrival, so that when his heart did burst, just as Pampa had predicted it would, the news flew around Bisnaga that the legendary foreigner who had named the city was dead, and also that Pampa Kampana had revealed that she possessed the power of foretelling when people would move on from this life into the next—in short, that she could not only whisper them alive but also whisper them dead. After that day she was more feared than loved, and her refusal to grow older only intensified the terror she began to inspire. Hukka Raya I, generous to his deceased adversary in love, summoned a Catholic bishop from Goa and kept Domingo Nunes's body on ice until the prelate arrived accompanied by a choir of twelve beautiful Goan youths whom he had personally trained, after which Nunes received a fine Roman send-off with all the trimmings. It was the first Christian funeral in Bisnaga, alien hymns were sung, the names of that exotic trinity of deities which bizarrely included a ghost were spoken, a plot of land outside the city wall was allocated for the burial of heathen foreigners, and that was that. Pampa Kampana stood beside her husband the king to bid her lover farewell, and it escaped nobody's attention that Hukka Raya I wore every day of his fifty years of life upon his lined and weathered face, and in fact struck most people as looking much older than that, the cares of monarchy and the exigencies of war having aged him beyond his years; but Pampa Kampana had scarcely aged at all. Her youth and beauty were as terrifying as her prophecy of Domingo Nunes's demise. The people of Bisnaga, who had loved her for her role in bringing the city into being, began to keep their distance from her after Domingo's funeral, and when she journeyed through the streets they backed away from her royal carriage, and averted their fearful eyes.

Her feeling of being cursed clouded her naturally sunny nature, and when she and Hukka were together the atmosphere in the room was filled with the perfumes of their melancholy. Each one misunderstood the other. Hukka thought his wife's sadness showed that she was in mourning for her dead lover, while Pampa Kampana ascribed the austere shadow that had fallen over Hukka to his newfound religious zeal, whereas in reality the king's thoughts were full of schemes which he hoped would win him back his wife's most tender affections, while she, sometimes, was wishing she could die.

For an hour each day they sat in the Hall of Public Audience, enthroned side by side, or rather lounging on a carpeted dais amid an amplitude of embroidered cushions, entertained by musicians playing the music of the south on the ten instruments of the Carnatic tradition, and waited upon by butlers carrying trays of sweetmeats and pitchers filled with fresh pomegranate juice, while the citizens of Bisnaga came before them with their various pleas, to be granted tax relief on account of the failure of the rains, or to be given permission to marry a daughter to a boy of a different caste, "because what to do, Your Majesties, it is love." During these sessions Hukka did his best to suppress his growing puritanism and generously to grant as many requests as he could, hoping that his display of softheartedness would soften the heart of the queen.

In between responding to his people's entreaties he tried to plead his own cause with Pampa Kampana. "I have been, I think, a good king," he murmured to her. "I am widely praised for the systems of administration I have created." But the creation of a civil service was unromantic, he quickly realized that, and to avoid boring Pampa Kampana he turned to matters of war. "In spite of my own desires, I have shown wisdom, and refrained from attacking the impregnable fortress of Golconda, leaving that heathen Diamond King to enjoy his kingdom a little longer, until our own army has been hardened by battle and can drag him down into the dust. However, I have gained many large tracts of land for the empire, passing the Malprabha river to the north and taking possession of Kaladgi, and reaching as far as both coasts, the Konkan as well as the Malabar. Also, after that upstart the sultan of Madurai killed Veera Ballala the Third, the last king of the old Hoysala Empire, I moved swiftly into that power vacuum and made the Hoysala territories our own . . ." Here he broke off, seeing that Pampa Kampana had fallen asleep.

In those days after the death of her lover Pampa Kampana began to feel oddly estranged from herself. She walked in the palace gardens through the tunnels of foliage the king had had constructed so that he could take his evening walks without being observed, and as she passed through those bougainvillea bowers she began to feel like a wanderer in a maze with a monster waiting at its heart: lost, that is to say, to herself. Who was she, she wondered. Maybe she was the monster at the heart of the maze, so that as she moved through that verdant labyrinth she was in reality getting ever closer to the beastliness of her true nature. Ever since the day of fire when her mother had chosen to become a stranger to her, after which a second mother, the goddess, had spoken to her through her own mouth, her identity had been transformed into a mystery she could not solve. Very often she felt like a means to an end—a deep channel through which the river of time could flow without flooding its banks, or an unbreakable container into which history was being shoveled. Her real self felt incomprehensible, impossible to approach, as if she too were burning in a fire. But it was becoming clear to her that the answer to the riddle was the point of the story of the world she had brought into being, and that she and Bisnaga would only learn that answer when they both simultaneously arrived at the end of their long tales.

There was one thing she did understand: that the force of her sexual desires grew stronger with every passing year, as if her body's ability to cheat time went hand in glove with an increase in the force of its physical needs. It occurred to her that she was more like a man than a gentlewoman in the matter of desire; when she saw someone she wanted, she set her sights upon him, she had to have him, and cared little for the consequences. She had wanted Domingo Nunes and she had had him, but she had lost him now, and the king with his growing puritanism was less and less to her taste. There were many preening, fawning options at court with whom a queen might indulge herself if she so chose, but for the moment she did not so choose. It was hard to be attracted to these former half-finished beings whose stories she herself had whispered into their ears. Whatever their ages, they felt to her like her children, and to seduce them would feel incestuous. And there was another question to think about: was she sucking the life and beauty out of the men she chose? Was that why they looked older than their years and died before their time? Should she abstain from all romances to spare the lives of the men she desired, and would she then begin to age like everyone else?

Such were Pampa Kampana's preoccupations. But the imperatives of her growing sexual hunger overrode her doubts. She began looking for a man; and the person upon whom her predatory and possibly lethal gaze alighted was her husband's brother: little buzzing Bukka, as sharp as the sting of a bee.

He was the only one who could cheer her up. He regaled her with risqué accounts of the bawdy late-night goings-on at the Cashew and invited her to spend an evening there with him and his drinking buddy Haleya, an idea so deliciously scandalous that the queen was tempted to accept his offer. But she restrained herself, contenting herself with his tall tales, by which, she noticed, she was not only amused but very frequently aroused.

Her attraction to the crown prince rapidly became obvious to everyone at court, and seemed impossible to comprehend. Bukka was no beauty of the Domingo Nunes type. By this time his body had bulged and sagged in several places, and he had the helpless look of a bulbous human root vegetable, a rutabaga or a beetroot. This sack of a man was oddly endearing to the lustful queen. And she had motives beyond mere desire. He was good with her girls, a naughty uncle whose antics delighted the princesses. It had come to Pampa Kampana in a dream that this year would be the last of her husband's life as well as the year of Domingo Nunes's death, and so she had to think about the future. In the absence of a clearly established line of succession the death of a king endangered all his closest relatives. Therefore it was important that she safeguard Bukka's long-established claim to the throne, because if he was wearing the crown then her children would be safe. And if she stood by his side no man in Bisnaga would dare to stand against them.

She asked him to walk with her through the foliage tunnels, and kissed him for the first time in those secret passageways constructed by her husband. "Bukka, Bukka," she murmured, "life is a ball that we hold in our hands. It is for us to decide what game to play with it."

Of course the news of Pampa Kampana's entanglement with the crown prince reached Hukka's ears almost immediately, foliage or no foliage, and the cuckold king, unwilling to move against his brother, was forced for one last time to leave home on a military expedition, to conceal his shame and also, by military triumph, to erase it. It was time to kill the sultan of Madurai, who had grown too big for his boots ever since he dethroned the Hoysala king, even though he had afterward failed to conquer the old Hoysala lands, which now belonged to the Bisnaga Empire. The sultan was a nagging thorn in the empire's side, and he needed to be dealt with. So Hukka Raya I set out on his last campaign, from which he would never return. His last words to the crown prince and the queen were very simple. "I place the world in your hands." There was no doubt in Pampa Kampana's mind that he feared he was going to his death. There was no need for her to confirm that he was. He hugged his brother and for a moment they were two poor cowherds again, just starting out on life's road. Then he left, knowing in his heart that his own road would run out soon, and thinking a good deal about the world of ghosts.

Ever since the funeral of Domingo Nunes, at which he had heard for the first time the liturgical terminology of Roman Catholicism, Hukka had been perplexed by the idea that one of the Christian gods was a phantom. He was familiar with gods of all types, metamorphic gods, gods who died and were reborn, liquid and even gaseous gods, but this concept of a ghost deity disturbed him. Did Christians worship the dead? Was the ghost somebody who had once lived, who had been elevated to the pantheon by the other gods on account of his godlike qualities? Or was this a god designated for the task of overseeing the dead while the Father- and Son-gods took responsibility for the living? Or a god who had died but failed to be resurrected? Or one who had never lived, a disembodied wraith present from the beginning of time, invisibly circulating among the living, sliding in and out of bedrooms and chariots like some sort of spy watching over the good and bad deeds of the world? And if the other Christian gods could be described as Creator and Savior, was the ghost the Judge? Or simply a god with no special area of concern, a god without portfolio? It was . . . a puzzlement.

His mind was running on specters because in those days rumors had begun to circulate about the emergence of a so-called Ghost Sultanate, an army of the dead—or perhaps the undead—made up of the spirits of all the soldiers, generals, and princes destroyed by the rising power of the Bisnaga Empire, all of whom were now hell-bent on revenge. Tales of their leader, the Ghost Sultan, had begun to spread. He carried a long lance and rode on a three-eyed horse. Hukka didn't believe in ghosts, or at least that was his public position, but privately he wondered if the sultan of Madurai's forces would be supported by these invincible ghost battalions, and if he would have to face the Ghost Sultan as well as the living one on the battlefield. That would make victory almost impossible to achieve. He secretly feared, too, that his growing religious intolerance, which in his almost wholly secular (and therefore debauched) brother Bukka's opinion ran counter to the founding idea of Bisnaga, might add to the fervor with which the ghost soldiers would oppose his forces, because, of course, they had all belonged in life to the religion which he no longer found tolerable.

Why had he changed? (The road to war was long and allowed much time for introspection.) He had not forgotten his hilltop conversation with Bukka on the day of the magic seeds. "Those people down there, our new citizens," Bukka had wondered, "do you think they are circumcised or not circumcised?" And he had added, "The truth is, I don't really care. It's probably a mixture, and so what." And they had both agreed. "I don't care if you don't care." "Then so what."

The answer was: he had changed because the sage Vidyasagar had changed. At the age of sixty the seemingly humble (though secretly predatory) cave dweller had grown into a man of power, who would have been called Hukka's prime minister if the term had existed in those times, and was no longer the pure (but also the impure) mystic of his youth. In the would-be revolutionary pamphlet known as the First Remonstrance—probably the work of the underground radical (and overground drunkard) Haleya Kote himself—Vidyasagar had been criticized by name for his proximity to the king. Nowadays he began his days neither in prayer, meditation, and fasting, nor in contemplation of the Sixteen Systems of Philosophy, but performing the duties of the senior lord of Hukka Raya I's bedchamber. He was the first person to see Hukka every morning because the king was obsessed with astrology and needed Vidyasagar to read the stars and tell him what the day held in store, even before he had breakfast. It was Vidyasagar who told the king what the stars said he should think about each day, and who should have access to the royal presence and who would be better avoided on account of an unhappy configuration in the heavens. Bukka, in whose less superstitious opinion astrology was a pile of bunkum, had begun to dislike Vidyasagar heartily, seeing his prognostications as plain political maneuvering. If he was the one who decided who the king could see, if he was the gatekeeper of the royal bedchamber and the throne room too, then his power was second only to the monarch's, and Bukka suspected the sage of using that power to oblige the king's ministers and supplicants to make large donations both to the Mandana temple complex and also, almost certainly, to himself. This was a power that already rivaled and might at some point be capable of overthrowing the monarchy. Hukka would hear no criticism of his mentor, but Bukka told Pampa Kampana, "When it's my turn I'm going to clip the priest's wings."

"Yes," she said with a vehemence that startled him. "Be sure that you do."

The newly politicized Vidyasagar expressed strong disapproval of Hukka's early embrace of a kind of syncretism, which had made him willing to embrace persons of all faiths as equal citizens, traders, governors, soldiers, even as generals. "There's no accommodation to be made with that Arab god," Vidyasagar told him firmly. However, the holy man was attracted to the uses of the monotheistic principle, and had elevated the adoration of the local form of Lord Shiva above all other deities. He had also watched with interest the large prayer gatherings of the followers of the Arab god. "We don't have anything like that," he advised Hukka, "but we should." The introduction of mass collective worship was a radical innovation which was beginning to be known as New Religion, and was much disapproved of by the Remonstrance, supporters of Old Religion whose pamphlets insisted that in Old and therefore True faith the worship of God was not a plural but a singular matter, an experience linking the individual worshipper and the god and nobody else, and these gigantic prayer meetings were really political rallies in disguise, which was a misuse of religion in the service of power. These pamphlets were largely ignored except by members of small intellectual coteries who lacked the common touch and therefore, being almost impotent, could be allowed to exist; and the idea of mass worship caught on. Vidyasagar murmured to the king that if he led these ceremonies there would be a valuable blurring between the worship of the god and the devotion felt for the king: which proved to be true.

The march against the sultan of Madurai was in line with the attitudes of Vidyasagar's New Religion. It was time to teach the upstart princeling, and his upstart religion, a lesson whose symbolism would reverberate around the land.

All of this had pushed Bukka and Hukka further apart than they had ever been, which was why, when Pampa Kampana kissed the crown prince in the green tunnel, he made no protest, but returned her affection with enthusiasm. For her part, she saw the rift between the brothers very clearly, and she had made her choice.

The global traveler to whom Domingo Nunes sometimes compared himself, the Moroccan wanderer Ibn Battuta, had paused on his meandering way to China—after being robbed in the Khyber Pass, and seeing a rhinoceros grazing on the banks of the Indus, and being kidnapped by bandits on his way to the Coromandel coast—to marry a princess of Madurai, and was therefore able to record his eyewitness account both of the hideous atrocities committed by the Madurai sultans and of the kingdom's fall. The short-lived Madurai sultanate was a quarrelsome place, the eight princes following one another onto the bloody throne by murdering their predecessors, one after the other, in rapid succession, so that by the time Hukka Raya I's armies arrived the sultan who defeated the Hoysalas—and whose daughter was now

Ibn Battuta's wife—was long gone, and since his time Madurai had been the scene of repeated power grabs, assassinations of the nobility, and public impalings of the common people, grisly acts intended to show both the nobles and the common people who was boss, but resulting in a level of hatred so profound that the army of Madurai rebelled and refused to fight, so Hukka's victory was achieved without bloodshed, and nobody mourned the last execution, which was of the last and most murderous of the octet of bloody sultans.

(Before Hukka could enter Madurai in triumph, Ibn Battuta made his escape, thinking it wiser for the foreign spouse of a member of the vanquished dynasty to absent himself from the scene; so there is no mention of the Bisnaga Empire in that great man's celebrated travel journals, and we may allow him to leave these pages without further comment. Of his abandoned wife there is no more news. She has faded from history, and even her name is a matter of some conjecture. Poor lady! It is always unwise to marry a footloose, traveling man.)

After Hukka entered Madurai he learned the tales of the gruesome dynasty whose rule he had just terminated, and he immediately thought of his own family, and regretted his recent estrangement from his brother the crown prince, and his longer alienation from his other siblings. He commanded the four cavalry riders with the fastest of all the horses in the army to gallop home to Bisnaga with a letter for Bukka, and to take similar letters to his three other brothers, Chukka in Nellore, Pukka in Mulbagal, and Dev in Chandragutti.

"These people in Madurai have been killing each other every few weeks for several years, it seems," he wrote, "sons killing fathers, cousins killing cousins, and yes, there's fratricide as well. The doings of this gory clan have made me love my family even more fiercely than I did before. So I am writing to tell you, my beloved kin, that I will not lift a finger to harm any of you merely to keep my hold on power. I trust you all not to move against me either, and I beg you to trust one another, and do no harm to your own blood. I'll be home in Bisnaga soon and all will be well, as it has long been. I love you all."

When Bukka received the letter he read it as a veiled threat. "The bloodbath in Madurai has given the king some bloody ideas," he told Pampa Kampana. "We need to be certain that we have a protective armed phalanx around us at all times from now on. These letters will have agitated our brothers also, and who knows? One or all of them may decide it's better to strike before they are struck."

Pampa Kampana's first thought was for her children, even though, being daughters—by this time they were beautiful teenage girls—they would be seen as less of a threat than sons. Maybe she needed to leave Bisnaga and seek shelter—but where?—the king's brothers were not to be trusted, everywhere else in the empire was under Hukka's control, and everywhere outside the empire was hostile. Bukka suggested that the princesses were safe while Hukka lived, but when the king died she should disguise her daughters as poor cowherdesses and send them to the Sangamas' remote village of origin, Gooty, built in the shadow of a great wall of rock, where there were people who would look after the girls. "This will only be necessary for a short time, until I have established control over the kingdom," he reassured her. "But in case I fail, whoever usurps my rightful claim, whether it's Chukka or Pukka or Dev, will never imagine the girls might be there," he said. "Since they became little kings in their little forts they have forgotten their roots and I doubt they even remember that Gooty exists. They weren't there for long, anyway, preferring to embark on a life of crime."

So began the first paranoid panic in the history of the Bisnaga Empire. In Nellore, Mulbagal, and Chandragutti the Sangama siblings began to eye their spouses, the Sisters of the Mountains, with increased suspicion, because maybe they had received secret messages from the king and were getting ready to kill their husbands. And Pampa Kampana secretly started preparing for her daughters' flight to the cows of Gooty. Bukka sent back to Hukka the most loving message he could manage and then prepared for trouble.

Such moments can presage the fall of empires. But Bisnaga did not fall.

Hukka fell instead. On his way home from Madurai, riding at the head of his troops, he suddenly cried out and dropped off his horse. The army came to a grinding halt and a royal tent and field hospital were erected with great haste, but the king was comatose. After three days he briefly awoke from his coma and his attending physician asked him questions to try to determine the state of his mind.

"Who am I?" the physician asked.

"A ghost general," Hukka replied.

The doctor pointed to his nursing assistant. "Who is he?" he inquired.

"He is a phantom spy," answered the king.

An orderly came into the field hospital tent bearing clean linens. "Who is he?" the doctor asked Hukka.

"He's just some spook," Hukka said dismissively. "He doesn't matter." Then he sank back into what proved to be his final sleep. And just as the army reached Bisnaga it was announced that the king was dead. Afterward as the story of his last words was whispered among the troops there were many who were prepared to say that they had seen the phantom army of the Ghost Sultanate approaching, they had watched with terror as the ghost general charged toward the king on his three-eyed horse, and witnessed Hukka Raya I's chest being pierced by the general's translucent lance. But for every man who was willing to spin such yarns there were ten who said they had seen nothing of the sort, and the field doctors' consensus was that the king had suffered a medical crisis in the brain and possibly in the heart as well, and no occult explanation was necessary.

The funeral rites of the first king of Bisnaga provided a solemn moment which, Pampa Kampana told Bukka, was the final act of the coming-into-being phase of the empire's history. "The death of the first king is also the birth of a dynasty," she said, "and another word for the evolution of a dynasty is *history.* On this day Bisnaga moves out of the realm of the fantastic into that of the historical, and the great river of its story flows into the ocean of stories which is the history of the world."

Things calmed down quickly after that. Pampa Kampana had not sent her girls into exile in Gooty to pretend to be cowherds. She had gambled her family's safety on her presumption that if she stood beside the crown prince, nobody would dare to raise a hand against him. And so it proved. Courtiers, nobles, and military leaders quickly acknowledged Bukka Raya I as the new ruler of Bisnaga and so did the Sisters of the Mountains. Bukka's three surviving brothers, immensely relieved that their wives had not killed them when they learned of Hukka's demise, journeyed to Bisnaga City to kneel before their new monarch, and that was that. Bukka Raya I would reign for twenty-one years, a year longer than his deceased brother, and these years comprised the first golden age of Bisnaga. Hukka's puritanical religious sensibilities were replaced by Bukka's happy-go-lucky lack of religious rigor, and the mood of so-what tolerance in which the city and empire had been born returned. Everyone was happy except for the priest-turned-politician Vidyasagar, who expressed to Pampa Kampana his displeasure at the return of an air of loose-moraled levity, at the indulgence shown toward members of other faiths, and at the new regime's theological laxity.

But she was no longer the traumatized little girl he had once taken into his cave and—in her unspoken words—abused. So she chose, quite simply, to ignore him.

7

On the first day of his reign Bukka sent for his old drinking buddy. Haleya Kote, whose life had been spent in army camps and cheap hostelries, was thrown off balance by the grandeur of the royal palace. He was escorted by expressionless women warriors past ornamental pools and splendid baths, past stone reliefs of marching soldiers and saddled elephants, past stone girls with flared skirts dancing in stone unison beside musicians drumming on stone drums and playing sweet melodies on flutes of stone. Above these friezes the walls were lined with silken cloths onto which pearls and rubies had been sewn, and there were golden lions standing in the corners. Haleya Kote felt overawed in spite of all his secret radicalism, and also afraid. What did the new king want with him? Maybe he wanted to erase the memory of his boozy past, in which case Haleya Kote feared for his neck. He was brought by the women warriors into the Hall of Private Audience and told to wait.

After an hour alone in the presence of shimmering silk and stone magnificence Haleya Kote's nervousness was much increased, and when at last the king entered, accompanied by a full retinue of guards, butlers, and handmaidens, Haleya became convinced that his last hour was at hand. Bukka Raya I was no longer little round Bukka of the Cashew. He was splendid—dressed in gold brocade, with a cap on his head to match. He seemed to have grown. Haleya Kote knew he could not actually have increased in size, that that was just an illusion created by majesty, but even that illusion was enough to heighten the grizzled old soldier's discomfiture. Then Bukka spoke, and Haleya Kote thought, *I'm a dead man.*

"I know everything," Bukka said.

So this wasn't about the drinking. Now Haleya Kote was even more convinced that his last day had come.

"You are not who you seem to be," Bukka said. "Or so my spies inform me." This was the new king's first admission that throughout his brother's reign he had maintained his own personal security and intelligence unit, whose officers would now replace the Hukka team, whose members would be encouraged to retire to small countryside villages and never return to Bisnaga City.

"My spies," Bukka added, "are very reliable."

"Who do they say I am?" Haleya Kote asked, although he already knew the answer. He was a condemned man asking to hear the sentence of death pronounced.

"You *remonstrate,* is that the word?" Bukka said very gently. "And indeed it is my information that you may be someone my late brother deemed a person of great interest, the actual author of the Five Remonstrances, and not simply a disciple of the cult. What's more, to conceal your authorship, you do not behave like the religious conservative the author would appear to be. Either that, or your declarations do not align with your true character, and are made to acquire for you a following you don't deserve."

"I will not insult your intelligence team by denying what you know," Haleya Kote said, standing very upright, as a soldier should at a court-martial.

"Now, regarding the Five Remonstrances," Bukka said. "I'm in complete agreement with the first. The world of faith should be separated from the temporal power, and from this day forward, that will be the case. As for the Second Remonstrance, I agree that these ceremonies of mass worship are alien to us, and they too will be discontinued.

After that things get a little stickier. The link between asceticism and sodomy is not proven, nor is the link between celibacy and that practice. Furthermore, it is a form of pleasure enjoyed by many in Bisnaga, and it is not for me to prescribe what kinds of pleasure are acceptable and which illegal. Then you require that we refrain from all military adventures. I understand that like many seasoned soldiers you have a hatred of war, but you in your turn must acknowledge that when the interests of the empire require it, then into battle we will go. And finally, your Fifth Remonstrance against art is the work of a true philistine. In my court there will be poetry and music and I will build great buildings too. The arts are not frivolities, as the gods well know. They are essential to a society's health and well-being. In the *Natya-Shastra* Indra himself declared the theater a sacred space."

"Your Majesty," Haleya Kote began, using the formal appellation of his former drinking partner, "if you would give me time to explain, and also beg for clemency."

"There is no need to beg," Bukka said. "Two out of five is not so bad."

Haleya Kote, experiencing a powerful mixture of relief and puzzlement, scratched the back of his neck, shook his head, and shuddered a little, giving the impression of being flea-infested, which, in fact, was very probably true. Finally he asked, "Why did you summon me to court, Your Majesty?"

"Earlier this morning," Bukka told him, "I entertained our great and wise sage, Vidyasagar, the Ocean of Knowledge, and I suggested to him that his masterwork-in-progress, his inquiry into the Sixteen Systems of Philosophy, was reportedly of a brilliance so extraordinary that it would be a tragedy if it ended up incomplete, unfinished, because of the distractions of his work at court. I also took the liberty to mention that astrology was not my personal cup of tea, so that the daily morning horoscope readings demanded by my brother would no longer be required. I must say that on the whole he took it very well. He is a man of infinite grace, and when he let out a single wordless ejaculation—a 'ha!' so loud that it frightened the horses in the stables—I understood this to be a part of his transcendent spiritual practice, a controlled exhalation from his body in which he expelled all that was now redundant. A letting-go. After that he took his leave and I believe he has retreated into his original cave of so long ago, near the perimeter of the Mandana complex, to begin a ninety-one-day program of meditation and soul-renewal. I know that we will all be grateful for the fruits of this disciplined activity and for the rebirth of his spirit in an even more bountiful incarnation. He is the greatest of us all."

"You fired him," Haleya Kote dared to summarize.

"It is true I have a vacancy at court," Bukka replied. "I can't replace Vidyasagar with a single adviser, because he is a man worth more than any other single living person. So I would like to offer you two-fifths of his responsibilities, namely, to advise on political issues. I'll find somebody else to be in charge of another two-fifths, which is to say, social life and art, the stuff you're too ignorant and bigoted to deal with. As for war, as and when that necessity arises, I'll take charge of that myself."

"I will try to become less bigoted and ignorant," Haleya Kote said.

"Good," said Bukka Raya I. "See that you do."

In Pampa Kampana's mighty rediscovered book, the *Jayaparajaya,* which looks with equal clarity and skepticism upon both Victory and Defeat, the name of the adviser chosen by Bukka to deal with social and artistic matters is given as "Gangadevi," who is described as a poet and the "wife of Bukka's son, Kumara Kampana," and who was the author of the epic poem *Madurai Vijayam,* "The Conquest of Madurai." The humble author of this present (and wholly derivative) text ventures to suggest that what we see here is a small subterfuge on the part of immortal Pampa—near-immortal in her physical incarnation, forever immortal in her words. We know already that "Gangadevi" is the name used by Vidyasagar to address the mute child who came to him in the aftermath of fiery tragedy; and "Kampana" of course is a name forever associated with Pampa herself. As for the "wife of Bukka's son," well! That would be a physical and moral impossibility, since Pampa Kampana would soon be the mother of Bukka's three sons—yes! This time around it was all boys!—and these sons would therefore have been unborn at the time of the Madurai expedition; and if they had been born, then to marry one of them would have been unthinkable and offensive to all. We must therefore conclude that "Kumara Kampana" never existed, that "Gangadevi" and Pampa Kampana are one and the same, that Pampa herself was the author of the *Madurai Vijayam,* and that it was her great modesty, her unwillingness to demand approval for herself, that was the reason for this flimsy veil of fiction, which is so easily torn away. However, we may further speculate that the very flimsiness of the veil suggests that Pampa Kampana actually wanted her future reader to rip it to shreds; which would mean that she wished to give the impression of modesty while secretly wanting the credit she pretended to be giving to another. We cannot know the truth. We can only surmise.

And so to resume: Pampa Kampana achieved the unusual feat of being queen of Bisnaga in two successive reigns, the consort of consecutive kings, who were also brothers; and Bukka gave her responsibility for overseeing the progress of the empire's architecture, poetry, painting, music, and sexual matters as well.

The poetry written during the reign of Bukka Raya I is rivaled only by the work done a hundred years later during the glory days of Krishnadevaraya. (This we know because Pampa Kampana included many examples of the work of both periods in her buried book, and those long-forgotten poets are only now beginning to gain the recognition they deserve.) Of the paintings made in the royal atelier, none survive, because during the apocalypse of Bisnaga its destroyers paid particular attention to the obliteration of representational art. Also, regarding the enormous quantity of erotic sculptures and friezes, we only have her word that they existed.

In spite of everything Bukka wanted to stay on good terms with the philosopher-priest Vidyasagar, because of the immense influence he still wielded over many Bisnagan hearts and minds. To keep himself in Vidyasagar's good books even after dismissing him from the palace, Bukka agreed to allow the holy man to levy his own taxes for the maintenance of the growing Mandana temple complex, in return for an assurance that the *mutt* would not involve itself in worldly matters.

As for Pampa Kampana: she paid Vidyasagar a visit in the cave to which he had retreated, the cave in which his weaknesses had been revealed and inflicted repeatedly upon her body. She came without any retinue of guards or handmaidens, and wearing only the mendicant's two strips of fabric, apparently turning herself once again into the ascetic young woman who had slept on the cave floor for so many years, and borne in silence everything he had done. She accepted his offer of a cup of water, and, after a few ritual compliments, outlined her plan.

As a central part of her program as culture minister, she told the great man, she proposed to build a spectacular new temple within the city walls, dedicated to a deity of Vidyasagar's choice, whose staff of priests and *devadasis,* temple dancers, would be for the high priest to appoint. For her part, she told Vidyasagar with straight-faced solemnity and no hint of a suggestion that she knew that her words would horrify him, she would personally select the most gifted masons and stone carvers in Bisnaga to create a magnificent edifice and cover the rising temple's walls, inside and outside, and also its monumental tower, its *gopuram,* with erotic bas-relief portraits featuring the beautiful *devadasis* and selected male counterparts in many positions of sexual ecstasy including, but not limited to, those spoken of in the Tantric tradition, or recommended in ancient times in the *Kamasutra* of the philosopher Vatsyayana of Pataliputra, of whom, she added, great Vidyasagar must surely be an admirer. These carvings, she proposed to the sage, should include sculptures of both the *maithuna* and *mithuna* types.

"As we are taught in the Brhadaranyaka Upanishad," she said, knowing perfectly well that to invoke not one but two sacred texts in the presence of the revered Vidyasagar was insolent behavior, to say the least, "erotic figures of the *maithuna* type are symbols of *moksha,* the transcendent condition which, when attained by human beings, releases them from the cycle of rebirth. 'A man closely embraced by a woman knows nothing more of a *without* or a *within,*'" she quoted the Upanishad. "'So also a man embraced by the spirit no longer separates the *within* and the *without.* His desire is satisfied, and his spirit. He has no desire anymore, nor pain.' As for *mithuna* sculptures," she went on, "these represent the reunion of the Essence. In the very beginning, the Upanishad tells us, the Essence, the *Purusha,* desired a second entity, and divided itself into two. Thus began man and wife, and so, when these are reunited, the Essence is once again whole and complete. And as is known it was by the union of the two parts that the whole universe itself came into being."

Vidyasagar in his mid-fifties, with a white beard so long that he could wind it around his body, was no longer the skinny twenty-five-year-old with wildly curly hair who had defiled little Pampa in this cave. Life in the palace had thickened his waist and denuded his scalp. Other qualities, too, had fallen away from him, modesty, for example, and generosity toward the ideas and opinions of others. He heard Pampa Kampana out and then replied in his loftiest and most patronizing tones.

"I fear, little Gangadevi, that you must have been listening to people from the north. Your attempt to justify obscenity by calling upon the ancient wisdoms is ingenious, if tortuous, but, to say the least, misguided. It is well-known to us here in the south that those pornographic sculptures in such faraway places as Konarak are little more than attempts to portray the lives of the *devadasis*, who, in the north, are little better than prostitutes, and are willing to contort themselves into many filthy postures in return for a few coins. I will allow no such display upon the pristine sites of our Bisnaga."

Pampa Kampana's voice was like ice. "In the first place, great master," she said, "I am not your little Gangadevi anymore. I have escaped that accursed life and am now Bisnaga's beloved Twice-Queen. In the second place, while my lips have remained sealed concerning your behavior in this cave all those years ago, I am prepared to unseal them at any moment, should you try to stand in my way. In the third place, this has nothing to do with north or south, but a willingness to admire the sacred human form and its movement in both monogamous and polygamous unions. And in the fourth place, I have just this moment decided that it will not be necessary to build a new temple after all. I will have these carvings added to the temples that already exist, the New Temple as well as the Monkey Temple, so that you can look at them every day for the rest of your life, and ponder on the difference between willing and joyous lovemaking and forcing oneself brutally upon another, smaller, defenseless human being. And I have a further idea which it is not necessary to share with you."

"Your power has grown greater than mine," Vidyasagar told her. "For the moment, anyway. I can't stop you. Do as you please. And as I can see from the continuation of your impossible youth, the goddess's gift of longevity is real and impressive. Please know that I will pray to the gods to grant me an equally long life, so that you will have me standing against your decadent ways for as long as we both shall live."

And so Pampa Kampana and Vidyasagar became, in a word, enemies.

This was Pampa Kampana's "further idea": to take erotic art away from the religious settings in which it had exclusively been seen up to that point, to set aside the need to justify it by calling upon the ancient texts, whether from the traditions of the Tantra or the *Kamasutra* or the Upanishads, whether Hindu or Buddhist or Jain, to separate it from high philosophical and mystical concepts, and to transform it into a celebration of everyday life. Bukka, a king who believed in the pleasure principle, gave her his full support, and in the months and years that followed carvings of *devadasis* and their male companions began to be seen on the walls of residential quarters, above the bars of the Cashew and other such hostelries, the exteriors and interiors of shopping establishments in the bazaar, and, in short, everywhere.

She found and trained a new generation of women woodcarvers as well as women stonemasons, because most secular buildings in Bisnaga, even large sections of the palace complex, were made of wood, and because women had more complex and interesting ideas about the erotic than men did. In those years when her sons were being born and she and Bukka were enjoying each other—she had never enjoyed being with Hukka in the same way—she set out to transform Bisnaga from the puritanical world envisaged by Vidyasagar, who had managed to persuade Hukka of its desirability, into a place of laughter, happiness, and frequent and variegated sexual delight. The project was a way of extending her own newfound happiness—which had permitted her to consign Domingo Nunes to the realm of memory rather than that of pain—and offering it to the general populace as a gift. It is likely, too, that the project was also, less innocently, a kind of revenge, undertaken precisely because the great priest wouldn't like it—the now-revered priest who had once been a monk who had not behaved, in the cave at Mandana, as monastically as he had encouraged everyone to believe.

It was Haleya Kote who came to Bukka to warn him that the plan might be backfiring.

"The thing about creating a life of delight," the old soldier told the king as they walked through the private leaf-tunnels of the palace gardens, "is that it doesn't really work from the top down. People don't want to have fun because the queen tells them to, or when, or where, or in the manner she prefers."

"But she isn't really telling them what to do," Bukka protested. "She's just creating an encouraging environment. She wants to be an inspiration."

"There are grannies," Haleya mentioned, "who don't like having wooden threesomes set into the walls above their beds. There are wives who are finding it difficult that their husbands look so long and carefully at the new sculptures, and husbands who wonder if their wives are being turned on by the wooden men, or, alternatively, the wooden women in these reliefs and friezes. There are parents who are finding it difficult to explain to their children exactly what's going on in the carvings. There are sad sacks and lonelyhearts made sadder-sackier and lonely-heartier by all the portraits of other people's joy. Even Chandrashekhar"—this was the barman at the Cashew—"says that looking at all that perfection of beauty and performance all the time, every day, is making him personally feel inadequate, because what ordinary guy could rise to such gymnastic heights. So you see. It's complicated."

"Chandra says that?"

"He does."

"How ungrateful people are," Bukka mused, "to find complication in a simple offering of public beauty, art, and joy."

"One person's art is another's dirty picture," Haleya Kote said. "There are still a lot of people in Bisnaga who follow Vidyasagar, and you know what he says about the carvings that are now crawling around the temples and infesting the public streets."

"'Crawling'! 'Infesting'! Are we talking about cockroaches?"

"Yes," said Haleya Kote. "That's exactly the word he uses. He's encouraging people to stamp out the invasion of filthy roaches fucking in wood and stone. Several of the new sculptures have already been defaced."

"I see," Bukka said. "And so? What is your advice?"

"This isn't my portfolio," Haleya Kote said, backing away from a possible confrontation with Pampa Kampana. "It is something you should discuss with Her Majesty the queen. But . . ." And here he stopped.

"But?" Bukka insisted.

"But, possibly it would be a good idea for the empire to follow policies that do not divide us, but unite."

"I'll think about it," said the king.

"I understand," he said to Pampa Kampana in the royal bedchamber that night, "that for you the act of physical love is the expression of spiritual perfection. But apparently not everybody sees it that way."

"This is disgraceful," she replied. "Are you taking the side of that old bald fat fraud against me? Because he's the one poisoning people's minds, not I."

"It may just be," the king gently said, "that your ideas are too progressive for the fourteenth century. You're just a little ahead of your time."

"A mighty empire such as ours," she replied, "is precisely the entity that should set out to lead the people toward the future. Let it be the fourteenth century everywhere else. It's going to be the fifteenth century here."

8

The three daughters of Pampa Kampana and Domingo Nunes, who were officially considered to be the offspring of Hukka Raya I, were Yotshna, "the light of the moon," a name chosen by Pampa to refer back to the Sangama brothers' claim of being descended from the Moon God; Zerelda, "the brave warrior woman"; and Yuktasri, "the brilliant, naughty girl." By the middle of Bukka's reign, when they were grown women in their late twenties, it was evident that Pampa's prophetic gifts had allowed her to foretell their characters perfectly. Yotshna had been a serene child and had grown into a calm beauty, as radiant as the full moon over the river, as alluring and romantic as the newborn crescent rising in the East. She was born with a stammer but before anyone could notice it Pampa Kampana whispered the cure into her ear to make sure that no wicked gossip could even think of uttering the words "just like Domingo Nunes." The middle girl, Zerelda, had been a tomboyish child, and occasionally perhaps a little too violent when playing with the daughters of courtiers, who dared not punch her back because of her superior rank and so were obliged to take their beatings without protest; and now, as an adult, she shocked the court by cutting her hair short and wearing men's clothes. Yuktasri, the youngest, had been the brightest girl in the royal schoolhouse, and her teachers told Pampa Kampana that if she hadn't been a princess she might have found a future in mathematics or philosophy, but her habit of playing practical jokes on classmates and teachers alike ought, perhaps, to be curbed. At sixteen, she was still the intellectual of the family, and shared one striking characteristic with her sisters: which was, that none of the three had shown any interest in finding a spouse.

Pampa Kampana did not try to force them to marry. She had always let her girls run free and grow into themselves in their own way. And now that they were women, not children, she proposed to Bukka her latest radical idea. When the goddess had spoken through her mouth she had urged Pampa to fight for a world in which men would *start considering women in new ways,* and this would be the most powerful novelty of all. Women, she said, should have the same rights of succession to the throne as men, and that if he agreed and the appropriate proclamation could be devised and approved by the royal council, it would then be necessary for a decision to be made as to whether the bloodline of Hukka or Bukka should determine the future of the dynasty. If she knew that this proposal would divide her family, setting her boys against her girls, she gave no sign of it, saying only that she was in favor of equality, and hoped that everyone she loved would feel the same way.

"In the Bisnaga Empire," she said in her address to the council, "women are not treated as second-class. We are neither veiled nor hidden. Many of our ladies are persons of high education and culture. Consider the marvelous poet Tallapalka T. Consider the exceptional poet Ramabhadramba. Also, women take part in every action of the state. Consider our beloved friend the noblewoman Lady Akkadevi, who administers a province on our southern border and has even led our armed forces into battle during more than one siege of an enemy fort.

"You see around you the formidable women of the palace guard. And you must know that we have women medicos, women accountants, women judges, and women bailiffs too. We believe in our women. In Bisnaga City there are twenty-four schools for boys and thirteen schools for girls, which is not equality, or not yet, but it is better than you will find anywhere beyond the borders of the empire. Why then should we not allow a woman to rule over us? To deny this possibility is an untenable position. It must be rethought."

At the time of the equality proposition the three sons of Pampa Kampana and Bukka Raya I were just eight, seven, and six years old. Their names, which Bukka himself had insisted on choosing, were Erapalli, Bhagwat, and Gundappa. According to Vidyasagar's astrological charts, *Gundappa* meant the child would be generous and high-minded; while *Bhagwat* meant he would be a dedicated servant of God; and *Erapalli* suggested an idealistic dreamer with much imagination. Bukka conceded to Pampa Kampana in private that the boys' actual characters largely disproved the value of the astrologer's predictions, for Erapalli possessed no imagination whatsoever and was in fact the most literal of young fellows, and Gundappa showed not the slightest interest in the higher things, and was, if the truth be told, more than a little mean-spirited as a child, and, later, as an adult as well. Bhagwat, it was true, was a deeply religious infant, bordering, Bukka admitted sadly, on fanaticism, so that was one correct astrological prediction out of three, which was not a good score, a lower percentage, even, than Haleya Kote's two out of five.

Motherhood never came easily to Pampa Kampana. She tried not to blame her mother Radha for that, but there was always a bubble of anger that welled up whenever the image of Radha's self-immolation swam before her eyes. Her mother hadn't cared enough about her to live. Pampa's was the opposite problem. She would outlive everyone. Whatever kind of mother she might be, she would still have to watch her children die.

Pampa Kampana did the best she could with her sons, in whom she was, to tell the truth, considerably disappointed. She brought them up to have perfect manners and to wear charming smiles on their faces. But these likable attributes only served to conceal their true natures, which were, to be frank, brattish. And when word got out that the king and his council were giving serious consideration to the queen's proposition, those natures—arrogant, entitled, perhaps even bullying—asserted themselves.

The three brothers—just eight, seven, and six years old!—stormed into the council chamber to make their feelings known, pursued by hand-flapping tutors and governesses, who were trying to calm them down.

"If a woman wears a crown," Bhagwat cried, "the gods will call us their bad children, and punish us."

Erapalli added, shaking his head, "When I'm a man, must I stay home and cook? And wear women's clothes, and learn to sew, and have babies? It's . . . stupid."

Finally little Gundappa made what he clearly believed was a conclusive, clinching argument. "I won't stand for it," he stated, stamping his foot. "I won't, I won't, I won't. We are the princes. Princesses are just *girls*."

Pampa Kampana was seated on the dais next to her husband. Her sons' behavior appalled her, and it was at this point that she made the shocking choice that would alter the history of Bisnaga and dramatically change the course of her own life as well.

"I do not recognize my own blood in these noisy little barbarians," she stated. "Therefore, with a heavy heart, I disown them, now and forever, and I ask the king and council to strip them of their royal titles. The three of them should be exiled from Bisnaga City and placed under armed guard in a remote corner of the empire. They can take their governesses and tutors with them. Obviously. In time a good education may improve their bad natures."

Bukka was shocked. "But they are little children only," he blurted out. "How can their mother speak of them in such a way?"

"They are monsters," Pampa Kampana said. "They are no children of mine. They should not be yours, either."

All hell broke loose. The first circle of hell was right there in the council chamber, where Bukka Raya I was plunged into the inferno of impossible choices—to support his wife and outlaw his children, or to protect the little princes and alienate Pampa Kampana, maybe permanently—while all around him were the members of the council, looking in his direction, trying to decide which way they would jump after he had made his own unhappy leap. If he exiled the boys it could destabilize the empire and perhaps even lead to civil war; if he refused Pampa Kampana's demand then who knew what occult devastation she might rain down upon Bisnaga? As she had created it, might she not also be its destroyer?

"We need time," he said. "This requires much consideration. Until we deliver our opinion, the princes will remain here under the protection of the palace guard."

No decision was the worst decision. The next day, as the news spread, fights broke out in the city streets, and there were many violent assaults on women by those who opposed the queen's position, and these crimes dragged Bisnaga into the second circle of hell. On the third day the stores in the bazaar were looted by criminal gangs seeking to profit from public disorder, and on the fourth there was even a brazen attempt to rob the city's treasury with its huge vaults of gold. By the fifth day the whole city was full of rage, this faction against that one, and on the sixth day each faction was accusing the other of heretical thinking, and on the seventh day the violence was out of control. For this entire week Bukka Raya I sat alone in his private chambers, almost immobile, barely eating or sleeping, pondering, seeing nobody, not even the queen. At last Pampa Kampana forced her way into his presence and slapped him across the face to snap him out of his reverie. "If you don't act now," she told him, "then everything will collapse."

To quote Pampa Kampana's own words at this important moment in the narrative (because my own might not be trusted when such discord must be described): "When Bukka Raya awoke from his confused slumber, he was as powerfully decisive as he had been indecisive before." In quick succession he accepted and agreed with Pampa's requests, insisted on and received the royal council's assent, sent his three little boys into exile, and dispatched the women warriors of the palace guard, as well as a substantial body of soldiers from the military cantonment, into the city streets to restore order.

(It is very striking that Pampa Kampana, describing these crucial and painful events in her book, writes about them without a trace of emotion, giving no hint of what must surely have been the case, that she must have felt anguished and conflicted at her sudden and absolute rejection of her sons; that Bukka too was deeply torn between his love of his wife and his paternal feelings for his children; and that to choose his wife over his sons was—to say the very least—an unusual and unexpected move for a man of his position, and his time. She simply records the facts. Off into exile went the arrogant little boys, and the princesses ruled the court. We begin to see that Pampa Kampana possessed a startling—an almost frightening—streak of ruthlessness.)

It didn't take long for the city to calm down. Bisnaga was no primitive civilization. In her early creative whispers Pampa Kampana had imbued its newborn citizens with a strong belief in the rule of law, and taught them to value the freedoms they would enjoy under the law's umbrella. The umbrella became the most important fashion accessory in the city, a sign of status, and a symbol of patriotic reverence for justice and order. In the streets of the city every day the umbrellas paraded in all the colors of the rainbow, with golden tassels dangling from the spokes, some brilliantly patterned in paisley swirls or abstract zigzags, some with tiger motifs or with birds flying all over them. The umbrellas of the wealthy were set with semi-precious stones and made of silk, but even the poor had simple umbrellas over their heads, and the variety of the designs spoke of the diversity of cultures, faiths, and races to be found in those streets, not only Hindu, Muslim, and Jain but also the Portuguese and Arab horse-traders, and Romans who came with great jugs of wine to sell and spices to buy; and the Chinese were there too. Bukka Raya I had sent an ambassador to Zhu Yuanzhang, known as the Hongwu Emperor, in the first Ming dynasty capital of Nanjing; and some years later, after a family coup led to the shifting of the capital to Beijing, meaning "Northern Capital," the new emperor's great general (and eunuch) Cheng Ho, who liked to travel, came to visit Bisnaga in return. He, too, had an umbrella, and the design of his golden Chinese parasol spawned many local imitations. The umbrellas revealed the cosmopolitan open-mindedness of the city, and it was that open-mindedness that led, after some days of discontent, to the people accepting Bukka's decree, so that Bisnaga became the first and only region in all the land where people could contemplate the idea of a woman sitting alone upon the throne.

But the trouble rumbled on. Bukka sent his spies into the city to find out what was bubbling down below the apparently peaceful surface. The news they brought back was troubling. The reality that had emerged during the troubles—the factions, the criminals, the rage simmering down there and the threat of further violence fed by that rage—was not an illusion. The people might be more divided than had been believed, and support for the exiled little princes might be greater than expected. The equality judgment might, in the future, be seen as destabilizing, the decision of an out-of-touch elite. When Bukka told Pampa Kampana about the spies' report, however, she was unimpressed.

"I suspect most of these doubters belong to the first, Created Generation and not to the Newborn," she said. "I was always concerned that Whispering was an imperfect tool, and that some, at least, of the Created would later suffer from unpredictable forms of existential difficulty, psychological problems caused by their uncertainty about their own natures and worthiness, and that these problems would lead them to be prejudiced against others who, in their misguided opinion, were being treated as worthier than themselves. Get me a list of these doubters," she told Bukka imperiously, "and I'll go whisper to them some more."

During the second half of Bukka's reign, Pampa Kampana took on this task of whispered reeducation. As we will see, it did not succeed. In this way Pampa learned the lesson every creator must learn, even God himself. Once you had created your characters, you had to be bound by their choices. You were no longer free to remake them according to your own desires. They were what they were and they would do what they would do.

This was "free will." She could not change them if they did not want to be changed.

Bukka Raya I had played second fiddle to his brother for two decades, but once he became king he took to it as to the manner born. If we look ahead in Pampa Kampana's great book, we find that in the years to come he would be considered the best and most successful king of the Sangama dynasty, the first of the three ruling houses of Bisnaga. Nobody now remembers the Shambhuvaraya kingdom of Arcot, and the power of the Reddis of Kondavidu dwindled into nothing long ago. Yet these were among the substantial kingdoms and consequential rulers who fell under Bukka's aegis. Goa was his, and even a part of Odisha or Orya. The Zamorin of Calicut was his vassal, and the Jaffna kingdom of Sarandib or Ceylon paid him tribute. And it was to Jaffna that Bukka sent the exiled no-longer-princes, Erapalli, Bhagwat, and Gundappa Sangama, to live out their days under house arrest, closely guarded by soldiers of the Jaffna king, as a favor to the emperor of Bisnaga.

This was both Bukka's most painful decision and also his greatest miscalculation. No king likes paying tribute to a more powerful monarch, or acknowledging the other as his suzerain. So as the boys from Bisnaga grew toward manhood, the king of Jaffna covertly joined forces with them and helped them to set up a system of communication—by boat across the strait separating Ceylon from the mainland and then on horseback—with their three uncles, Chukka, Pukka, and

Dev, all of whom had poorly disguised royal ambitions too. The night-riders, dressed all in black, galloped regularly to Nellore, Mulbagal, Chandragutti, and back again, and so the six Sangamas, the three angry teenage nephews and their three ex-bandit uncles, all of them filled with flaming, murderous ambitions, were able to make their plans.

The failure of Bukka's intelligence service to notice the brewing conspiracy could be ascribed to one single distraction: Zafarabad. The rise of the Zafarabad sultanate to the north of Bisnaga, on the far side of the river Krishna, was a genuine threat to the empire. The shadowy figure of Zafar the first sultan was so rarely seen in public that people began to speak of him as the Ghost Sultan, and to fear that in Zafarabad the phantom army of the dead had been reborn and therefore could not be killed again. There were rumors that the three-eyed mount of the Ghost Sultan, the phantom stallion Ashqar, had been seen strutting in the streets of Zafarabad like a prince. It was plain to Bukka that Sultan Zafar was modeling his new kingdom on Bisnaga. Just as the Sangamas claimed to be the children of the Moon God Soma, so Zafar and his clan announced they were descended from the legendary Persian figure Vohu Manah, the incarnation of the Good Mind, and they went so far as to identify Bisnaga with Aka Manah, the Evil Mind that was the enemy of the Good. This sounded like nothing less than a declaration of war, and so did the choice of the name of "Zafarabad," which meant "City of Victory," just as "Bisnaga" did, in its uncorrupted form. To give the new sultanate the same name as the empire was a clear announcement of intent. The Ghost Sultan meant to erase Bisnaga and take its place. Even the three-eyed magic horse was a part of the challenge. If indeed it did exist, it was a rival to the celestial white horse upon which the Moon God rode, and whose descendants Hukka and Bukka had always claimed—without providing any proof—were their own sacred battle steeds.

Bukka was a well-loved king, so when he chose to march upon

Zafarabad the decision was popular. Cheering crowds lined the streets as the king rode through the great gate to where his army was waiting, its one million men, its one hundred thousand elephants, its two hundred thousand Arab horses, its air of utter invincibility against which not even ghosts would stand a chance. Only Pampa Kampana was filled with foreboding, and Bukka's last words to her felt like a warning, or an omen. "This is where you get your wish," he told her. "In my absence, you will be the queen regent. You alone will rule."

After he left at the head of his army, Pampa Kampana, alone in her private rooms in the *zenana,* the women's wing, asked to see Nachana, the court poet. "Sing me a happy song," she told him, which should have been an easy request to fulfill since almost all of Nachana's work was a celebration of the empire and its rulers—their wisdom, their prowess in battle, their cultured elegance, their popularity, their looks. But when Nachana opened his mouth only mournful verses poured out of it. He closed his mouth, shook his head in puzzlement, opened his mouth again to apologize for his mistake, then tried again. Even sadder stanzas fell from his lips. Again he shook his head, frowning. It was as if some dark spirit were controlling his tongue. It was a second omen, Pampa realized. "Never mind," she told the discomfited poet. "Even genius sometimes takes the day off. Maybe you'll do better tomorrow."

As the humbled poet was leaving Pampa's presence, her three daughters came in. Yotshna, Zerelda, and Yuktasri were a trio of mature beauties as formidable as their mother. Nachana bowed to them as he left, and delivered this parting shot: "Your Majesty, your daughters have now become your sisters." And with this final failed attempt at flattery he was gone.

The line struck Pampa Kampana's heart like an arrow. "Yes," she thought, "it's happening again." People were growing old all around her while she remained unchanged. Her beloved Bukka was sixty-six now, with bad knees, and he was often short of breath; he was really in no condition to ride to war. Meanwhile, if she paused to work it out, she herself was approaching her fiftieth birthday, but she still looked like a young woman of perhaps twenty-one or twenty-two. So, yes, the girls looked like her older sisters, not her children—maybe even her aunts, for by now they were spinster ladies in their thirties. She had a vision of a day in the future when they would be in their mid-sixties or older and she would still, to all appearances, be a young woman of perhaps twenty-seven. She would probably be looking under thirty when they died of old age. She feared that she might once again have to harden her heart, as she had with Domingo Nunes. Was she going to have to learn how to stop loving them, so that she could let them go while she lived on? What would it do to her, to bury her children one by one? Would she weep or remain dry-eyed? Would she have learned the spiritual technique of detachment from the world, which would ward off grief, or would she be annihilated by their departure and long for her own death, which obstinately refused to come? Or maybe they would be lucky and all die young together, in a battle or an accident. Or maybe they would all be murdered in their beds.

Her daughters wouldn't let her sit alone with that thundercloud over her head. "Come with us," Zerelda cried. "We're going to swordsmanship class."

Pampa Kampana had wanted them to learn pottery, as she had, and her mother Radha too, but the three sisters were uninterested in the potter's wheel, which continued to be Pampa Kampana's solitary hobby. She had raised her daughters to be better than men, better-educated than any man and more outspoken, and they could also ride horses better than men and argue better and fight harder and more effectively than any male warrior in the army. When Bukka sent his ambassador to China, Pampa Kampana told him, "They have extraordinary combat skills in that country, I hear. Youngsters learn about bare-hand fights and swords and spears too, long knives and short daggers also, and blowpipes with poisoned darts, I think. Bring me back the best martial arts instructor you can find." The ambassador had done as she commanded, and now Grandmaster Li Ye-He was installed as chief instructor of Wudang Sword at the Green Destiny *kwoon*—which was to say, "school"—of Bisnaga, and all four royal women were his star students.

"Yes," Pampa Kampana agreed, shrugging off her sadness. "Let's go and fight."

The *kwoon* was a wooden building made by Bisnagan craftsmen (and craftswomen) in the prescribed Chinese fashion, under the direction of Grandmaster Li. There was a central quadrangle, open to the sky, and this was where the fighting mat was rolled out every day. Around the quadrangle the building rose up for three stories, with balconies overlooking the fighting square, and there were rooms for study and meditation as well. Pampa Kampana found very beautiful the presence of this alien building near the heart of Bisnaga, one world penetrating another for the benefit of both. "Grandmaster Li," she said, bowing, as she entered the *kwoon* with her daughters, "I bring my girls to you. You should know that they all tell me they intend to find you a Bisnagan wife."

All four women tried every day to make this kind of remark in the hope of coaxing a reaction, a smile, perhaps even a blush, out of the instructor. But his face remained impassive. "Learn from him," Pampa Kampana advised her daughters. "Such magnificent self-control, such awe-inspiring stillness, is a power we should all try to acquire."

As she watched her daughters working out on the fighting mat in the *kwoon,* dueling in pairs, Pampa Kampana noticed, not for the first time, that they were developing supernatural skills. In the midst of a bout they could run up walls as if they were floors, they could leap gravity-defying distances from balcony to balcony on the upper levels of the school, they could spin so fast that they created little tornadoes around themselves, which bore them vertically into the air, and they could use an aerial somersault technique—somersaulting, so to speak, up an invisible staircase in the air—which Grandmaster Li avowed he had never seen before. Their sword skills were so extraordinary that Pampa Kampana understood they could defend themselves against a small army. She hoped she would never need to put that belief to the test.

She worked with Grandmaster Li as well, but in solitude, preferring to be simply a proud mother while her daughters had their lessons, and to attend to her own education by herself. In her private sessions with Li it quickly became clear that they were equals. "I have nothing to teach you," said Li Ye-He. "But to fight with you sharpens my own skills, so it would be more truthful to say that you are teaching me." In this way, Pampa Kampana learned that the goddess had granted her even more than she had previously suspected.

In the solitude of her regency, seeing omens everywhere, Pampa Kampana had begun to be full of foreboding. Since she shared everything with her daughters, she told them about her worries. "I may have overreached myself when I insisted on the equality thing," she said. "We may all pay the price of my idealism."

"What are you afraid of?" Yotshna asked. "Or should I say, whom?"

"It's just a feeling," Pampa Kampana said. "But I worry about your three half-brothers, and I worry about your three uncles, and there's someone I worry about even more than I worry about the six of them."

"Who's that?" Yuktasri pressed her.

"Vidyasagar," Pampa Kampana said. "He's the danger man."

"Don't worry about anything," Zerelda comforted her mother. She was the best fighter of the three daughters, and was confident of her mastery. "We'll protect you against anyone and everyone. And," she added, calling out to her teacher, "you'll protect the queen too, won't you, Grandmaster?"

Grandmaster Li approached and bowed. "With my life," he agreed.

"Don't make promises like that," Pampa Kampana said.

"The world appears to be *many*," the sage Vidyasagar liked to say, "but in truth *many* does not exist, and there is only *one*." After he lost his prime ministerial appointment and completed his cave retreat, he had left Bisnaga for many years, traveling all the way to Kashi to meditate by the holy river and deepen his knowledge. Now he was back. Seated once again in his place of honor under the spreading banyan tree at the heart of the Mandana temple complex with his long white beard wound like a belt around his waist and with a *devadasi* behind him holding a simple umbrella over his bald head to protect it from the sun, he adopted the *padmasana* or lotus posture and remained still, with his eyes closed, for long hours every day. Crowds gathered around the returned holy man, hoping he would speak, which often he did not. The longer his silences lasted, the larger the crowds grew. Thus he increased his army of disciples without appearing to seek any kind of following at all, and his influence spread through the city and beyond it, even though he made no apparent attempt to influence anyone. When he spoke it was in riddles. "There is nothing," he said. "Nothing exists. All is illusion." A daring disciple tried to elicit from him a comment that could be interpreted as, well, political. "Does the banyan tree not exist? Or Mandana? Or Bisnaga itself? The whole empire?" Vidyasagar did not answer for a week. Then he said again, "There is nothing. There are only two things, which are the same thing." This was unclear, and the disciple asked again, "What are the two things? And how can two things be one thing?" This time Vidyasagar did not answer for a month, during which time the crowd around him became immense. When he spoke he used a soft voice, so that his answer had to be repeated many times, the words rippling out across the multitude like waves on the surface of the sea. "There is *Brahman*," he said, "who is the ultimate and only reality, who is both cause and effect, who does not change but in whom all change is contained. And there is *atman,* which is in everything that lives, which is the only true thing in everything that lives, which is in fact the only thing that lives, and which is one hundred and one percent the same as *Brahman.* Identical. Same to same. Everything else is illusion: space, time, power, love, place, home, music, beauty, prayer. Illusion. There are only the two, which are one."

By the time these whispers had rippled through the crowd, being subtly altered by repetition as they moved, they sounded like a call to arms. What Vidyasagar was saying, the crowd understood, was that there were Two, and there should only be One. Only One could survive and the other must be—what?—absorbed? Or overthrown?

Bukka Raya I had insisted throughout his reign on the separation of the temple from the state, and Vidyasagar had not crossed that line. "If we did so," he told his disciples, "a fire would rise up along the line and consume us." Everyone understood this to be a reference to the magic protective line or *rekha* drawn by Lakshman the brother of Ram to defend Ram's wife Sita while the brothers were away, a line that would erupt in flames if any demon tried to cross it. Thus people also understood, first, that Vidyasagar was staying within the realm of religion by using a *Ramayana* metaphor, and second, that he spoke in a spirit of modesty and even extreme self-deprecation by comparing himself and his followers to demons, *rakshasas,* which clearly, in reality—in that reality which was an illusion—he was not, and nor were they. But at another level his followers also understood that by this dictum he had created an *us* who were not *them,* an *us* who wanted to cross that line and secretly supported the intrusion of religion into every corner of life, political as well as spiritual, and a *them* who opposed such *demonic* ideas. So gradually two camps grew up in Bisnaga, the Vidyaites and the Bukkaists, although these camps were never named as such, and everyone went along, at least on the surface, with the idea that they were all One. But beneath the surface the illusion dissipated and it was clear that they were Two, and that the Two were getting harder and harder to reconcile. If the Vidyaites noticed that these developments went against the grain of Vidyasagar's nondualism, his preaching of the identity of *Brahman* and *atman,* they did not mention it, focusing instead on the idea that the empire was a kind of illusion, and believing that the truth, which was religious faith, meaning their own true faith to the exclusion of all other false beliefs in hollow gods, would soon arise to take charge of everything that Was.

Meanwhile, in another corner of Bisnaga, Haleya Kote's Remonstrance had undergone a remarkable change. In its pamphlets and wall graffiti it had abandoned its opposition to sodomy, war, and art, espousing, instead, free love, conquest, and creativity of all kinds; and as a result it had begun to gain followers, many of whom said that the leaders of the movement need no longer conceal themselves, but should come out and stand for the Bukkaist values which so many in Bisnaga supported—to take up their role, in fact, as leaders of the Bukkaist tendency against the Vidyaites. (Although, we repeat, the divisive words "Bukkaist" and "Vidyaite" were never openly used.) Haleya Kote heard these voices, but remained silent.

When one has been in the shadows for an eternity, the sunlight feels too bright to bear.

Bukka had told Pampa Kampana about Haleya Kote's secret life, of course. She did not argue with his decision to keep the Remonstrance underground. "Ask your friends to work on escape routes," she told him. "If things go badly in the future—the near future, I fear—then an underground network may be something we all need."

Messengers arrived from the front. The expedition against Zafarabad was not going well. Haleya Kote came to give the queen regent the news. After the first skirmishes Bukka had to retreat south of the river Bhima and concede the northern shore to the sultan. Next, the sultan annexed Warangal, which had been a part of the Bisnaga Empire, and killed its ruler. Pampa Kampana was surprised and even distressed to learn that Bukka had sent envoys to the court of the Delhi sultan asking for that prince to help Bisnaga against his own co-religionists, which looked like a desperate move, and was unsurprisingly rejected. Then things had improved. Bukka had surged back toward the north and captured Mudgal. The messengers' report described Bukka's savage massacre of the people of Mudgal, which horrified Pampa Kampana. "That isn't the man I know," she said to Haleya Kote. "If that's how he's behaving now, it means his project is in danger, and so are we."

She was correct. The next messengers described an assault by the army of the Zafarabad sultan upon Bukka Raya I's forces at Mudgal. The weight of this assault panicked many members of the Bisnaga army, and whispers of the Ghost Sultanate, rumors that its phantom warriors were at the head of the Zafarabad vanguard, spread rapidly through the ranks, instilling terror and panic. When an army is afraid, it can't fight, even if it outnumbers its opponents. Bukka had fled his camp, the messengers said. His army had retreated in haste, and the advancing sultan had murdered ninety thousand people who had been left behind. Another even worse military defeat followed. "The king is coming home, but the enemy is in pursuit," the messengers said. "We must prepare for an attack, or at the very least a siege."

The Bukka who came home from the wars was, indeed, unlike the one who had departed. The way a man dealt with victory revealed one kind of truth about him: was he a magnanimous victor or a vindictive one? Would he remain humble, or develop an inflated opinion of himself? Would he become a victory addict, greedy for repetitions of his triumph, or would he be content with what he had achieved? Defeat asked even more profound questions. How deep were his inner resources? Would the moment be the unmaking of him, or reveal a previously unseen resilience and resourcefulness—qualities unknown even to himself? The king entering his palace in the bloodied leather and metal garments of the battlefield was a man surrounded by question marks, as if by a cloud of mosquitoes. Even Pampa Kampana did not know how he would answer.

He didn't speak to her, but only shook his head, and the cloud of interrogatory mosquitoes shook with him. He went into his private rooms and gave orders that nobody should enter. He remained there for week after week and it was left to Pampa Kampana to arrange the city's siege defenses with the help of Haleya Kote and her three daughters. Vidyasagar came to see her on the ramparts, where she was busy from dawn until dark, and told her that Bisnaga's defeat was a consequence of the king's abandonment of "intimacy with the gods in general and Shiva in particular." If that intimacy could be renewed then the advance of Zafarabad would fail; and military success would follow. "Many people in Bisnaga—most of our people, may I suggest—are in agreement with this analysis," he told her. "There are moments when a king should be instructed and guided by the people, and not the other way around."

"Thank you," she told him. "I will make sure the king knows this wise advice." Then she got on with her work and didn't give Vidyasagar's wise words another thought, because she was making sure the battlements were well stocked with cauldrons of oil to be heated and poured over anyone who tried to assault the walls, and that the soldiers manning the ramparts were well armed and also well rested, sleeping in shifts and taking up their posts in strict rotation. The army of Zafarabad was very close. Within days the attack—if it was to be an attack—or at least the siege would begin.

Pampa Kampana had begun to despair, but then one Friday morning when the earth was trembling because of the weight of marching feet, both human and animal, and when the dust cloud enveloping the army of Zafarabad was visible in the near distance, Bukka pulled himself together, marched out of his private quarters in full, clean battle array, and cried out, "Let's give that Ghost Sultanate a welcome that will make them scurry back to Ghost World." Though he had never been a large man, he rode through the streets of the city like an angry colossus and then at the head of his troops he led the charge into the sultan's army screaming a scream so terrifying that even that regiment of ghost soldiers, if that was what they were, could think of nothing except to flee as fast as possible and in complete disarray.

In the conflict with Zafarabad, Bukka had been the aggressor, seeing the danger of his northern neighbor's growing strength, and opting for a preemptive strike, which did not succeed. The river Krishna remained the boundary between the two realms. Not one *guntha* of land was gained or lost—not one *cent*—not so much as a single *ankanam*. Both sides held their territory, and an uneasy truce was made.

But after his last triumphant charge, Bukka became unwell. His condition worsened slowly but steadily and he fell into a deep sleep. As the news of his failing health spread beyond the palace walls people began to speculate on the cause. The idea that the king had been poisoned by a ghost dart took hold. "He is fighting the poison, but it is winning," the taxidermist said. "A ghost kills you slowly, because the move from our world into that world requires time," wailed the vendor of sweets. "He stands on the bank of the Sarayu river like Lord Ram," cried the painter of signs, "and soon, like Lord Ram, he will step into its waters and be lost."

Pampa Kampana spent every day and night at Bukka's bedside, applying cold compresses to his brow, and trying to squeeze water drop by drop into his mouth. He was asleep and did not awake. She understood that he was dying, that he would be the next person she had loved to leave her alive and mourning. On the third day of Bukka's illness Haleya Kote asked to be admitted to the king and queen's presence. Pampa Kampana knew at once, from the expression on his face, that things were going badly outside the king's bedchamber as well as inside it.

"We have been blind," Haleya Kote said. "Or rather we were only looking at the danger from the north, so we did not see the growing problems in the east, west, and south."

Chukka, Pukka, and Dev Sangama, accompanied by Shakti, Adi, and Gauri, the Sisters of the Mountains, and their personal armies, were converging on Bisnaga from their strongholds in Nellore, Mulbagal, and Chandragutti, Haleya told Pampa Kampana. "They have evidently persuaded those ferocious Sisters, their wives, that their oath to safeguard Bukka's position on the throne expires when he passes away, and that, after that, their loyalties must lie with their husbands." Additionally, he went on, the three deposed princes, now arrogant, entitled young men instead of arrogant, entitled little boys, and even angrier than they had been as children, had been allowed to leave Jaffna, accompanied by a sizable Ceylonese force of men, and they, too, were headed for Bisnaga to stake their claims to the throne. "I am sorry to tell you," he concluded, "that even though Bukka Raya decreed it and the council approved his decree, support for your eldest daughter's right to rule is not extensive, neither in the army cantonment nor on the city streets. 'Queen Yotshna' is still a step too far for most people."

"Six claimants to a throne that has not yet been vacated," Pampa Kampana said. "And who will choose between them?" Haleya inclined his head. It was a question to which they both already knew the answer. The answer was sitting under a banyan tree at Mandana with his eyes closed, apparently removed from these events, not a co-conspirator at all, not even remotely to be thought of as an individual who had corresponded and conspired with all six claimants, but merely a saint under a tree.

"Whoever it is, and whoever takes the prize," Haleya Kote told Pampa Kampana, "the danger to you and your daughters is very real. Especially as the question of their true parentage is still present in many wicked minds."

"We will not run," Pampa Kampana said. "I will sit by my husband's bedside, and if he leaves us I will make sure he does so with all the honors of the state. This is my city, which I built from seeds and whispers. Its people, whose stories are my stories, whose being-in-the-world comes from me, will not chase me out."

"It's not the common people I'm worried about," Haleya Kote said. "But let it be as you wish. I will remain by your side, with all the defenders I can find."

With the death of Bukka Raya I, two of the three founders of Bisnaga were gone and only Pampa Kampana remained. The day after Bukka died peacefully without waking up from his last sleep, the last rites, *ant-yeshti,* were performed at the burning ghat which would afterward become the site of his memorial. In the absence of a male child—the male children being still in transit, at the head of an army—the role of chief mourner was undertaken by Haleya Kote, who bathed himself thoroughly, then in fresh clothes circumambulated the body on the pyre, sang a brief hymn, put some sesame seeds in the dead king's mouth to serve as a symbol of the magic seeds with which he had created the city, sprinkled the pyre with clarified butter, made the correct linear gestures toward the gods of death and time, performed the act of breaking the water pot, and lit the fire. After that he, Pampa Kampana, and her three daughters walked around the flames several times, and finally Haleya Kote picked up a bamboo stave and pierced Bukka's skull to release his spirit.

All this was done with the proper solemnity, but after the mourners left the burning ghat a detachment of soldiers separated Haleya Kote from the four royal women, who were taken back to the palace and sequestered in the *zenana,* the women's wing, under twenty-four-hour armed guard. It was not clear who had given the order for this to happen, and the guards refused to answer Pampa Kampana when she asked them. The priest Vidyasagar was some distance away under his banyan tree, lost in meditation, and had not spoken a word. Yet somehow everyone knew who was in charge.

That night Pampa Kampana, enraged by her sequestration and filled with disbelief that Bisnaga would treat her in this way, was unable to think clearly. She commanded the woman warrior guarding the entrance to her rooms, "Go and get me Ulupi, right now." Ulupi, you will recall, was the gigantic, hissing captain of the guard, the one with the hooded eyes and flickering tongue. But the warrior at the door merely shrugged. "Not available," she said, making it clear that she who had been queen until a day earlier was considered to be nobody now; that Bisnaga had turned away from its matriarch in contempt.

Pampa Kampana's face reddened. Her daughters, seeing this, came up and led her off. "We need to talk," Zerelda told her mother.

Pampa Kampana took seven very deep breaths. "Very well," she said, "talk."

The three women gathered around their mother, coming in close, so that they could whisper. It occurred to Pampa Kampana that after having whispered all the histories of Bisnaga's citizens into their ears she was now having her own story whispered to her by her offspring. Karma, she thought.

"In the first place," whispered Yotshna, "nobody around here will fight for our rights, or even our safety. Agreed?"

"Yes," said Pampa Kampana, sadly.

"In the second place," Yuktasri continued, "maybe you haven't heard the rumors about the royal council. A headless council, now that there is no king. Have you noticed that nobody came to you from the council confirming your reappointment as queen regent until the question of the succession is settled?"

"Yes," said Pampa Kampana.

"One rumor," Zerelda told her, "is that they wanted to force us to enter the fire at the king's funeral pyre. That didn't happen, but it was a close thing."

"I didn't know," said Pampa Kampana.

"Nobody on the council can decide who should rule," Yotshna said. "So when all are assembled, Vidyasagar will be the kingmaker."

"I see," said Pampa Kampana.

"The most important thing now," Yotshna said, "is for us to get you to a safe place until we understand what the new world will be like."

"And if there's any place for us in that new world," Zerelda added.

"So a safe place for all of us," said Yuktasri.

"And where is that," Pampa Kampana asked, "and how will we get there?"

"As to how we will get away," Yotshna said, "we have a plan."

"As to where we'll go," Zerelda continued, "we hoped you might have some ideas about that."

Pampa Kampana thought for a moment. "Okay," she said. "Get us out of here."

"You have ten minutes to pack," Yotshna said.

Grandmaster Li Ye-He was our savior,
rolling over the zenana *like the thunder*
on Mount Kailash,
his blades as powerful as thunderbolts,
flashing in the night like the light
of freedom.

I give here my poor translation of Pampa Kampana's imperishable verses. I cannot come close to her poetic genius (I have not attempted to match her in meter or rhyme) but I offer it to suggest to the present reader the intrusion into the narrative of a moment belonging to a universe of marvels; for not only did Grandmaster Li arrive flying over the rooftops like a giant supernatural bat and then drop into the *zenana*'s inner courtyard like a panther who devoured whatever crossed its path, not only did he cut a path of death all the way to the four ladies; but then the princesses, as agile as he, two of them holding their mother by her hands, followed him as he ran up walls and along the heights of the city, bounding as if on winged feet from temple to tree to battlement, until at last the five of them dropped silently to the ground beyond the defenses of the city at the place where Haleya Kote was waiting, all in black, with six black horses saddled and ready to ride.

Where shall we go, our Mother,
Away from those who mean us harm?
My darlings, my beloveds, my dears,
Let us go to the Enchanted Forests
As they did in the ancient stories
And be safe.

PART TWO

| *Exile* |

9

The jungle stands at the heart of the great ancient tales. In the Mahabharata *of Vyasa, Queen Draupadi and her five husbands, the Pandava brothers, spent thirteen years in exile. Much of that time was spent in forests. In Valmiki's* Ramayana, *the lady Sita and the brothers Ram and Lakshman are exiled, mostly in forests, for fourteen years. In Pampa Kampana's* Jayaparajaya, *she tells us that her time in exile, which is to say* vanvaas, *plus her time in hiding in disguise, which is* agyatvaas, *added up to a total of one hundred and thirty-two years. By the time she reemerged in triumph, everyone she had ever loved was dead. Or almost everyone.*

In the jungle the past is swallowed up, and only the present moment exists; but sometimes the future arrives there ahead of time and reveals its nature before the outside world knows anything about it.

As they galloped away from Bisnaga it was Pampa Kampana who took the lead. "So many forests," she said. "The Dandaka forest where Lord Ram took refuge, and Lord Krishna's Vrindavan. Also, elephant-Ganesh's sugarcane forest, Ikshuvana, and Kadalivana, monkey-lord Hanuman's banana forest. In addition, there's Imlivana, the tamarind forest of Devi. But we will go to the most powerfully enchanted forest of them all, the Forest of Women."

She does not say in her book how long they rode, how many nights and days, or in what direction. So we cannot say for sure where the Forest of Women was located, or if some part of it stands there still. All we know is: they rode hard and they rode long, through coarse hilly terrain and green river valleys, barren land and lush, until at last the forest stood before them, a green rampart concealing great mysteries.

At the edge of the forest Pampa Kampana had a warning for Haleya Kote and Grandmaster Li. "In this forest, which exists under the protection of the forest goddess Aranyani," she said, "men can have a serious problem. It is said that any man who enters here will be transformed into a woman at once. Only men who have achieved complete self-knowledge and mastery over their senses can survive here in male form. So we must thank you and warn you, it would be safer to say goodbye."

The men considered this unexpected obstacle for some time.

Then Grandmaster Li said, "I swore an oath to protect you with my life. That promise does not expire until the day I die. I will go with you into the Forest of Aranyani, come what may." He dismounted from his horse and took up his sword and his other possessions. "Go well, horse," he said, and patted it on the rump. Off it went. Zerelda, his star pupil, looked at him admiringly and, Pampa Kampana noted, even a little fondly. "If anyone has self-knowledge and mastery over his senses," Zerelda told him, "you do. The forest will not harm you in any way."

(At this point in her narrative Pampa Kampana introduces a digression about the loyalty of horses, how they did not betray people who truly cared for them, and how she had spoken to them to ask them to cover their tracks on their return journey, walking through streams and across stony ground to make sure the runaways' destination could not be learned. We have chosen not to include this perhaps overlong passage.)

• • •

Haleya Kote shifted in his saddle uncomfortably. "I'm not a guy like our pal Ye-He here," he said. "I don't meditate, or attend to the purification of the self. I'm not a wise man like Vidyasagar, studying the Sixteen Systems of Philosophy. I'm just somebody who accidentally became a friend of our dear departed king, a fellow who likes a drink from time to time, and who used to be okay in a fight. I've never been a woman. I don't know if I'd take to it very well."

Pampa Kampana rode up beside him and said softly, "But you are also a man who does not deceive himself. You are not a fake. You know exactly who and what you are."

"Yeah, probably," Haleya Kote replied. "I'm nobody special, but I'm me."

"In that case I believe you may be fine."

Haleya Kote thought for a moment.

"Okay," he said at last. "Fuck it. I'll stay."

They set the rest of the horses free and stood for a moment gazing at their verdant destiny. Then into the trees they went, and the rules of the outside world fell away.

The wood closed around them, and was full of noises. There was much birdsong, as if a chorus had flown up to greet them: the yellow-throated bulbul, the jungle babbler, and the rufous tree pie could be heard; and tailorbirds, wood swallows, and larks; the barbet, the coucal, the forest owlet, the parrot, and the jungle crow were here; and many more to which they could not give names, birds of dreams, they thought, not of the real world. For here it was the real world that was unreal, its laws had been blown away like dust, and if there were other laws here, they did not know what those laws might be. They had arrived in *arajakta,* the place without kings. A crown, here, was no more than an unnecessary hat. Here justice was not handed down from above, and only nature ruled.

Haleya Kote was the first to speak. "Ladies, if you'll excuse the vulgarity, I have checked myself, and it feels like I am not changed."

"Oh, wonderful," Yotshna, the eldest princess, cried, and for a second time Pampa Kampana noted just a little too much emotion in one of her daughters' voices. "That's such good news for us all."

"Grandmaster?" Zerelda asked. "And you?"

"I am happy to say," replied Li Ye-He, "that I too appear to be intact."

"Our first victories," Zerelda declared. "These are good omens. They show that we will overcome whatever challenges the forest may send in our direction."

"Are there wild beasts here?" Yuktasri, the youngest, asked, trying not to let her fears show in her voice. Her mother nodded. "Yes. There are tigers as big as a house, and predator birds larger than the *rukh* of Sinbad, and giant snakes capable of swallowing a goat, and maybe dragons too. But I have magic that will keep us safe."

(We must ask ourselves how great her powers could actually have been, and if the forest truly did contain wild beasts that never bothered them because of her witchcraft—as her story suggests—or if it was mercifully free of such dangers, and she was just making a sort of joke. Was it true that the goddess who gave her the gift of long life, and the power to give seeds the power to grow a city, and the power that enabled her to whisper men's lives into their ears, also endowed her with the ability to enchant the enchanted forest? Or was this poetry, a fable like so many others? We must reply: either it's all true, or none of it is, and we prefer to believe in the truth of the well-told tale.)

Now they heard music. There were tabla drums playing rapidly somewhere up above them, speaking in their private language. And someone was dancing, invisible feet mirroring the speech of the drums.

They could hear the dancer's anklet bells jingling. Someone was dancing in the trees, up on the high branches, or perhaps in the air between the trees.

"Is that Aranyani?" Yuktasri asked, unable to keep the note of awe out of her words.

"The goddess is never seen," Pampa Kampana replied, "but if we have her blessing in this place, we will often hear her dancing near us. If she refuses us, then the dangers grow. Get used to the jingling bells. They are a part of what will protect us."

"If I may intrude," Haleya Kote intruded, "this is all very interesting, but we need to answer the questions of where we will stay, and also what we will drink, and eat."

"Yes!" said Yotshna, smiling too wide a smile. "Very good point."

Now that we know the full story of Bisnaga, that wooden hut, that palace in the forest where Pampa Kampana was queen in exile, and where she plotted her return in triumph, has become legendary. "Aranyani is not the only Being in this forest," Pampa Kampana told her companions at the beginning of their work. "Every grove of trees, every stream has its own familiar spirits. We must ask permission to cut and build before we start. Otherwise whatever we do will be undone immediately, and if the spirits grow angry with us it will not be possible to remain." So they made their appeals and when they had finished a light rain began to fall. The thick forest prevented the water from soaking them, but little rivulets ran down off the leaves and branches all around. "It's fine," Pampa Kampana said. "The rain is the blessing we need."

After the rain, the four women and two men built their new home in a little glade where the trees retreated to allow the sun to shine down after the rain. They asked permission of the goddess and also of the lesser deities of tree and leaf, they used their fighting skills with swords and axes, and the trained strength of their bare hands which could chop their way through trees as if they were made of cotton. We see them in our mind's eyes whirling through this grove, surrounded by giant trees without names, trees of myth and legend, weaving their new home into being in a dizzying display of athleticism and grace, lifting themselves off the ground to tear off higher branches, and spreading over their sylvan shelter a broad canopy of leaves. The drummer in the air and the invisible dancer both paused for a moment to watch the extraordinary sight, then resumed, and the house came into being to the music of the hidden gods.

The old soldier, Haleya Kote, proved to be the one who had thought ahead about practical matters. From the bulging bags he had loaded onto his horse and which, after the horses had left, he had carried without complaint, slung across his back, he now produced two cookpots, and also enough wooden cups and bowls for them all to eat and drink from, and flints to light a fire. "Force of habit," he said, shrugging with embarrassed pleasure when the queen and princesses thanked him. "It's not what you ladies are used to, but it will have to serve."

As to their first meal, Pampa Kampana tells us that it was the forest itself that provided for them. A shower of nuts fell around them from above, and banana trees like those in the forest of Hanuman gave up their plenty. There were fruits they had never seen before hanging from unknown trees, and bushes of berries so delicious that they made one weep. They found a fast-flowing stream of cold sweet water close by and by its banks grew *anne soppu,* which was water spinach, and Indian pennywort, which could be used medicinally, to ease their anxiety, and even improve their memory. They found air potatoes and clove beans, black licorice–flavored sunberries and wild red okra and delicious ash gourds.

"So we will not starve," Pampa Kampana said. "I also have brought seeds, which we will plant, and more varieties of food will grow. But let us talk about fish and meat."

Grandmaster Li spoke first. He had been a vegetarian all his life, he said, and would be more than content with what the forest had granted them. Haleya Kote cleared his throat. "In my military years," he said, "there was only one rule. Eat what you can get, whatever and wherever it is, and eat as much as you need to keep you going. So I have eaten bunnies as well as cauliflowers, billy goats as well as cucumbers, and little baa-lambs as well as plain boiled rice. I have tried to avoid cows, many of which are poorly nourished, and the meat not so good. It's chewy—apart from any other reasons for eschewing it. I also avoid eggplant but that's only because I can't stand the stuff. If there are deer in the forest, spotted chital, hog, blackbuck, or other types of food that moves about under its own steam, I'm ready to hunt it down."

Pampa Kampana's daughters told Pampa Kampana what she already knew. "Vegetables only," said Zerelda, smiling conspiratorially at Grandmaster Li. "Anything and everything," said Yotshna, stepping a little closer to Haleya Kote. As for Yuktasri, she hitched up her garments, walked into the stream, and stood there up to her knees in the rushing water, with her eyes closed and her arms outstretched. "Rohu carp, katla carp, pulasa fish, now come near," she said in a soft voice. "Pink Rani fish, walking catfish, snakehead fish, can you hear." According to Pampa Kampana, after a few moments a fish of a species they had never seen before leaped up out of the water into Yuktasri's arms. She brought it back to the group. "I like fish," she said. Her mother Pampa Kampana, who had long abhorred the meat of animals, surprised herself by thinking that maybe fish would not be so bad, would not evoke the dreadful memory of her mother's burning flesh. They had indeed entered a new world.

That first meal around the fire built by Haleya Kote, when they were all exhausted and hungry, felt like a banquet to all six vagabonds. The fact that they had abandoned their homes and fled, that the future was alarmingly uncertain, that being queens, princesses, grandmasters, or former soldiers, drunks, and underground radicals turned royal advisers meant nothing anymore, and that the forest was full of unexplained strangeness and no doubt other dangers of its own—at that warm and well-fed moment seemed not to matter. Pampa Kampana leaned against a tree, closed her eyes, and was lost in her thoughts, while the other five laughed and joked.

"I don't care how long we have to stay here if we can all be together like this," said Zerelda Sangama, leaning her head toward Grandmaster Li until it almost—but not quite—rested on his shoulder.

"Agreed," her sister Yotshna said. (She was sitting a little too close to Haleya Kote.)

Young Yuktasri said, "Good fish."

"Time to sleep," Pampa Kampana said, getting up. "Tomorrow it will be time to find out exactly what's going on in Bisnaga, and what we can do about it."

During the night the forest bats flew over them, around and around, like a protective army of the air.

It was a part of the enchanted quality of the forest that Pampa Kampana and the others were immediately able to understand and converse with all the living things within it. Of course this made the newcomers feel less alien in their new surroundings, but it was also, very often, oppressive, because the forest was full of conversation, the endless gossip of the birds, the sinuous whispers of the snakes, the high distant calls of the wolves, the loud bullying voices of the tigers. After a time the six of them would find a way of adjusting their minds and shutting out the nonstop cacophony, but in the beginning the princesses constantly had to put their hands over their ears and even thought about filling those shapely organs with mud to silence the din.

Pampa Kampana had no such difficulty, and immediately began to join in many of the conversations with evident pleasure, and even issued commands and offered instructions. She might no longer be a queen in Bisnaga but here in the forest her aura of magical power, conferred upon her by divine authority long ago, was impossible to argue with. Aranyani the goddess of the forest had accepted her as a sister and so that was how all the forest creatures thought of her. On their second night, a female panther dropped down from a tree and addressed them in a language they did not know but found that they could understand. "Don't worry about us," she said. "You have a mighty protector in this place." The next morning, even before the dawn chorus began its chit-chat, Pampa Kampana awoke and went out of their new home to talk to the birds. She dismissed some of the woodland species as being insufficiently serious for her needs, and concentrated on the parrots and the crows. "You," she told the parrots, "will fly to the city and hear what people say and come back and repeat it all to me, word for word. And you crafty creatures," she told the crows, "will go with them to understand what it means, the words beneath the words, and then you can be my wise advisers."

Seven parrots and seven crows obediently flew away in the direction of the great city. They were on relatively friendly terms, the crows and parrots, because both species were disapproved of by many of the other birds. In the forest world the crows were rank outsiders, considered to be treacherous and self-serving, and were distrusted. Even their voices were ugly when compared to the bulbuls and the larks; they did not sing, but cawed, hoarsely. If the forest birds were an orchestra, then the crows were always out of tune. Also, nobody had forgotten the war, two hundred years earlier, between the owlets and the crows, a war in which the crows were widely believed to have behaved dishonorably. Pampa Kampana knew about this anti-crow sentiment, and found it despicable. For hundreds of years before the war the crows had been obliged to act as servants—as serfs—to the more aristocratic birds, the owlets above all, and in her opinion the war had been a battle for liberation. By the end of the war many of the owlets were dead and the crows no longer answered to anyone, and, frankly, in Pampa Kampana's opinion, the more beautiful birds with more mellifluous voices needed to reassess their prejudices. Yes, there had been many casualties, but this had been a war of independence and should be understood as such. "It's too bad," she lectured the gallery of dawn birds, "that you beautiful winged creatures can be as bigoted as flightless human beings."

As for the parrots, they weren't songbirds either, which made them, so to speak, lower-caste; and there were so many of them that the other birds resented them for taking up too much space. Pampa Kampana had deliberately chosen the two outsider species to be her eyes and ears. After all, now she and her companions were banished outsiders also.

The delegation of parrots and crows returned three weeks later. They brought much news. When the six claimants to the throne arrived in Bisnaga (they told Pampa Kampana), it was Vidyasagar who ordered all of them to leave their troops outside the city gates, and to enter with no more than a personal security entourage. "There will be no bloodshed in our streets," he decreed. "Everything will be resolved without resorting to murder." By this time (the birds reported) Vidyasagar was well over seventy years old, and if the gods had indeed granted him a longevity equal to that granted to Pampa Kampana by the goddess whose name she bore, they had unfortunately not given the sage the gift of immunity from aging. So he was alive, but, it must be said, more than somewhat decrepit. His hands were bony claws; he had lost a good deal of weight and now looked, to be frank, scrawny. For courtesy's sake the birds did not dwell on the condition of his teeth.

"I don't care how he looks," Pampa Kampana told them. "Tell me what was said and done."

"Appearances had a lot to do with it," said the head parrot, whose name, approximately, was To-oh-ah-ta. "Vidyasagar took one look at the white-haired Sangama uncles, Chukka, Bukka, and Dev, and told them they were too old for the job—which was rich, coming from him!—and said that the empire needed young blood, a ruler who would stabilize matters by ruling for a long time."

"Meaning," the head crow, whose name, approximately, was

Ka-ah-eh-va, clarified, "that he, Vidyasagar, would be the real boss, and the young king would do what he was told."

"The three brothers of Hukka and Bukka the Firsts left Bisnaga City without argument," the head parrot reported. "People say that they were relieved not to have to kill anyone or be killed, not to have to murder their wives or be slain by them, and that they could live out their days in comfort in their distant fortresses, with their formidable women. So, this was a happy ending for them."

"Weaklings," said the head crow. "They never had the guts or will or strength to gain the crown, and everybody knew it. We don't need to concern ourselves with them anymore. They always were bit-part players, and they don't have any more lines."

"What about my sons," Pampa Kampana asked. "What of Erapalli, Bhagwat, and Gundappa, whom I disowned, but who, it seems, have now triumphed over me?"

"Interestingly," said To-oh-ah-ta, "Vidyasagar has anointed the middle son, Bhagwat."

"Meaning," commented Ka-ah-eh-va, "that Bisnaga will now be ruled by a religious fanatic, who will be advised by another extremist."

"I must also report," the parrot said, "that, in the first place, Erapalli and Gundappa Sangama have acquiesced in Vidyasagar's decision, so there will be no bloodshed, not for the moment, at least."

"But neither of them is happy," the crow added. "So look out for blood down the line."

"And in the second place," continued the parrot, ruffling its feathers in irritation at the crow's interruption, "Bhagwat Sangama has chosen, as his regnal name, the name of his uncle, a decision which has been widely interpreted as a slap in the face of the dead father who rejected him. So he will be Hukka Raya the Second. Hukka Raya *Eradu.* People are already calling him 'Eradu' for short. Or, in the rougher parts of town, less politely, 'Number Two.'"

"Does he say anything about me?" Pampa Kampana asked.

"I don't think he misses his mother," said the crow, a little cruelly. "We heard his coronation speech."

"From now on," the parrot parroted, *"Bisnaga will be ruled by faith, not magic. Magic has been queen here for too long. This city was not grown from magic seeds! You are not plants, to come from such vegetal origins! You all have memories, you know your life stories and the stories of those who came before you, your ancestors, who built the city before you were born. Those memories are genuine and were not implanted in your brain by any whispering sorceress. This is a place with a history. It is not the invention of a witch. We will rewrite the history of Bisnaga to write the witch out of it, and her witch-daughters too. This is a city like any other, only more glorious, the most glorious in all the land. It isn't a conjuring trick. Today we declare Bisnaga to be free of witchcraft, and decree further that witchcraft will be punishable by death. Henceforth our narrative, and our narrative only, will prevail, for it is the only true narrative. All false narratives will be suppressed. The narrative of Pampa Kampana is such a narrative, and it is full of wrong-headed ideas. It will be allowed no place in the history of the empire. Let us be clear. A woman's place is not on the throne. It is, and will henceforth be, in the home."*

"You see," said the crow.

"Yes," said Pampa Kampana. "I see very clearly. That backstreet name, 'Number Two,' suits him very well."

For the first time in a very long time, Pampa Kampana was thinking about defeat. It was not possible even to think of a return to Bisnaga. Worse than that, it seemed as though Number Two's polemic had widespread support among the people—or at least among a substantial group of them. This was her failure. The ideas she had implanted had not taken root, or, if they had, then the roots were not deep, and were easily uprooted. Bisnaga was becoming alien to the world she had created when she whispered it into life. And she was in the jungle, which was not a prison, but which would begin to feel like one soon enough.

"I must start planning for the long term," she thought. "Who knows how long it will be before the wind changes. My daughters will grow old. What I need is granddaughters."

Two very different lines of descent had emanated from Pampa Kampana. Her sons with Bukka Raya I were men who exuded a harsh perfume of embitterment that was her fault, because of her rejection of them; and one of them was now king. King "Number Two." He was Vidyasagar's creature, and so his reign would be a puritanical, oppressive time, and the free-spirited women of Bisnaga would suffer greatly. She closed her eyes and looked into the future and saw that after Number Two things would get even worse. The dynasty would descend into squabbling, growing religious intolerance, and even fanaticism. Such was the line of her sons. Pampa Kampana's daughters, however, had grown up to be forward-thinking, brilliant, scholars and warriors too; the most original children a mother could wish for. They had also inherited most of her magical abilities, whereas in the lowbrow literalism of the male Sangamas no trace of the wonderful could be found. Even their religious belief was ploddingly simple-minded and banal. The higher mysticisms eluded them entirely and religion became, for them, no more than a tool for the maintenance of social control.

"What I need around me," Pampa Kampana decided, "is a lot more girls."

It was a hard time to raise the subject of procreation. Her three daughters were having trouble dealing with the idea that their forest exile might not be brief, and might even last for the rest of their lives. The last things they wanted to discuss, as they neared their fortieth birthdays, were babies. They were shaken and uprooted, like trees in a hurricane. They were full of disbelief that their half-brother the new king would endanger them in this way, but at the same time they were old enough to know that when a king died the royal family's most dangerous enemies were within the family circle. They were strong-minded women, with deep reserves of character, so they set their jaws and worked with great determination to make their new lives the best that they could be. "If we have to be *junglees* from now on," Yotshna Sangama told her mother, "then we will be the most fearsome *junglees* anyone ever saw. That's the jungle law, right? Either you're on the top or you're on the bottom. Eat or be eaten. I intend to be the hunter, not the prey."

"We're not at war here," her mother reproved her gently. "We are accepted. We need only learn to coexist."

Yes, there must be granddaughters, she thought; maybe even great-granddaughters. For obvious reasons this was something she had to keep to herself. She turned over in her mind the idea that some of her granddaughters might have Chinese blood, which would make possible a grand alliance with the Ming. She also feared that the old soldier to whom Yotshna was attracted might be too old for fatherhood. And Yuktasri, what of her?

As if to answer her question, her youngest daughter asked her as they sat around their campfire at night, "Are there other women in the forest? Sometimes at night I imagine I'm hearing laughter, songs, and shrieks. Are they human, or *rakshasa* demons?"

"There are almost certainly other women somewhere," her mother replied. "Refugees like ourselves from one cruel kingdom or another, or just wild women of the wood, who have chosen to live their lives away from the coarse presumptuousness of men, or women who were abandoned by their mothers as babies at the forest's edge and have known nothing else but the forest, having been suckled by wolves."

"Good," Yuktasri said emphatically. And *oh*, her mother thought. *Oh.*

10

It quickly became evident that the forest creatures meant them no harm. During those early days, the denizens of the forest came in groups to greet the newcomers. Snakes hung down from the trees, and bears and wolves all came to pay their respects. The drummer in the air welcomed them, Aranyani danced invisibly over their heads, and the atmosphere around them was festive. Gradually the members of their party relaxed, and Grandmaster Li and Haleya Kote accepted that it wasn't necessary for one of them to stand guard at all times, and gave up the idea, which the four women had found more than a little patronizing anyway.

"This woodland festival to celebrate our arrival," Pampa Kampana said ruefully, "reminds me of how things used to be in Bisnaga in the good old days."

In the old days everyone in Bisnaga had celebrated everyone else's festivals. At Christmas Pampa Kampana had put up a tree in the palace and asked Domingo Nunes to teach her the songs and prayers that praised his "three gods," in their original language, and also what those alien words meant, *adeste fideles, laeti triumphantes,* translated into words she could understand. Baby Jesus became someone she could say she knew, a little bit, at least. And as for the followers of the "one god," she prevented herself from ever saying that, in her opinion, just one god sounded much less interesting than her large and variegated pantheon of deities; instead, she invited the one-godly to take part in the festival of light, the festival of color, and the festival of nine nights celebrating the victory of the goddess Durga over the demon Mahish-asura, which was to say, the victory of good over evil, because, she argued, surely that was something everyone could celebrate, whatever their preferred mode of worship, and however singular or plural their gods might be. This was what she had wanted for Bisnaga, this cross-pollination, this mingling. Now that was all fading away. The crow and the parrot made repeated visits to the city and reported to her that tensions between the communities were running high. Now there were areas of town where it was not safe for the one-godly to go, and there were unprovoked assaults at night. The news broke her heart, but, she told herself, for the moment her business was here, building the future with her daughters, until history provided her with the springboard for her return.

In the forest the conventions of the outside world lost their meaning and melted away. There were no schedules or timetables. One ate when one was hungry and slept when one was tired. It was a theater in which one could discover oneself, invent oneself anew, or clarify oneself by meditation. Hopes hung on every branch. Fears were things to be controlled. Desires were there to be fulfilled.

Pampa Kampana spent much of her time meditating. *Arajakta,* the condition of being without kings, was held by philosophers to be equivalent to a state of chaos or disorder. Yet here in the forest, in the very place of *arajakta,* it felt like something closer to a state of grace. Could it be that the world would be better off without kings? But then the animal kingdom too chose chieftains, leaders of the pack, top dogs. So perhaps a better question was, how should such leaders be chosen? The animal way—by fighting—was not the best. Could there be a way—was it even possible?—to let the people choose?

The idea shocked her. She set it aside for further consideration at another time.

• • •

Yuktasri Sangama turned into a nocturnal creature. Without asking anyone's permission she adopted a pattern of sleeping much of the day, snoring lustily, and rising as the darkness fell. Then she stepped across the invisible protective *rekha* and went into the forest. The first time she did this Pampa Kampana woke up and had to restrain herself from following. She saw shadows moving in the forest, and heard laughter, and understood that the wild women of the forest had come to meet her daughter, and that that was the company Yuktasri sought and needed. The next day she drew Yuktasri aside and asked, as gently as she could, "Tell me about them." At first her daughter was reluctant to answer but once she started talking she couldn't stop. Her eyes were alight with excitement as she spoke, and Pampa Kampana saw a happiness in her which was unlike anything the young woman had felt in her old life.

"In the beginning," Yuktasri said, "they thought I was a spoiled aristocrat. They wanted to push me around, to throw me between them like a toy. But they couldn't catch me. I ran up a tree trunk in my bare feet and chopped branches with my hands and the branches fell on their heads and then I got some respect. They speak a strange language which I at first thought they had made up so that they can talk to one another, like a mixture of many tongues and some wolf-talk too. But soon enough I realized that—even though they speak it with a terrible accent of their own—it's actually the same language the pantheress spoke, which we instinctively understood. They call it the Master Language, or something meaning something like that, and the magic of the forest works, so that even though I don't know the words I know what they mean. It's as if someone is whispering translations into my ear. Are there interpreter-spirits in the forest, whispering to us all? I think there must be. Most of the women don't bother to wear clothes and their hair is a mess and to be frank they are dirty and they stink as well. I don't care. I want to get to know them all. Last night they only sent a small group, six of them, like a scouting party. But the forest is large and they have several encampments. I want to learn everything, every track and trail, and how and what they hunt, and what they do for fun. They say they will teach me. In return, they want me to teach them everything I learned at the Green Destiny *kwoon.* The vertical running, the flying leap, the climbing tornado, the staircase somersault, the chopping. They don't have swords but they want to learn stick fighting."

"If the forest is a safe place for them," Pampa Kampana wanted to know, "why are they so fascinated by the martial arts?"

"They are worried," Yuktasri said. "There are rumors of hostile monkeys."

"Monkeys? What sort of monkeys? Monkeys are sacred creatures to us, as you know. They are the children of Lord Hanuman and the descendants of the tribes of his ancient kingdom of Kishkindha."

"These are not temple monkeys," Yuktasri said. "They are wild, and the forest is full of them, some brown, some green. But we don't need to worry about the green and brown ones. They mean no harm. The ones the women fear most are pink, and alien to this place. Definitely not the children of Lord Hanuman or the remnants of Kishkindha. Foreigners."

"Foreign pink monkeys?"

"They say the pink monkeys have almost no hair on their bodies, and their bare skin is a horrible pale color. They say the pink monkeys are large and unfriendly and travel in swarms and want to take over the forest."

Pampa Kampana was puzzled. "But the forest is under Aranyani's protection, so that can't happen."

"I don't know," Yuktasri said. "Maybe her magic doesn't work against them."

"Has anyone seen these pink monkeys?" Pampa Kampana asked.

"I don't think so," Yuktasri replied, "but the women keep saying, they're coming. And apparently there are no women monkeys. It's just an army of males."

"Sounds to me that this might be a story they tell themselves,"

Pampa Kampana said. "It doesn't sound real. A story, maybe, about their general dislike of men. Also, if Aranyani's spell works, maybe they would turn into females when they entered the forest, and change their plans and settle down."

"Oh," Yuktasri said, "if you heard them tell it, you wouldn't say that. This is the song they sing." And she sang it.

O the Monkeys are a-coming,
they're as pink as wagging tongues,
And they're not like any monkeys
in any song we've ever sung
Not lithe or sweet or hairy,
and as big as any man,
O the monkeys mean to harm us,
and to rule us if they can.
O pink monkeys are a-coming,
and their tails are very short,
And they speak a cruel language
which we never have been taught,
It is not the Master Language
of the forest and the wood
But they mean to be our masters,
let that be understood.
Tell all the forest creatures,
tell the Wolf and Bird and Deer,
Tell the Tiger, Bear, and Panther,
that the danger's very near,
And the danger's coming closer,
and soon it will be here,
And we must fight together,
without quarrel, doubt, or fear.
Oh, the goddess will protect us,
You may think and you may say,

For o'er this magic forest
It is she who holds the Sway.
But the monkeys are ungodly,
And though her power is strong
This may just be the time when
Something stronger comes along.
O the Monkeys are a-coming,
they're as pink as wagging tongues,
And they're not like any monkeys
in any song we've ever sung.

The song sent a chill through Pampa Kampana. I am hearing a message from the future, she told herself, a future beyond my imagining, of which these creatures are harbingers. I want to think that this is not my fight. I am engaged in a different struggle. But this may become our fight as well.

She was a child of Lord Hanuman's world, and Bisnaga was, in a sense, the child of his monkey-kingdom of Kishkindha, and so she had always thought well of monkeys, and believed in their benevolence. Maybe that, too, was changing now. Another defeat. Maybe this is what human history was: the brief illusion of happy victories set in a long continuum of bitter, disillusioning defeats.

"All right," she said aloud. "Can I meet these women of yours?"

"Not now," Yuktasri said. "I'm not ready for that yet."

Every morning for two hours Grandmaster Li and Zerelda Sangama practiced their skills with swords, long fighting knives, short throwing knives, tomahawks, sticks, and feet. As they fought it felt as if the whole forest came to a standstill and crowded around to watch. Yuktasri watched admiringly like everyone else, but afterward she said quietly to her sister, "I know you and Grandmaster Li are the best, but please don't intervene in my life. I'm the one the forest women want, not you."

"The women are all yours," Zerelda assured her. "I've got other things on my mind."

What she was thinking about was Grandmaster Li's Beijing, and other unknown cities with stranger names. Of all the Sangamas she was the only one who had an itch for foreign travel, a desire to see the world beyond her own part of it. Pampa Kampana, perceiving this, understood her daughter's attraction to the Chinese Grandmaster and feared the spirit of adventure might whisk her child away from her forever. A similarly adventurous nature had brought Li Ye-He south to Bisnaga, and in the forest he told Zerelda tales of his journey by land and sea; as well as tales told to him by his friend Cheng Ho, general, eunuch, and constant voyager, in search of treasure, around and across the ocean to the west; and, in addition, stories Cheng Ho had heard from the descendants of people who had met the Italian Marco Polo at the court of Kublai Khan in the time of the Yuan dynasty.

"I have heard," Grandmaster Li said, "that there is a city across the water with your name. In the city of Zerelda, time flies. Every day the citizens, who know that life is short, rush about with large nets trying to capture the minutes and hours that float around just above their heads like brightly colored butterflies. The lucky ones who capture a little time and gulp it down—it's easily edible, and quite delicious—have their lives elongated. But time is elusive, and many fail. And all the inhabitants of Zerelda know that there will never be enough time for them, and in the end they will all run out of it. They are sad, but put on cheerful expressions, for they are a stoical people. They try to make the best use of the time they have."

"I want to go there," Zerelda cried, clapping her hands. "And I also have to see the city of Ye-He, your namesake metropolis, where, as I have been told, the people, who possess the power of flight, live on the treetops while the birds, who are flightless, peck around for worms on the ground. In the trees one can find many stores selling warm clothing, because those who fly know that the air, as one rises up through its layers, rapidly becomes very cold, and it's necessary to wrap up when you don't have feathers to protect you. Because of this they, the featherless aerialists, understand that every gift, no matter how wondrous, also creates problems, and so they are a modest people, with modest expectations, who do not ask too much of life."

Pampa Kampana, eavesdropping on their conversations, was unsure if they were telling each other travelers' tales they had truly heard, or sending one another coded messages of love and desire in the form of these fabulous descriptions. "What is clear," she told herself, "is that they are planning to leave." She put a brave face on it, for grown-up children do finally leave home, and mothers must content themselves with memories and yearnings, but it was hard to hold back the tears. Then she heard Grandmaster Li saying, "Soon it will be the time of year at which General Cheng Ho likes to come by boat to visit the port of Goa and eat an excellent fish curry," and she realized that the time of their departure would not be long delayed.

She decided to take the initiative and be the one to suggest the big move, so that Zerelda would not have to feel guilty for abandoning her mother in exile. "Travel is good," Pampa Kampana said, "but also dangerous. Remember that Number Two is king of all the land up to and including Goa, and that we are all declared to be witches, so we are fugitives from what he would call his justice. If you want to meet General Cheng Ho safely and embark on his boat without any trouble, we have to make a careful plan."

Zerelda burst into tears. "We'll come back," she said. "It's just a little trip."

"If things go well for you both, you'll never return," her mother told her. "And in your place, considering our poor situation here, neither would I."

Grandmaster Li spoke up. "I have already explained to Princess Zerelda that all of this is no more than a fantasy in which we are indulging ourselves, a way of traveling in our imaginations, and I have further explained that it cannot happen, because I am bound by my oath."

"You must miss your own country," Pampa Kampana said, "because, after all, you have been away for a long time, and this decline in our fortunes is not something you could have anticipated; and while you appear to be as expert in fantasy traveling as you are in the martial arts, it's no substitute for the real thing. Therefore I release you from your oath. My daughter loves you and I see that she loves, too, the kind of journeying life you have in mind. So we must find a way for you to eat a fish curry in Goa with General Cheng Ho, and then go on with him or without him, to China or Timbuktu or wherever the spirit moves you, or the wind blows you, to experience whatever chance has in store. But before you leave, to keep you safe, there is someone with whom I must speak."

(It is at this point in her great work that Pampa Kampana writes about her first visit to the goddess Aranyani, and of the gift the goddess gave her. Such passages in the Jayaparajaya *are not, we believe, to be interpreted literally. They are a part of the poetic vision that infuses the whole masterwork, and like all such visions must be interpreted as metaphors or symbols. It is for wiser minds than the present author's to explicate the nature and meaning of such symbols and metaphors. We can only humbly draw attention to this requirement. For ourselves we will strive earnestly to understand how poetry tells us truths which plain truth-telling prose cannot reveal, being insufficient for the purpose.)*

She was enveloped (*or so she tells us*) in a sudden whirlwind which wreathed her in circling leaves and bore her up and away and out of sight. Up there in the brilliance above the forest's canopy, hovering in the air above the topmost tip of the highest tree, was a golden ball of light, even brighter than the sun, that dazzled her eyes. Around and above the golden ball a group of ferocious *cheel* birds, the pariah kites who look out for the world's outcasts, was hovering. The voice that spoke to her from this ball was not ordinary, it seemed simply to exist in the air and be an aspect of the air. "Ask me," it said. When she returned to the forest glade, brought down slowly by the whirling air that had raised her up, she said simply, "I asked for a certain gift, and she gave it to me."

She refused to explain further. "When the two of you are ready to leave, you'll understand," she said. "And when that time comes, come to me, each of you holding a crow's feather in your hand."

After that she retreated into the forest to meditate for seven days. When she returned she was smiling calmly, and if she was grieving, she did not show it. "Are you ready?" she asked Zerelda and Ye-He and they said they were. Each of them held a crow's feather. "I have a feather too," she told them, "but mine came from a *cheel*. It's sensible for you two to be commonplace birds that nobody will look at twice, but if I'm going to guard you on your journey, I need to look as fierce as possible."

"What are you talking about?" Zerelda Sangama asked.

"Metamorphosis," said Pampa Kampana. "It only succeeds if it's not whimsical or frivolous, but arises out of your deepest need."

Once she cast the spell which Aranyani had granted her the power to cast, they would all three be transformed, and would remain as birds until they released the feathers they held in their claws. "Don't drop the feathers while you're flying," she warned, "or you will turn back into yourselves and plummet to your deaths out of the sky. Also, the feathers will only work three times—bird, person, bird, person, bird, person. Look after them. You never know when you might need their help to escape some bad situation."

"So we can take nothing with us?" Zerelda asked.

"The clothes that you're wearing, the gold in your pockets, the bags slung over your shoulders, the swords in their scabbards on your backs," Pampa Kampana said. "Those will return when you regain your form. But that's all. If it's not connected to your body, you can't have it on your journey."

"When we meet General Cheng Ho," Grandmaster Li advised, "then I will put down my feather, but you, Princess, must keep hold of yours and sit on my shoulder until we are on his ship and away from the shore, safely out of Hukka the Second's reach."

"What about you?" Zerelda asked. "Won't you be in danger in Goa?"

"The moment we are with Cheng Ho and his party I'll be safe," replied Grandmaster Li. "We have found, we Chinese, that in this country people can't tell us apart."

Pampa Kampana gave each of the voyagers a pouch of gold coins from her secret hoard. "Good luck," she said, "and goodbye, because although I'll be flying over you, we won't be able to speak." Her face was expressionless. When Zerelda came up weeping to say her farewells, Pampa Kampana's features were set in stone. "Let's just go," she said.

It was her first departure from the forest, her first shift from exile, *vanvaas,* into disguise, *agyatvaas,* and it was only when the three of them, two crows and a kite, were up in the sky and flying toward the sea that Pampa Kampana realized that she had forgotten something important. Ye-He and Zerelda were embarking on a life together, but they were not married. She considered this matter silently as she flew and discovered to her surprise that she didn't care. "I have started living like a savage, according to the forest law," she realized. "There nobody is married and nobody cares." She asked herself if at some point Zerelda might want the formality of a wedding and she answered herself, "It's too late for you to do anything about this."

All the way to Goa she reflected, with a sense of shock, on her own shoulder-shrugging attitude. Was she a bad mother? Or might her attitude be another visitor from the distant future, when marriage would feel archaic and unnecessary, and nobody would give a damn about it? "That is a future beyond my imagining," she thought. "So, yes, bad mother, probably, that's it."

Darkness rushed up as if invisible hands were drawing a curtain quickly over the day, and then with a twinkling of lights there was Goa, and beyond Goa, the sea, and in the harbor—they swooped down to look—was the largest wooden ship Pampa Kampana had ever seen. There were many decks, enough room on board for several hundred men, and there was a Chinese flag of some kind painted on the stern. General Cheng Ho had already arrived, and he traveled with a private army, apparently. Good. Zerelda would have defenders if she needed them.

Pampa Kampana stayed up in the sky, hovering, watching Li Ye-He and Zerelda fly down to the hostelry where Cheng Ho habitually went for his spicy fish curry. One crow touched down on the ground and then Grandmaster Li stood there, with the other crow perched on his shoulder. After a brief pause, the grandmaster went indoors. Then time stopped for Pampa Kampana. For a timeless hour she sat on the roof of the inn listening to noises of revelry. The general's party came out, singing lustily, and headed back to the ship. Then after a further timelessness there was the shadow of a man faintly visible in the prow of the ship in the darkness, with an even less visible black shadow sitting on his shoulder, looking up toward the invisible *cheel* in the midnight sky and raising a hand in farewell.

As Pampa Kampana flew back to the forest of Aranyani, she kept her feelings under tight control, which was her way. "At least," she thought, "I'll never have to watch her grow old and die, never have to sit by that old lady's side terrifying her by looking like the ghost of her younger self staring back at her in her final hours. At least we will both be spared that upside-down ending. And I won't know when she dies, or how, so I can go on thinking of her as she is now, at the height of her beauty and power. Yes. That's what I want."

Time drifted aimlessly, as if floating on tides of sadness, in the period after Zerelda's departure. Years passed without anybody noticing. Nobody seemed to be getting older: neither the men nor the women. That phenomenon, too, eluded their attention, as if the enchanted forest had so ordained it.

The departed Zerelda's sisters' emotions did not fade. They had experienced her going as a kind of betrayal and reacted to it more in anger than with grief. The encampment in the forest blazed with activity as the princesses released their rage into construction projects. Their residence grew larger with the passage of time, with multiple rooms connected by a labyrinth of corridors, and now there was a thick soft carpet of fronds on the floors and there were tree stumps carved into comfortable seats by the skill of their blades, and whittled wooded blocks for pillows, curved into the shapes of their necks. But it did not feel like a peaceful home, because it had been built with wrath. After Pampa Kampana returned from the sky and was restored to human form, she withdrew into herself, spending days and even weeks alone, while Yuktasri disappeared into the forest with the forest women for long periods, and when she came back to their encampment she looked wilder, her hair standing out from her head, her garments torn, and mud on her face. Yotshna, the most sentimental of the sisters, sought to heal herself by plunging into love. She turned toward Haleya Kote and declared her affections. The old soldier, besotted with her as he was, did his best to discourage her.

Haleya Kote was maybe fifty years older than Yotshna Sangama. He had been born before her father. It was ridiculous for her even to think of him as a romantic prospect. He told her that from the beginning. "My knees creak when I stand up," he said, "and I exhale *whoof* when I sit down, as if somebody let all the air out of me. I can't walk as fast as you—damn it, I can't run as fast as you walk—and I can't think as fast as you either. I'm uneducated, my eyesight isn't what it should be, I read slowly, I've lost most of the hair on my head, the hair on my chin is white, and my back hurts. I've killed men, and I was wounded so often in the old days that I'm more than half dead myself. I was a pretty bad soldier, not a very successful underground rebel, a more successful drunkard, and an adviser to your uncle whose main function was to tell him dirty jokes from the old military days. What kind of man is that for you? You only started thinking about it because there was no other man around except Grandmaster Li and he was destined for Zerelda and now he's gone anyway. My most important achievement in life is that I didn't get turned into a woman when we entered the forest. That's more or less it. You're young. Be patient. We'll get out of here in a while and the right guy, young, handsome, charming, dashing, will be waiting for you in Bisnaga when we return."

"It's so insulting that you think that's all I want," Yotshna told him. "Some young good-looking fool. I've had them swarming around me all my life at court and, to be frank, *yecchh*. The reason you didn't turn into a woman is that you're not a stupid boy. You're a man, and you've lived long enough to know who you are. Very few men know who they are and that's why they can't get in here. A man who knows who he is, is gold."

"My breath smells," said Haleya Kote, "and I snore more loudly than Yuktasri in my sleep. I have half a century of memories of a time before you existed, when there was no Bisnaga, when the world was full of things that would be incomprehensible to you, because they happened so long ago. In my dreams I sometimes wish I was back there, young like you, and strong and full of determination and hope, knowing nothing about the harshness and cruelty of the world that beats optimism out of the young and makes them old. I don't want to be the one who drives the optimism out of you."

"I love it when you speak so romantically," Yotshna told him. "That's when I know you really love me."

"Will you love me when I get sick and start to fail, to descend, as is inevitable, toward death?" he said. "Do you really want to nurse a dying man and have to grieve for all the love you wasted on him?"

"Love is never a waste," she said. "You'll look after yourself and the enchantment of the forest will look after you too, and so will I, and if we have ten or even fifteen happy years, I will be content. And yes: I will care for you until the last day, when the time comes for that end."

"This can't happen," he said. "It mustn't happen."

"I know," she replied, "but it will."

11

The time came when Pampa Kampana was no longer resigned to exile. She needed to know exactly what was going on in Bisnaga City so that she could make decisions about her next moves. She informed Haleya Kote that she had work for him to do inside the city walls. "I can't rely on crows and parrots forever," she said. "I need experienced eyes and ears. And you have secret pathways in and out of the city."

Yotshna was furious with her mother. "You're doing this because of me," she accused Pampa. "To get him away from me. You're willing to put his life in great danger just to stop me having the man I want."

"In the first place," Pampa Kampana told her daughter, "that's not true. I know you well enough to understand that you will not allow any action of mine to stop you if you're determined enough. In the second place, don't underestimate Haleya. He is well versed in underground work and in the arts of *agyatvaas,* and I'll help him, too."

"You'll turn him into a crow?"

"No," Pampa Kampana said. "I was not granted unlimited powers of transformation. I can only use them on two more occasions, and must wait until it's absolutely essential to shape-shift. Haleya Kote will have to go in human form."

"You won't do for us what you were ready to do for Zerelda and

Ye-He," cried Yotshna. "That means you do want him dead, and if he dies, I will hold you responsible, I will never forgive you, and I will find a way to have my revenge."

"You really do love him," Pampa Kampana said. "That is good to know."

The city of Bisnaga had grown up in the shadow of a rocky mountain range, those same mountains on which Hukka and Bukka Sangama sat on the first day, watching in disbelief as the future sprang up out of Pampa Kampana's enchanted seeds. Both ends of the city wall touched the mountains, which themselves completed the ring of the city's defenses, and gave Bisnaga the confident appearance of being impregnable. But Haleya Kote and the Remonstrance had long ago discovered deep cavities among the boulders, and after years of slow burrowing they had deepened those caves into tunnels and created hidden pathways to the outside world, intended to be escape routes in the event of their discovery and persecution. "I can get in and out," the old soldier assured Pampa Kampana, "and in the city the members of the Remonstrance will hide me, if any of them still exist. In any case I can look after myself, don't you worry. But without a horse to carry me it's going to be a slow journey. Maybe I can steal a horse along the way, and another to get back."

During Haleya Kote's absence Yotshna Sangama refused to speak to her mother, and as the days wore on she became convinced that he must be dead. She imagined his capture, his torture, his terrible last moments, and wondered if he had died with her name on his lips. He was a hero whom her mother had wantonly sacrificed, and for what? What could he find out in Bisnaga that would affect their lives? Nothing, she thought. So he had died for nothing, which was not how a hero should die.

But he came back unharmed, riding a stolen horse, just as he had said. "Everything went according to plan," he comforted the sobbing

Yotshna, who rushed into his arms as soon as he had dismounted, sent the horse on its way, and reentered the forest—once again, without being transformed. "There was never a dangerous moment. Nobody's on the lookout for an old nobody like me."

"You look terrible," Yotshna greeted him. "The risks, the danger, the journey have all aged you. You look like you're a hundred years old."

"You look as beautiful as ever," he replied. "I told you I was too old for you."

Haleya Kote's safe return was the good news, but the news he brought was hard to absorb. Number Two had replaced the royal council with a governing body of saints, the Divine Ascendancy Senate or DAS, headed up by a certain Sayana, the brother of Vidyasagar, and the city was now under this new senate's strict religious control, as it "demolished" the philosophies of Buddhists and Jains as well as Muslims to celebrate the New Orthodoxy created by the thinkers of the Mandana *mutt* under the supervision of Vidyasagar, and made the New Orthodoxy—which was nothing more than the rephrasing of Vidyasagar's earlier New Religion—the basis of Bisnagan society. This change was a mirror image of developments in the sultanate of Zafarabad, where Sultan Zafar had died (thus proving that he was not, after all, the Ghost Sultan of legend) and had been succeeded by another Zafar, another Number Two, a zealot of his own faith, who had installed a religious "council of protectors" of his own. So in place of the old tolerances, in which members of all faiths participated fully in the life of both kingdoms, there was a separation, and a sad migration to and fro between the kingdoms of people who were no longer safe in their homes. "This is just stupid," Pampa Kampana said. "Whoever decided that our gods or theirs would want this kind of suffering had a basic misunderstanding of the nature of godness." According to Haleya Kote most of the citizens of Bisnaga were unhappy about the new hard line, but kept their mouths shut because of Number Two's creation of a squad of enforcers who reacted unkindly to any show of dissent. "So there's this quite small hard-core group in charge, and most older people fear and detest it, but unfortunately a proportion of the young go along with it all, saying that the new 'discipline' is necessary to safeguard their identity."

"And the army?" Pampa Kampana asked. "How do the soldiers feel about the dismissal of members of the other religion, which must include many senior officers?"

"So far the army has remained quiet," Haleya Kote said. "I think the soldiers fear being asked to move against their fellow citizens, which would be hard for them, and so they insist on their neutrality."

Vidyasagar himself was very rarely seen. Age had him in its grip. "He refuses to die," Haleya Kote told Pampa Kampana, "or that's what people say, but his body is not of the same opinion as his spirit. They say he's like a living man in a body that's no longer alive. He speaks through a dead mouth and gestures with dead hands. But he's still the most powerful person in Bisnaga. Number Two refuses to go against his wishes, however crackpot they may be. He wanted to change the names of all the streets, to get rid of the old names that everyone knows and replace them with the long titles of various obscure saints, so now nobody is sure where anything is anymore, and even long-time residents of the city are obliged to scratch their heads when they need to find an address. One of the new things the Remonstrance is fighting for these days is to get the old familiar names back. This is how crazy things are."

The Remonstrance had grown. Haleya Kote found many members willing to house him, feed him, shield him from unwelcome attention. It was no longer a small, insignificant cult, could now count its secret supporters in the thousands, and had changed its demands, dropping its less palatable early proposals and adopting, instead, an inclusive, kindly, syncretist worldview, which had turned it into a popular, although banned, opposition party. Its platform had the unusual characteristic of looking forward by looking back—in other words, it wanted the future to be what the past had been, and so turned nostalgia into a new kind of radical idea, according to which the terms "back" and "forward" were synonyms rather than opposites, and described the same movement, in the same direction.

There were handwritten leaflets scattered all over town, and graffiti on walls, but neither remained where they were put for very long. The gangs of the regime swept up the leaflets and burned them, and the graffiti artists knew that their archenemies would be close at hand, so they had to work fast. A single word was as much as anyone could put up, and by the next morning it had been washed away. So it was hard to protest, and yet the effort continued. The Remonstrance contained many highly motivated persons. Haleya Kote heard more than once the story of the heroic protester who dared to stand alone at the heart of the bazaar distributing pamphlets. When the DAS squad arrived to arrest him they found that the sheets of paper he was distributing were blank. No text was written on them, there were no drawings or coded symbols, nothing at all. Somehow this blankness angered the DAS team even more than slogans or cartoons would have.

"What does this mean?" they demanded. "Why isn't there any message written here?"

"There's no need," the protester replied. "Everything is clear."

Yotshna Sangama came out of their residence carrying water. "Let the man rest and drink," she scolded her mother angrily. "He just got back from this long and dangerous errand you sent him on, he has had a long and dangerous journey home, it has all put years on his face, and you insist on interrogating him at once, without even allowing the poor fellow to sit down."

Haleya Kote drank deeply and thanked her. "Don't worry, princess," he said, placing an intimate hand on her forearm. "It's better that I get everything off my chest. My memory isn't what it was and I should say it all before I start forgetting."

"Hm," Yotshna gave an unconvinced snort. "I see the queen here can still twist you around her finger. Maybe one day you'll start listening to me."

She walked off and left Haleya Kote and Pampa Kampana alone. What about Number Two's brothers, Pampa now wanted to know, unimaginative Erapalli and mean-spirited Gundappa. What were they up to? Making trouble or keeping the peace? "As for the brothers," Haleya Kote told her, "Number Two has sent them off to conquer Rachakonda, where people still follow the old *gungajumna* culture. That's the word they use in that locality to describe the blending of Hindu and Muslim culture. In Rachakonda the two cultures flow into each other just like the rivers Ganga and Yamuna, and become one."

"Just like things used to be in Bisnaga," Pampa Kampana said.

"Number Two doesn't approve of it, and nor does the DAS," Haleya Kote said, "so Erapalli and Gundappa have instructions to destroy the great fort at Rachakonda and kill enough people to cure the rest of these ideas. Then the two of them can rule the region together."

"And the uncles in their castles," Pampa Kampana asked her last question. "What news of those three old bandits?"

"They never amounted to much," Haleya Kote said. "Their stories hardly got started before they stopped. Now they are old and sick and far from Bisnaga and you don't have to worry about them. They won't last much longer."

When Haleya Kote had finished his report, Pampa Kampana nodded slowly. "Your news about the Remonstrance is encouraging," she said. "The seeds of change have been planted, but it will take time before the new plants grow. I must go to Bisnaga myself soon. I have hidden away like a rat in a hole and done nothing for too long. It's time I started whispering to people again. If many of the young are seduced by Number Two's nonsense, then it will be hard work. The wheel always turns in the end, but if that's true about the young then it could take a long time. Still, we have to make a start."

"I heard that," Yotshna cried, rushing out of the residence to where her mother and Haleya Kote were standing in the glade. "Don't you dare tell me you'll both go to Bisnaga, literally jumping into the jaws of death, and leave me here in the forest alone?"

"You won't be alone," Pampa Kampana said. "Yuktasri is here."

"No she isn't," Yotshna Sangama wailed. "She's a savage in the jungle now, along with the other savages, spouting nonsense about pink monkeys. I'm the only one of all of us that hasn't lost her mind, and now you'll abandon me to go mad by myself alone in this dreadful place."

"I have to be there," Pampa Kampana said. "If one wants to change the direction of history, one can't do it from a distance."

"What if they catch you," Yotshna exclaimed. "You'll make the wrong kind of history then, won't you."

"They won't catch me," said Pampa Kampana. "And time has gone by, and that cools all tempers. Also, people forget. History is the consequence not only of people's actions, but also of their forgetfulness."

"You're hard to forget," her daughter told her. "And this is insanity."

"Don't worry," Pampa Kampana tried to reassure her. "We'll steal horses, so we won't be away too long."

As she passed beyond the outer edge of the enchanted forest, accompanied by Yotshna and Haleya Kote, Pampa Kampana realized for the first time that Aranyani's magic had blurred the exiles' perception of the passing of the years, and, in that world without mirrors, had blinded them all to the changes in their own bodies—or, more accurately, it had preserved them unchanged, keeping them as they had been when they first entered. Now she understood why Haleya Kote, on his return from Bisnaga, had looked so much older. When he left the forest his true age had revealed itself in his features, so he now seemed almost impossibly antique, no doubt granted such a long life by the magic of the wood. She began to work out her own age, to which she had never given any thought—in some way that she did not understand the forest had banished all such considerations from her consciousness—and she was alarmed to find, as she made her calculations, that she must be at least eighty-six years old; but because of the goddess Pampa's gift of youth—not eternal youth, but long-lasting enough!—she still possessed the youth, vigor, and appearance of a young woman of perhaps twenty-five.

She was interrupted in her calculations by Yotshna's horrified voice. "What have you done?" she shrieked. "What has happened to me?"

"I have done nothing," Pampa Kampana replied. "The years have passed, but in the forest we have been living in a dream."

"But you," Yotshna shouted, "you look like a girl. You look like you could be my daughter. Who are you, anyway? I don't even know who you are."

"I've told you everything," Pampa Kampana said, with a deep unhappiness in her voice. "This is my curse."

"No," cried Yotshna. "It's mine. *You* are my curse. Look at Haleya Kote. He looks like he won't live another hour. So you found a way of taking him from me, after all."

"I will live," Haleya Kote said, "and I will come back to you. I promise you that."

"No," Yotshna wept. "She will find a way to kill you. I know she will. I'll never see you again." And with that she fled weeping into the depths of the forest.

Pampa Kampana shook her head in sorrow, and then gathered herself. "Let's go," she said to Haleya Kote. "There's work to be done."

Pampa Kampana returned to Bisnaga wrapped in an all-covering blanket, crawling through the secret tunnel of the Remonstrance and being guided by Haleya Kote to a safe house, the home of a widowed astrologer calling herself Madhuri Devi, a small matronly lady of about forty, who willingly agreed to shelter her. (When Haleya Kote told Madhuri Devi the name of her new guest, the astrologer's eyes widened in disbelief, but she asked no questions and welcomed Pampa Kampana into her home.) As it happened this was a time of much upheaval in both the capital of the empire and also in the citadel of its rival, Zafarabad, so nobody was thinking about the former twice-queen, and the memories of the old folks who remembered her or had heard her spoken of were fading, too. What occupied everyone's minds was the turbulence in the ruling dynasty, and among the rulers of Zafarabad as well. Hukka Raya II had died suddenly, and so, across the empire's northern border, had Sultan Zafar II, both Number Twos departing almost simultaneously. Fierce battles for power broke out in both kingdoms.

Zafar II did not die peacefully in his sleep like Hukka Raya II. His uncle Daud, accompanied by three other assassins, rushed into his bedchamber and stabbed him to death. One month later, the assassin was assassinated himself, while at prayer in the Friday Mosque of Zafarabad. Another noble, Mahmood, took the throne, after blinding Daud's eight-year-old son to end any arguments about the succession. All Zafarabad was in a condition of chaos and dismay.

Meanwhile in Bisnaga, things were not much better. Hukka Raya II had three sons, Virupaksha (named after the god who was the local incarnation of Lord Shiva), Bukka (yes, another Bukka), and Deva (named, simply, God). Virupaksha took the throne, and in a few short months lost much territory, including the port of Goa, and was then murdered by *his* sons. These sons were dealt with in their turn by Virupaksha's brother Bukka, who then became Bukka Raya II, and didn't last long either, being killed and succeeded by the third brother, Deva, who believed that, as the actual, so-named incarnation of the godhead, he possessed a divine right to the throne. (He would bring an end to the cycle of dynastic murders and rule for forty years.)

During the years of turmoil a second Portuguese horse-trader, Fernão Paes, arrived in Bisnaga, and was sensible enough to keep his head down and do no more than sell his horses and prepare to leave at a moment's notice. But business was good, and he became a frequent visitor. He kept a journal, and in it he described the murderous Virupaksha and Bukka II as being "only interested in getting drunk and fucking, usually in that order." Deva Raya would have gone down the same weak-minded road but he was the most easily influenced of all of them, and so, as will be seen, his story would be different, which was why he managed to stay alive and die unremarkably, of old age.

"The world's turned upside down," thought Pampa Kampana. "It's up to me to turn it the right way up again."

Even though much time had passed, and the new king Deva Raya thought of Pampa Kampana's escape as an old, long-concluded story, there was still the DAS, and somewhere there was still ancient Vidyasagar, and it was necessary to be careful. There was an alcove in Pampa's bedroom and Madhuri Devi insisted that during daylight hours her guest should position herself inside it, and then Madhuri would push a wooden almirah in front of it to hide her. At night she would move the almirah back so that Pampa Kampana could come out. As an extra precaution, Madhuri would buy provisions in two places, the main bazaar which she regularly used, and where she was well-known, and also a second, smaller market in a distant corner of the city, where nobody knew who she was; so that people did not have reason to wonder why she was buying more food than one person needed, and so begin to suspect that she might be shopping for two. Pampa Kampana understood that her host was a seasoned and professional underground operative and did not question her rules. In her hidden alcove she adopted the lotus position through the long hot daylight hours, closed her eyes, and allowed her spirit to travel through Bisnaga as it had in the early days of her whispering, to listen to the thoughts of the citizenry, and to eavesdrop on the machinations of the kings. For a long time she did not begin to whisper. She listened, and waited.

It was not yet time to make her move. She did not seek out Vidyasagar because if she entered his thoughts the wizened centenarian would certainly become aware of her intrusive presence nearby, and after that he would have the city turned upside down to find her, and her secret hideout would not remain secret very long. She saw him only in his effects, in the survival and strength of his brother Sayana, very old himself by this time but still immensely powerful, and, in Madhuri Devi's opinion, the dark unseen hand behind all the killings. "His purpose all along has been to get Deva onto the throne," she told Pampa Kampana, "because Deva's vanity and god-complex makes him susceptible to outrageous flattery, and therefore he's the easiest of all the contenders to control." And if that had been Sayana's plan, then it was really Vidyasagar's plan, and Deva Raya was the old man's pawn.

"I will make it my business to get this young king out of the old brothers' clutches," said Pampa Kampana, "and that will be the beginning of the renewal, and the return of the Bisnaga we loved."

"It may take longer than you think," Madhuri Devi said.

"Why do you say that?" Pampa Kampana asked.

"According to the stars," said Madhuri Devi, "you will be married to a king of Bisnaga one more time, but it won't be this one, and it won't be soon."

"Madhuri, you're so kind to give me shelter, but I don't really put much store in the stars," Pampa Kampana said, and then added, after a few moments, "How long will it be?"

"I don't know how this is even possible," Madhuri Devi said, frowning, "but then I don't know how you're possible at all. You're somebody my grandparents used to talk about when I was a little girl, and yet here you are looking younger than me. Anyway, the stars are very certain, and they say, in approximately eighty-five years from now."

"Too long," said Pampa Kampana. "We'll have to see about that."

• • •

In his own time, people called young Deva Raya a great monarch, but Pampa Kampana in the *Jayaparajaya* refers to him as the "Puppet King," because he allowed not one but two unseen masters to pull his strings, falling under the spell of the two rivals whose struggle was at the heart of the secret history of Bisnaga: first, Vidyasagar the priest, and then the priest's "protégée" whom he had abused, who rejected him and became his greatest adversary—Pampa Kampana herself, the empire's once and future queen.

In the early days of his rule Deva Raya was the obedient creature of Sayana and the DAS, which was to say, of Vidyasagar, the absent puppet-master. He ordered the beautiful Hazara Rama temple to be built in the heart of the Royal Enclosure and it became the private place of worship of the kings of Bisnaga from then on, until the very end. And the puritanism of the DAS and its intolerance of other faiths continued. Also under the expansionist influence of the DAS he was very often away at the wars. For almost twenty years he fought everyone in the neighborhood, defeating them all, including Mahmood of Zafarabad. All of this added to his glory, but it meant that Bisnaga City was left for long periods in the hands of Sayana, who was beginning to be very old and sick, and behind Sayana there was Vidyasagar who had become old and sick many years earlier. The DAS-controlled royal council, too, had atrophied. Its long spell in power, and the immense age of its senior members, had encouraged laziness and incompetence, which, in turn, bred—in the less antique members—a good deal of fiscal corruption, and a liking for deviant sexual practices which the official policy of the organization strongly condemned. The citizens of Bisnaga began to want a change.

This was the opening Pampa Kampana needed. She began to whisper through all the concealed hours of the day and most of the night as well. "You don't eat," Madhuri Devi told her worriedly. "If you are human, then you must eat at some point." Pampa Kampana agreed politely to set aside thirty minutes a day during which they could share a meal and converse. The rest of the time she sat with her eyes closed, visiting the minds of the people. "You don't sleep," marveled Madhuri Devi. "At least, not when I'm looking. What kind of a being are you? Is this a goddess who has come into my house?"

"I was inhabited by a goddess when I was very young," Pampa Kampana replied. "It changed me in many ways, some of which even I don't yet understand."

"I knew it," said Madhuri Devi, and fell to her knees.

"What are you doing?" Pampa Kampana cried.

"I'm worshipping you," Madhuri Devi said. "Isn't that the right thing to do?"

"Please don't," Pampa Kampana said. "I have lost one daughter to a foreigner and the sea, and left two behind in a forest. I see now that the task ahead of me will take many years and maybe before it's done my daughters will all be dead, and Haleya Kote will be gone for sure, and maybe you will have come to the end of the road as well, and yet there's a thing in me that doesn't care about any of that, a thing that only cares about the task I have been set. I have turned away from my daughters as my mother turned away from me. That's not the kind of person you should revere. Get up off your knees at once."

The whispering wasn't as straightforward as it had been in the beginning. That had been the time of the Created Generation, born from seeds, and they were blank slates, empty heads, and when she wrote their stories on those slates they accepted the narratives she was planting in their heads without making any fuss. She was making them up, and they were becoming the people she invented. There was little or no resistance. But the people she had to whisper to now were not her inventions. They had been born and raised in Bisnaga, they had actual family histories going back two or even three generations, and so they were not pliable fictions. Also they had been encouraged by the authorities of the present day, the DAS people, to believe that the true story of the birth of Bisnaga was a lie, and that a lie was the truth: that Bisnaga was not seed-born, but an ancient kingdom with a history that did not originate in the imaginings of a whispering witch.

And another thing: the city had grown. Now there was a multitude to address, and this time she would have to persuade many of them that the cultured, inclusive, sophisticated narrative of Bisnaga that she was offering them was a better one than the narrow, exclusionary, and, to her way of thinking, barbarian official narrative of the moment. It was by no means certain that the people would choose sophistication over barbarianism. The party line regarding members of other faiths—we are good, they are bad—had a certain infectious clarity. So did the idea that dissent was unpatriotic. Offered the choice between thinking for themselves and blindly following their leaders, many people would choose blindness over clear-sightedness, especially when the empire was prospering and there was food on the table and money in their pockets. Not everybody wanted to think, preferring to eat and spend. Not everybody wanted to love their neighbor. Some people preferred hatred. There would be resistance.

Haleya Kote came to see her in the middle of the night when she had emerged for a few hours from her alcove of secret inwardness. Yotshna had told him he looked terrible, and now he looked even worse than when she said that. "I haven't got long to go," he told Pampa Kampana, "and I have a promise to keep."

"Go," she said. From a fold of her garment she took out a little pouch of gold coins. "Go and find this new foreigner, this Sir Paes, and buy the fastest horse he has to sell. Go and embrace her and tell her I send her my love."

"She loves you too," said Haleya Kote. "Won't you come also?"

"You know I can't do that," Pampa Kampana said. "I have to sit in a hole behind an almirah and try to create a mass movement. Once I was a queen. Now I'm a revolutionary. Or is that too grand a word? Let's say, I'm a witch behind a wardrobe."

"Then I'll say goodbye," Haleya Kote said, "and I'll go on my last ride."

(In the Jayaparajaya *Pampa Kampana tells an extraordinary tale of that ride. We must ask ourselves how she could know what happened, since she wasn't there. It would be forgivable to conclude that the entire episode is an invention. The poet shrugs off such suspicions. The birds told her, she writes. Years later, she tells us, when she emerged from her seclusion, the crows and parrots spoke to her in the Master Language.)*

"It was hard for him to go back," said the crow. "First he had to bribe the Portuguese trader to bring the horse through the city gate to a secret meeting point. Then on the way to the forest he began to feel unwell."

"As he neared the forest he developed a fever and entered a state of delirium," said the parrot, "and he was shouting nonsense as he rode."

The crow took up the story. "By the time he reached the forest his mind had gone completely, and he no longer knew who he was. All he knew was that he had to get into the forest to see her."

"But, as you know, for men who don't know who they are, or have forgotten, the forest is a dangerous place," the parrot said.

"He ran into the forest shouting her name," the crow continued. "But then he screamed as the forest's magic took hold of him, and he fell to the ground, and didn't get up."

"She came running," said the parrot, "but she was too late."

"When she reached the fallen figure, it was no longer Haleya Kote, her beloved," the crow declared, with great solemnity.

"It was a dying woman who looked a hundred years old," the parrot sadly said.

"And the woman was wearing the old soldier's clothes," added the crow.

12

When the king's adviser Sayana finally died Pampa Kampana decided it was time to act. There was no sign of Vidyasagar anywhere by then. If he was indeed still alive he was probably lying on a cot somewhere like an ancient baby, helpless, clinging to life out of sheer spite, but unable to do any living. His time was over. The ruling officers of the DAS were similarly toothless and wizened. It was as if cadavers were in charge of things, the dead ruling the living, and the living were tired of it.

From her alcove behind the almirah she began to whisper into the king's ears. In the depths of his palace Deva Raya clutched at his head, not knowing where these extraordinary new thoughts were coming from all at once—not understanding how it was possible that he was having such inspirations, never having been the inspirational type before—and finally beginning to give himself the credit for arriving at a condition of true genius. The voice in his head told him so. It flattered him by saying that it, the voice, was the manifestation of that genius. He had to listen to, and be guided by, what it—what he himself!—was telling him to do.

The voice in his head told him to forget war and bigotry.

—You are Deva, godly, yes you are, but why be simply a god of Death? Aren't you sick of coming home from battle spattered with blood and gore? Don't you want to be a god of Life instead? Instead of armies, you could send diplomats, and make peace.

—Yes, yes, he thought, I'll do exactly as I'm now suggesting to myself, I'll send diplomats and make peace with them all, why not? Even with Zafarabad as well.

—And bigotry, the whisper reminded him. Forget bigotry, too.

—Yes, yes, he thought. I'll prove how tolerant I've become! I'll marry a Jain! Bhima Devi, she's nice, I'll marry her, and I'll pray at her favorite temples too. And I'll take a Muslim second wife. I'll have to find one of those, but I'm sure I can come up with one. I've heard there's a Muslim goldsmith in Mudgal whose daughter is very beautiful. I'll look into it. And what else, my brilliant brain, what else?

—Water, Pampa Kampana whispered.

—Water?

—The city has grown so large, there isn't enough water for everyone to drink. Build a dam! Build it below the confluence of the Tunga and the Bhadra, where they become the ample and fast-running Pampa, and then build a great aqueduct to bring the fresh river water into the city, and place pumps in all the squares so that the thirsty may drink and the dirty may bathe and wash their clothes, and then people will love you. Water creates love more easily than victory.

—Yes, yes! A dam! An aqueduct! Pumps! Water is love. I will be the God-King of Loving Dams. I'll make love flow everywhere in the city and I will become the People's Darling, their Best-Beloved. Anything else?

—You must be a patron of the arts! Bring poets to the court, Kumara Vyasa for the Kannada language, Gunda Dimdima for Sanskrit, and the king of poets, Srinatha, for the Telugu tongue! And you know what? I bet you can write excellent poetry yourself!

—Yes, yes, poetry, poets. And romances! I can write those, and I will!

—Bring mathematicians also. Our people love mathematics! And bring shipbuilders, not just for warships, but for trading vessels, and royal barges in which you can visit the three hundred ports in the empire! And make sure that plenty of these new people, painters, poets, calculators, designers, are women, who deserve it no less than men!

—Yes, yes! All this and more I will do. My thoughts are more brilliant than myself, but from now on I will be as magnificent as my thoughts.

—Oh, and one more thing. Get rid of those mummified old priests surrounding you and hissing their old-fashioned notions in your ear, and bring back the old royal council. You can put everyone in there, the poets, the mathematicians, the architects of the aqueduct and the dam, the diplomats, and their brilliance will reflect extra radiance upon your own.

—Good idea! I'm glad that came to me all of a sudden. I'll do that right away.

And now, Pampa Kampana thought, my murderer of a grandson is a puppet on my strings.

In those days the people of Bisnaga had a complicated relationship with memories. Perhaps they distrusted them unconsciously, without even knowing or believing that at the beginning of time Pampa Kampana had planted fictional histories in their ancestors, and created the whole city out of her fertile imagination. At any rate they were people who had little regard for yesterdays. They chose—like the denizens of Aranyani's forest!—to live wholly in the present, without much interest in what came before, and if they needed to think about any day other than today, then that day was tomorrow. This made Bisnaga a dynamic place, capable of immense forward-looking energy, but also a place that suffered from the problem of all amnesiacs, which was that to turn away from history was to make possible a cyclical repetition of its crimes.

Ninety years had passed since Hukka and Bukka Sangama had

scattered the magic seeds, and by now most people thought of that story as a fairy tale, and were sure that "Pampa Kampana" was the name of a good fairy, not a real person, but somebody in a story. Even Deva Raya, her grandson, thought so. He knew the story of how his father Bhagwat Sangama, the rejected child of the sorceress, became Hukka Raya II and vowed revenge on Pampa, his unloving mother, Deva Raya's grandmother, and on Pampa Kampana's favorites, her daughters, as well. Even if half of it was true, Deva Raya thought, that story was over. If his grandmother was alive, she would be around one hundred and ten years old, which was absurd, of course. And all that nonsense about her powers of sorcery, that was absurd too. She had probably been a mean old woman, but no sorceress, and now she was gone, and that old world could disappear along with her. All he wanted was to listen to the voice of his own genius in his head, pointing the way toward the future. Now it was time for aqueducts, mathematicians, ships, ambassadors, and poetry. Yes, yes!

As for Vidyasagar: Pampa Kampana's enemy was entering his last days, having failed in his scheme to live as long as her and thwart her plans. She didn't need to fear him anymore.

There were battles in the streets after Deva Raya made his sudden, radical change of direction. The thugs of the discarded power structure didn't give up easily. From the cots of their antiquity the dismissed old guard guided their stormtroopers and tried to establish control over the streets. They were not used to being thwarted. They were accustomed to having their way, to being feared and therefore obeyed. But they faced unexpected opposition. The years of whispering bore unexpected fruit. From everywhere in Bisnaga, from backstreets and grand thoroughfares, from the quiet retreats of the elderly and the loud gathering places of the young, people poured out of doorways and resisted. The flag of the Remonstrance, a hand with the index finger raised, as if to remonstrate, was seen on every avenue, and that symbol was daubed on many walls. The transformation wrought by Pampa Kampana stood revealed in all its marvelous force. This was the birth of the New Remonstrance, as it came to be known: no longer anti-art, against women, or hostile toward sexual diversity, but embracing poetry, liberty, women, and joy, and retaining from the original manifesto only the First Remonstrance against the involvement of the religious world with that of government, the Second Remonstrance opposing mass religious gatherings, and the Fourth, which favored peace over war. The goon squads of the *ancien régime* retreated in disarray. That regime had seemed all-powerful, invincible, but in the end its whole apparatus crumbled in days and blew away like dust, revealing that it had rotted from the inside, so that when it was pushed, it was too weak to go on standing.

The king in his palace, bewildered by the speed of these events, heard the voice, which he thought of as the voice of his own genius, whispering in his ears.

—You have done it.

—Yes, yes, he assured himself. Yes, I have.

A new day dawned in Bisnaga. Pampa Kampana abandoned her alcove and emerged into the daylight. Her disguise, her *agyatvaas,* turned out to be her own appearance. In the second-golden-age years that followed the great Change, and the rise of members of the Remonstrance to prominent places in the government of the state, Pampa Kampana was unrecognizable, seen by one and all as a woman in her middle twenties, known only by a small inner circle to be the great founder of the city who was approaching one hundred and ten years of age. The astrologer Madhuri Devi, her closest confidante and now one of the high leaders of the Remonstrance, was appointed to the royal council, and recommended her friend to the king as a woman of unusual qualities, whom it would be well to employ in the service of the state.

"What's your name?" Deva Raya asked, when Pampa Kampana was brought into his presence.

"Pampa Kampana," Pampa Kampana replied.

Deva Raya roared with laughter. "That's a good one," he cried, wiping his eyes. "Yes, yes, young lady! You're my grandmother, of course you are, and you're lucky—I don't bear my father's grudges, and we need a matriarch of your wisdom on my team."

"No, thank you, Your Majesty," replied Pampa Kampana haughtily. "In the first place, if you don't believe me now, when I am nobody, then you will not trust me then, when I am a counselor at your side. And in the second place, as my friend Madhuri Devi the astrologer has told me, this is not my time, which is still many decades in the future, when I will marry a different king. I could not marry you anyway, because that would be incest."

Deva Raya laughed his booming laugh again. "Madhuri Devi," he cried, "your friend is a great humorist. Maybe she would agree to join us as a court jester? I haven't laughed like this in years."

"If you'll excuse me, Your Majesty," Pampa Kampana said, trying not to sound affronted, "I will take my leave."

Deva Raya's reign was a time of great success for Pampa Kampana, and she might easily have taken much justifiable pride in it. But in her verses describing those days, she was harshly self-critical.

"I begin to feel," she wrote, "as if I am more than one person, and not all those persons are admirable. I am the mother of the city—even though few people believe I am she—but I am away from my own daughters and during this separation I do not feel like their mother at all. The years pass and I have not so much as ascertained if they are alive or dead. What elderly women they will have become if they still live, green-eyed ladies unknown to me and who do not know me either, even though I still remain superficially who I was a lifetime ago. That person, the person I see reflected in water or glass, I do not know who she is either. My daughter Yotshna asked me that question—'Who are you?'—and I cannot answer it.

"This eternal youth is a kind of damnation. This power to affect the thoughts of others and to alter history is another curse. The witchcraft, the sorcery of magic seeds and metamorphosis, whose limits even I do not know, is a third. I am a ghost in a body that refuses to age. Vidyasagar and I are not so different after all. We are both specters of ourselves, lost within ourselves. What I know is that I am a bad mother, and my sons and daughters would all agree with that statement. Sometimes I feel I am not a person of any kind, that I no longer exist, that there is no longer an 'I' that I can identify with myself. Maybe I should go by a new name, or many new names in the interminable future that stretches ahead. When I say what my name is I am not believed because I am, of course, impossible.

"I am a shadow, or a dream. One night when darkness falls I might simply become a part of that darkness and disappear. I feel, often, that that would be no bad thing."

On the day Vidyasagar died and the city was plunged into mourning and prayer, Pampa Kampana in the grip of a different melancholy made her first visit to the drinking place called the Cashew and ordered a jug of the powerful feni liquor that Haleya Kote used to drink long ago in the company of a man who would be king. She had emptied half the jug when a man approached her, a foreign-seeming fellow with green eyes and red hair.

"A beautiful lady like yourself should not be sitting here with a jug full of solitary sadness," the man said, speaking with a heavy accent. "I would like to lighten your burden, if you will permit."

She scrutinized him closely. "It's not possible," she said. "You're long dead. I'm the only one who doesn't die."

"I assure you that I am alive," the stranger replied.

"Don't be ridiculous," she said. "Your name is Domingo Nunes, as I should know because we were lovers for many years, and this is an apparition caused by the alcohol, because you certainly no longer exist."

And it was on the tip of her tongue to say, but she did not say it, "Also, by the way, you are the father of my three daughters."

"I have heard the name of Nunes," the stranger replied, marveling. "He was one of the pioneers who paved the way for my business here. But he is someone from a long time ago, too long ago for you, surely. I am also Portuguese. My name is Fernão Paes."

Pampa Kampana examined him even more intently. "Fernão Paes," she repeated.

"At your service," he declared.

"It's crazy," she said. "You really do all look alike."

"May I sit with you?" he asked.

"I'm too old for you," she said. "But I'm a sort of foreigner here too. Nobody recognizes me. I built this city and I'm a stranger in it. So we are both strangers. We are both just passing through. We have things in common. Sit down."

"I don't know what you're talking about," Fernão Paes confessed, "but I'd like to find out."

"I'm one hundred and eight years old," Pampa Kampana said.

Fernão Paes smiled his most ingratiating smile. "I like older women," he declared.

He had become wealthy selling horses to the king and his nobles and cavalry, so he built a stone mansion in the Portuguese style, with large shuttered windows facing outward to the city, a green garden watered by one of the first canals to be built to bring water from the enormous reservoir created by the new river dam. He had a field of sugarcane also, and even a small piece of woodland. Pampa Kampana moved out of the astrologer's house and into the foreigner's residence. "I'm a homeless person now," she understood. "I have to rely on the generosity of others."

Fernão Paes was a man of emotional substance and complexity, who could love Pampa Kampana even though he didn't believe the stories she told him about her life. When a man traveled across continents and oceans he heard life stories in which no sane person could possibly believe. He met an impoverished sailor in the port of Aden who swore that in happier times he had discovered the secret of transmuting base metals into gold, but the formula had been stolen from him when he was captured by corsairs in the Mediterranean Sea, and now, owing to a blow on the head, he could not remember it, et cetera. And he had met a dwarf who said that she had formerly been a giant, until a sorcerer's magic spell had shrunk her, et cetera, et cetera; and a young boy in Brindisi who had the sharpest eyesight of anyone Paes had ever met, who claimed he had been born as a hawk until a sorcerer's magic spell brought him down to earth transformed into a hawk-eyed child, et cetera et cetera et cetera.

There were people everywhere in the world telling stories of how they were not what they seemed to be, how they had been better before, or worse, but certainly different, different in a hundred ways. Paes had even met a hundred-year-old woman begging for alms by the shore of the Red Sea, who told him that when she was twenty-one years old an angel had fallen in love with her and carried her off to heaven, but when living human beings arrived in heaven it did not go well for them, they aged very rapidly and died within hours, so I begged the angel to bring me back to earth, she said, and when I landed I looked like this, sir, and this was only two years ago, sir, and you must believe that two years later I am still only twenty-three years old. Because Fernão Paes had listened to that old woman pretending to be young it wasn't so unusual for him to hear a young woman pretending to be old, so he went along with what Pampa Kampana told him, and did not judge her. The whole world was mad. That was his deepest belief. He was the only person who was sane.

Pampa Kampana in Paes's house at first thought herself to have fallen in love but then realized that what she was experiencing was relief. Ever since her return from the forest she had felt upset, even offended, at the disbelief with which she had been greeted by everyone except Madhuri Devi, a skepticism which had culminated in the discourteous laughter of the king, but now her feelings of being insulted had been replaced by a sensation of pleasure in her new anonymity. For the first time since she was nine years old she could be excused from being Pampa Kampana, or rather she could be "this" Pampa Kampana, the nobody with the famous old name, instead of the "real" Pampa, who, in the opinion of almost everyone, no longer existed except in memory. She was being given a second chance at life, and had been granted the possibility of having an ordinary place in the world instead of a relentlessly extraordinary one. This man, Paes, was lively and adventurous, appeared to be sincere in his feelings for her, and, best of all, was absent for long stretches of time, traveling back and forth between Bisnaga and the lands of Persia and Araby in search of fine horses to sell. "Truly, this is the best of all possible men," she told herself. "He's loyal and loving and has put a good roof over my head and food in my belly, and most of the time he isn't even here."

In this way Pampa Kampana entered the second phase of her exile, during which she was physically present in Bisnaga but agreed with the general opinion that she was not the person she knew she was, but simply a different, unimportant person with the same name. Her one continuing anguish, compounded by Fernão Paes's astonishing resemblance to Domingo Nunes, had to do with her daughters, who did not require mothering, that was true, they were elderly ladies by now, but not to know how they were, well or unwell, happy or unhappy, alive or dead, that was difficult. Zerelda had chosen a path in life that suited her, a traveling life not unlike Domingo Nunes's, *so she inherited that from him*, Pampa Kampana thought, and Yuktasri was at home with the wild forest women and had even become one of them, Pampa Kampana reassured herself often, so that was two out of three. Yotshna was the problem. Yotshna was the one with a grievance, the one who would not forgive her mother. It was Yotshna's accusatory eyes that haunted Pampa Kampana in her dreams.

Fernão told her he was puzzled by the king. "When I first came to Bisnaga, everyone was murdering everyone," he said one morning at breakfast. (He ate breakfast like a savage: quantities of leavened bread, chunks of cheese made from cows' milk, and coffee drowned in cows' milk too, which he called *galão*—things that no right-minded person would eat at the beginning of the day.) "And I wrote in my journal," he went on, "that Deva Raya and his murderous brothers only cared about getting drunk and fucking. I should have added, *and killing one another.*"

Ah, my male line of descent, Pampa Kampana thought. Worthless scum, all of them. The fathers who were my sons and their sons as well.

"Then Deva Raya fell under the influence of Vidyasagar, Sayana, and the DAS, and he sobered up and even became puritanical," Paes continued. "Then all of a sudden he changed again, rejected the priests, and everyone celebrated his new open-mindedness, and now there are festivals and parties, and people say he's a great king and this is a golden age. It's my opinion that the fellow has no mind of his own, he needs someone to tell him how to behave and what to do, but it beats me who has drawn him away from the theocrats. There's some secret individual or individuals somewhere, whispering in his ear."

Yes, my dear, Pampa Kampana thought, but when I told you, you didn't believe me.

"Maybe it's Madhuri Devi," she said. "The New Remonstrance seems to have become the ruling party, the group the king uses to run things."

Pampa Kampana's friendship with Madhuri Devi had continued, and the old astrologer, now a royal counselor, often talked to her about goings-on in the palace. Even though Madhuri now had quarters in the palace complex she had hung onto her old home, and she and Pampa met there privately, to drink tea and gossip. "The fact is, Deva Raya has lost all interest in the business of being king," Madhuri said. "He leaves everything to us and has gone back to his carousing youthful ways, except that he really isn't capable of very much wildness anymore."

"Drinking and fucking," Pampa Kampana mused. "Especially fucking, apparently. Everybody in the market is talking about his army of wives."

"The fucking is mostly theoretical," said Madhuri Devi. "Yes, twelve thousand wives. This is to demonstrate his sexual prowess. I doubt he has been able to do anything energetic with any of them. He isn't very fit, or well. He just likes to dress up in green satin robes with necklaces of jewels and many rings on his fingers, and lounge with his head in a wife's lap and with other wives clustering around him. There is a plan to take all the wives out for a procession around the city to show them off to the people. Four thousand wives will be on foot, to show that they are little better than domestic servants. Four thousand will be on horseback to indicate higher status. And four thousand will be carried in palanquins. That's the worst part."

"Why?"

"He wants those four thousand wives to burn themselves on his funeral pyre when he dies. This is the condition on which he has made them queens, and because they have accepted he has placed them in the position of greatest honor."

"There will be no more burning of living women on dead men's pyres in Bisnaga," Pampa Kampana said with great ferocity. "Never again."

"Agreed," said Madhuri Devi. "I think it's a bit of the old DAS mentality that is still stuck in his head."

While she watched Fernão Paes eat his foreign savage's breakfast Pampa Kampana was remembering her mother, and the terrible flames, and deciding to whisper once more, and as soon as possible, into the ear of the king. Then Fernão Paes, having eaten, jumped up to start his day. Before he left for the stables he had one more word of wisdom for Pampa Kampana. "When people start talking about a golden age," he said, "they always think a new world has begun which will last forever. But the truth about these so-called golden ages is that they never last very long. A few years, maybe. There's always trouble ahead."

In the hot season before the rains came they slept on the flat roof of Fernão Paes's house, on *charpai* rope beds enclosed within white mosquito netting that made Pampa Kampana imagine that the whole world was a ghost and she the only living creature in it. Contained in that white cube in the darkness she felt as if unborn, waiting to enter life and make of it something new, something never seen before. She began to feel hopeful, and dreamed of herself riding a *yali,* a sort of leogryph, across the threshold of life into the future. In those days Deva Raya had ordered the construction of a new temple, the Vitthala, which would take ninety years to complete. In these early days of the temple's construction a row of stone *yalis* pranced under the open sky, waiting for the great edifice to grow around and above them. When one entered or left such a temple, or when one began a new enterprise, it was good to ask a *yali* for its blessing. Pampa Kampana understood her *yali* dream as an auspicious sign of a new start.

She also knew that such superstitions were nonsense, and not to be relied upon any more than the astrological divinations of her friend.

One night when the air was pregnant with the moisture which had not yet begun to pour down, Pampa Kampana was woken up by the cawing of a crow near her ear. She woke up and understood that her other world had come to draw her away.

"Ka-ah-eh-va," she said softly, so as not to wake Fernão Paes under his neighboring mosquito net.

"Well, not exactly," the crow said in the Master Language. "But, family of, yes. You can call me that if you wish."

"You bring me a message," she said. "My daughters, how are they?"

"There is one daughter," the crow said, "and the message comes from her."

"What about my other daughter?" Pampa Kampana asked, although she knew what the answer must be.

"Died long ago," the crow said tersely. "They say, of a broken heart, but I don't know. I'm just a messenger. Don't kill me. I'm just a crow."

Pampa Kampana took a deep breath and controlled her tears.

"What's the message?" she asked.

Yuktasri's message was this: *"War."*

13

The pink monkeys came at first in small groups and behaved courteously. They were able to communicate in a garbled, ugly attempt at the Master Language. It was comprehensible, although their pronunciation was laughable. They said they were, in essence, simple traders, employees of a trading company from far away, but news had reached even that remote location of the riches of the forest of Aranyani, where it was possible to find produce that grew nowhere else in the world, berries whose unknown flavors brought tears of joy to the eyes of those who ate them, and gourds of a rich sweetness no other gourds could rival, and there were fruits with no names because they had never entered the outside world where things had to be named in order to exist; and there were also nameless fish that swam in the jungle's rivers, so succulent that men, and monkeys, might cross the world to taste them.

We ask your permission to receive some of the bounty of the forest, the pink monkeys said, and we will repay you in any currency that would be meaningful to you. Maybe it's time you learned the value of silver and gold, the pink monkeys suggested to the brown and green monkeys and, through them, to the forest in general and even to Aranyani herself. The sound they made to describe these coins was like a word from the language of the east coast, *kacu*, which, because they couldn't pronounce things properly, they called *cash*. "*Kacu, cash,* is the future," they said. "With *kacu* you can have a place in that future. Without it, unfortunately, you will become irrelevant, and in the end the future will arrive like a forest fire and burn your jungle to the ground."

The green and brown monkeys were both seduced by the pink monkeys' courtesies and scared into cooperation by their threats. The other jungle creatures ignored the embassies of these bizarre aliens with the terrible accents. Only the wild women of the forest, and, it is said, the goddess Aranyani herself, understood the danger to their way of life. "The future" was a menace they had no desire to confront. But for a long time they didn't know how to act.

(We may perhaps best understand the pink monkey narrative as an aspect of the Jayaparajaya*'s fascination with Time—Time divided into yesterdays, todays, and tomorrows. The monkeys we first encountered in these verses, the gray Hanuman langurs of Bisnaga, are, we may say, the poet's gesture toward the mythical past of the great legends, while these pink newcomers represent an as-yet-unknown tomorrow, a tomorrow that will fully arrive long after the poet's work is done. This, at least, is the proposition which, with all due modesty, is here advanced.)*

When Pampa Kampana told Fernão Paes she had to leave, and would appreciate the gift of a horse, the foreigner made no argument. "At the very beginning you told me that you were just passing through my life," he said, "so I can't complain that you misled me in any way. And if as you say you are a miraculous ancient being who was once the lover of Domingo Nunes then I must also accept, even if I can't believe it, that you see me as little more than an echo of, or a substitute for, your earlier beloved. At any rate I'm grateful for the gift of your time, and a horse is the least I can offer in return."

She had one last meeting with Madhuri Devi in the old house with the alcove. "I will never see you again," she told the former astrologer, "but I know I am leaving my city and the empire in safe hands. Make sure you find safe hands to hand them to when it's your time."

"I have never thought of you as a supernatural being, although you are," Madhuri Devi replied. "But now I see your solitude and the sadness that it brings. We are just fleeting shadows on a screen for you. How lonely that must be."

"I whispered in the king's ear last night," Pampa Kampana said. "So don't be surprised if he announces his decision to ban the burning of widows in the whole of the empire, and to restore the status of women in Bisnaga to the way it used to be."

"The New Remonstrance would not have allowed the burning anyway," Madhuri Devi said. "But thank you, it's easier if the king already agrees."

"No more burning widows," Pampa Kampana said, instead of saying "goodbye."

"No more burning widows," Madhuri Devi replied. Then they parted, knowing it would be forever.

After Pampa Kampana left Bisnaga for the second time, the so-called "second golden age" came to an abrupt end, as if by her departure she had brought down the curtain on those years. Deva Raya died, and happily no women were burned on his pyre. The twelve thousand wives were released into the world to make their way in it as best they could. Incompetence and corruption followed. We may pass over the sequence of incompetent kings, each murdered by the next ruler. There were decapitations and straw-stuffed heads. And finally the last, pathetic Sangama king was decapitated by a general named Saluva, and the founding dynasty of Bisnaga came to an end.

Pampa Kampana has little to tell us about the short-lived "Saluva dynasty," even though in this period the fortunes of the empire were much restored, but she writes with affection about a certain Tuluva

Narasa Nayaka, another general, whose "Tuluva dynasty" soon supplanted the Saluvas, and who regained the rest of the lost territories, kept Zafarabad and the other adversaries at a distance, and was the father of the man during whose reign Pampa Kampana would learn the most profound lesson in love of her long life. In her epic poem she taunts us, her readers, with this hint of a love story to come, but then refuses to elaborate further, writing only, with her characteristic simplicity of expression:

"Before all that, we had to fight the monkeys."

As she rode out of Bisnaga Pampa Kampana, saddened by her last conversation with Fernão Paes, in which he had understood that he was no more than an echo of the past, was thinking about Domingo Nunes, and the three daughters whose father he had been, a father pushed into the shadows, his paternity never recognized. I wronged him, she told herself, and maybe that is why I have no grandchildren of his line. It is the revenge of his blood. Her daughters, who had inherited some, at least, of the magic with which the goddess had filled their mother, would be the end of a line, not the beginning of a dynasty. Magic would fade from the world and banality would replace it. As she rode back toward Aranyani's forest, which was to say into the very heart of the fabulous, she was already mourning the victory of the humdrum, the mundane, over that other reality. The victory of the line of ordinary boys over that of extraordinary girls. And perhaps of pink monkeys over the forest of women.

Yuktasri Sangama was waiting for her at the edge of the forest, looking like her mother's ghost. She was indifferent to the disparity in their appearances. "I know what it means to be your daughter," she said to Pampa Kampana. "It means, to become your grandmother before I die." She had no interest in discussing that any further. "I waited too long to call you," she said. "Things are bad here, and the final conflict will begin very soon."

The beginning of the problem was the willingness of the forest's green and brown monkeys to invite groups of pink monkeys into their trees. Soon some of the pink leaders had persuaded the green monkeys that they needed to be afraid of the brown tribe, while other pink leaders persuaded the browns of the malicious intentions of the greens. The peace of the forest was broken, and the pink monkeys shrewdly sided with the greens in one area of the forest, the browns in another, and helped them to defeat their "rivals," asking only to be rewarded with control of part of the tree-worlds of the defeated tribes. In a startlingly short time the pink monkeys had acquired footholds in the forest, and they used these to expand the areas of their control. They even hired many of the green and brown monkeys to help them in their enterprise. After that the wealth of the forest was at their mercy. "We did nothing," Yuktasri told her mother. "We thought this was something between the monkey people and it wasn't for us to intervene. We were stupid. We should have guessed that the pink ones would keep coming, and coming, and coming, there would be wave after wave of them, until they had taken over the whole forest."

The goddess Aranyani could surely prevent the invasion, Pampa Kampana suggested, but Yuktasri shook her head. "She can surround the forest with her line of power, her protective *rekha*," Yuktasri said, "but it won't work if forest dwellers themselves invite the intruders in. And now the pinks are forest dwellers too, and many greens and browns support them, and talk about wanting to divide the forest into green zones and brown zones, and they are too dumb to understand that their attitude will lead to there being only one zone, neither brown nor green. Monkeys, what can you do?" Yuktasri said, her betrayal of the habitual respect of jungle denizens for one another indicating how bad the situation had become. "You can't teach them anything."

"How can I help?" Pampa Kampana said. "I don't even live here anymore."

"I don't know," Yuktasri replied. "But I thought, if I'm going to die fighting the pink invasion, I want you here too."

"Because you need your mother," Pampa Kampana asked, "or because you want her to die in the battle as well?"

"I don't know," old Yuktasri answered. "Maybe both."

(Here there is an unexplained break in continuity in the Jayaparajaya *manuscript. It is possible that the author destroyed some pages, perhaps because the confrontation with her daughter was too painful to preserve in detail, or simply because Pampa Kampana turned away from that private matter to complete her account of the crisis. In her next passage she moves away abruptly from this mother–daughter scene and describes her second visit to the unseen forest goddess Aranyani. Here is that scene, as Pampa Kampana has written it. It should be noted that this is the only instance in the entire body of ancient literature in which the forest goddess revealed herself fully to any human being.)*

She, Pampa Kampana, spread out her arms and called the goddess's name. Then the whirlwind came as before, and she was hidden inside the whirling leaves, and carried into the sky. The angry *cheels* were there, wheeling above the roof of the forest as before, and the golden ball of light, and she, Pampa Kampana, was standing on the topmost branch of the highest tree. But this time the ball of light dissolved into air and there she was, Aranyani, floating on the sky, presenting herself to Pampa Kampana without pretensions, not in the golden crown and bejeweled radiance of a god but plainly dressed in simple woodland clothes.

"Ask me," she said, as she had said once before.

"When I was nine years old the great goddess Pampa herself entered me," Pampa Kampana said. "And if an aspect of her remains within me, maybe there is a greater strength in my body than I know, and if that strength is released it can combine with yours and together we can rid the jungle of this plague of short-tailed hairless foreigners."

"Yes, the power is within you," Aranyani told her, "and it is a far greater power than my own; and yes, I can release it. But when such a force bursts out of a mortal human body it is very probable that the human body will be destroyed. If you do this I cannot promise you that you will survive."

"I have failed my daughters all their lives," Pampa Kampana said. "At least this one time I can answer one of my children's calls for help."

"There's something else," Aranyani said. "The moment is near when the gods must retreat from the world and stop interfering in its history. Very soon human beings—and monkeys of all colors, for that matter—will have to learn to manage without us and make their stories on their own."

"What will happen to the forest when it is no longer under your guardianship?" Pampa Kampana asked her.

"It will suffer the fate of many forests in the age of men," Aranyani said. "Men will come, and either there will be open fields under cultivation here or else there will be houses and roads, and maybe a small ghost forest will remain, and women will say, look, there stands the memory of the forest of Aranyani, and men will not believe them, or care."

"And this does not concern you?"

"Our hour is over," Aranyani said, "and it's your time now. So even if you—or the goddess coming out of you—and I together manage to win this battle, after that neither animals nor humans can count on us to protect or guide or help. The victory may be real, but also temporary. You should understand that."

"*Forever* is a meaningless word," Pampa Kampana said. "*Now* is my only concern."

When Aranyani descended in majesty toward the forest floor all living things bowed down in fear and respect. None of them had seen a divine being before and the only proper response to it was gratitude and awe. That was the day of the expulsion of all pink monkeys from the jungle. They went quietly, or, at most, muttering under their breath about the injustice of their removal and the certainty that, one day, they would return. They were escorted out by the wild women, but everyone knew that the main force of the invaders was approaching, and this was just a preliminary move. Pampa Kampana and the goddess went together to face the enemy. As they neared the northern perimeter beyond which the battle would take place, Yuktasri Sangama approached her mother for the last time. "I'll say goodbye," she said, "and thank you."

They went forward together
The two great ladies
Goddess and Woman
Stood glorious together
Against the thin pink line
Of our invaders
And wrought horrible destruction
On our foes.

(She tells us—Pampa Kampana tells us—that the wild women told her, long afterward, that Yuktasri had *died peacefully and happily as she saw you win the war;* and the jungle animals told her what they had seen, and she had translated their Master Language account into her own immaculate verse.)

The War was not really a Battle
It was a single Instant of Doing
They became two Golden Suns
Goddess and Woman
Flaming, blinding, burning
Utterly consuming the Enemy
In their fire.

After this extraordinary, cataclysmic event Pampa Kampana's inert body was carried by the jungle women to her old home in the jungle and laid down to rest on a bed of soft mosses and leaves. Her eyes and mouth were open, and had to be closed, and the women thought her dead, and planned a funeral pyre, but then the voice of Aranyani filled the air as the goddess spoke for the last time to the creatures of the earth, saying, "She is not gone, but sleeping. I have placed her in this deep, healing sleep, and I will cause great thickets of thorns to grow around her, and you must leave her there, until she is awakened by an act of love."

Time passed.—Can you feel it passing?—Like a ghost in a corridor floating past white curtains blowing at open windows, like a ship in the night, or a high migration of birds, time passed, shadows lengthened and shrank back, leaves grew and fell from branches, and there was life and death. And one day Pampa Kampana felt something like a soft breeze touching her cheek, and opened her eyes.

A young woman's face was above hers, so like her own face that it seemed to her that she was floating above her body and looking down at herself. Then her thoughts cleared. The young woman was dressed like a warrior, with a great sword sheathed across her back.

"Who are you," Pampa Kampana said.

"I am Zerelda Li," the other replied, "the daughter of the daughter of the daughter of the daughter of the daughter of Zerelda Sangama and Grandmaster Li Ye-He. All my kin have departed this life in various ways, leaving me with only one living relative, about whom my mother spoke with her dying words, the same words her mother said to her, and her mother, and her mother, and hers. 'The matriarch of our house is a woman named Pampa Kampana,' she told me. 'And she is still alive. Go to the forest of Aranyani, and make her give you what she owes you.' I was holding her hand very tightly. 'What does she owe me, Mother?' I asked her, and she answered, 'Everything.' Then she died."

"And so you have come," Pampa Kampana said.

"None of my ancestors believed what they were being told,

thinking it impossible that you could still be in this world. For some reason I had no doubt that it was all true, and so I began my search, which was long and hard. I had to cut my way through the thorns to find you," said Zerelda Li, "with this sword, which you will recognize. Then I kissed you, I hope you don't mind that, but apparently that's what has revived you."

"An act of love," Pampa Kampana said. "And your mother was correct."

"That you owe me everything?"

"Yes," said Pampa Kampana, "I do."

Time returned to greet her, and history was reborn. It was the year 1509. Pampa Kampana was one hundred and ninety-one years old, and looked like a woman of thirty-five or so—thirty-eight at the most. "At least," she said to Zerelda Li, "for the moment, I still look older than you. And yes, I see that you have inherited this famous sword. But have you inherited the swordsmanship of your ancestor as well?"

"I have been told that I am as good as the famous Zerelda Sangama and Grandmaster Li Ye-He combined," the young woman replied.

"Good," said Pampa Kampana. "We may need those skills."

Pampa Kampana now used the power of metamorphosis for the second of the three times which were the goddess's gift. She gave Zerelda Li a *cheel* feather from one of her pockets and held another herself, and then they were flying, flying toward Bisnaga, where the greatest king in the history of the empire was about to take the throne, and the love story at which Pampa Kampana had hinted would soon begin; at first it would not be her own story, but one that would cause her heartache, and afterward turn into the strangest description of love she had ever known.

PART THREE

| *Glory* |

14

There were twenty-two *rayas* of Bisnaga before the final destruction of the city, and Krishna Raya was the eighteenth and most glorious of them all. Not so long after he became king he began to add *deva,* god, to his name to indicate his high opinion of himself, and he became Krishnadevaraya, Krishna-god-king, but at the start of his reign he was just Krishna, named after the beloved blue-skinned deity, yes, but neither blue nor godly; although "beloved" fitted him well. During his life and after his death his court poets celebrated him in three languages, and their portraits were uniformly laudatory, and there were many statues made of him and these flattered him too—he became more handsome in stone, his body grew slimmer and more muscular, and if the sculptor had put a flute in his hand and some adoring milkmaids at his feet he could easily have been mistaken for the god after whom he was named. In reality he was, to be frank, a little chubby, and his face showed the marks of a childhood attack of smallpox which he had happily survived. However, he boasted a luxuriant handlebar mustache, a strong jawline, and it was said, though this may have been simply more of the flattery of his courtiers, that his sexual prowess was second to none.

For an account of his ascension to what was now being called the Lion Throne, or sometimes also the Diamond Throne—for an actual throne had by this time replaced the original royal *gaddis,* or mattresses—there presently exist not one but two rediscovered manuscripts. As always in this retelling we rely primarily on Pampa Kampana's work, but the journal of an Italian traveler, Niccolò de' Vieri, who visited Bisnaga in Krishnadevaraya's time, has also come to light—that Vieri who nicknamed himself Signor Rimbalzo, Mister Bounce, because for much of his life he bounced from place to place. Between them they provide seven different narratives of how Krishnadevaraya became king. (Vieri's tales are more bloodthirsty than Pampa Kampana's, which may tell us more about the yarn-spinners than about the historical event.)

Vieri tells us that there was bad blood between Krishna and his much older half-brother, Narasimha. They were both sons of the first king of the Tuluva dynasty, Tuluva himself, a low-caste army commander who had seized the throne; but their mothers, both ambitious former courtesans—Tippamba was the mother of the older son, and Nagamamba of the younger—hated each other and brought up their sons to do the same. When Tuluva was dying, Narasimha ordered the king's chief minister to blind his younger brother Krishna and bring him the eyes as proof (writes Niccolò de' Vieri). However, this minister, Saluva Timmarasu, about whom much more will be said, killed a goat and brought the goat's eyes to Narasimha instead, and then made sure it was Krishna who succeeded the king when he died.

Pampa Kampana, however, tells us that there was no bad blood between the half-brothers, and in fact Narasimha willingly gave up his right to the throne and handed Krishna the signet ring of kingship.

But no!, cries Vieri, what happened is that Narasimha's mother, the vicious Tippamba, plotted to murder Krishna, and Timmarasu had to hide him to keep him safe.

Nonsense, responds Pampa Kampana, the truth is that the brilliant Prince Krishna was playing his flute on the riverbank and all came to listen and wonder, saying, truly, the god walks among us, and that settled it.

To which Vieri answers with the story of how on his deathbed

Tuluva, the father of both Narasimha and Krishna, told the two sons that whoever could pull the signet ring off his finger would be king. Narasimha tried, but the finger was too swollen, because the old man was too full of death; then Krishna simply cut off his father's finger and grabbed the ring for himself.

It is plain that Pampa Kampana in her telling has little time for the gruesome and violent legends in which the foreigner Vieri seems to rejoice. She suggests that, in reality, old King Tuluva placed a dagger in the center of a large carpet and challenged his sons to seize it without walking on that rug. Narasimha was at a loss, but Krishna just rolled up the carpet until the dagger was within his grasp, and so won the day.

Vieri retorts with a rumor of a fight to the death between the two half-brothers, at the end of which Krishna stood over the other's corpse and held aloft his bloodied sword and so won the crown.

All these tales can be treated with respect or dismissed as tall tales, as the reader prefers. For our purposes the most important version—although perhaps the hardest to believe—is the eighth one, in which Pampa Kampana is present herself, along with Zerelda Li.

On the day of their father's death *(Pampa Kampana tells us)* Krishna and his half-brother walked together to the palace gates to announce the passing of Tuluva Raya to the gathered crowd. As they came forward, Krishna looked up into the sky and saw two *cheel* kites circling overhead, high up in the heat-shimmered air. Once, twice, thrice they circled, until he believed their presence might be an augury.

"If they circle around us seven times," he said, "then it's certain they come with a message from the gods." And indeed the two kites did make seven circles, coming down gradually, lower and lower on each circle, until they were flying right over the two princes' heads. Then they dropped to the ground at the two men's feet and to everyone's amazement they metamorphosed into two of the most beautiful women anyone had ever seen: sisters from heaven, or so it seemed. In a swift movement they knelt at the feet of Prince Krishna, bowed their heads, and offered him their magnificent swords. "We place ourselves at your service, and at the service of the empire of Bisnaga," they said. After that there wasn't any argument about the succession to the Lion Throne. The half-brother Narasimha disappears from Pampa Kampana's manuscript and is never heard of again. We must hope that Krishna Raya allowed him to live in comfortable anonymity for the rest of his days.

The spectacular arrival in Bisnaga of Pampa Kampana and Zerelda Li was a gamble that paid off. There were risks in such a bravura entry, there was the danger that such beings as they were revealing themselves to be would engender fear and hostility rather than acceptance. But Pampa Kampana had been determined to enter Bisnaga through the front door this time, instead of crawling through a tunnel. This time, she wanted to be seen for who and what she was. Fortunately, their timing was excellent. The newly crowned Krishna Tuluva—now Krishna Raya—was convinced that Pampa Kampana and Zerelda Li were supernatural beings, *apsaras* (celestial nymphs who were known to be shape-shifters), sent down from above to bless his reign; and after that their safety was assured. They were given lavish accommodations in the palace, and expressed their gratitude for it, although Pampa Kampana, who remembered the days of living in the queen's quarters, was obliged to smother a surge of disappointment. It was plain that the young king was intoxicated by the two women who had descended from the skies, thought to be sisters by one and all, and was already thinking about romance, although his preference was unclear, even to himself. But in the beginning he was engulfed by matters of state and understood that love and marriage would have to wait.

By this time the grand old sultanate of Zafarabad had broken up into five smaller kingdoms, Ahmadnagar, Berar, Bidar, Bijapur, and Golconda; and nobody spoke about a "Ghost Sultanate" anymore.

This is how history moves; the obsession of one moment is relegated to the junkyard of oblivion by the next. All five of the new sultans, undeterred by their smaller territories, were hungry for expansion, especially the sultan of Golconda, rich in diamonds, who was happy to be freed from the domination of the old Zafarabad regime, and had plans of his own to establish a new dominance over the region. In addition, the Gajapati dynasty's kingdom to the east had grown more powerful, and they too had designs on the lands of the Bisnaga Empire. The arrival of a new, young, untested king on the Lion Throne encouraged them to try their luck.

When Krishna Raya's army was ready to march against the oncoming, combined forces of Bidar and Bijapur, Pampa Kampana and Zerelda Li asked for an audience with the king. "Do not number us among the brocaded ladies of the royal court, accustomed to lounging among silken fabrics and eunuchs, singing love songs all day, smoking opium and drinking sweet pomegranate juice," Pampa Kampana told him. "You will find no better warriors in your service than ourselves." Krishna Raya was impressed. "The old *kwoon* constructed in the time of Grandmaster Li still stands," he said. "We will bring the finest women warriors of our palace guard there, and let's see how well you do against them."

"We have been trained by the very best," Zerelda Li said. "So we would prefer to be tested against men as well as women."

"Don't underestimate the fighting women here," said the sizable woman who was the head of the palace guard. "My forebear was the invincible Ulupi, and I have taken her name in her honor. You will find me the equal of any man."

The king was amused. "Enough, enough," he said, laughing. "Ulupi Junior will fight you both, my two *apsaras*, and we will find a mere man to put you to the test as well."

He summoned Thimma the Huge (so called both because it was a fair description and also to avoid confusion with Saluva Timmarasu, Krishna Raya's prime minister). It was said of this immense, silent hulk that he was more elephant than man, his arms like two long trunks that could swing an enemy into the air and hurl him great distances, his gigantic feet able to crush opponents beneath their unimaginable weight. He needed so much to eat that, like a working elephant, he had to carry his food in a sack around his neck, and if he was not fighting or sleeping then he was eating. On the battlefield his mere arrival was enough to make entire platoons of adversaries turn and flee. His weapon of choice was the club, but on entering the *kwoon* he picked up a spear as well. The balconies of the *kwoon* were full. Nobody gave the two women much of a chance, even if they had arrived from the skies, and the watchers began to bet against them. Thimma and Ulupi Junior were heavy favorites. Only the king, as an act of friendship to the new arrivals who had blessed his claim to the throne, placed a large bet on the supernatural ladies, on whom he received very long odds.

Then the combat started, and all those who had backed the two local heroes quickly understood that their money was lost. The spectacle of the two *apsaras* whirling up into the air to attack their opponents from above, running up walls and along the rooftops of the *kwoon* to dive down, attack, and retreat again, was dizzying not only to the spectators but to their opponents, who were soon reduced to standing back-to-back in the center of the *kwoon*'s fighting arena, swinging and lunging at empty air. The aerial ballet of the two women, punctuated with bouts of swordplay that were almost ecstatic in their beauty, left Thimma the Huge and Ulupi Junior exhausted, with only a smashed club, a bisected javelin, and a broken sword to fight with. When Thimma finally sank to his knees panting, the king threw a scarlet cloth into the arena to indicate that the battle was at an end. After that day there was no argument about the most fearsome fighters in Bisnaga, and Krishna Raya declared, "All four of these warriors will come with me to the wars, and no force on earth will be able to withstand us."

The oldest spectators, who were familiar with the old stories, said to one another, "The only women who could ever fight like that were Pampa Kampana and her three daughters, especially Zerelda Sangama." That memory ran swiftly around the galleries of the *kwoon* and dropped down into the arena and reached the ears of the combatants and the king.

"Then call me Pampa Kampana," said Pampa Kampana, "and I will be her second coming. Or, to be precise, her third."

"And call me Zerelda," said Zerelda Li, "and I will be that great lady reborn."

The gold coins Krishna Raya had won by betting on the two women were used to buy food to distribute to the poor. In this way both the king and the victorious ladies began to be seen as virtuous benefactors of the people, and were much loved. "It's a new age in Bisnaga," people began to say, and so it proved to be.

When the army paused at night, on the road north to Diwani to face the armies of Bijapur and Bidar, Pampa Kampana and Zerelda Li shared a tent, and this, after the nonstop activity that had followed their first meeting, was where they finally had time to begin to know each other.

"Tell me your story," Pampa Kampana said, and the young woman, who by nature was a reticent and inward person, made so by the strangeness of her life, opened up to this apparition of a youthful ancestor who was the very incarnation and point of origin of that strangeness. "I was born on a ship," she said, "and nobody can put down roots in the sea. This is how it has been for us ever since Zerelda Sangama and Grandmaster Li joined General Cheng Ho. We have been women on ships, making our way here, there, everywhere, finding men, not marrying them—following the lead of Zerelda Sangama and Grandmaster Li, who never married, but remained true to one another all their lives—and having daughters, and carrying on, bearing Zerelda Sangama's given name—Zerelda after Zerelda after

Zerelda, ending with me, the sixth of that line!—and we kept the grandmaster's family name as well, down all our generations. So we have all been Zerelda Li, the first, the second, the third, and so on. As for me, I had my mother and that was all. My father was mislaid in a port somewhere. There were no other children on board; so from the beginning I was treated as an adult and expected to behave as such. I grew up silent and watchful and I think the men on board—tattooed, gold-toothed, peg-legged, eye-patched, piratical types of whom a normal girl would be terrified—were actually a little scared of me, and very scared of my mother, and so they kept their distance.

"The ship itself was my only neighborhood, it was the street where I lived, but there was a new world waiting every time we came into port and that new world became a part of my world too, for a while. Java, Brunei, Siam, the far lands of Asia, and in the opposite direction the lands of Araby, the Horn of Africa, the Swahili Coast. When we brought the giraffe of Malindi back to China the emperor said it was proof of the Mandate of Heaven that blessed and authorized his rule. We brought ostriches too but they were not held to be divine, being too foolish-looking. This was my life, everywhere and nowhere, and I discovered I possessed the gift of holding the shape of things in my mind. I became a map of the world.

"I learned that the world is infinite in its beauty but also unrelenting, unforgiving, greedy, careless, and cruel. I learned that love is for the most part absent and, when it appears, is usually fitful, fleeting, and finally unsatisfactory. I learned that the communities men build are based on the oppression of the many by the few, and I did not understand, I still do not understand, why the many accept this oppression. Maybe it is because when they do not accept it and rise up, what follows is a greater oppression than the one they overthrew. I began to think that I did not like human beings very much, but I loved mountains, music, forests, dancing, wide rivers, singing, and of course the sea. The sea was my home. And finally I learned that the world takes your home away without any remorse. Somewhere on the eastern coast of Africa a yellow fever came aboard. I was spared, but many died, including my mother. All I had left was what she had taught me, the high arts of battle, and her dying words, the dying words of all the Zereldas. 'Find Pampa Kampana.' And so here I am, and now you know everything."

"Your map of the world," Pampa Kampana said, "do you have an actual map in your head? Can you see how the world joins up? How *here* connects with *there,* and is affected by it and changed by it? Can you see the shape of things?"

"Yes," said Zerelda Li. "I see it very clearly."

"Then I will tell you who I am," Pampa Kampana said. "I am a map of time. I carry almost two centuries within me and will absorb half a century more before I'm done. And just as you can see how *here* connects to *there,* so I perceive how *then* is joined to *now.*"

"Then let's both make our maps," Zerelda Li proposed, clapping her hands. "I'll set mine down on paper if you will agree to do the same with yours. I will ask the king for a Map Room and cover every inch of the walls and even the ceiling with pictures of the great world beyond the sea, and you must ask for an empty book that you will fill with history and dreams and maybe tell the future as well, while you're at it."

There, in that spartan military encampment, on the road to war, Pampa Kampana's masterwork was born. She began in earnest to write the *Jayaparajaya,* even though to do so meant revisiting the horror of the fire that consumed her mother; and Zerelda Li began to draw the maps that would be thought, for fifty-five years, to be the most perfect works of the cartographer's art. But the Map Room did not survive the destruction of Bisnaga, and no shred of Zerelda Li's genius remains for us to marvel at today.

The battle of Diwani didn't last long, and would be better described as a rout. As the armies of Bijapur and Bidar fled the field the vanquished sultans prostrated themselves at Krishna Raya's feet, expecting to be trampled by the battle elephant, Masti Madahasti, on which he sat in his golden howdah, looking down at them with the wide yellow-toothed grin of victory. But Krishna held his elephant back. "He has sensitive feet," he informed the prone sultans, "and I don't want to injure them if I can help it. So, I suggest that you can live, and go back to your petty thrones, but from now on both your sultanates will be subservient to the Bisnaga Empire, and you will accept my supremacy, and pay me tribute. I hope you will accept this generous offer, because if not then Masti Madahasti here may have to risk his tender feet after all."

"There's just one thing," said the horizontal sultan of Bijapur. "We are not prepared to convert to your religion with its thousand and one gods, and if you insist on that, then let the elephant do its worst. Is that not so, my friend Bidar?"

The sultan of Bidar considered for a moment. Then, "Yes," he said, "I suppose so."

Krishna Raya let out a loud laugh, a laugh containing little mirth. "Why would I insist on such a thing?" he asked. "In the first place, such conversions are dishonest. We know from our history that the founders of Bisnaga, Hukka and Bukka Sangama, were forcibly converted by the Delhi sultan, and obliged for a time to pretend to accept your tediously unitary God; but they escaped the first chance they got and gave up all that nonsense at once. In the second place, were you to convert, you would lose the support of your own people and therefore be unable to convince them of the value of loyalty to the Bisnaga Empire, and after that you would be of little use to me. And in the third place, if by some miracle your people followed you and converted en masse, who then would occupy all those beautiful mosques you have built in your sultanates? So, keep your faith, my elephant doesn't mind if you do. But if you show disloyalty to the empire in even the slightest degree, then Masti Madahasti may have to risk his tender feet after all and pound you both to death."

In that age of decapitations, straw-stuffed heads, assassinations, and elephant crushings, news of Krishna Raya's merciful act spread rapidly, and was thought to be greatly to his credit. Thus began the legend of the new God-King, as godlike as the god after whom he was named, a legend which, very soon, Krishna Raya unfortunately began to believe himself. On that day, however, Pampa Kampana noticed a more immediate motive for his act of forgiveness. As Krishna Raya was pardoning the defeated sultans, his eyes moved away from their humbled bodies and darted between Zerelda Li and Pampa Kampana herself. They were mounted on horseback and positioned to his elephant's right. Ulupi Junior and Thimma the Huge were to his left, on foot, but the king's gaze never once strayed in their direction. Zerelda Li kept looking straight ahead and gave no indication that she was aware of the king's scrutiny, but Pampa Kampana looked right back at him until his grin widened, becoming even more yellow, and he actually blushed.

Pampa Kampana put her hands together and applauded him for his wisdom. He bowed his head to recognize her gesture, because the approval of his two *apsaras* was something he found that he greatly desired. It was plain that something had begun.

It was *Mahamantri* or Great Minister Saluva Timmarasu who had taught the young Krishna Raya about the importance of the number seven. There were, he said, seven ways to handle an adversary: you could try to reason with him, or bribe him, or stir up trouble in his territories; you could lie to him in peacetime and trick him on the battlefield; you could attack him, obviously, and this was the recommended method; or finally—not to be recommended—you could forgive him. When Krishna Raya forgave the two sultans at Diwani, almost everyone approved and praised his humane act. Timmarasu, however, greeted him on his return to the palace with the words: "I hope that wasn't really forgiveness, because that would be a sign of weakness, but if it's a trick, it's a good one."

"I attacked and defeated them first," said Krishna Raya, "then I offered them the bribe of survival using the appearance of forgiveness, and acting the part of a reasonable man. We will send spies to Bijapur and Bidar to make trouble for them, so they will be preoccupied with local dissensions and therefore unable to try anything against us again, and we will lie to them if they accuse us of having done so. You can call this a trick if you wish. I prefer to think that I am using all seven techniques at once."

Timmarasu was impressed. "I see that the student has outstripped the teacher," he said.

"You saved my life more than once," Krishna Raya said, "so you will always be at my right hand, and I will go on learning what you have to teach."

"In that case, welcome home," Timmarasu said. "And I must immediately inform you about the seven vices of kings."

Krishna Raya sat back on the Lion Throne. "I can already dismiss two of them," he said. "I don't drink, and I don't gamble, so you don't need to tell me the *Mahabharata* story of how Yudhisthira rolled the dice and lost his kingdom and his wife. Everybody knows that story. Spare me, too, the allegory of the god of death and the poisoned waters of the lake."

"You have also shown that you avoid harshness in war," Timmarasu said. "But the vice of arrogance is already present in you. That is something we need to work on."

"Not now," said the king, with a dismissive gesture. "Three more to go."

"The hunt," Timmarasu said.

"I hate the hunt," Krishna Raya said. "A barbarian practice. I prefer poetry and music."

"Wasting money," Timmarasu said.

"Money will be your job," said the king, laughing, although it was not clear if he was making a joke. "The purse-strings of the treasury are in your hands, and the power of taxation. If you get greedy or waste money, I'll chop off your head."

"That's fair," said Timmarasu.

"What's the last vice?" Krishna Raya asked.

"Women," his minister replied.

"If you're going to tell me I can only have seven wives," Krishna Raya replied, "don't. There are some matters regarding which the number seven is inadequate."

"Understood," Timmarasu said. "Though I may have more to say about this at another time. For now, I'll just offer my congratulations. Five out of seven isn't bad. You'll make a fine king."

Then he came up close to the king and slapped him hard in the face. Before Krishna Raya could begin to express his shock and anger, Timmarasu said, "That is to remind you that the common people suffer pain every day."

"And that is more than enough education for one day," said the king, rubbing his face. "It's lucky for you that I have only just now said that I'm willing to be schooled by you."

15

Regarding the "vice of women": soon after the victory at Diwani, Krishna Raya chose to transform the royal *zenana,* the women's wing adjacent to his own residence the Lotus Palace, into a glorious simulacrum of the world of his divine namesake, and so he announced to the citizens of Bisnaga that one hundred and eight of their most beautiful daughters would have the honor of being selected as royal *gopis.* He would spare them the job of milking cows, because, after all, it should be obvious that he was not proposing to turn the royal residence into a cow palace. The Sangamas had been cowherds to begin with, so maybe in the time of Hukka and Bukka their palace had smelled of dung, but that dynasty was long gone, it was ancient history, and therefore there would be no cows. The milkmaids, who would not be required to milk any odorous udders, would be well cared for, living in great ease—one might almost say splendor—and their only duty would be unconditional love. When he chose to play the flute they would dance for him, and the dance would be the *Ras Lila,* the dance of divine adoration. There would be three ranks of consorts, the lowly messengers, the middling maidservants, and above them all there would be his queen, to whom, once he had chosen her, he would give the name of the eternal Radha; and the eight *varisthas,* the top *gopis,* who would be his constant companions, and to whom he would give the names they bore in the ancient tales, Lalita, Visakha, Champaka-Mallika, Chitra, Tungavidya, Indulekha, Ranga, and Sudevi. The role of Radha would require the deepest search, because it would be necessary for her to be the very incarnation of Bliss Potency. "But let the search begin!" he decreed. "When I have them all, I will rename the *zenana* also, and call it the Holy Basil Forest, after the sacred grove of the god; and the reign of love will be established across the empire."

This was also the moment when, to use his own words, he "reluctantly, and with all due modesty and a deep sense of being unworthy of the honor, gave in to widespread popular demand," and allowed his regnal name to be changed. He would be Krishnadevaraya, the God-King, for the rest of his life.

When Saluva Timmarasu heard that the king intended to issue this proclamation he began to worry. "Pride comes before a fall," he thought, "and to equate oneself with a god risks bringing down upon oneself the wrath of the god himself." But he saw that the king would not be dissuaded and decided that his own best interests lay in managing the project as efficiently as possible, to avoid falling out of favor. So the parade of young women began, and Timmarasu's selections were pleasing to the king, until one hundred and five of the positions had been filled by ladies who were eager to please, because for almost all of them the overnight rise in their fortunes utterly transformed the lives of their families, and the horizon of their own limited possibilities seemed to spread until the whole world was within their grasp. If Krishnadevaraya wanted unconditional love as the price of their new lives, they were happy to provide at least the appearance of that love. It was well worth it. Thus they, too, the one hundred and five, were creating a simulacrum, a mimic life, a falsehood. But it looked like the real thing, and so, in a way, it became real, or, at least, everyone treated it as if it was real, which was almost the same thing.

Saluva Timmarasu was a man of humble origins, not learned in the texts, a brusque worldly fellow who had made his way up by soldiering; a plain man, who knew himself to be inadequate to the task of rehearsing these pseudo-*gopis* in the characters they must now inhabit to please their royal master. He therefore turned for help to the one he thought of as the senior of the two celestial beings who had flown down into their lives, and who, being celestial, would know about the characters and antics of the timeless personages inhabiting that other world. It so happened that, unknown to Timmarasu, this Senior Celestial Being was also the person in Bisnaga who was most learned in the books, the one who had spent her childhood years from the age of nine in the company of the sage Vidyasagar, studying and striving to understand the ancient texts. This was Pampa Kampana, of course, and if Timmarasu was accepted by the king as his personal tutor, then Pampa Kampana became Timmarasu's teacher, as well as the instructor and confidante of his one hundred and five consorts.

At first Pampa Kampana didn't want to do it. Her advanced views on the position of women in society were incompatible with a royal household of over a hundred wives. She wanted to approach the king and say, just choose one wonderful woman and rule with her, side by side. But Timmarasu suggested this would be unwise. "He is deeply struck by you and Miss Zerelda Li as well," the minister said, "because of your magical nature and your unrivaled prowess in combat. But he is beginning to think of himself as a god, and so in his own opinion he outranks mere metamorphic *apsaras.* Don't get on the wrong side of him now, at the beginning of things. Slowly, slowly is the way to make him change. Also, I've seen the way he looks at both of you. One of you, or both of you, may be granted a very high rank."

"There are things I have to tell Krishna Raya about us—about *me*—that I hope will make him take me very seriously indeed," Pampa Kampana said. "But you are right. Everything in its own good time. Let us wait until Bisnaga has a queen."

"As to that," Timmarasu said, "I expect and intend to be influential in the king's choice. That is a matter not of love, but of state."

"I see," said Pampa Kampana. "So I'll find out eventually whose side you are on."

She began her assignment with the eighth-ranked consort, formerly a flower-seller's daughter, now renamed "Sudevi," and chosen for her complexion, which was the color of a lotus stamen. "There's a lot for you to do," Pampa Kampana old her. "You must always be sweet-natured, no matter what the provocation. You must bring the king water whenever he is thirsty, and massage his body with perfumed oils after he comes home from the day's exertions. You will train parrots to perform for him, and roosters to fight. You will also be the guardian of the flowers in the *zenana,* making sure they are fresh in their vases. Certain flowers blossom when the moon rises. Those are auspicious flowers. Learn their names and make sure there are plenty of them in the palace. Also, you will keep bees. And once the queen is crowned, you will braid her hair, and spy on the other *gopis* to make sure they are not plotting against her. Can you do this?"

"I will do this with love," said the eighth-ranked *gopi.*

The seventh-ranked *gopi* was "Ranga," originally a washerwoman's daughter. "Your job," Pampa Kampana told her, "is to flirt incessantly with the king when the queen is absent, and, when the queen is present as well as the king, to make her laugh by telling her a nonstop stream of jokes. In the summer heat, you must fan them, and in the winter cold, bring coal for their fireplaces. But you must also study logic, so that if the king chooses to philosophize, you can join in the conversation with impressive competence and verve. Can you do this?"

"The logic part won't be easy," said the seventh-ranked *gopi,* "but I'll make up for it by flirting extra hard."

When the sixth-ranked *gopi,* now called "Indulekha," formerly the daughter of a palace cook, was brought before her, Pampa Kampana said, "Oh, you're the hot-tempered one, probably because of all that heat in the kitchen. You will make for the king meals that taste like nectar, and fan him while he eats. In addition you will master the charming of snakes so that they may dance for him, and the arts of palm-reading, so that you can tell him his fortune every morning, ensuring that he is well prepared for the day. Once there is a queen, she and the king will use you to send messages to each other, so you will know their secrets; and you will be the mistress of her wardrobe and her jewels. If you should ever be so foolish as to tell any other living person a royal secret, or to steal . . ."

"I will never be that foolish," shouted the sixth *gopi,* "so kindly don't accuse me of being either a blabbermouth or a thief."

The *gopi* of the fifth rank, now known as "Tungavidya," a schoolteacher's child, had been chosen for her high intelligence and wide-ranging knowledge as well as her mastery of the arts. "You are here," Pampa Kampana said, "to stimulate the king with your expertise in the eighteen branches of knowledge, including morality, literature, and everything else. Also to dance. And I believe you can play the vina and sing in the *marga* style. That is suitable. It can also be that if the king wishes to make a political alliance he may call upon your diplomatic expertise. And if the king and queen should quarrel, your diplomacy will be required to smooth things over, although at such times your senior, Chitra, will always take the lead, and you will do as she asks."

"That's all fine," said the fifth *gopi,* "but I hope I will be allowed some romance as well."

"Chitra," the fourth-ranked *gopi,* was one of the few chosen ladies who came from an aristocratic household, and was therefore a nose-in-air type who was reluctant to be schooled by Pampa Kampana. "I know how it goes," she told Pampa. "I intercede in the royal disagreements, and I garland the king and queen every day. I speak and read many languages, and can interpret any text to tell the king what the author really means, rather than what is apparent on the surface. I know how food will taste just by looking at it, and so I can also discern if it's poisoned or not. I can fill pots with different quantities of water and play music on them with drumsticks. I will be in charge of the palace gardens, so that I can bring the king herbs that transport him into a transcendental state, and others that will heal him when he's sick. The household animals will be in my care. And I will behave with extreme affection and high sensuality toward the king, but remain absolutely demure in the queen's presence. None of this is very difficult."

"We will see," Pampa Kampana said.

Her last pupil was "Champaka," or "Champaka-Mallika," the Magnolia Queen, from a humble woodsman's household. "I don't have much to tell you," Pampa Kampana said, "except everything I've told the others, combined. You are the most exalted of the ladies of the household, behind only the as-yet-unknown queen and her two as-yet-unnamed closest companions. You will have the ultimate responsibility for everything the ladies ranked below you must do, but you will be, or will become, skilled in the art of delegating. If you succeed in inhabiting your role, you will be fourth-ranked in Bliss Potency, and will be called upon to cause bliss to the king when the senior three are tired or disinclined. Your hands are skilled, or must become so, so that you can make sculptures from clay, and also sweetmeats to eat, so delicious that all will call you 'Sweet Hands.'"

"I can't cook," said the Magnolia Queen. "Everybody says so. What happens if I fail?"

"Don't fail," Pampa Kampana said, her patience at an end. "Learn. And do it soon."

To Pampa Kampana's surprise, her great-great-great-great-granddaughter Zerelda Li found the long-drawn-out process of the selection of the royal consorts entirely unobjectionable; in fact she was pleased that Pampa was participating in the enterprise, and helping the ladies to grasp the importance and variety of their new responsibilities.

"Who knows," she said, and her air of starry-eyed innocence astonished Pampa Kampana, "maybe he'll choose me as one of the two Chief Companions, or even—yes! Why not?—as his queen."

"What are you saying?" Pampa Kampana said. The heat with which she spoke surprised them both, and may have been the product of her reluctant mentoring of the newly appointed royal consorts. "You've traveled the world, so you must have seen there are better ways to be a woman than that."

"Yes, I've spent my life wandering, rootless, not knowing where I came from, where I belonged, or who, if I ever found that place, I might become," Zerelda Li replied. "If there's a chance now for me to become a real part of something, to join myself to an ancient tradition and become part of the ruling dynasty as well, then I will happily do it, and you should understand why. To stand by the side of the king will allow me to believe that my journeying is at an end, and that I can finally put down roots."

"I have always believed that a woman can put down roots in herself," Pampa Kampana said, "and not define herself by standing next to any man, not even a king. Didn't you come across any women who thought like that in all your travels?"

They were in the old Green Destiny *kwoon*, sharpening their martial skills, and the argument—their first moment of dissension—added an edge to their training. "In the maps I have in my mind," Zerelda Li said as they battled, "I see places where women are slaves, or servants, and where they are free they are still disrespected. In China their feet are bound and crippled when they are little girls. In the Stone Town of Zanzibar women are not allowed in public places. In the Mediterranean and in the South China Sea there were women pirates, that's true, but one was overthrown by her son-in-law and the other married her adopted son and ended up running a brothel in Macau. Being a queen is a lot better than any of that."

"I've been a queen," said Pampa Kampana, setting down her sword. "It isn't all that great." At the end of their training they went to the baths. "In old Bisnaga," Pampa Kampana told her grandchild, "women were lawyers, traders, architects, poets, gurus, everything."

"When I am queen," Zerelda Li said, "all that will be true again."

"If you are queen," Pampa Kampana corrected her, sighing.

"When," Zerelda Li insisted. "Haven't you seen the way he looks at me?"

At this point Pampa Kampana said something she hadn't intended to say, something that came from a place within her whose existence she hadn't suspected.

"He looks at me in the exact same way," she said.

After that Zerelda Li did not speak to her for a week, but shut herself up in her Map Room in the Lotus Palace, had food brought to her while she worked, and slept in there on a bed she had brought in for her. When she finally opened the doors, everyone saw that she had made, over and over, maps of only two countries, both of which, Pampa Kampana suspected, were imaginary: the country of Zerelda, which Grandmaster Li had invented to entrance his beloved, and the land of Ye-He, by which invention Zerelda Li's forebear, Pampa Kampana's daughter Zerelda Sangama, had found a language in which she could tell Li Ye-He that she, too, loved him. The city of fleeting time and butterfly nets, and the city of flighted humans and flightless birds, were both depicted in dazzling colors and extraordinary detail. Here, in a corner of Zereldaville, was an old woman in a wheeled chair being pulled by her daughters, desperately grasping at the flitting hours she could no longer capture, while, watching her with expressions that mingled pity and contempt, were young boys munching on time sandwiches and fruits that looked like clocks, and believing themselves immortal; while here, in a neighboring panel, were ecstatic women flying above the clouds of Ye-He-Town, naked as the day they were born and dancing together in the air without a care in the world—and then the same women, shivering with cold, buying coats from the garment shops in the clouds, not because they had been overcome by shame at their nudity, but because they were freezing to death at that altitude. In the faces of the citizens of the two towns the stoicism of the Zereldans and the worldly wisdom of the Ye-He-ites shone out.

Finally, when her work was complete, she allowed her grandmother to see what she had made. Pampa Kampana began to weep because the maps were so beautiful, and she praised the work for a long time. But eventually, in a low, loving voice, she felt obliged to say, "My beloved child, these are, are they not, places to travel to in dreams, not places that one can visit in one's waking hours."

"On the contrary," Zerelda Li replied. "Every map that I have made is a portrait of where we are standing right now. They are all maps of Bisnaga."

The Map Room was thrown open. The king was the first visitor and he, too, was moved to tears by the beauty of Zerelda Li's cartography. After him, the senior courtiers visited, and it was necessary for them to cry as well, to prove they were not less moved than the king, and after that everyone who visited that room was obliged to shed quantities of real or imaginary tears, so that people began to call it—though not within the king's earshot—"the Room of Compulsory Crying."

The recently renamed Krishnadevaraya summoned the court to the Lion Throne Room—the courtiers filed in, wiping their red-rimmed eyes—and publicly declared his love for the mapmaker Zerelda Li. He told her that he proposed to rename her, too, as "Radha-Rani," Queen Radha, after the beloved of the god, and asked her to choose her own closest companions, "one of whom, I assume," he told her, "will be your fellow *apsara*, your sister or whatever you say she is." Then three things happened in quick succession:

First, that Zerelda Li declared that she would humbly accept the gift of his love;

. . . and second, that Pampa Kampana, somewhat red-faced and intemperate, stated that she had no wish to be either of the closest companions, neither a pseudonymous "Lalita" nor a counterfeit "Visakha." "If you permit it," she told the king, "I will remain plain Pampa Kampana as long as I live."

"I'm confused," Krishnadevaraya replied. "As you are obviously not the real, legendary Pampa Kampana of long ago, but have merely adopted that name as a flag of convenience, why is it a problem to adopt another new name instead, a name that would lend you great prestige and renown?"

"The time may come, Your Majesty," Pampa Kampana said, "when I can explain to you who and what I am. For now, I beg to be excused." And with that she left the throne room;

. . . and third, that *Mahamantri* Timmarasu, positioned beside the Lion Throne at the king's right hand, bent down and murmured, "I ask with great urgency for a private word in Your Majesty's immaculate ear."

Krishna, who had already learned that when his chief minister spoke in that particular tone of voice it was a good idea to pay attention, descended from the throne and went into his private quarters. Only Timmarasu was allowed to accompany him. When they were alone, the minister shook his head sadly.

"You should have discussed this with me," he said. "The choice of a number-one wife is a matter that cannot be decided by mere physical attraction."

"I love her," said Krishnadevaraya. "And that must be enough, and decisive."

"Nonsense," Timmarasu said firmly. "If you'll pardon the expression."

"Then what factors are enough, and decisive?" Krishnadevaraya demanded.

"Reasons of state," Timmarasu said. "In such a matter, nothing else is relevant."

"And to what reasons of state might you be referring?" asked the king.

"The southern border," Timmarasu said. "It's time for an alliance. After the victory at Diwani, things to the north are stabilized, at least for the moment. But in the south we need some help. We need, in short, King Veerappodeya of Srirangapatna, an able ruler and a feared military commander, to conquer and then administer a number of southern regions for us, notably the city and principality of Mysore."

"But what does that have to do with my love for the *apsara* Zerelda Li?" demanded the king, petulantly, his face coloring as his anger mounted.

(He was known to have a short fuse, and Timmarasu would eventually discover the consequences of the king's rage. But it was also true that when Krishnadevaraya's temper subsided he felt remorseful and went to great lengths to compensate the victims of his anger for their suffering. As we shall see. That is not a matter for now.)

"The only way to secure King Veera's affection and support," Timmarasu told the king, "is for you to marry his daughter Tirumala."

"What, *that* Tirumala?" Krishnadevaraya roared, and his voice echoed through every corner of the palace, reaching the ears of Zerelda Li, Pampa Kampana, and the entire court as well. "The notorious Telugu princess of whom people say, she's a monstrous bully, tyrannical in her habits and unloving in the extreme?"

"You know how it is," Timmarasu said soothingly. "A strong man is admired as a leader, but a strong woman is reviled as a shrew. By this union you will show all the women of the empire that a time has returned in which female strength will be treated with respect."

"So it will make me the beloved benefactor of every woman in Bisnaga," said the king.

"It will," said Timmarasu.

"And I'll have my *gopis* anyway, so I won't have to spend very much time with this lady," the king mused.

"They say she's a military lady," Timmarasu said, "so maybe you will want her to fight alongside your other great heroines, Ulupi Junior, Zerelda Li, and Pampa."

"They won't get on," the king prophesied.

"They must," Timmarasu said. "Because you will command it, and you are the king."

Krishnadevaraya thought for a moment. "What am I supposed to do now?" he asked, and his voice was not thunderous anymore, but almost piteous. "Just minutes ago I told the world that Zerelda Li would be my Radha. Am I supposed to demote her before anything has even begun?"

"The royal court is a school of hard knocks," said Timmarasu. "There are ups, and there are downs. It will be a valuable lesson for the girl to learn."

"Then I must go out and tell her that she cannot be Radha but she can be Lalita, which is just one step down. It's still a very important position."

"I believe Tirumala will ask her mother to accompany her to Bisnaga," Timmarasu said. "She may not be with us all the time, but the position of closest companion must be hers. So the second-place 'Lalita' role must go to her."

"You want me to push Zerelda Li down into third place?" Krishnadevaraya cried. "She can't be Radha or even Lalita, so she must be Visakha. This may be hard for her to take."

"She is a sort of foreigner," Timmarasu said, brutally. "There is in her more than a touch of the Chinese, and maybe of other races, too. Tell her no foreigner has ever occupied so high a position in the empire. There was once a foreigner in charge of explosions, but this is a far more elevated position. Tell her it's impossible to place her higher, because that would perhaps indicate to the Chinese emperor that you were willing to accept some degree of Chinese authority in Bisnaga. This may lead to an invasion, a fleet arriving at Goa, followed by a war we do not want. It would be better, really, if you did not give her any rank at court at all."

"You go too far," Krishnadevaraya said to Timmarasu. "This is the woman that I love. I must hurt her for your 'reasons of state,' but I will continue to love her. Tirumala may become the queen empress of Bisnaga, but Zerelda Li will always be the queen empress of my heart."

"Really?" Timmarasu demanded. "This isn't just some infatuation of yours? You have hardly spoken to the girl since she arrived. You don't know her."

"It is not an infatuation," said the king. "When you see someone fighting on the battlefield their entire nature becomes apparent. When life and death are the only questions there's no room to hide. I saw her at Diwani. She was magnificent. She is extraordinary. I can't think of a better woman to have by my side for the rest of my life. Well, the other *apsara,* the one who calls herself Pampa Kampana, is perhaps even more extraordinary, but in spite of her apparent youth and beauty she gives off, for some reason that I don't understand, the air of a very old woman, and even though I respect and admire that old soul which she seems to possess, I need youth that acts like youth. These are the reasons for my feelings. They are not superficial. They are profound. And I will make one more point that may be to the liking of your calculating way of thinking. It may even be a 'reason of state.'

"If it's true that, as she says, she is descended from Zerelda Sangama, then a union with her unites the Tuluva and Sangama dynasties and makes our claim to the Lion Throne—my claim and our children's claim—impossible to refute. We don't need to mention this to Tirumala or her father, but this may be my preferred line of succession—the best line of succession for my house."

Timmarasu scrutinized him closely. "I see that you are telling the truth about your feelings, and that you are also thinking ahead in an interesting way," he said at length. "So I will protect and enable your love. But Tirumala must be the senior queen. We will face the question of what happens to any offspring at a later point. Now we must return to the throne room and make everything clear."

"Very well," Krishnadevaraya said. "Let's get this over with."

After she left the throne room, Pampa Kampana went to sit alone in her chambers, and asked herself what the matter might be. Her own recent behavior was a puzzlement to her. Why had she spoken so competitively to Zerelda Li about the king's glances toward her—"*He looks at me in the exact same way*"? Why had she left the throne room in an inelegant, red-faced fit of pique? It was true that she had wanted no part of Krishnadevaraya's ersatz Vrindavan, his "Holy Basil Forest" filled with counterfeits of the retinue of the god. It was true that she resented having been dragged into the whole foolish business, as the girls' educator and mentor, by Minister Timmarasu. It was also true that Radha had been her own mother's name and so it was painful to see it bestowed upon another. But none of that should have created a rift between Zerelda Li and herself. Also, she could readily understand Zerelda Li's eagerness to be a part of her new world, her yearning to enter into the heart of a culture which was hers, but still largely unknown to her; her desire to belong. What, then, was going on, Pampa Kampana wondered. Why was she so upset?

Was she herself in love with the king?

Ridiculous idea. His vanity, his godly delusions, his pockmarked face. There were a hundred reasons why she wouldn't want a man like him. He was the opposite of her type. And anyway, she hardly knew him.

But was she in love with him?

And how long do you have to know somebody to fall in love with them, anyway? Seven years? Or seven minutes?

The reign of love will be established across the empire. He had said that, and it was greatly to his credit. In all her long life she had never heard any king—any *man*—privilege love above all other values. She, too, in her heart of hearts dreamed of such a thing, of a Bisnaga in which all divisions—of caste, of skin color, of religion, of thought, of shape, of region—would be set aside, and *premarajya,* the kingdom of love, would be born. She had never confessed to anyone, perhaps not even to herself, that she harbored so sentimental a desire in her heart, and then this Krishnadevaraya had just said it out loud for everyone to hear.

The reign of love.

He probably didn't even know what he meant, Pampa Kampana told herself. It was just a phrase he tossed out, a rhetorical emptiness. But if she were the one standing next to him, she could teach him what it meant. If she were restored to her former place of glory she might whisper words of love into the king's ear, and the ear of his Great Minister, and into every ear in the land. She could make it her life's work, the life that still remained to her after almost two hundred years.

But she could do that anyway, couldn't she? She had whispered to a whole city once before. Why didn't she just go ahead and spread the gospel of love, if that, as she was now telling herself, was her dearest wish?

Her place of glory. Was it because of glory that she had been thrown off balance? Was that what she really wanted, after all this time, after everything? The desire for renewed glory, masquerading as the desire for a not-particularly-desirable man, and his crown?

She was obliged to admit to herself, even though it made her feel ashamed of herself, that this was probably the right answer. Zerelda Li was not the only one to have spent long years in exile, not the only one who craved belonging, and a kind of validation. But Zerelda Li knew almost nothing about Bisnaga other than what her mother had told her, and what her mother knew was only what had been passed down to her through many generations. She had no lived experience of it; she was now hungry for that experience, certainly, but a hungry woman was, frankly, a woman who hadn't been fed.

Pampa Kampana, on the other hand, knew everything. She knew what she had done to make Bisnaga what it was, and she remembered the bitterness of her forest exile. To have something and lose it, she thought, was a good deal worse than never having had it at all, and not even really knowing what it was. She wanted everything back: to be seen once again as the magical creature she was, the human person with the goddess dwelling within her, who had created an empire from a sack of seeds, and whispered its history into its ears, and, by doing so, had made it real. She wanted to sit alone with the king and tell him the true story of his kingdom and of her central part in its making, and to have him see that this was not some fairy tale handed down over two centuries, but the truth, embodied in the woman who was telling him the tale, who looked to be not more than thirty-seven years old but had in reality seen her one hundred and ninetieth birthday come and go. That would be better than a crown. And if recognition brought love with it, the king's love and maybe also the love of the people, if a crown were to be offered, then she would gladly accept that, all of it, as a kind of confirmation.

She accused herself of vanity.

Zerelda Li burst into the room, running, crying, and laughing at the same time. "I'm not going to be queen after all," she cried, "but I'm going to be junior queen!" and in a tumble of words, sobs, and giggles she told Pampa Kampana about the political match with Tirumala of Srirangapatna, "but I don't care, because she's probably a hag, isn't she, if the only way she can get a husband is through some cold-blooded political arrangement, not so *romantic,* is it, and who cares about *her,* anyway, because he took me into his most private of private rooms and told me I am his one and only true love, he said that the love god loosed all five of his arrows and struck him five times and that's that, he loves me for the rest of my life, it's so beautiful, he's so, so, *sincere.*"

"I see," Pampa Kampana said, embracing the young woman who had rushed into her arms. "Well, congratulations."

"Junior queen is still queen," Zerelda Li sobbed into Pampa Kampana's shoulder. "Right?"

"Yes, indeed it is," Pampa Kampana said.

Zerelda Li wiped her eyes. "Do you know about the five arrows of Kama?" she asked, still a little tearfully.

"Yes," Pampa Kampana said; but there was no stopping the young woman. "Well, I didn't," Zerelda Li said, "but he explained it so beautifully. He said the arrow decorated with white lotus flowers, *Aravinda,* struck his heart, and made him feel excited, youthful, and happy. The second arrow, decorated with *Ashoka* flowers, hit him on the mouth and made him cry out for love. The third arrow, with the mango tree flowers painted on the shaft, *Choota,* penetrated his brain and made him mad with adoration. The fourth arrow, the jasmine flower arrow, *Navamallika,* struck his eye, and after that when he looked at me he saw a great radiance of beauty such as only the greatest goddesses exude. And the fifth arrow, the one with the blue lotuses, *Neelotpala,* struck his navel. Actually, he said, it doesn't matter where the fifth arrow hits you. Wherever it lands it fills you with love, you feel like you're drowning in a sea of love, and all you want to do is drown."

"That was very prettily spoken," Pampa Kampana conceded. "I see why it has affected you so deeply, as if you were the one struck by the arrows."

"I think maybe I was hit too," Zerelda Li said, "but because I didn't know then about Kama the god of love and his bow made of sugarcane, I wasn't aware of it."

Pampa Kampana held her tongue, and only smiled a small enigmatic smile.

"Are you happy for me?" her great-great-great-great-granddaughter exclaimed. "You have to be. I need you to be *very* happy for me. I need you to be ecstatic."

"I owe her everything," Pampa Kampana thought. "My own daughter said so with her dying word, and her daughter, and hers, and so on. So I will give her everything. Hers is the glory. I will stand aside for her, remaining plain Pampa in the shadows, and I will learn that the deepest meaning of love is renunciation, giving up one's own dream to fulfill the dream of the beloved. Also, I am tired of watching those I love grow old and die. Let the dying love the dying. The undying belong only to themselves."

"I am ecstatic for you," Pampa Kampana said, embracing her granddaughter tightly. "I am filled with divine joy."

16

Pampa Kampana was at her favorite fruit stall in the grand bazaar tasting the first perfect mango of the season, an Alphonso from Goa, when the foreigner Niccolò de' Vieri came into view, strolling down the street as if he owned it. He wore a soft burgundy-colored hat on his head and had a matching scarf draped loosely at his neck. He sported a thick russet beard whose color chimed with his clothes, and on his blouse a winged golden lion, rampant, could be seen. He looked like someone on his way to have his portrait painted. And the long hair on his head was bright red and his eyes were emerald green.

"It's not possible," Pampa Kampana said aloud. "But here you are, for the third time."

Niccolò de' Vieri—aka Signor Rimbalzo, the bouncing man—heard her. Like everyone in Bisnaga, he knew the tale of the two *apsaras* who had flown down from the sky. He wasn't sure he believed it—it sounded like the kind of fabulous saga an ambitious ruler might make up and put about to justify his seizure of power—and, as we have seen, he had heard other accounts of how Krishnadevaraya became king. But as his gaze fell upon Pampa Kampana he found himself thinking, "I will believe anything this woman tells me and do whatever she asks me to do." He bowed formally and replied, "If this were the third time I would surely remember the first and second, because such meetings would be impossible to forget."

"You speak our language well," Pampa Kampana said, "but where do you come from, foreigner?"

"My home is La Serenissima, La Dominante," he replied, flamboyantly, as was his way. "The city of bridges, the city of masks, the city without a prince, which is to say, the Republic of Venice, more lovely to behold than any city on earth, whose true beauty and truest nature is invisible, being found in the unique and multifarious spirit of its citizens, who travel the world but never leave home, because they carry it within them always."

"Oh," Pampa Kampana said. "Well, at least this time you aren't Portuguese."

It turned out that Vieri was staying in what, ever since Fernão Paes's day, had been known as "the foreigner's house," that stone mansion with large, outward-facing windows, which had once boasted a green garden and a field of sugarcane but was now an inn whose lands had disappeared under new construction as the city grew. He invited Pampa Kampana to visit him there if she so desired. "Even your voice is the same," she said. "You have that beard now, but underneath it I'm pretty sure you have the same face. I should be grateful, I think. Once in each generation you reappear to cheer me up."

"Nothing would make me happier than to cheer you up," Niccolò de' Vieri said.

The vendor of fruits, the gentle, pot-bellied Sri Laxman who took great pride in his produce, interrupted. "Mangoes also make you happy, isn't it," he said.

"Mangoes make me joyful," Pampa Kampana said. "Send me a basketful of Alphonsos, and another basketful to this foreign gentleman's abode, just so he can see what the Portuguese are capable of."

The Alphonso mango was a varietal created by the Portuguese in Goa, the product of their skills in grafting, and named after the general Alphonso de Albuquerque, who established his country's colonial presence on the west coast. Niccolò de Vieri picked up a mango from Sri Laxman's display and tossed it lightly in the air. "Anything the Portuguese can do," he said, "the Venetians can do better, and in more elegant clothes."

The vendor in the neighboring stall was Sri Laxman's brother, Sri Narayan. He sold pulses, grains, rice, and seeds. "Buy from me also, sir, madam," he called out in mock outrage. "Rice brings happiness also. Seeds bring forth the bounty of the earth, and what is more joyful than that."

"Today isn't the day for seeds," Pampa Kampana said. "But your day will also come."

"When one can simply command the unconditional love of any woman in Bisnaga," Krishnadevaraya said to Zerelda Li in the royal bedchamber, "it is impossible to give any of them my unconditional love in return. But you are different because you came to me out of the sky. If I can have a divine lover without being consumed by the power of her divinity, then I must contain in myself that selfsame power. You have revealed me to myself, and for that I will never fail to love you."

"Thanks to you," Zerelda Li replied, "I feel for the first time in my life that there is solid ground for me to stand on, and I feel my roots growing down out of my feet into that earth. So you have also given me myself, and for that I will never fail to love you."

"All true love is self-love," Krishnadevaraya said. "In love the other is united with the self, and becomes the equal of the self, and therefore to love the other is also to love the other in the self, for they are equals, and the same."

Zerelda Li sat up in bed and ate a pistachio sweetmeat from a dish on the nightstand.

"When does she arrive?" she asked. "The hag? And her mother as well?"

"Tomorrow," said the king.

"Then you and I cannot be equals after today," she said. "It's just impossible."

"It is possible for a thing to be impossible and possible at the same time," Krishnadevaraya said. "This is one of those things."

"We'll see," Zerelda Li said, pulling him down toward her, her confidence growing. "The proof will be in how you behave."

Princess Tirumala of Srirangapatna—not a hag at all, but a strikingly handsome woman with, it must be said, a haughty, even cruel, but undeniably impressive nose, a nose that had inspired at least one great poem—arrived at the gates of Bisnaga seated on a golden throne in a golden chariot drawn by a dozen horses the color of gold, covered in golden carapaces, dazzling in the sunlight. Behind Tirumala stood her father, King Veera, and her mother Queen Nagala, wearing high golden headdresses, wide golden neckpieces, and belts of gold studded with precious stones. Everyone had heard of the wealth of the emperor of Bisnaga, and the royal family of Srirangapatna was making sure they didn't look like the poor relations from the south.

Krishnadevaraya awaited them at the ceremonial doorway of his palace, and the manner of his dress astonished, one might even say shocked, the newcomers. Instead of the traditional bare-chested style familiar to southerners, Krishnadevaraya wore a long brocaded tunic in the Arab fashion, called a *kabayi,* and a high, conical Persian-Turkic cap, also brocaded, known as a *kulldyi,* or a *kuldh;* and his only jewel was the signet ring of kingship on his finger. King Veera, unable to restrain himself, replied to Krishnadevaraya's elaborate formal greeting with a discourteous jabbing forefinger accompanied by the equally discourteous, brusque words, "What's this?"

Krishnadevaraya was angered. "Down there in the provinces Our news may not have reached you," he replied, magnificently entering the plural, "but We are pleased to style Ourselves as the sultan among

Hindu kings. Your daughter will not only be a queen, but a sultana as well, and by the end of Our reign all the five Deccan sultanates will be Ours. Two of the five, Bijapur and Bidar, are already Our vassals. This is why—for example—you will see everywhere in Our palace the exceptional *bidri* handicrafts of Bidar—the boxes and hookahs and vases and closets made of blackened copper and zinc and inlaid with the most delicate silver traceries and designs . . ."

"Yes, yes, all right," King Veera interrupted impatiently. "Assimilation of Muslim handicrafts is okay, why not. But why dress like them?"

"I like the clothes," Krishnadevaraya said, "and much else about their way of life as well. Now, if you permit, I will welcome your daughter, my wife-to-be."

Princess Tirumala at the door of her new home put her celebrated nose in the air. "If I am to enter here," she said, "I wish to be accorded the rank of Tirumala Devi. If you are a Deva, then it is fitting that you should have a goddess at your side. And my mother, staying with me, will be Nagala Devi while she is in residence. And our garments will not be those of any northern sultanas. There will be no Arabic-Persian-Turkic blasphemies for us."

Great Minister Timmarasu saw the rage rising in Krishnadevaraya's eyes and intervened. "Agreed," he said quickly. "And now, let the festivities begin."

The bride's entourage—there were many lesser chariots following in the wake of the royal golden car—swept into the palace. There were some cheers from the watching crowds, but not too many. The match didn't appear to be popular in the city. And later that night, Krishnadevaraya's spies in the crowd reported to him that as the wedding party passed through the throng, many people murmured the words *Shrimati Visha.* Krishnadevaraya frowned. "That's bad," he said.

Zerelda Li was with him in his bedchamber, even though it was his nuptial night, and he should have been elsewhere, in another bed, on which flower petals had been scattered to prepare for the deflowering, and next to which incense burned, while handmaids dressed the bride in her nocturnal finery and braided her long hair, oiling it with coconut oil, and musicians played softly in a distant corner; or else he should have received his bride in this place.

"I'm sorry," Zerelda Li said. "I'm still learning the language. *Shrimati* I know of course, that's 'Madam.' But *Visha*?"

"In her own language, Telugu, it would be *Visham,*" the king explained. "*Visha, Visham,* doesn't matter. Means the same thing. 'Venom.' So, *Shrimati Visha,* Madam Poison."

"Who are they talking about?" Zerelda Li asked. "The mother or the daughter?"

"It's unclear," Krishnadevaraya said. "We are making discreet inquiries into the origin of the name, and the reasons for it; but at this moment, we don't know."

Zerelda Li sat up in bed. "I see," she said. "Then I'll have to be careful what I eat."

Krishnadevaraya kissed her, and lovingly took his leave, and went elsewhere to attend to the duties of the wedding night.

It didn't take long for the instant hostility that developed between Tirumala Devi and Zerelda Li to break out into open war. Krishnadevaraya made very little attempt to hide from the senior wife his preference for his junior queen. Tirumala Devi was by nature a proud, even a haughty woman, and this understandably hit her hard, so that her feelings toward her new home, Bisnaga, grew bitter and resentful. She had expected her husband to appreciate her administrative skills and delegate some of the burden of overseeing the empire to her, but this did not happen at first. She also expected to ride into battle at his side, and was abashed to learn that the king had already chosen his preferred quartet of battle companions, Ulupi Junior and Thimma the Huge to his left, and Pampa Kampana and Zerelda Li to his right. "If you insist on accompanying me," he told Tirumala Devi, "I would prefer that you take responsibility for the running of the army camp, the kitchens and the field hospitals and so on, and leave the fighting to us." She had no choice but to bow her head in agreement. At that moment such matters were only theoretical, because Bisnaga was not at war. Time enough, she thought, to insist on her proper place when a military campaign began. In the meanwhile her hatred of Zerelda Li festered within her.

Soon enough it was time for the festival of Gokulashtami, celebrating the birthday of Lord Krishna, who had been born at midnight, so the *gopis* of the court had been singing and dancing all day and deep into the evening until the midnight hour, bringing sweet and savory snacks for the king to eat, snacks which were known to be the favorite of the god himself: betelnut and fruit and sweet *seedai,* small fried balls of rice flour and jaggery which the ladies took it in turns to place in the king's open mouth, until he cried, enough, because it was impossible to eat one hundred and five. The last little ball was fed to him by Zerelda Li, which she did with so much sensuous suggestiveness that Tirumala Devi, his senior queen, seated at his right hand, cried out in rage, "Know your place, you slant-eyed foreigner!" Zerelda Li reacted by laughing in the senior queen's face. "I know my place very well," she said, "and I don't think you have a place anything like as enjoyable as mine." She blew a kiss in the king's direction and backed away, bowing deeply, with her palms conjoined. When she had gone, Krishnadevaraya turned to Tirumala Devi and said, "I never want to hear such bigotry from your mouth again, or I may ask the palace seamstresses to sew your lips shut forever." The queen reddened and jerked back, as if she had been slapped across the face, but she held her tongue.

At the climax of the evening's celebrations the *gopis* performed the dance-drama of the *Ras Lila* in the inner courtyard of the palace, exactly as the king had ordained that they should. Zerelda Li took the central role of Radha, even though she had been denied that role in life, and revealed in her performance that her talents as a dancer rivaled even her mastery of the sword. Her flirtatious approaches to, and sudden retreats from the king earned her a new nickname at court. In his poem celebrating the events of that night, the poet Dhurjati named her "the elusive dancer." *This is how I will hold you,* her dance said to Krishnadevaraya, *by slipping out of your grasp whenever you think you've caught me, and so making you want me even more desperately than you already do.* Tirumala Devi, knowing that she herself would be incapable of performing so supple and potent an erotic display—understanding, at that moment, that Zerelda Li's Bliss Potency was far greater than her own—wanted to leave the courtyard, but protocol dictated that she stay and watch her enemy seducing her husband before her very eyes.

Fireworks had been the gift of Domingo Nunes to Bisnaga, and by now the firework makers' skill had grown so great that they could launch into the midnight heavens fiery images of dragon-breathed monsters doing battle with the god and being slain by him, and giant pictures filling the sky of Krishna and Radha coming together in a series of flaming, but still tender, embraces. When this concluding display was done the king rose and thanked all those who had entertained him. "It is the best birthday I can remember," he said, and withdrew, alone, leaving the enraged Tirumala Devi and her equally ill-tempered mother Nagala to their own devices. Dragon fireworks were dancing in their eyes, and whirling demons, too.

"Did you hear that?" Tirumala Devi said to her mother. "He imagines this is his own, actual birthday, as if he truly is Lord Krishna and not just a mortal man. Can it be that he actually believes he is the great god come down to earth?"

"I fear, my darling," her mother replied to her, not bothering to lower her voice, so that her words were heard by all the assembled court, "that your exalted husband, Krishnadevaraya the great, may have gone a little mad."

Timmarasu the Great Minister approached. "It is unwise, ladies, on such an auspicious day to be heard making such inauspicious remarks. I suggest you go to your quarters and pray for forgiveness. I am sure, the king being the generous man that he is, that your prayers will not go unheard."

The two women retreated indoors. There are those who afterward claimed that the mother was heard saying to her daughter, "We have other means besides prayer for achieving the ends we desire." But this story remains uncorroborated and unconfirmed.

Zerelda Li was not incorrect (Pampa Kampana writes)
When she said she needed to be careful
About what she put into her body.
For food, the great sustainer of life,
Can also be a way of ending it
If it passes through the wrong hands.

The first victim of poisoning in the royal palace of Bisnaga was a court poet, or so Pampa Kampana began to believe, and she held Nagala Devi and Tirumala Devi responsible for it in her book, even though one of the things Krishnadevaraya and Tirumala Devi had in common was their shared love of poetry. Places of honor at the court were given by Krishnadevaraya to the so-called "Eight Elephants," the master poets whose genius held up the sky, as the king liked to say. Among them were the two maestros Allasani Peddana and Tenali Rama; the doomed versifier, Dhurjati; and Krishnadevaraya himself, though some saw this as evidence of the king's rapidly growing immodesty and arrogance. Also, Tirumala Devi had brought a poet to Bisnaga in her retinue, one Mukku Thimmana, whose name meant "Nosey Thimmana," because his most famous poem was the one to which we have previously alluded, an ode to the beauty of a woman's nose, and Tirumala Devi had been given reason to believe that the nose in question was her own highly distinctive facial feature.

Krishnadevaraya agreed to include Mukku Thimmana in his living pantheon, in spite of the numinous power of the number seven; and so there were Eight Elephants instead of seven.

Then Dhurjati died, grabbing at his belly after dinner in his private quarters, and being discovered dead with his hands still clutching his gut, and a little foam still bubbling in the corners of his mouth. Nobody was willing to say for sure that he had been murdered—who would want to murder an individual who was so universally loved?—and the medical consensus was that something had burst inside him and unleashed a fatal toxicity into his body. Such things happened, and it was a great sadness, but there was nothing to be done about it. And after that there were Seven Elephants again. If one wanted to be superstitious one might almost believe that an eighth elephant was an affront to the natural order, and the natural order had taken measures to set things right.

Pampa Kampana remembered Dhurjati's final work, that long, beautiful lay celebrating the night of Gokulashtami when Zerelda Li, the "elusive dancer," had danced before the king, infuriating the senior queen. Was it possible, she asked herself, that an awful revenge had been wrought upon the poet for overpraising the wrong queen, the junior who did not know her place? Was this a warning shot, intended to tell Zerelda Li to beware of overreaching, and to accept her secondary status once and for all? The whispered phrase "Madam Poison" was still circulating in the bazaar, and after Dhurjati's death those whispers were a little louder than before. Pampa Kampana was beginning to believe them. It was hard for her, at that time, to go before the king and accuse his senior queen.

But the king had suspicions of his own.

It soon became clear that Tirumala Devi was on the warpath not only against Junior Queen Zerelda Li, but the entire troupe of surrogate *gopis* as well. She marched into the *zenana* pleasure rooms to confront the king during his daily playtime. The lesser wives scattered at her approach. "This second-rate paradise, this mimicry of the Basil

Forest, what is it?" Tirumala Devi demanded. "Maybe it's your love of Muslim culture, the many-wives-and-concubines thing, the spirits of their seven heavens, those *houris* 'untouched by man or jinni.'" You should put on manly clothes and give up this girly garbage."

Krishnadevaraya was unrepentant. "Your own father has quite a stable of wives," he said. "This has nothing to do with Hindus or Muslims. I honor my namesake Lord Krishna by re-creating his place of joy here in our own Bisnaga."

"You know what I think would be a real paradise?" Tirumala asked him, revealing a line of thought surprising in its similarity to Pampa Kampana's. "It would be a place, or maybe a time, when one woman was enough for one man."

"That paradise already exists for most people," Krishnadevaraya replied. "It's called poverty."

"Maybe we should rename it," said his senior queen, "and think of it as wealth. Maybe you, for whom no number of women is enough, are the one who's poor."

"I heard you were the argumentative type," said the king. "I like it. Don't stop."

"Get properly dressed," she told him. "Then we'll see about conversation."

"By the way," the king added as she was leaving, "you heard that poor Dhurjati died."

"Yes," she said with a shrug. "Something burst inside him, probably his heart. You know what they say about poets. They are in mourning from the day they are born, and they all die of sadness, because nobody can ever love them enough to satisfy them."

"They say other things also," said the king. "They whisper the words *Shrimati Visha*, for example, when you or your mother pass by."

"Death is inevitable," she replied. "The poor see murder everywhere. I see only fate, which I call karma, as is only right and proper, but you, in your Muslim clothes, with Urdu constantly on your tongue, would probably describe it as kismet."

"Here's some advice for you," the king said. "The poisoner usually ends up drinking the poison himself. Just something for you to think about."

"It's that junior queen of yours who is the poisonous one," Tirumala Devi cried, before sweeping away with her head held high. "That foreigner. She's the one to worry about, if poison's on your mind."

The "foreigner" Zerelda Li was visiting Pampa Kampana in "the foreigner's house." She came in a silver carriage with attendants and guards, but she entered the house alone and became, during her visit, a simple child of the family, and not a junior queen. She found Pampa Kampana alone and huddled in a window seat watching the bustle of the city outside, with the melancholy air of one who feels her time has passed, and the lover in whose home she lives is nothing more than a way of helping the hours that remain to creep by as noiselessly as possible. "He is not special," she admitted to herself. "His hair is like a beautiful fire and his eyes are jewels and his manners are of the old school, which is nice. But he is an imitation of an earlier man in another life. Actually, he is an imitation of the man who was himself an imitation of the real man. I am too old to fall in love with imitations of imitations, even one with the right hair, eyes, and manners, who makes love in the way I remember and still prefer, even though he is not Portuguese. I have seen the original, I have heard the music of that love, and I can't be satisfied with an echo of an echo. Niccolò is pleasant, and has seen the wide world as he says Venetians do, but in the end, he's beside the point."

And then she thought, perhaps that's what I have become as well, after all these years, as I approach my two hundredth birthday. Maybe I, too, am beside the point.

"Great-great-great-great-grandmother," Zerelda Li said, "what is it you want?"

"I want two things," Pampa Kampana replied. "And the first thing is, I want you to have what you want. If you want this king, and all that goes with him, if that makes you belong and shows you who you are, then I owe it to you to make sure you have that for as long as you want it, and don't accidentally die of poison before you're tired of life."

She got up from the window seat and beckoned to Zerelda Li to follow her. "The woods near Bisnaga are not like the enchanted forest of Aranyani," she said, "but neither were the groves around Vidyasagar's cave where I grew up. Those ordinary woods gave him all the things he needed, and these woods have enough for my purposes too. I've been foraging there quite a lot while you've been busy with palace intrigues."

"Foraging for what?" Zerelda Li asked and Pampa Kampana grinned widely with self-satisfied pleasure. "Vidyasagar was a man of many parts," she said. "There was his wisdom, for which he was adored by many, and his statecraft, which was devious and made him a man who was feared by many as well. There were some parts, nocturnal ones, which I can never forgive, but I have locked those memories in a room so deep that on some days even I can't find the way there, or the key, and there is no reason to go looking for that key today. And there are some parts which will be useful to us. Useful, I should say, to you."

They were in Pampa Kampana's room, and in a corner of the room there stood a small clay pot with a long neck that made it look a little like a strutting rooster. "Vieri tells me that this pot is a thousand years old and comes from a country whose people used it to hold the blood of defeated rivals. The dried remnants of that blood were still inside when he gave it to me, and I knew, because Vidyasagar taught me, that blood of this kind, when augmented with the right herbs, creates a drink that makes the drinker invulnerable to anything she eats or drinks."

"An antidote," Zerelda Li understood.

"I gathered the herbs," Pampa Kampana said. "I crushed them

and dropped them in through this long neck. I heated it all over a fire, and I said the words that Vidyasagar taught me, and now it's ready."

She put a wooden bowl down beside the clay rooster, picked the pot up by its neck, and smashed it down into the bowl. A thick dark liquid oozed out from the broken shards.

"A thousand years old, you said," Zerelda Li marveled with a little shock in her voice.

"Yes," said Pampa Kampana. "It has been waiting a long time to do what it was meant to do." She saw that Zerelda Li was still looking disapproving. "Great age," she added sourly, "doesn't buy you any privileges these days. I used to make pots, so for me to smash one to bits is not an easy thing."

She scooped the thick dark liquid into a glass vial and sealed it with a small cork. "Wear this around your neck," she said. "Use food tasters and take every precaution, but if all else fails and you feel the poison in your body, take a sip. You don't need to take much. A few drops will save your life."

"How will I know if the food or drink is poisoned?" Zerelda Li asked. "Rich flavors can mask the taste of the venom, can't they?"

"Your body will tell you," Pampa Kampana said. "When the body is threatened, it sends out an alarm. You'll know the signal when it comes. Which obviously I hope it never does."

"And your other desire?" Zerelda Li demanded, hanging the vial around her neck, under her clothes. "Are you going to tell me what that is?"

"What are you talking about?" the older woman asked.

"You said there were two things you wanted," Zerelda Li reminded her. "What's the second thing?"

Pampa Kampana was silent for a long moment, then made her decision, and spoke.

"I am the mother of Bisnaga," she said. "Everything that has happened here, happened because of me. My seeds gave birth to the people, my art caused the walls to rise. I have sat upon the throne beside both the founding kings. What do I want? I want my true nature to be recognized. I don't want to be invisible. I want to be seen."

Zerelda Li listened with great seriousness and attention. Then she said, "I'll talk to him. I'll explain. I'm sure he will be thunderstruck when he starts believing. I'm sure he will welcome you into the palace and give you the highest rank, higher even than the senior queen. I will try. But you know what would convince him better than I can?"

"No," Pampa Kampana said.

"More walls," said Zerelda Li.

Under the influence of the mystical power of the number seven, Krishnadevaraya had decided that the expanding city should be defended by not one, but seven circles of surrounding walls. The population had grown spectacularly, and burst out of the original enclosure. Whole new neighborhoods were being built outside the fortifications, and the citizenry who lived there were unprotected against attack. New walls were urgently required.

"It's a long time since I made the first wall rise," Pampa Kampana said. "I was much younger then, and stronger. And that was before the war against the pink monkeys almost killed me and I slept until you woke me up. We changed into birds to get here, that's true, but even that gift is all but used up, and I don't know what else remains. I don't know if I can still build even one new wall, let alone six more."

"Try," said Zerelda Li.

The next day Pampa Kampana visited Sri Narayan and bought a large sackful of assorted seeds. "No fruits today, madam?" Sri Narayan's fruit-vendor brother Sri Laxman called across. "Mango season soon be over, madam. Mango also has seed. Better you buy some quick, before they go."

To please him, she bought some mangoes and put them in her sack. Sri Narayan snorted in irritation. "He can sweet-talk better than I," he said. "But what mango-shango can grow in this stony ground?"

"Not only mangoes will grow from mango seeds," she said. "Or from your seeds either."

After she left the brothers scratched their heads.

"That meant what?" Sri Narayan wondered.

"Some nonsense," Sri Laxman replied. "The lady is an excellent lady but sometimes I am afraid she is a little bit crack." And he tapped himself on the forehead to make his point.

Pampa Kampana slept early, and Niccolò de' Vieri crept into bed later, without disturbing her. Then when it was still dark she awoke and stole out of the room without waking him. At dawn, she passed through the city gates, barefoot, and wearing only two lengths of homespun cloth, with marks on her forehead which indicated her seriousness of purpose, and a large gunny sack filled with seeds (and some mangoes too) slung over a shoulder. She went out alone into the rocky brown plain and looked up at the surrounding hills, as if she was letting them know that they were about to experience a great change. Then she walked forward into the emptiness and nobody saw her for many weeks. Afterward in the *Jayaparajaya* she described her long wanderings across the plain, up the hills, down into the valleys, and told how she chanted and sang as she walked.

Yes, the land is barren, (she wrote)
But song can make fruits grow
Even in a desert
And the fruits of songs become
The wonders of the world.

At length she came down again into the wide Bisnaga plain, her skin dusty and her lips parched. It was dawn again, and the shadows of the hills retreated and sunlight flowed over her, a river of heat. Pampa Kampana stood very still for the next seven hours, ignoring the sweat that began to run down from her head, the perspiration flowing out from all her body's pores, the dust on her skin turning to mud, the shimmer of the heat in the air, the drumbeat of the heat in her ears. After seven hours she closed her eyes and raised her arms and her miracle began.

The stone walls rose up everywhere that she had planted their seeds, along the riverbank, through the plains, and up and down the hills of that harsh terrain. The river washed the stones, the plains were dominated by their eminence, and the ranges of hills surrounding Bisnaga City raised the new defenses up toward the sky. There were watchtowers awaiting sentries, crenellated ramparts lacking only archers, and cannons, and cauldrons of hot oil. There were gates strong enough to resist the heaviest of battering rams. From that day until the last day no enemy would ever set foot in the heart of the empire, and on that last day the enemy only entered because the people had lost hope. Only despair could make the walls crumble and fall, and the coming of that despair was still long years away.

Six new circles of high stone walls, born of enchanted seeds, and seven circles in all: *the wonders of the world.*

The raising of the walls did not end until after sunset, it went on deep into the night, but well before the miracle was complete there were crowds rushing out of Bisnaga, on foot, on horseback, in carriages, to stand open-mouthed and stare at the city's rising defenses. The king himself rode out and could not believe his eyes. Pampa Kampana, a solitary figure in the heart of the great Bisnaga plain, stood with her eyes closed and her arms raised and nobody, at first, connected this solitary ascetic woman with the surging stone all around. The crowds grew larger and people jostled Pampa Kampana in their ignorance. Still she stood there, silent, unseeing, commanding the massive fortifications to rise up, stone on stone, perfectly dressed, the walls even and smooth, as if an army of invisible, spectral master masons was at work, an army capable of summoning stone out of the air and working at impossible speed. As the sun set behind the seven stone circles the people of Bisnaga were filled with a mixture of fear and joy, as men and women are when the miraculous crosses the frontier from the world of gods and enters the everyday, revealing to women and men that that frontier is not impenetrable, that the miraculous and the everyday are two halves of a single whole, and that we ourselves are the gods we seek to worship, and capable of mighty deeds.

Zerelda Li rode out beside the king and at night when she saw the crowds beginning to push and shove the small female figure with the upraised arms she galloped through them to defend Pampa Kampana. "Get back!" she cried. "Can't you see she's the one responsible for it all?"

After the miracle of the walls the whole of Bisnaga believed in Pampa Kampana's power, and understood at last that they lived in a city which she had brought into being, which she had *seeded;* they knew that the old mythologies were literally true. Everyone from Sri Narayan who had sold her the seeds and his brother the sweet-talking fruit vendor Sri Laxman, to Niccolò de' Vieri, the foreigner whose bed she had left to begin her work, was in awe. The king himself was obliged to concede that he was not the only person in the empire touched by a god or goddess. Zerelda Li told him the true story of Pampa Kampana, as she had been told it in her turn, and Krishnadevaraya did not dismiss it. The proof was all around him, made of stone.

"I have been blessed with her glory," he said, "and it will magnify my own."

Finally, at midnight, Pampa Kampana sank to her knees, exhausted, and pitched forward, unconscious, into the dust. She was brought back to Bisnaga in the king's own carriage, attended by the king and Zerelda Li on horseback, and Great Minister Timmarasu as well. (Tirumala Devi was absent, sulking in her rooms, knowing that her influence at court had just been powerfully diminished.) She was put to bed in the rooms reserved for visiting kings and queens, and Zerelda Li slept beside her on the floor, lightly, with her hand on the hilt of her sword: like a crouching tiger, ready to destroy any foe who might approach.

She woke up one month later. Zerelda Li was there, moistening her lips with water as she had done throughout Pampa Kampana's long sleep.

"Are the walls standing?" Pampa Kampana asked, and when Zerelda Li said they were, they were high and strong, the older woman smiled and nodded.

"Now I will see the king," she said.

When she entered the throne room, unsteady on her feet and with one hand resting on Zerelda Li's shoulder, Krishnadevaraya came down from the Lion Throne, fell to his knees and kissed her feet, sending a message to the watching wives and courtiers and to the whole empire beyond the palace. "Forgive me, Mother," he said. "I was too blind to see and too deaf to hear, but now my ears are open and my eyes have seen the truth. You are not merely an *apsara,* even though an *apsara* is a wonder too. I understand now that the goddess herself lives in you and has sustained you ever since you gave birth to our world, almost two hundred years ago, and that your youth and beauty are the manifestation of that divine sustenance. From now on you will be named the mother of us all, mother of the empire, and your rank will be higher than that of any queen, and I will build a temple where we must worship the goddess within you every day."

"I don't need any rank or crown or temple," Pampa Kampana said. Her voice was faint, but she did not allow it to tremble. "And I don't need to be worshipped. I wanted to be known, that's all, and perhaps to be allowed to stand alongside *Mahamantri* Timmarasu and offer advice and guidance as the empire enters its time of greatest glory."

"Excellent," the king said. "Then let the time of glory begin."

"On that subject," Tirumala Devi interjected, coming forward to kneel at the king's feet, "allow me to inform Your Majesty with sublime happiness that I am honored to be bearing your firstborn child."

Zerelda Li's face colored brightly, and she too moved forward, leaving Pampa Kampana behind, and stood before Krishnadevaraya. (Her refusal to kneel was a silent but scornful criticism of her rival's obsequious genuflection.) "To which I would like to add," she told the king, "that, as I am certain you will be overjoyed to learn, so am I."

17

Well! The competing pregnancies of Tirumala Devi and Zerelda Li certainly set the mongooses among the cobras, as the saying goes! In the months that followed, the court—and beyond the court, much of the empire—was plunged into an agony of speculation, dispute, and indecision. What if Zerelda Li had a boy and Tirumala Devi a girl? How would that shift the balance of power in the palace? What if they both had boys or both had girls? Should the thorny old subject—the bee in Pampa Kampana's bonnet—of the right of women to inherit the throne be raised again? What unintended consequences might such a debate make possible? If Tirumala Devi was demoted in seniority because of the outcome of the baby lottery, how would that affect Bisnaga's alliance with her father, King Veera of Srirangapatna? If King Veera backed away from the alliance, how weak might the empire's defenses at its southern border become? And if Bisnaga became preoccupied with trouble in the south, might that leave it vulnerable to new assaults from the Five Sultanates to the north? Might Bidar and Bijapur, vanquished at the battle of Diwani, rise again and join forces with Golconda, Ahmednagar, and Berar—re-creating the army of the now-fragmented Zafarabad sultanate—in a dangerous joint attack? What was the best attitude to adopt? How should courtiers align themselves, or was non-alignment the best policy? How possible was it that a Tirumala faction might seek to harm Zerelda Li, or vice versa? Oh, how uncertain the universe felt all of a sudden! Were the gods angry with Bisnaga? Was this pregnancy conundrum a test imposed by the Divine, and how should one act to pass the test and placate the gods? What did *Mahamantri* Timmarasu have to say about this? Why was he saying nothing? Why was the king himself silent? If the empire's leaders did not know how to offer guidance, how could the people possibly understand what was for the best?

During those months the two ladies at the heart of the matter treated each other with an icy courtesy that fooled nobody, least of all the ladies themselves. When she heard that Zerelda Li was suffering from morning sickness, Tirumala Devi sent her a nameless drink which she said would settle the junior queen's stomach immediately. Zerelda Li poured the contents of the bottle into a plant pot in her quarters and let it be known that the flower in that pot immediately shriveled up and died. Soon afterward Zerelda Li heard that Tirumala Devi had developed a craving for sweet things and was unable to resist sugary confections, even though she was dismayed at the amount of weight she was putting on. At once the junior queen sent the senior monarch a sequence of baskets containing quantities of the most irresistible sweetmeats in the land, the local delicacies Mysore *pak* and *kozhukkattai*, as well as Goan *bebinca* and Tamilian *adhirasam*, and even some more exotic delicacies from far away, *sandesh* from Bangla and *gujjiya* from the territory of the Delhi sultanate; one basket a day, every day for weeks, and Tirumala Devi's hatred for her rival increased even as her own waistline expanded.

Krishnadevaraya's trusted minister Saluva Timmarasu privately advised the king that nothing should be done that prejudiced the senior queen's status. Even if Zerelda Li's child was male and Tirumala Devi's turned out to be female, the junior queen's son should not be named heir to the throne. Instead, Tirumala Devi should be given further opportunities to produce a boy child, and that boy should be first in line of succession, whenever he arrived.

Krishnadevaraya shook his head. "That doesn't sound right," he said.

Timmarasu dared to contradict him. "You mean to say, my king, that it doesn't sound just, and I daresay it would be unjust. But there are occasions when an injustice is also the right course of action for a king to pursue."

"Let us ask the mother of the empire if she agrees," said the king.

Pampa Kampana was not well. Ever since the miracle of the walls she had felt dizzy, perpetually tired, with aches in her bones and an irritation in her gums. "You need to rest," Zerelda Li told her. "You're not yourself." But Pampa knew that in a deeper way she was precisely feeling like herself, feeling the way a person of her antiquity should feel. For the first time in her life, she felt old.

She had not returned to the house of Niccolò de' Vieri, and her instincts told her that whatever happened now, whether she recovered her strength and clarity of purpose, or slowly faded into nothingness, the time of Signor Rimbalzo, Mister Bounce, was over. She sent a message to the fruit vendor Sri Laxman asking him to send Alphonsos to the "foreigner's house," and to include the wax-sealed paper her messenger carried, containing words for the Venetian's eyes only. "These are the last Alphonsos," this message read. "Mango season is over." When Vieri received the gift and read the message he understood that it was her way of saying goodbye. He packed his bags immediately and left Bisnaga forever less than twenty-four hours later, bouncing away to the next place on his never-ending journey, carrying her words and the memory of his love, two burdens he would not put down until his dying day. He was the last foreigner to enter her life. That aspect of her story, too, was ending.

She remained in the suite for visiting monarchs but was deeply withdrawn into herself, noticing none of the grandeur of her accommodation, the stone and silver *bidri*-ware water-pipes from conquered

Bidar, the bronze Chola period *Nataraja* portraying Shiva as the lord of the dance, and the paintings of the unique Bisnagan school, whose artists characteristically chose to portray neither the gods nor the kings but the common people at work and, just occasionally, taking a hard-earned rest. To all of this Pampa Kampana was, for the moment, blind. She might as well have been living in an unfurnished cave such as the one she had lived in for nine years with Vidyasagar, or a jungle hut like the one she and her daughters had built in Aranyani's forest. She said very little, remaining lost in thought, and spent much of her time obsessively examining her face, hands, and body to see if old age, which she had begun to feel in her bones, might finally be catching up with her appearance.

She should not, she told herself, be worrying about the arrival of gray hair and wrinkles like some vain flibbertigibbet. Her power rested in herself, not in her looks. —Yes, but, she answered herself, if she started looking like a crone, the king would look at her differently. —Maybe, she argued back, he would treat her with the gravity, the respect, that old age commanded and deserved. Maybe her authority would actually increase.

But in fact she could not see the evidence of the years in her skin. The goddess's gift of youth was apparently not yet lost, not on the outside, at least. Inside, she had begun to feel the weight of every accumulated year of her two centuries of life. Inside, she began to feel that she had lived too long.

Zerelda Li came to see her, heavily pregnant, and looking outraged. Pregnancy was being unkind to her, she was suffering its myriad ills, but that was not the reason for her foul mood. "The king wants to see you," she told Pampa Kampana, sounding simultaneously out of breath and furious. "You have to come right away."

"What's the matter?" Pampa Kampana asked.

"That matter is, he wants you to decide if my child will be a person of importance, a person of some consequence in this damned empire, or if my baby should be shoved to one side like a little piece of shit," Zerelda Li told her. "And, just so I can be prepared, can you tell me how you intend to answer the question?"

Pampa Kampana told her. What she said did not make her granddaughter happy.

The "mother of the empire" was no longer accustomed to the deference with which she was now being treated. It had been a long time since she walked these halls as a two-time queen, and this new respect went deeper even than the formal salutes offered to a monarch. This, she realized, was reverence, something like the reception accorded to her old adversary the sage Vidyasagar in his prime. She was not sure that she liked being revered, but, if she was honest, she was also not sure that she didn't like it. She still wasn't feeling strong, and entered the throne room leaning on a frowning Zerelda Li, whereupon waves of courtiers subsided around her like a receding tide. Krishnadevaraya was waiting, and as she approached the Lion Throne both the emperor and Minister Timmarasu knelt down to touch her feet. Tirumala Devi had heard that Pampa Kampana had been asked to judge between the unborn children, and she had arrived in the throne room at speed, or at least as quickly as her body permitted, determined to overthrow any judgment except the one she wanted. She did not bow, or genuflect, or touch Pampa's toes. She stood erect and grim, like an avenging angel. Zerelda Li's eyes found Tirumala Devi's, and neither woman looked away. A deadly fire flowed along their line of sight.

"Well, well, I see that feelings are running high," Pampa Kampana said airily. "Let's try to cool things off. My judgment is this: it would be ludicrous to settle the question of the royal succession before the candidates have even learned how to breathe the world's air or fart. Which of them would be best able to rule? Let's ask that question again in eighteen years or so, by which time, maybe, we will know the answer. Only then let us argue about girl or boy."

It was an answer that pleased nobody and confused many. Both Tirumala Devi and Zerelda Li began to speak loudly, demanding the king's intervention, and the attendant throng of courtiers split into argumentative factions. Krishnadevaraya himself did not know what to make of Pampa Kampana's judgment. Minister Timmarasu, firmly in the Tirumala camp, whispered urgently in his ear.

Pampa Kampana spoke again. "While our king is healthy and in full command of his mind and spirit and of the empire too," she said, "it is absurd that we are wasting time on the rights of unborn babies. Our only concern, as we were taught more than a millennium and a half ago by the great emperor Ashoka, whose name means 'without sorrow,' should be for the greatest good and maximum happiness of all the citizenry. When we have done our best to create that paradise on earth, that place without sorrow, then by all means let's discuss who can best continue to guard it."

"Ashoka was a Buddhist," Tirumala Devi said. "He did not believe in our gods. How can we have faith in an ancient king who adored a man who renounced kingship?"

"Ashoka was the beating heart of our land," Pampa Kampana replied. "If you do not know the heart, you cannot understand the body."

Tirumala Devi did not argue the point. But when calamity struck, she was the first to say that it was the judgment of the gods upon Pampa Kampana, not only for her bad advice, but also for her "blasphemy."

Zerelda Li, junior queen of Bisnaga, most-beloved consort of Krishnadevaraya the Great, died in childbirth, and her son was also born dead. One week later, Tirumala Devi gave birth to a child, also a boy, also stillborn. She, however, survived. The triple tragedy felt like an omen of doom to everyone in Bisnaga, and was read outside the borders of the empire as a sign of weakness. Krishnadevaraya emptied the throne room and was not seen in public for forty days. It was understood he was seeing nobody except Timmarasu. It was understood that Tirumala Devi was being comforted by her mother and that Pampa Kampana had asked to be left to mourn her great-great-great-great-granddaughter, the last of her line, by herself. It was as if the head of the empire had been chopped off, and consequently the body lay inert. Bisnaga's enemies readied themselves to invade.

Zerelda Li's body wrapped in flames had released a flood within Pampa Kampana. Her failure adequately to mourn all those she had lost had caught up with her and all that ungrieved grief overwhelmed her. She had asked the king to allow her to hold the bamboo stave and break Zerelda Li's skull to release her spirit and even though that was man's work according to tradition the king in his generosity allowed it. After she had performed that duty Pampa Kampana lost consciousness and collapsed and had to be carried away to her quarters to recover. Again, this scene was the cause of much discussion. To Bisnaga and its friends it revealed the broad-mindedness for which Bisnaga had often been praised, and suggested that the old project of raising the value of women, which had led Bisnaga to promote women in all walks of life from the earliest days of its existence, had gained new momentum under this king. It showed that his early promise that "the reign of love will be established across the empire" had been no hollow boast. To Bisnaga's enemies it was another sign of weakness, of a crumbling power center.

This was how the world was in those days. Tragedy gave birth to armies, and the symbolic or allegorical meaning of individual human responses to disaster—heartbreak, generosity, loss of consciousness—had to be tested on the field of war. Everything was a sign, and the signs lent themselves to many interpretations, and only the battlefield—only force—could decide which version was most true.

Krishnadevaraya understood this better than anyone, and gave the order, via *Mahamantri* Timmarasu, to prepare his armed forces for war.

• • •

Pampa Kampana awoke from her collapse into a new reality. Zerelda Li was gone and with her all Pampa's hopes of a new line of magical girls. Her fabulist dynasty had ended. The future belonged to Tirumala Devi, who, once she emerged from her own sorrowful retreat, would no doubt be given many more opportunities to produce an heir, and no doubt at least one of them would be a boy, and would live. The old order would not change. Krishnadevaraya might be glorious, he might win many battles, but he would not become what the women of Pampa Kampana's line might have made him.

All Bisnaga was shaken by the deaths of one queen and two potential kings. Krishnadevaraya himself, who should have been readying himself for his military campaign, had instead taken off his habitual attire of a "sultan"—the clothing of which Tirumala Devi and her mother so strongly disapproved—and had put on the two pieces of homespun cloth preferred by mendicant alms-gatherers and holy ascetics. He had sequestered himself in the Monkey Temple, kneeling, with his head bowed and lost in prayer, asking Lord Hanuman for guidance. The whole city held its breath and waited for him to emerge.

Some days passed in this fashion.

Then before dawn one morning Pampa Kampana was woken by a nervous serving girl and informed that the king was waiting outside, still half-naked in his pauper's rags. "Bring him in," she commanded, and gathering her own garments about her got out of bed to greet him.

When he entered he would not let her kneel or make any other gesture of obeisance. "There's no time for that," he said. "I have a lot to tell you. In the temple, when I closed my eyes and waited for an answer from Lord Hanuman, all I could see was your face. At last I understood. In you and you alone there lies the guidance that I seek, and so I must at once offer you a new and deeper kind of love, not the common love men show to women, but the higher love shown by the devotee to the manifestation of the Divine." And after saying those words he was the one to kneel down and touch her feet.

The speed at which these new developments were arriving bewildered Pampa Kampana. "This is much too soon," she said. "All our thoughts should be fixed upon mourning the dead. Declarations of love, higher or lower, should be set aside for another time. What you say is inappropriate, my lord."

"You mean, I think, that it would be considered unseemly out there, in the corridors of the palace, and in the city street," Krishnadevaraya replied. "But sometimes what a king must do to perfect his majesty goes against that grain. I have no time to waste. The great matter of my life is upon me. I see years stretching ahead when my days will be filled with blood and my nights of peace here at home will be few. It is my wish that you act as queen regent in my absence, which is the meaning of my visions in the temple, and for that to be possible we must be married at once. Yes, you will be the junior queen, that's the vacancy to be filled, but in every other way you will be at the apex. Tirumala Devi says she is a fine administrator and perhaps she is but I exalt you above her, and Timmarasu agrees with what I say. You see that reasons of state must triumph over social convention. A king must act when it is time to act. He must love when it is time to love, and not when it is too late or when people think it seemly. You are my glory made flesh, and so you must rule in my place. Tirumala has many qualities, but she is not glorious."

"It is a strange use of that word, love," Pampa Kampana said. "It's all mixed up with other words that aren't loving at all. Also, you were Zerelda Li's lover, and therefore you can't be mine. That would be too great an indecency. So, yes, I will marry you, and rule Bisnaga in your absence, but it stops there. We will sleep in separate beds."

There was a great turbulence within her. She had owed Zerelda Li *everything*, and had set her own dreams aside so that the younger woman could achieve hers. But now the child was no more, and *everything* was being offered to Pampa herself, for the second time, and with even greater force than the first. The reverence she had been shown ever since she made the walls rise up—the miracle that made Bisnaga's capital city a fortress which could not be breached—was, finally, little more than a courtesy, a gesture of astonishment and gratitude. But now she was being invited into the heart of the empire, which also meant into the heart of the king. She was being offered the reality instead of the polite appearance, and it was no longer necessary for her to deny her own dreams in order to fulfill Zerelda Li's hopes. It was the strangest declaration of love she had ever received, a love that felt, at one and the same time, like an abstraction, an impropriety, and even a kind of blasphemy. She had been touched by a goddess but she was not one, yet now she was being offered the place, if not of the goddess herself then of her representative on earth, or something close to that. She had been loved in many ways by many men, had been called promiscuous as a result, and might even at times have admitted to the justice of the charge, but this was a love she had never been offered, not a thing of the body, but, instead, a higher exaltation, in which the love and care of Bisnaga itself was mingled with the obsession—the "vision"—of the king. She, who had so often been so eagerly desirous of physical love, began to see, through her turmoil, that carnal love had been a mere substitute for what she truly wanted; that she wanted what she was being asked to accept.

In my life (she tells us in her book, the book of which this book is but a pale shadow), *I have wanted many things I could not have. I have wanted my mother to walk out of the fire unharmed. I have wanted a companion for life even though I knew that I would outlive any companion who came my way. I wanted a dynasty of girls who would rule the world. I wanted a certain way of life even though I knew when I wanted it that I was dreaming of a distant future that might never arrive, or arrive in some half-hearted, damaged way, or arrive and then be destroyed. But it appears that the thing I wanted most of all was this:*

I wanted to be king.

"I told you once before that I don't want you to build me a temple," she said to Krishnadevaraya. "But there is an invisible temple that you and I will build, and its building blocks will be prosperity, happiness, and equality. And also, of course, your overwhelming military success."

"There are two more things," the king said. "In the first place, I will continue to attempt to make Tirumala Devi the mother of my heir."

"I don't care," Pampa Kampana said, although she did, although she consoled herself with the thought *but you aren't going to be here very much, are you, so that won't be easy,* and that felt good. "What's the second thing?" she asked.

"The second thing," Krishnadevaraya said, "is, beware of my brother."

(This is the first time in the Jayaparajaya *that Krishnadevaraya's brother is mentioned. It comes as a surprise to the reader, as perhaps it did to Pampa Kampana at the time.)*

Two hundred and fifty miles or more to the southeast of Bisnaga there still stands the eleventh-century fortress of Chandragiri. To the oblivion of this ancient fastness—ancient, we should add, even in the time of the Bisnaga Empire—Krishnadevaraya had consigned his younger brother, Achyuta, an individual of such low character, so ill-suited to royalty, so violent, cruel, and cowardly, that the king, unwilling to spill his own family's blood, locked him away, heavily guarded, and hardly ever acknowledged his existence. "But he's sneaky," Krishnadevaraya told Pampa Kampana. "He will try to bribe and murder and cheat his way out, as he has since the day I sent him there. Send spies you trust to make sure he has not corrupted his guards. Keep your eyes on him or he will burst forth and bring destruction and chaos in his wake."

Pampa Kampana, preparing for regency, absorbed this information, but for her there were people closer to home who needed to be placated, or at least spoken to. The first person she sought out was Saluva Timmarasu, the power behind the throne, who had successfully insisted that Tirumala Devi be named senior queen, and who might therefore be something less than an ally to Pampa Kampana in her new role, even if the king said he was supportive. She found him on the roof of the palace, feeding his pigeons. He was a big old man, bald, with many chins and huge hands, and watched the birds as they sat on his palms and pecked at seeds. He greeted her without looking up. "When I first met you," he said, "you, too, were a bird. In my eyes, that is greatly in your favor. These little gray ones here are my friends and my most trusted messengers. In many ways birds are creatures of a higher order than human beings."

She understood that he was making a gesture of friendship and replied with one of her own. "And I got to know you properly when we had to choose all those ridiculous girls to pretend to be *gopis* and please the king." Timmarasu threw back his head and laughed. "The king gets bored easily," he said. "Those ladies are now quietly growing old in the *zenana*, ignored, even forgotten. Soon we will be able to retire them and send them back where they came from, wherever that was. But I remember Queen Zerelda Li's dance. That was worth watching."

This was his way of bringing up the subject of Tirumala Devi, whom the dance had greatly displeased. "I hope," Pampa Kampana said, "that the senior queen will not feel the need to resort to any underhand tactics during the period of my regency."

Timmarasu's expression darkened. "You must understand that my recommendation of the marriage to the daughter of King Veera of Srirangapatna was purely political," he said. "It was a necessary alliance. You should not take it as expressing any preference."

"Good," Pampa Kampana said. "Then we are friends."

"It is my impression," Timmarasu said, "that Queen Tirumala is too preoccupied with dynastic ambitions to take on the daily work of running the empire. She wants to lie with the king and make babies, and I believe the king has explained to you that that will happen. This allows the senior queen to feel that she will win in the end, by producing the heir to the Diamond Throne."

"Let's see how that goes," Pampa Kampana said, and took her leave. As she turned to go, Timmarasu called after her.

"Regarding the matter of poison et cetera et cetera," he said. "That kind of melodrama will not happen in Bisnaga while I am alive and keeping an eye on things. I have made this very clear to the ladies concerned. They know they are being watched."

"Thank you," Pampa Kampana said. "I'll mention it to them also. And I'll watch as well."

"The king is a fool," Nagala Devi said. "Marrying you is idiocy, and appointing you queen regent adds insanity to folly. You will pardon my daughter the senior queen and myself. We will not be attending the wedding ceremony, or the ceremony of—let us agree—your very temporary ascension to the Lion Throne, the Diamond Throne, call it by whatever name you like."

"The palace is full of death," Tirumala Devi said. "My son is dead. You have brought this curse upon us and you will not be forgiven." She was smoking opium, lounging in her heavily carpeted and cushioned chamber, and the air was full of the drug's perfume, as well as the thick scent of patchouli oil. The poet Nosey Thimmana stood by her side.

"Nosey has composed a new masterpiece for us," Nagala Devi said. "Nosey, recite it for our guest."

It soon became apparent to Pampa Kampana that the poem was a malicious satire about Zerelda Li's famous dance, describing it as graceless and clumsy, a performance which had embarrassed all who witnessed it.

"I'll take my leave," Pampa Kampana said. "A lie does not become the truth simply because it is spoken. This is a slander against the dead. Poet, you dishonor yourself."

"Are you sure you would not like a drink before you go?" Nagala Devi asked, indicating a glass jug filled with a pink liquid.

"She's too scared to drink with us," Tirumala Devi said scornfully. "Let's just tell her what I am sure she does not know."

"Another lie?" Pampa Kampana said.

"A simple truth," Tirumala Devi said. "While you are languishing here in Bisnaga, attending to clerical matters and roof repairs and legal disputes, I will be accompanying the king on his campaign. By the time we return I am sure the next king will be returning with us, in my womb, or riding by my side."

"It's not true," Pampa Kampana said.

"Ask him yourself," said the senior queen, and laughed in her rival's face.

The war elephants of Bisnaga were held in as high regard as the human aristocrats of the city, and the Elephant House in the Royal Enclosure was one of the most majestic buildings in the capital, a grand red edifice of brick and stone boasting eleven giant arches behind which were the homes of the emperor's personal beasts, two within each of the arches, and of their mahouts—their trainers and caregivers—as well. When Krishnadevaraya needed a quiet place to prepare his mind for action, this was his chosen retreat, just as the rooftop of his Lotus Palace was the favored place of Minister Timmarasu and his pigeons. The king walked among his gray giants, stroking their flanks, murmuring to them in the mahout language they understood, and oftentimes he sat on a simple wooden stool in the depths of the building, beside his favorite of favorites, the largest and most fearsome elephant in the land, Masti Madahasti of the sensitive feet, who was reluctant to trample enemies underfoot for fear of bruising his soles, but would loyally do so if instructed by the king. There, now, sat Krishnadevaraya, breathing the calming aroma of elephant dung, and the elephants remained silent and allowed him to marshal his thoughts. It was here that Pampa Kampana found him on the eve of his departure for the wars which would occupy the greater part of the next decade of his life. She came in wreathed in thunderbolts and destroyed the serenity of the place.

There is no need to describe the argument. She protested that she hadn't been told that the senior queen would ride alongside the king. He replied that he had made clear his need for an heir. She fulminated further, he roared back. We may imagine them there, gesticulating and arguing amid a growing agitation of elephants, elephants rearing up, trunks raised, and crying out in their own language, which it is not given to us to understand. Finally the king raised his hand, palm outward, and there was an ending. Pampa Kampana turned on her heel and left him with his trumpeting friends.

The next morning before dawn, the army of Bisnaga went forth, a mighty force of more than forty thousand men and eight hundred elephants with Krishnadevaraya in his golden howdah atop Masti Madahasti, and Tirumala Devi, as well as Saluva Timmarasu, on other royal elephants at the front, and Nagala Devi and Pampa Kampana waving them on their way from the royal cupola on the outermost city wall—Nagala triumphant, Pampa mortified, but determined to make a triumph of her time on the throne in the absence of the king, his chief minister, and his senior queen.

Now that we have read Pampa Kampana's book and know the full story of the empire, we have begun to refer to the next decade, approximately between the years 1515 and 1525 of the Common Era, the time of war and regency, as "the third golden age" of the Bisnaga Empire, but we make the caveat that it was an age that began with a quarrel, and we remember the old saying that what begins with discord never lasts long. It did, surprisingly, last for a good ten years; so maybe old sayings should be left to rest in the comfortable resting-places which the old hope for and sometimes find.

The book describes the triumphant campaigns of Krishnadevaraya as if she had been there, as if she and not Tirumala Devi had been riding on the elephant next to his, as if she and Thimma the Huge and Ulupi Junior had fought alongside him in every battle. Krishnadevaraya communicated regularly with the queen regent to keep her informed of his progress, so those communications may form the basis of Pampa Kampana's account. Or the reader may feel that Pampa Kampana simply imagined herself looking out through the warrior-king's eyes. Or both things may be true.

"For the moment the northern border is safe," Krishnadevaraya told his generals. "Also, thanks to the alliance with my father-in-law King Veera, the south is reasonably secure. Therefore the assault our enemies are planning will come from the east, and so our plan must be to launch a preemptive attack."

To the east was the fabled land of Kalinga, against which the legendary Emperor Ashoka had launched his bloodiest war eighteen hundred years earlier, a war in which over one hundred thousand men had died, and which had led, it was said, to the emperor's conversion to Buddhism. To walk in Ashoka's footsteps was an attractive idea, even if Krishnadevaraya was not of a Buddhist inclination. But the gateway to Kalinga was the Eastern Mountain, and the king of the Eastern Mountain was Krishnadevaraya's most powerful enemy, Prataparudra of the Gajapati dynasty, known by many as Krishnadevaraya's twin, because they were equals in grandeur, and, it's said, they looked like each other, too. So to win his great war Krishnadevaraya would have to face the mirror of himself, and to win, it was this version of himself he would have to destroy.

The Eastern Mountain was a three-thousand-foot-high wall of thickly forested rock and on top of it was the fortress-citadel. Pratapa's commanding general Rautaraya was up there with thousands of men and good provisions. There was no way up. A siege was the only possibility.

Two long years went by before starvation forced General Rautaraya to surrender. During these years Krishnadevaraya made seven pilgrimages to the renowned local temple complex of Tirupati, to pray to Lord Vishnu in marathon, flamboyant sessions, begging the god for an heir. (After prayer he also made sizable financial donations to the temple coffers to help the god look kindly on his request.) And secondly, he and Tirumala Devi took what may politely be called direct nocturnal actions of their own to make the prayers come true.

And so during that two-year siege Krishnadevaraya and Queen Tirumala Devi became the parents of two children, a girl first—Tirumalamba, an elongated version of her mother's name—and then, to great general excitement, a boy! And both children lived. This news traveled back to Bisnaga rapidly. It is interesting to note that Pampa Kampana's history barely mentions the new arrivals. Her silence, one might say, speaks volumes.

After the birth of the boy, to whom Tirumala Devi gave another version of her own name, Tirumala Deva, the Eastern Mountain finally surrendered, as if in response to the auspicious event. Krishnadevaraya gave the command of the conquered fort to his chief minister Timmarasu's son. He also took many trophies from the Mountain. One was Prataparudra's aunt. Another was a grand statue of the god whose incarnation he said he was. The aunt was eventually returned undamaged. The Krishna statue was not returned. It was sent to Bisnaga and installed in a special chapel of the palace.

Pampa Kampana's first regency, one and a half centuries before her second, had been followed by an eternity of exile. She knew that in this, her second time around, she needed to do things differently. To establish her authority over the court, she decided to adopt a daily routine that closely followed the king's, so that all might remain familiar with the shape of the day. She rose before dawn and drank a large cup of gingelly oil, the amber oil extracted from toasted sesame seeds, and then asked her handmaidens to massage the same oil into her body. After that it was the king's habit to exercise with weights. Instead of lifting heavy pots, however, Pampa Kampana went to the old *kwoon* of Li Ye-He and practiced with her sword by the light of flaming braziers, inspiring awe in all who watched from the balconies above her. In this way she sweated out the oil she had drunk. Then for some time she rode her horse around the wide Bisnaga plain outside the outermost gate. When the sun rose she dismounted. It was time for the religious part of the day, the part that fitted Pampa Kampana most awkwardly, like an ill-made garment. She went to the Hazara Rama temple for dawn *puja,* putting on a version of the clothes Krishnadevaraya liked to wear when at prayer: a loose white silk dress embroidered with golden roses, with a diamond collar around her neck, and a tall brocaded conical hat. After prayer she went to sit in the *mandapa,* a pillared hall open to the elements, each pillar intricately carved to look like animals or dancers, and here she heard the matters of the day, the reports of her ministers, the complaints of discontented citizens. She would evaluate the reports and pass judgment on the petitions, and then issue her daily orders, while the noblemen of Bisnaga stood silently in lines before her with their heads bowed, only lifting up their eyes if she addressed them by name. If she wished to honor one of them especially she would invite him to share a betel nut. Nobody else dared chew betel at court. So skillfully did she preserve and mimic the routines of the king that people said, "It's as if the king never left us, and is still here, after all."

Behind the facade of such dutiful mimicry Pampa Kampana set about quietly changing the world. She ordered the creation of new schools for girls to correct the imbalance in numbers between girls' and boys' places of education. In these new schools, and also, more gradually, in all existing schools, she proposed that education should no longer be centered on theological instruction, no longer placed exclusively in the hands of Brahmin priests trained at the sprawling Mandana *mutt,* the complex of temples and seminaries where the influence of Vidyasagar and his Sixteen Systems was still inescapable. Instead, she set out to create a new professional class of people who would be called, simply, "teachers," who might be members of any caste, and who would possess and seek to impart the best available knowledge in a wide variety of fields—history, law, geography, health, civics, medicine, astronomy. These so-called "subjects" would be taught without any religious slant or emphasis, with a view to producing new kinds of people, broad in knowledge and mind, still well-versed in matters of faith but with a deep additional understanding of the beauty of knowledge itself, and of the responsibility of citizens to coexist with one another, and with a commitment to advancing the well-being of all.

At this point in her narrative Pampa Kampana, in a spirit of generous truth-telling, introduces the imposing personage of Madhava Acharya, which is to say Pontiff Madhava, the head of the Mandana *mutt* and the preserver and reinvigorator of the philosophy of old Vidyasagar, the *mutt*'s founder.

"O mighty Madhava!" *(She addresses him directly in the text, as if he were standing in front of her.)* "Set not your face against me, for I am not your foe!" From this we may deduce that Pontiff Madhava was in fact an adversary of Pampa Kampana's reforms, a powerful opponent whom she needed, with some urgency, to placate.

The high priest was approximately in his middle forties, had risen rapidly through the Mandana seminary system and recently assumed the leadership of the *mutt.* He was, Pampa Kampana tells us, an unusually tall man, a full head taller than most men in Bisnaga, and would have towered over Krishnadevaraya himself except that courtly protocol obliged him always to lower himself in the presence of the king. Of his character she tells us little, suggesting only that it was forceful and commanded respect, and that he was prone to outbursts of a foul temper—a temper, people said, that was the equal of the king's own explosive rage, and which was greatly feared in the Mandana temple world.

When the king set off to the wars, accompanied by his chief minister, senior wife, and two most powerful warriors, Madhava Acharya—unimpressed by the regency of a woman—thought he saw a power vacuum and moved swiftly to take advantage of it. He delivered a stirring series of orations, symbolically seated cross-legged under Vidyasagar's favorite banyan tree, and made the case that Bisnaga had moved too far from the ways of Vidyasagar—too far, he came very close to saying, from the ways of the gods. He reinstated the mass worship meetings that had fallen out of favor long ago, and the crowds were large, giving Madhava a power base which all could easily see. Pampa Kampana's reforms were hard for Madhava to endure, and his first fulminations against them, in particular against the removal of the priesthood from the heart of education, could not be ignored.

It was at this point that Pampa Kampana thought of reviving the Remonstrance, or at least creating a new movement from its ashes.

Radical ideas can run out of gas, and after the New Remonstrance had entered the government of Bisnaga during the time of Deva Raya and become a part of the establishment rather than a protest movement, the time soon came when it no longer seemed relevant or necessary, and had dissolved. That was ancient history by now, but once Pampa Kampana's spies had assured her of the popularity of her education reforms she charged those spies with assembling a movement that would defend them. Also, she hints in her narrative, she began her *whispering* again, and that won many people in Bisnaga to her cause. The whispering was even harder than the last time. Once again, she was feeling her age. Or maybe there had been a change in the world, and there were people who could no longer be moved by her sweet murmurings, people whose loyalty lay elsewhere and could not be shaken, immutable people, following Madhava Acharya as if he was a prophet and not merely a priest. Fortunately, there were others whose ears were happy to receive her silent whispers, and it seemed likely that these others still outnumbered the devotees of the Madhava cult. So she went about her nocturnal work, even though it was more demanding, more tiring than before; and once she was sure of the numbers she could mobilize if she needed to, she asked Madhava Acharya for a meeting at the *mutt*.

". . . For I am not your foe!" We can reasonably assume that these words were actually spoken by the queen regent to the head of the Mandana *mutt,* probably in person. We have, after all, her own detailed description of that summit meeting, an account in which she abandons her usual lyricism to provide a hard-nosed account of how to make a political deal.

They met alone, in a sealed and guarded room in the heart of the Mandana complex. To show her respect, Pampa Kampana did not ask Madhava Acharya to lower himself below the height of her head, even though, as the queen in place of the king, she had the right to demand it. It was her way of saying that they met on equal terms. Madhava Acharya declared himself charmed by her gesture and then got down to business. It soon became clear to both of them that each could place a substantial crowd of people on the streets of Bisnaga at a moment's notice, so that was a stalemate. Pampa Kampana had at her disposal the battalions that had remained behind to guard the city, which gave her an advantage, but, as Madhava Acharya was quick to point out, if she were to use those soldiers against the citizens of Bisnaga itself, she would quickly lose the advantages of her popularity and might well face a mutiny in the soldiers' ranks as well as an uprising in the streets. So that advantage might notionally exist but in practical terms it did not.

To break the deadlock, Pampa Kampana first made an offer and then played a trump card. Ever since the time of Bukka I, the Mandana *mutt* had been granted limited powers of direct taxation to fund its work. The queen regent now proposed a significant increase in those powers, which would make Mandana wealthier than it had ever been, and would fund the establishment of a parallel education system at the *mutt,* which would focus on matters of faith and tradition, while her own new schools covered other things.

In other words: a bribe.

That was the offer. To force Madhava Acharya to accept it, she followed it by showing him a letter written in the king's own distinctive handwriting, fully supporting all her decisions as regent. Once Madhava had read this letter he knew he could not unleash political turmoil in Bisnaga, or the king, when he returned, would exact a swift revenge; and he understood that the bribe that had preceded the playing of the trump—or, let us say, the offer of a compromise—allowed him an honorable way of backing down.

"You are indeed an able ruler," he told Pampa Kampana. "I accept, of course."

Only when Krishnadevaraya returned from the wars did Pampa Kampana confess to him that she had carefully practiced writing in his hand, and that the letter she had shown to Madhava Acharya had been an outright forgery. "I throw myself upon your mercy," she said, but Krishnadevaraya roared with laughter. "I could not have found a better regent," he cried. "For you found the way to bend Bisnaga to your will, even those parts of it that were not well disposed to your decisions. It is not one's decisions that matter when one is king, but one's ability to impose them on the people without bloodshed. I could not have done better myself. Also," he said, frowning, "I did write you many letters. It was as if I heard your voice whispering in my ear, saying, *Tell me everything.* Are you sure this one letter wasn't one of those?"

Pampa Kampana smiled lovingly. "If one is to tell an important lie," she said, "it's best to hide it among a crowd of unarguable truths."

This is a (genuine, unforged) letter from Krishnadevaraya to Pampa Kampana: *"Beloved Queen Regent, when I think of you I am filled with wonder, for you, who have made miracles, are a miracle in yourself. Sometimes I find it hard to believe it even though I know it to be true: you have seen everything, you have known all of us from the beginning until this moment, and all the answers to our questions can be found in you. I ask myself sometimes about those beginnings, Hukka and Bukka long ago, what was in their thoughts, what were they fighting for? At the birth of Bisnaga they fought, I think, for survival, to establish themselves, cowherds who became kings. You know their hearts better than any living person. Tell me if I am right, for now, as the years of battle stretch out, I am asking myself the same questions. Why am I fighting? If it is to defend ourselves against enemies who thought we were weakening, then the victory at the Eastern Mountain has shown everyone that we are strong. Our defenses in all directions are now assured. Is it for vengeance, then? No, for that would be the lowest of motives. A vengeful king does not send his enemy's auntie home unharmed, and she can certainly bear witness to how kindly she was treated while she was in our care. Certainly I do not fight for religion's sake, because Prataparudra is our co-religionist, and some of my finest generals and soldiers worship their supposed one god, and nobody has any problem with that. Maybe I fight for land, for the simple desire to expand the empire until it is the greatest thing that there has ever been. In that sense the conquest of land may also be born of the desire for glory. Many will say that my motives are a combination of all of these, but I have discovered that it is none of them, and it is my enemy Pratapa who has revealed the truth to me.*

"I write this to you, Beloved Queen Regent, as I march ever deeper toward the heart of Kalinga, aiming my force now against the fort at Kondavidu, where Pratapa's wife is in residence and his son is the governor; and I have intercepted a messenger bearing a message from Pratapa to this son. In this message Pratapa insults not only myself but all our line, calling us barbarians, not of blue-blood stock, because our ancestors were ordinary soldiers, not aristocrats. He further demeans the entire history of Bisnaga, saying it is a place created by cowherds, low-grade people, lower-caste, and so good behavior cannot be expected of us. 'Do not surrender to such a man as Krishna,' Pratapa writes, 'for he is no better than a common savage, and I fear for the safety of the queen and yourself if you should fall into the hands of a man without breeding.' This, after receiving his aunt back, safe and sound!

"And so I surmise that perhaps the entire history of Bisnaga has been driven by our need—my need and the need of all who came before me—to prove ourselves

the equals—no! The betters!—of arrogant princes such as these. It doesn't matter what gods they worship. It is their snobbery and conviction of caste superiority we must overthrow. Only one kind of social class matters: that of the victor. That is why I fight. Maybe it is not why Hukka and Bukka fought. You will tell me if I am right or wrong. But as for myself, that is why."

And Kondavidu fell, and Prataparudra's son committed suicide, and Pratapa's queen became Krishnadevaraya's prisoner. But—perhaps to prove he was no barbarian—he treated her and her retinue courteously, and returned them to his enemy unharmed, with a note saying, "So we treat our foes in the kingdom of love." And after Kondavidu, in victory after victory Krishnadevaraya showed extreme kindness to his vanquished opponents, as if he was fighting a war of etiquette. "You know," Minister Timmarasu worriedly advised him at one point, "just for the sake of tradition, of what is conventional, it might be advisable, from time to time, to cut off a few heads and stuff them with straw and send them on a tour of the region. It's what people expect. Hangings, tortures, beheadings, heads on sticks . . . people enjoy the spectacle of victory. And fear is an effective tool, but good manners don't really instill respect."

Influenced by this advice, Krishnadevaraya marched north and destroyed Pratapa's capital city, Cuttack. On this occasion he authorized the execution of the one hundred thousand soldiers defending the city—"There," he said ferociously to his chief minister, "as many decapitations as during all of great Ashoka's Kalinga campaign long ago. That's for you." But he ordered that no harm should come to the city's ordinary residents. He also made large placatory donations of gold coins to all the nearby temples. Thus—in spite of the hundred thousand severed heads—he believed he had maintained his reputation as the king who conquered with love.

(He had not.)

Pratapa sued for peace. At the signing of the treaty at the Simhachalam hill, Krishnadevaraya met his vanquished opponent face-to-face for the first time, and asked him a simple question. "So you see, do you not, that we are the same after all, you and I, mirrors of one another, and there's no difference between us?"

Prataparudra knew that he was being asked to apologize for his emphasis on the gulf in class, dynastic history, and caste between his own dynasty and the kings of Bisnaga. He made a last stand against such humiliation. "I confess," he said, "that I do not perceive the likeness."

"If you are so blind and vain," Krishnadevaraya told him, screaming with fury, "then let us tear up this piece of paper and I will burn your defeated empire to the ground, and kill every member of your family I can find, beginning, naturally, with you."

Pratapa bowed his head. "I was mistaken," he said. "Now that I look more closely, I see that we are exactly the same."

As a part of the peace treaty, Prataparudra gave his daughter Tuka to Krishnadevaraya in marriage. Tirumala Devi, who was present at the surrender meeting at Simhachalam, was furious. She stormed into the king's tent and berated him. "In the first place," she said, "there is the offense to me. And in the second place, are you too stupid to see that this 'marriage' is part of a plot against you?" Krishnadevaraya tried to calm her down, but at the wedding ceremony itself, Tirumala Devi intervened just before Tuka fed the king the traditional sweetmeat. Tirumala Devi insisted that a food taster eat a piece of it first, and when the man fell down dead the assassination attempt was foiled.

"I told you so," Tirumala Devi said to the horrified king.

Tuka did not attempt to deny her part in the plot. Instead she shouted, "How can this low-grade man, this king from the gutter, be fit to marry a high-born person like myself?" After that she was sent to the most remote part of the empire to live out her days in solitary captivity and the king, moved to a fit of rage, ordered that her quarters be made harshly uncomfortable and the food given to her be as unpleasant as possible.

"Don't worry," said Tirumala Devi. "I'll take care of that."

The book of Pampa Kampana does not provide a clear resolution to the story of Tuka, but there is a heavy hint about how it ended in the following verses:

Do not tempt Madam Poison
by seeking to be a poisoner,
or your fate may be sealed
by your folly.

Six years had passed since Krishnadevaraya left Bisnaga City at the head of his men (and women). Now at last it was time to go home.

18

Krishnadevaraya, returning to his palace, discovered that Bisnaga City during the regency had become the fabulous place of which Pampa Kampana had always dreamed. Its wealth was everywhere on display, in the finery worn by the people, in the goods available for purchase in its stores, and, most of all, in the lavishness of its languages, which had been raised to a point of ecstasy by the great poets to whom she had given homes to live in and stages from which to speak. Trading ships from Bisnaga were traveling everywhere and spreading the news of its wonders, and now foreign visitors—traders, diplomats, explorers—thronged its streets, applauding its beauty and comparing it favorably to Beijing and to Rome. *Every man may come and go and live according to his own creed. Great equity and justice is observed to all, not only by the rulers, but by the people, one to another.* These words were written by a red-haired, green-eyed Portuguese visitor to Bisnaga named Hector Barbosa, a scrivener and an interpreter of the Malayalam language based in Cochin, and the latest incarnation of the foreign men who had populated Pampa Kampana's life. This time, however, she resisted his charms. "I've had enough of your reappearances," she told the mystified Barbosa. "I've got work to do."

She allowed him, however, to tell her his traveler's tales. From Barbosa and other newcomers she heard rumors of the strangeness of the faraway world, of, for example, a town called Toruń in the far north of the place called Europe, where they baked great quantities of gingerbread, and where a man had begun to suggest that the sun, and not the earth, was the center around which everything moved; and of a city called Firenze or Florence in the south of Europe where they drank the finest wines on earth, painted the greatest paintings, and read the most profound philosophers, but where the princes were cynical and cruel. She remembered learning from Vidyasagar that an Indian astronomer, Aryabhata, had proposed a heliocentric system a thousand years earlier than the fellow from Toruń, but his ideas had been rejected by his peers; and she knew also that cruelty and cynicism of the Florentine kind were not the exclusive characteristics of foreign princes. "Anyway," she wrote, "it's good to learn that *over there* is not so very unlike *over here,* and that human intelligence and human stupidity, as well as human nature, the best and worst of it, are the great constants in the changing world."

Bisnaga had become a world-city. Even the birds in the sky seemed different, as if they, too, had traveled here from far away, drawn by the growing fame of Bisnaga. Fishermen told her that there were new fishes in the sea at Goa and Mangalore, and Sri Laxman had begun to display and sell unheard-of alien fruits. Welcoming the king home, and giving up her regency, Pampa Kampana greeted him thus: "I return to you your city, heart of your empire, which is now a wonder of the world."

She had built a new pavilion for him, the Conquest of the World Pavilion, where the great poets of the land assembled each day to sing his praises in several languages while the most beautiful women of the court fanned him with yak-tail fans. There were musicians and dancers in the streets to greet the returning heroes, and there were fireworks too, as fine as any that Domingo Nunes had created in the old days. It was a glorious return, all of it intended by Pampa Kampana to distract from the fact that Tirumala Devi, returning with two children, a daughter and a son, intended to make it plain to everyone that she—not only the senior queen but also the queen mother of the next king—that she, and not the outgoing queen regent, was the real power in the land alongside Krishna the Great.

Nagala Devi, now the grandmother to the future king, made sure Pampa Kampana understood her new situation. She came to stand beside the ex-regent, ostensibly to watch the carnival in the streets with her, but actually to gloat. "Whatever you are," Nagala Devi said, "a very old woman disguised by magic as a much younger one, or just a brilliant fraud, it no longer matters. As queen regent you were a sort of servant promoted above your station for pragmatic reasons. Now you're just a servant again, and any ambitions you may have had, have been nullified by the birth of the Crown Prince Tirumala Deva and the Princess Tirumalamba his sister. Once Krishnadevaraya dies you will be nobody. Actually, it feels like you're nobody now."

Then—soon after Krishnadevaraya's return—the drought began. Without water even the most prosperous land begins to wither, and Bisnaga during the great dryness was no exception. Fields cracked open and swallowed cows. Farmers committed suicide. The river shrank and drinking water had to be rationed in the city. The army was thirsty and a thirsty army is no good in a fight, unless it's a fight over access to water. Foreigners began to leave town in search of rain. The people, always hungry for allegory, began to wonder if the drought was a curse upon the king, if in spite of all his temple offerings he had displeased the gods and this unending barrenness was a judgment upon the slaughter of the one hundred thousand. This feeling intensified when it became known that one hundred miles to the northeast, at Raichur, situated in the *"doáb,"* the land between the two rivers Pampa and Krishna, it was raining hard, and the famous freshwater spring in Raichur's high citadel was flowing freely, so water was plentiful, and the harvest promised to be good.

The increasing frequency of the king's bouts of bad temper was becoming alarming to Minister Timmarasu and to Pampa Kampana as well. At first they thought his irritability might have been caused by exhaustion, by the stress and fatigue of six years away from home, but even now, in the bosom of his capital, fanned by yak-tails and constantly entertained, his mood was often foul. Then the day came when he walked into the throne room clapping his hands and brimming with energy. "I have it," he announced. "We have to conquer Raichur and then we will be masters of their rain."

This was close to insanity, but neither Pampa Kampana nor Timmarasu could prevent Krishnadevaraya from putting his plan into action. "I had a vision," he declared. "My father the old soldier came to me in a dream and said, 'Without Raichur the empire will remain incomplete. Take that fortress and it will be the jewel in your crown.'" He ordered the army to get ready to march.

"Raichur is in the hands of Adil Shah of Bijapur," Timmarasu warned, "and to move against him after the long amicable peace with that sultanate ever since the battle of Diwani, after which, Your Majesty will recall, Bijapur acknowledged our preeminence . . . such a move may look like bad faith, and provoke the other sultanates to rise up and come to the defense of their co-religionist."

"This isn't about religion," Krishnadevaraya roared. "This is about destiny."

The battle for Raichur proved to be the most perilous conflict of his reign. Krishnadevaraya marched north with half a million men, thirty thousand horses and five hundred war elephants, and faced Adil Shah's army waiting on the far side of the river Krishna with an equal force. Nobody could say who would prevail. But in the end it was Adil Shah's army that fled the field.

Krishnadevaraya sent Adil Shah a contemptuous message. "If you want to live, come over here and kiss my feet." When he read this the deeply insulted sultan ran away, swore to fight again another day, and was saved, for the moment, from choosing between humiliation and death; but the doors of the fort were smashed down, and the white flag of surrender raised. The soldiers of Bisnaga rushed to the spring and drank as deeply as they could, and no other sultan of the Deccan, having learned of the fall of Raichur, dared march against Krishnadevaraya, and the empire of Bisnaga had all the land below the river Krishna in its grasp. And the next day, back home in Bisnaga City and across all the lands of the empire, the drought ended and the rains came. The streets burst back into life.

In the king's absence, Pampa Kampana was Queen Regent again, which infuriated Tirumala Devi and Nagala Devi, in whose opinion the Crown Prince Tirumala Deva should have had that honor, even though he was just a boy, and his decisions should have been guided by his mother and grandmother. But Timmarasu had seen how well the city had flourished under Pampa Kampana's guardianship and he had vetoed that idea. After that the senior queen and her mother were Timmarasu's sworn enemies. For a time, however, they had other matters on their mind, because both the prince and princess were unwell.

The unbearable dry heat of the drought unleashed a sickness that was killing people all over Bisnaga and even the cool of the thick-walled palace rooms did not offer enough protection. It was an unpredictable illness whose cause nobody knew; a curse piled upon a curse. The young people's fevers rose very high, then returned to normal, then rose again. They coughed, then they did not cough, then they coughed. There were days of diarrhea, then no diarrhea, then there it was again. Up and down, up and down: it was like riding an ocean wave. Tirumala Devi and Nagala Devi suffered along with the youngsters, and it is true that a part of their suffering was caused by motherly and grandmaternal love and concern, but it must be said that they also knew that their own futures were tied to the life of the young ones, in particular the life of the crown prince. Princess Tirumalamba recovered her health first and could not help noticing that this happy news caused her mother and grandmother a good deal less joy than the recovery of Prince Tirumala Deva ten days later. This was wounding, made her feel unloved, and embittered her toward the women in her family for the rest of her life. After she was married off at the age of thirteen to a certain Aliya Rama, a much older, ambitious, conniving fellow with royal aspirations of his own, she separated herself from Tirumala Devi and Nagala Devi, and turned to face in a new direction.

Golden ages never last long, as the horse-trader Fernão Paes once said. Krishnadevaraya's time of glory was coming to an end. The drought tarnished the gold, the rains came to burnish it again, the king returned from Raichur in triumph, the heat sickness went away, but a short while later the deterioration began, and the beginning of it was the death of the crown prince Tirumala Deva. The king had come home with a great plan. He would abdicate the throne in his son's favor, ensuring a trouble-free succession, and after that he would act as the lad's mentor and guide, forming a trinity of high advisers along with Timmarasu and ex–Queen Regent Pampa Kampana. But no sooner had Krishnadevaraya announced his intentions than the boy fell sick again, his forehead was on fire while the rest of his body shivered, and this time there was no recovery. He slid rapidly down into darkness, and died.

The king broke the skull of his burning son and entered a state of screaming, ranting agony driven by grief, rage at the gods, and furious suspicion of everyone in the vicinity. The palace was plunged into chaos as courtiers tried to avoid the royal presence lest they be accused of having had a hand in the boy's death. Rumors of foul play burst out beyond the palace walls and filled the city's bazaars. The most repeated theory was that a traitor at court, in the service of the vanquished Adil Shah, had somehow managed to poison the prince. And the moment poison was mentioned people's thoughts turned to the two notorious Poison Ladies, the senior queen and her mother, but nobody could understand why they would wish to assassinate their own son and grandson. So confusion reigned. Then Queen Tirumala

Devi and her mother Nagala Devi themselves came forward with an accusation that changed Bisnaga's history.

"The king sat on his Diamond Throne, weeping, inconsolable, looking for someone to blame," Pampa Kampana tells us, "and the two wicked ladies with their nails as long as daggers and painted the color of blood pointed their fingers at wise old Saluva Timmarasu, and also at myself."

"Can't you see? Are you blind?" Tirumala Devi declaimed. "This woman, this fraud and murderess, has become drunk on power and plans to seize the throne with your dishonest minister's help. They are whispering about you behind your back. 'The king is mad,' the whispers say, 'the king has lost his mind and cannot rule, and it is the duty of the two most able persons at court to take his place.' The whispers are spreading everywhere. People are starting to believe them. They wake up every morning with the whispers in their heads.

"Your son was the first victim of these two traitors. If you do nothing, you will be the second. I ask you again: are you too blind to see what's in front of your face? Only a blind man could fail to see something so obvious. Has the king my husband gone blind?"

Krishnadevaraya in his agony shouted at his minister. "Timma? What do you say to this?"

"It is contemptible," Timmarasu said. "I say nothing. I let my years of faithful service speak for me instead."

"You told me to kill more people," Krishnadevaraya cried. "It's what people expect, you said. Then I did, I beheaded the soldiers, one hundred thousand of them, *is that enough for you,* I asked you, *will that satisfy the people?* But then people started to call me insane. *The king is mad.* I see it. I see your plan. That was your idea all along."

He turned to Pampa Kampana. "And you? Will you also refuse to plead your case?"

"I will say only that it is a kind of derangement in the world when a mere accusation, supported by nothing, feels like a guilty verdict. That way madness lies for us all," said Pampa Kampana.

"Madness again," the king bellowed. "You seduced the people while I was away. Yes, yes. You made yourself queen of their hearts and now you want to clear your path to this throne. Women should be kings, that's what you always say, isn't it? Women should be kings as well as men? This is what's behind your actions. It is very clear."

Pampa Kampana said no more. A terrible silence fell. Then the king stood up and stamped his foot. "No," he declared. "The king is not blind. The king sees very well what is in front of his eyes to see. But these two will see no more. Seize them! Blind them both!"

Forty more years would pass before the final collapse of Bisnaga, but its long, slow downfall began on the day of Krishnadevaraya's wild, willful, terrible command, the day on which Saluva Timmarasu and Pampa Kampana had their eyes put out by hot iron rods. Neither of them resisted when the women warriors guarding the court manacled and chained them. The women guards were weeping, and when Thimma the Huge and Ulupi Junior walked the two sentenced figures out through the gates of the Royal Enclosure they were weeping freely as well. They moved slowly toward the blacksmith's forge with their captives, down the great bazaar street crowded by horrified people wailing in disbelief, slowing down as they neared the forge, as if they were unwilling to arrive. Moments later, as the shrieks of pain rose up from the forge, first a man's cry, then a woman's, it was possible to hear the blacksmith sobbing also, unable to bear the thing he had been obliged to do. These tears and cries did not die away, but rather grew in volume and spread out across the city, flowing down broad thoroughfares and along narrow streets, pouring in through every window and door, until the air itself was weeping, and the earth gave up great sighs. Some hours later the king ventured out in his carriage to assess the temper of the city and the gathered crowds pelted him with shoes to express their disgust.

"Remonstrance!" people cried. "Remonstrance!" It was an unprecedented rebuke to power, a roaring in the street, and after that people thought of Krishnadevaraya differently, and the sun of his glory set and did not rise again.

After the blinding, Timmarasu and Pampa Kampana sat trembling in the forge on stools brought to them by the blacksmith, who was unable to stop apologizing, even after they forgave him; and the best doctor in Bisnaga came running to them with soothing poultices for their bloody ruined eye sockets; and strangers brought them food to eat and water for their thirst. Their chains were removed and they were free to go wherever they chose, but where could they go? They remained in the blacksmith's forge, dizzy and close to fainting from pain, until a young monk ran up from the Mandana *mutt* with a message from Madhava Acharya.

"From this day forward," the monk said quietly, reciting the Acharya's words, "you will both be our most respected guests, and it will be our honor to serve you and care for your every need."

The two unfortunates were guided carefully into a waiting bullock-cart which moved slowly through the streets toward Mandana. The monk drove the cart; Thimma the Huge and Ulupi Junior walked beside it; and it felt as if the whole city watched it on its journey to the *mutt.* The only noise to be heard was the sound of inconsolable grief, and a single word, rising above the tears.

"Remonstrance!"

19

In the beginning there was only the pain, the kind of pain that made death feel desirable, a blessed relief. Finally that extreme pain subsided, and for a long time afterward there was nothing. She sat in darkness, ate a little when food was brought to her, and drank a little from the brass pitcher of water that had been placed in the corner of the room with a metal mug inverted over its neck. She slept a little although that felt unnecessary; blindness had erased the boundary between waking and sleeping, they felt like the same thing, and there were no dreams. Blindness erased time as well, and she quickly lost count of the days. On occasion she heard Timmarasu's voice and understood that he had been brought into her room to visit her, but their blindnesses had nothing to say to one another, and he sounded weak and sick and she understood that the blinding had burned most of his remaining life out of him. Soon enough those visits ended. There were also visits from Madhava Acharya but she had nothing to say to him, which he understood, and simply sat quietly with her for a period of time that might have been minutes or hours, they were all the same now. There were no other visitors and that didn't matter. She felt that her life had ended but she was cursed to go on living after its end. She was separated from her own history, and no longer felt like Pampa Kampana the maker of miracles whom the goddess had touched long ago. The goddess had abandoned her to her fate. She felt as if she were in a lightless cave, and even though at night someone came in and lit a stove to keep her warm the flames were invisible and cast no shadows on the wall. Nothing was all there was and she was nothing too.

They had tried to make the room comfortable for her but comforts were unimportant. She was aware of a chair and a bed but used neither, remaining squatting in a corner, her arms stretched forward, resting on her knees. Her rear was pushed up against a wall. She woke like this and went to sleep in the same position. It wasn't easy for her to wash, or to agree to be washed, or to perform her natural functions, but she was aware that that happened from time to time, that people were tending to her, cleaning her, putting clean clothes on her body, brushing and oiling her hair. Except at these times she stayed in her corner, undying, undead, waiting for the end.

There was one unwelcome disturbance. A hubbub at the door and a voice saying, "The king, the king is here." And then he was there, a particular, loud, voluble absence within the engulfing, undifferentiated, silent absence, and she felt his touch and understood that he was kissing her feet and begging to be forgiven. He was prostrate on the floor blubbering like a bad-mannered child. The sound was nauseating. She needed it to stop.

"Yes, yes," she said. They were her first words since the blinding. "I know. You were angry, you got carried away, you weren't thinking straight, you weren't yourself. You need forgiving? I forgive you. Go and beg at the feet of old Saluva who was like a father to you. This was a death blow to him, and he needs to hear your stupid apology before he dies. As for me? I'll live."

He pleaded with her to return to the palace and live in comfort like the queen she was, and be waited on hand and foot, and be cared for by the best physicians, and sit at his right hand on a new throne of her own. She shook her head. "This is my palace now," she said. "There are too many queens in yours."

Tirumala Devi and her mother Nagala Devi had been confined to quarters, he told her. What they had done was unforgivable. He would never see them again.

"Nor will I," said Pampa Kampana. "And it seems you find forgiveness harder to give than to receive."

"What can I do?" Krishnadevaraya pleaded.

"You can leave," she answered. "I will never see you again either."

She heard him leave. She heard the knock on Timmarasu's door. Then came the old man's roar of wrath. With the last of his strength the brutalized chief minister cursed his king and told him that his misdeed would be a stain on his name for all time. "No," Saluva Timmarasu bellowed. "I do not forgive you, and I would not, even if I lived out a thousand thousand lifetimes."

That night he died, and the timeless silence returned, and closed in upon her.

The first dreams that came were nightmares. In them she saw again the blacksmith's guilty face, the iron rod lowered into the furnace, and removed with its tip red-hot. She felt Ulupi Junior behind her, holding her arms, and Thimma the Huge towering over her, holding her head still. She watched the approach of the rod, felt its heat; then she woke up, shaking, sweating her lost eyesight out of every pore in her body. She dreamed about Timmarasu's blinding too, even though she knew he was gone and didn't have to fear anything anymore, neither the frown of the great nor the tyrant's stroke. He had been mutilated first, so she had had to watch, and see her own fate before it happened. It was as if she had been blinded twice.

But yes, there were images again, the darkness was no longer absolute. She dreamed her whole life and did not know if she woke or slept while dreaming it; everything from the fire that took her mother to the furnace that burned her eyes. And because the story of her life was also the story of Bisnaga itself, she remembered her great-great-great-great-granddaughter Zerelda Li instructing her to record it all.

She called out to whoever was there, watching over her. "Paper," she said. "And a feather, and some ink."

Madhava Acharya came to sit with her again. "I want to say to you," he said, "that by your example you have taught me kindness, and shown me that it expands to include all people, not only the true believers but the unbelievers and other-believers also, not only the virtuous but also those who know not virtue. You told me once that you were not my foe and I did not understand, but I understand now. I have been to see the king and told him that his own virtue has been tarnished by his misdeed, but I must still care for him as I must for all our people. I talked to him about his own poem, *The Giver of the Worn Garland*, which tells of the Tamil mystic we know as Andal; and I said, 'Although you did not know it, all the time you were writing about Andal you were in fact writing about our Queen Pampa Kampana, all the beauty of Andal is Pampa Kampana's beauty, and all the wisdom is Pampa Kampana's wisdom. When Andal wore her garland and looked into the pond the image she saw there, the reflection in the water, was Pampa Kampana's face. Thus you have mutilated the very thing you sought to celebrate, you have deprived yourself of the very wisdom in which your poem rejoices, and so you have committed a crime against yourself as well as her.' I told him this to his face, and I saw the anger rise there, but my place at the head of Mandana protected me, at least for now."

"Thank you," she said. Spoken words came with difficulty. Perhaps written words would be easier.

"He allowed me to go to your rooms and bring some clothes," Madhava Acharya told her. "I did this personally. I have also brought all your papers, your writings, in this satchel which I place here before you, and whatever paper, quill, and ink you need will be brought to you also. I can send our finest scribe to you, to guide your hand until it learns its way. From now on it is your hand that must see what your eye cannot, and it will."

"Thank you," she replied.

Her hand learned quickly, returned easily to the familiar relationships of paper and inkwell, and her carers expressed astonishment at the delicacy and accuracy of her script, the straightness of the lines of words as they marched across her sheets. She began to feel her selfhood returning as she wrote. She wrote slowly, much more slowly than in the past, but the writing was neat and clear. She could not describe herself as happy—happiness, she felt, had moved out of her vicinity forever—but as she wrote she came closer to the new place where it had taken up residence than at any other time.

Then the whispers began. At first she wasn't clear what was happening, she thought people were talking in the corridor outside her room, and she wanted to ask them to please be quiet or at least take it elsewhere, but she soon understood that there was nobody outside. She was hearing the voices of Bisnaga within herself, telling her their stories. Things had gone into reverse, as if rivers had started flowing upstream. When she was a child a religious saint had taken her in, but that safe place had become unsafe, and friendship had soured into enmity; now another holy man, who had been an adversary, had metamorphosed into a friend and had given her safety and care. And in the early days of Bisnaga she had whispered people's lives into their ears so that they could begin to live them; now the descendants of those people were whispering their lives into her ears instead. From the vendors of things taken as offerings to the city's many temples—flowers, incense, copper bowls—she heard that sales had dramatically increased, because the blindings—followed by the death of *Mahamantri* Timmarasu—had filled people with uncertainty about the future, and they were praying to the gods for help. From the street of foreign traders she heard more worries and doubts, was Bisnaga about to collapse in spite of all its military success, should they be thinking about packing their bags and getting out before it was too late? Chinese voices and Malays, Persians and Arabs, spoke to her, and she only comprehended a little of what they said, but she could well understand the panic in their voices. She heard the voices of maidservants retelling the worries of their mistresses, and she heard astrologers prophesying a grim future. The female guards of the palace were full of grief and there were those who went so far as to think of mutiny. Temple dancers, the *devadasis* of the Yellamma temples, expressed their unwillingness to dance. Pampa Kampana even thought she could identify individual storytellers, here was Ulupi Junior grieving, and Thimma the Huge, here. All of Bisnaga was in crisis, and the voices of that crisis filled her waking thoughts. She heard the discontented mutterings of soldiers in the military cantonment, the gossipy voices of junior monks, the foul-mouthed scorn of courtesans. The king, so recently returned in triumph from his wars, was held in lower esteem than at any point in his reign, and people's heads were full of the possibility of a palace coup. But who would dare rise up, and how, and when, and would it succeed, and if it did, oh, what then, and if it failed, oh, what if it failed? In what are now becoming known as the "blinded" verses of the *Jayaparajaya*, Pampa Kampana gave voice to the anonymous, to the ordinary citizens, the little people, the unseen, and many scholars assert that in these pages of the immense work Bisnaga comes most vividly to life.

She herself wrote that the whispers were a blessing. They brought the world back to her and took her back into the world. There was nothing to be done about the blindness but now it was more than just darkness, it was filled with people, their faces, their hopes, their fears, their lives. Joy had left her, first when Zerelda Li died, and then when her eyes were taken from her and she had understood that she had not escaped the curse of burning. But now, little by little, the whispered secrets of the city allowed joy to be reborn, in the birth of a child, in the building of a home, in the heart of loving families she had never met; in the shoeing of a horse, the ripening of fruits in their orchards, the richness of the harvest. Yes, she reminded herself, terrible things happened, a terrible thing had happened to her, but life on earth was still bountiful, still plenteous, still good. She might be blind, but she could see that there was light.

In the palace, however, the king was lost in darkness. Time had stopped all around the Lion Throne. He began to be quite unwell. Courtiers spoke to one another about seeing him wandering the corridors of the palace talking to himself, or, according to some reports, seemingly deep in conversation with ghosts. He spoke to his lost chief minister and asked for advice. None was given. He spoke to his junior queen, taken from him in childbirth, asking for love. No love was returned. He walked in the gardens with his dead children, he wanted to teach them things and push them on swings and pick them up and toss them in the air, but they didn't want to play and were unable to learn. (Strangely, he had less time for his living daughter, Tirumalamba Devi. His departed children who would never grow up seemed more on his mind than his adult girl.)

(Here Pampa Kampana's text speaks of Tirumalamba Devi as an adult. We are obliged to comment that, as careful—not to say pedantic!—readers of the text may have calculated, Tirumalamba must in "reality" still have been a child. To these readers, and to all who encounter the Jayaparajaya *in our pages, we offer the following advice: do not, as you experience Pampa Kampana's tale, cling to a conventional description of "reality," dominated by calendars and clocks. The author has previously—in her account of her six-generation-long "sleep" in the forest of Aranyani—shown that she is prepared to compress Time for dramatic purposes. Here she shows her willingness to do the opposite as well, stretching Time instead of abbreviating it, making it do her bidding, allowing Tirumalamba to grow up inside her magically expanded hours—the clocks paused outside her bubble but continuing to tick inside it. Pampa Kampana is the mistress of chronology, not its servant. What her verses instruct us to believe was so, we must accept. Anything else is folly.)*

Krishnadevaraya went into all the temples of Bisnaga to offer prayers and ask to be released from his torment, but the gods turned deaf ears to the man who had blinded the creator of the city, in whom the goddess had dwelled for more than two hundred years. He wrote poetry but then he tore it up. He asked the gathered poetic geniuses of the court, the Seven Remaining Elephants, whose talents were the pillars that held up the sky, to compose new work whose lyricism would renew the beauty of Bisnaga, but all of them confessed that the muse had departed and they were unable to write a word.

The king is mad, the whispers said.

Or it might have been that the king, filled with repentance and shame, consumed by the horror of self-knowledge—the knowledge that his lightning storms of rage had finally broken his own world and deprived him of its two most valuable citizens—was possessed by the need for expiation, and had no idea how or where to find it.

His health worsened. He took to his bed. The court physicians could find no cause. He seemed simply to have lost a reason for living. "All he wants," the whispers said, "is to find some measure of peace of mind before he leaves."

At some point during his rapid decline he remembered his brother, imprisoned in the fort at Chandragiri. In a state that many at the court believed to be the beginning of a terminal delirium, he cried out, "Here is one wrong I can right!" He gave the order to release Achyuta from his place of exile and escort him to Bisnaga City. "Bisnaga needs a king," Krishnadevaraya proclaimed, "and my brother will rule when I am gone." Very few people at the royal court had ever met Achyuta, but the rumors of his bad personality, his cruelty, his violent nature, were known to all. But nobody dared to speak against the king's decree, until Princess Tirumalamba's husband Aliya tried to intervene.

Aliya visited Krishnadevaraya on what people were beginning to think of as his deathbed. "Your Majesty, excuse me," he said, bluntly, "but your brother Achyuta is well-known to be a savage. Why send for him when I am here? As your only surviving child's husband, known to all as a serious man, a responsible man, surely that would be a better, less risky route for the succession to follow?"

The king shook his head, as if he was having difficulty remembering who Tirumalamba was, and who this older man, her husband, might be.

"I must make peace with my brother," the king replied, waving a weak, dismissive hand. "Although Chandragiri is not such a bad place," he added almost piteously. "The Raj Mahal there is fairly comfortable. However, I must set him free. As for you, just look after this daughter of mine properly, and when he is king her uncle Achyuta will treat you both with all the respect you certainly deserve."

Aliya went to Queen Tirumala Devi and her mother Nagala Devi. "As senior queen," he said, "you must intervene with the king. Isn't the crown the reason why you wanted Tirumalamba to marry a man of consequence, an older, more authoritative figure than some callow youth? Wasn't this your way of getting your family on to the throne of Bisnaga? Well then. Now is the hour when you must make your move."

Tirumala Devi shook her head sadly. "My daughter hates me," she said, "and she has turned away from her grandmother too. She thinks that when she was sick we didn't care if she lived or died and our attention was focused solely on our son. Now she has averted her gaze from us both. There is nothing for us to gain by helping put her, and you, on the Lion Throne."

"And is that true?" Aliya asked. "About your attention?"

"What a question," said Nagala Devi. "It's obvious rot. She always was a petulant child."

Aliya returned to the weakening Krishnadevaraya. "You made a great mistake with *Mahamantri* Timmarasu and the lady Pampa Kampana," he said. "Don't make this second colossal error before you leave us."

"Send for my brother," Krishnadevaraya commanded him. "He will be your king." It was the last decision of his life. A few days later he was dead. The once-great Krishnadevaraya, master of all of the south below the river whose name he shared, greatest victor who ever ruled the city of victory, in whose time Bisnaga became more prosperous than ever before, died in a kind of unspoken disgrace, much reduced in honor, and people were blind to his achievements, as if he had blinded all Bisnaga when he put out Pampa Kampana and Minister Timmarasu's eyes.

The whispers told Pampa Kampana that his last word had been a bitter rebuke to himself.

"Remonstrance."

PART FOUR

| *Fall* |

20

After her father died Princess Tirumalamba Devi wandered the streets of Bisnaga like a lost soul, with Ulupi Junior following her from a distance, in case of need. But nobody approached the sad princess with bad intentions. Her sadness was like a veil protecting her from the unwelcome gaze of uncouth strangers. In the main bazaar street Sri Laxman and his brother Sri Narayan offered her fruit, pulses, seeds, and rice, but she passed on by with a small rueful shake of the head. On the banks of the river at dawn she watched worshippers praising Surya the god of the sun, but she herself had lost the desire to worship any god. The hilly landscape of immense rocks and boulders dwarfed her and increased her feeling of insignificance. She felt like a mosquito or an ant. Her father had died without recognizing her rights and had insulted her husband by dismissing him without discussion. Her mother and grandmother were poisonous shrews. She was alone in the world, except for the old man to whom she was married, who spent his days lost in intrigue, trying to get his allies into positions of influence before the new king arrived in town. He had no time for her troubles. She drifted in and out among the quarters of the foreigners where porcelain, wine, and fine muslin could be found, and through the neighborhoods of noble families, and the gullies of the courtesans too. Only the Royal Enclosure where she had grown up, with its emerald pools and architectural beauties, failed to interest her. She meandered past the irrigation canals and the Yellamma temples whose dancing girls were the best in town. *I no longer have a place in this place where everyone knows their place,* she thought. In this way, lost and aimless, she found her way to the Mandana *mutt,* and her feet, which knew what she needed better than her head, brought her to Pampa Kampana's door.

The whole city was holding its breath. Stories of Achyuta's approach, his wild nights at hostelries on the road, the drunkenness, the gluttony, the women, the brawls, ran ahead of the royal party, and Bisnaga rightly feared that its new age would be very different from the regal grandeur of Krishnadevaraya in his prime, and the culture of art and tolerance which Queen Regent Pampa Kampana had fostered during the king's years of military absences. Something louder and cruder was on the way. It was time to keep one's head down and one's nose clean. There was no telling in what direction Achyuta Deva Raya might aim his fabled vulgarity, to say nothing of his violent streak. Stories of men strung up by Achyuta and left hanging by the wayside because of some real or imagined act of disrespect rushed down the road from Chandragiri, like heralds of the new order, and struck fear into every heart.

"May I come in?" Tirumalamba Devi softly asked, and the woman squatting in the far corner of the room moved a hand very slightly in a gesture of invitation. The princess came in quickly, taking off her sandals, and moved forward to touch the blind woman's feet.

"Don't do that," Pampa Kampana said. "In this place we meet as equals or not at all."

Tirumalamba Devi sat down near her. "You are the mother of Bisnaga and have been so cruelly treated by its children, who are also yours," she said, "and I am a child cruelly treated by my mother and my grandma too. So maybe I'm looking for a mother and you are in need of a child."

After that they were friends. Tirumalamba Devi came every day, and soon Ulupi Junior left her there alone, telling her that she didn't need security in this place, in which everyone was safe from harm. Sometimes the woman in the corner did not want to talk and they sat silently together. It was a good silence in which both women felt cared for, a silence that brought them closer. On other days Pampa Kampana wanted to talk, and told the younger woman stories from her earlier life, about the bag of seeds with which Hukka and Bukka gave birth to the city, and the battle against the pink monkeys, everything. Tirumalamba Devi listened in awe.

And every day Pampa Kampana tried to write. Tirumalamba Devi saw how hard it was for her, in spite of the skill of her hand. Finally she spoke up. "What I see," she told Pampa Kampana, "is that because of your eyes, your hand moves very slowly, much more slowly than your mind, and that is hard for you. You can actually compose with great rapidity, isn't it, but you can't set it down fast enough, and the enforced slowness must be very frustrating, yes?"

Pampa Kampana made a small movement of the head, meaning to say, *perhaps, but I have no other choice.*

Tirumalamba Devi found the courage to make a bold suggestion. "When immortal Vyasa was composing the *Mahabharata,* he also did so at a very fast pace, no?" she asked. "But Lord Ganesh, who was taking the dictation, could keep up with him, no? Even when his pen broke, he broke off one of his elephant tusks and wrote with that. Isn't it? For this reason we also call him *Ekdanta,* Ganesh One Tooth."

"I am not Vyasa," Pampa Kampana said, and a rare smile spread across her face. "And you still have all your teeth, I'm sure, and I also know that your ears are not so big."

"But I can write as fast as you can recite," Tirumalamba Devi said with shining eyes. "And if my pen breaks, I'll do whatever it takes to go on without stopping."

Pampa Kampana considered this.

"Can you dance?" she asked. "Because Lord Ganesh is a fantastic dancer. Can you ride on a rat? Will you wrap a serpent around your neck like a scarf, or around your waist like a belt?" Now her smile was very wide.

"If that's what it takes," Tirumalamba Devi said firmly, "then I will learn."

Achyuta Deva Raya entered the Lotus Palace looking for someone to kill. He was a swarthy man in his fifties, thick-bearded, gap-toothed, pot-bellied, angry as only a man obliged by his detention in a remote place to suffer the attentions of country dentists can be. He was dressed as if for combat, in a leather jerkin over a chain-mail vest, well-worn boots on his feet, a sword at his waist and a shield on his back. His companions were a disorganized band of drinking ruffians that had provided his only social life in Chandragiri, and behind them came his official royal escort, a band of women warriors from the palace guard whose expressions bore witness to their anger at the lascivious approaches made by the king's friends on the road, the king's own inappropriate behavior, and their professional embarrassment at the brutish bad manners of the new monarch whom they were obliged to bring into the room of the Lion (or Diamond) Throne.

Waiting to greet him was what remained of the royal family: Krishnadevaraya's senior queen Tirumala Devi and her mother Nagala Devi, Princess Tirumalamba Devi, and her husband Aliya Rama, whose decision to style himself as Aliya Rama Raya, while technically justifiable because of his marriage to Krishnadevaraya's only surviving child, was certain to be seen by Achyuta as a red rag, inflammatory, even a declaration of war. "When a man has been exiled as long as I have," Achyuta said, "he returns looking for revenge. The one responsible for my ruined life—my noble brother—is no longer here to face my wrath. But, in his absence, you people will do."

"Twenty years is a long time," Aliya replied, "and we can see that your banishment has not been kind either to your appearance or to your character. However, welcome, Uncle—I use the term of respect even though I am your senior by several years. Bisnaga is yours, as the late king decreed, and be assured that nobody here will consider rebellion against his will. But you should know that the people of the palace—the city's aristocrats, its ministers and civil servants, and these formidable women of the guard—are loyal to the empire itself, not only to the occupant of the throne. They are loyal to those who have treated them well during the twenty years of your absence. Let me put it to you more plainly. They love the late king's daughter, his only living child. And I am her chosen husband. So they are loyal, also, to me. The people outside the gates are the same. It is Bisnaga they love, and the king is the servant of their beloved, and must never betray it. Therefore be careful how you act, or your reign may be brief."

"In addition," Tirumala Devi said, "my father King Veera of Srirangapatna, my mother's husband, guardian of your southern border, is watching closely, and should he be displeased, it would not go well for you."

Achyuta turned to Princess Tirumalamba Devi. "And you, young lady, what do you say? Do you have some threats for me too?"

"My closest friend and second mother, the lady Pampa Kampana, sees everything through blinded eyes," she answered. "So, learning from her example, I will say everything through closed lips."

Achyuta scratched the back of his neck. Then his hand strayed to his sword and he grabbed the hilt, released it, grabbed it again, released it again. Then he scratched the top of his head with his right hand, ruffled his thick, unkempt, and graying hair, and furrowed his brow; while his left hand reached into his right armpit, like a man hunting for fleas. Then he shook his head, as if in disbelief. He looked over to his drinking buddies with an expression that said, *Well, you're not much use, are you.* Then all of a sudden he burst into loud laughter and clapped his hands. "Family life, eh?" he cried. "You can't beat it. It's good to be home. And so, let's eat."

In the years that followed, the story of Achyuta Deva Raya's coronation feast, vividly told and retold, became the defining narrative of his reign. Everyone in Bisnaga carried around a mental image of the king and his drunken companions eating like swine and drinking like men who had been lost in a desert for many years; while the royal family and nobles of the court sat in silence, with folded hands, eating nothing; and while Aliya Rama Raya stood at the back of the dining hall, refusing even to sit and break bread with the new ruler, and plotting his next move.

Tirumalamba Devi gave Pampa Kampana a detailed description of the evening, and that is what we now have in the *Jayaparajaya*, transformed by the author into verse, but written in the princess's neat hand. After Tirumalamba had finished her account, Pampa Kampana gave a deep sigh.

"These two men," she said, "your husband and your uncle. Between them, they will be the destruction of us all."

The last two leading men in the drama of Bisnaga were so unalike that people began to call them "Yes and No," or "Up and Down," or "Plus and Minus" to describe their opposed natures. "Forward and Back" was also used, and in this case Achyuta was definitely the one considered to be the backward party. He was the unsubtle one, the type who barges in through your front door, hits you over the head, and steals your house. Aliya was stealthy. If he stole your house you wouldn't know it was going until it was gone. You'd be standing in the road, homeless, wondering where everything went. Achyuta made people think of a bear with angry bees flying around his head, perpetually agitated, swatting at the buzzing air. Aliya was still, like an archer just before he releases his deadly arrow. Achyuta was thick-bodied and gross, while Aliya reminded everyone of a skeleton—a walking skeleton with a long hard face and arms and legs so long and thin that there seemed to be no flesh on them, just skin and bone. Achyuta was excitable; Aliya was almost preternaturally calm. Achyuta was religious, in the sense of being hostile to followers of other religions; Aliya was cynical, and didn't give a damn about your faith as long as you were of value. Achyuta, by general agreement, was not very intelligent. Aliya Rama Raya was the smartest man in the palace.

And yet, under Achyuta, Bisnaga survived. It no longer prospered in the old way, and it lost territories and influence, but at the end of his reign, it was still there. By the time Aliya was done, the empire was finished as well.

Several years passed before Tirumalamba Devi persuaded Pampa Kampana to leave the Mandana *mutt.* She only left her room when she was told that the *mutt* had a pottery room with a wheel and a kiln, and so after a long time, and in spite of her blindness, she began to throw pots again. It seems probable that she herself made the pot which, in the end, would contain the manuscript of her life's work. But for a long time the pottery room and her own cell were the only places she wanted to be.

In the end it was the new Pampa statue that persuaded her. Achyuta Deva Raya had been determined to make a show of his deep religious conviction and had commissioned this tribute to the goddess who was the local incarnation of Parvati, Shiva's wife and Brahma's daughter, after whom the river of Bisnaga was also named. The sculptor was a certain Krishnabhatta, the same Brahmin genius whom Krishnadevaraya had asked to carve the giant, terrifying figure of Lord Narasimha, the Man-Lion incarnation of Vishnu, out of a single monolith: Narasimha with the goddess Lakshmi on his left thigh and the dead body of the demon Hiranyakashyap on his lap. That statue had not been finished until after Krishnadevaraya's death, but it was forever associated with his glory, and Achyuta ordered Krishnabhatta to make a Pampa-figure of equal size and grandeur, also carved out of a single block of stone, which would be placed in direct opposition to the Narasimha statue. It would be as if Achyuta's magnificence, embodied in stone Lady Pampa, as large as Lord Narasimha and just as fearsome, was staring down the greatness of his predecessor.

"You have to come," Tirumalamba Devi said to Pampa Kampana. "Because, so soon after its completion and blessing ceremony, everyone is already saying the statue is a tribute to you, the mother of us all, and that it's Achyuta Deva Raya's way of apologizing for the crime against you committed by his brother." She giggled. "It's driving my uncle insane."

"Okay," Pampa Kampana finally said. "My fingers will see what my eyes cannot."

On the day Pampa Kampana left the *mutt,* with a white cloth wrapped around her head to shield her ruined eyes, and an umbrella held over her by Madhava Acharya himself in spite of his advancing years, all of Bisnaga came out to honor her. She heard the crowd's cries and songs and was greatly moved and began, for the first time since her bloodied retreat, to consider the possibility of living in the world again, of finding her way back to some sort of love after the great hatred of the hot iron rod. When she reached the statue the sculptor himself guided her hands across its surface, describing its details and explaining its symbols.

With the help of Tirumalamba Devi and Madhava Acharya, she made an offering of flowers to the goddess, and took care to congratulate not only the sculptor but also the king for this supreme act of devotion. "It's beautiful," she said softly, and her words, repeated by many voices, rippled across the throng. "I see it clearly, as if it had restored my sight."

News of the event reached the palace quickly and infuriated Achyuta, who saw that the work he had commissioned to bring glory to himself had unintentionally become a tribute to the blind woman of Mandana. (There were those who thought he should have known what would happen, and we, with the benefit of hindsight, can't help but agree, but Achyuta was not a far-sighted man, nor, as has been noted, was he the most intelligent of rulers. As a result he was taken aback and angered by the people's reaction to the Pampa statue, and perhaps his anger was increased by his realization of his own stupidity.)

"To hell with her," he shouted from the throne. "She's pretending to be the goddess now? There's no room in my Bisnaga for witches or blasphemers. If blinding wasn't enough to get rid of her, I'll burn her alive."

Pampa Kampana's book makes no record of the names of Achyuta's ministers but it appears that, whoever they were, they persuaded the king that the public burning of a woman held in high esteem by so many would be inadvisable. They could not, however, prevent him from descending upon the Mandana *mutt* and demanding to be shown to her room. Madhava Acharya led the way and they found her sitting in her usual corner, reciting, while Princess Tirumalamba Devi wrote down her verses.

"If I can't burn you," he told her, "I can certainly burn your book, which I don't need to read to know that it's full of unsuitable and forbidden thoughts, and then you will die and be forgotten, and nobody will know your name, and the statue will be mine again and remain so for all eternity. What do you say to that?"

Tirumalamba Devi leaped to her feet and placed herself between Achyuta and the blind woman. "You'll have to kill me first," she said. "Madam has a divine gift and to do what you threaten would be an act of sacrilege."

Pampa Kampana stood up also. "Burn all the paper you want," she said. "But every line of what I have written is held in my memory. To get rid of it you'll need to cut off my head and stuff it with straw, as sometimes happens, in my book, to defeated kings."

"I, too, have memorized this immortal text," Madhava Acharya said. "So your axe will have to visit my neck as well."

Achyuta's face reddened. "The time may come soon," he said roughly, "when I accept all your offers with pleasure. For the moment, to hell with you all. Keep out of my way, and you," he pointed furiously at Pampa Kampana, "are forbidden to visit my statue."

"That's fine," said Pampa Kampana. "My history will not be written in stone."

Once the king had gone, she turned to the priest. "What you said wasn't true," she said. "You risked your life for a lie."

"There are times when a lie matters more than a life," he replied. "This was such a time."

She settled back into her corner. "Very well," she said. "Thank you both. Now perhaps we may proceed."

"Sometimes I hate men," Tirumalamba Devi said when Madhava Acharya had gone.

"I had a daughter who thought that way," Pampa Kampana told her. "She preferred the company of women and was happiest in Aranyani's enchanted forest. And if by 'men' you mean our recent royal visitor, that is understandable. But Madhava is a good man, surely. And what about your husband?"

"Aliya is all plots and conspiracies," Tirumalamba answered. "He's all secrets and schemes. The court is full of factions and he knows how to set one group against another, how to balance this interest against that one, and Achyuta can't keep up; that kind of complication makes him dizzy. So Aliya has become a second power center, equal to the king, which is all he wants, at least for now. He's a labyrinth. You never know which direction to go in. How can one love a maze?"

"Tell me this," Pampa Kampana said. "I know princesses are imprisoned by their crowns and find it hard to choose their own path, but in your heart, what do you want from life?"

"Nobody ever asked me that," Tirumalamba Devi said. "Not even my mother. Duty, duty, et cetera. Writing down your verses is the only thing that fills my heart."

"But for yourself, what?"

Tirumalamba Devi took a breath. "In the street of the foreigners," she said, "I get envious. They just come and go, no ties, no duties, no limits. They have stories from everywhere and I'm sure that when they go somewhere else we become the stories that they tell the people there. They even tell us stories about ourselves and we believe them even if they get everything upside down. It's like, they have the right to tell the whole world the story of the whole world, and then just . . . move on. So. Here's my stupid idea. I want to be a foreigner. I'm sorry to be so foolish."

"I had a daughter like that too," Pampa Kampana said. "And you know what? She became a foreigner and I think she was happy."

"You don't know?" Tirumalamba asked.

"I lost her," Pampa Kampana replied. "But maybe she found herself." She put a hand on the princess's knee. "Go and search for a *cheel* feather," she told her.

"A feather? Why?"

"Keep it safely," said Pampa Kampana.

"They say you came here as a bird," Tirumalamba said, awestruck.

"Let's go back to work," Pampa Kampana said. But before she started reciting again she added one more thing. "I have known foreigners," she said. "I have even loved one or two. But you know what's the most disappointing thing about them?"

"What?"

"They all look exactly the same."

"Can I ask you the same question that you asked me?" Tirumalamba said. "Is there still something you hope for, something you want? I know, your lost eyesight, of course, excuse me, another stupidity. But some secret desire?"

Pampa Kampana smiled. "Thank you," she said. "But my time of desiring is over. Now everything I want is in my words, and the words are all I need."

"Then, by all means," said Tirumalamba Devi, "let's get back to work."

It was the rainy season when everything heated up. Early in the morning Aliya Rama Raya had breakfast with his wife in their private chambers in the Lotus Palace, in silence, listening to the deceptively cheerful sound of the falling rain, and saying nothing on account of the servers. When they had finished eating and drinking, Aliya walked around all their rooms and made sure there were no unwelcome ears listening, no loose-tongued flunkies or gossipy maids. Then at last he spoke.

"I can hardly talk to the man," Aliya told Princess Tirumalamba Devi, "his level of thought is so crude. He thinks like he eats, which is to say, piggishly."

The loose, tense power-sharing arrangement between Achyuta the brutish king and Aliya his devious rival was unsatisfactory to both men, and their dispute had dragged on down the years and pulled Bisnaga in two opposite directions, which was unsatisfactory to everyone.

Tirumalamba made a careful answer. "Madhava Acharya says he's very godly, no?"

"Yes," Aliya said, "but he understands nothing. *We* are good, *they* are bad, that's the sum total of his religion. Underneath that, I think, he's afraid of *them.* And now that there's a new *they* rising in the north—these Mughals—he's even more scared."

"But we have *them* everywhere in Bisnaga," Tirumalamba said. "We have their places of worship in many neighborhoods, and they live among us, and are our friends and neighbors, and our children play together, and we say we are Bisnagan first and godly second, isn't it? We say that. Some of our senior generals are also *them,* na? And in the Five Sultanates, *we* are everywhere there also. Senior personages, shopkeepers, all. Even some wives in their palaces are *we.*"

"I have reached out in a friendly way to the Five Sultans," Aliya told her. "Seems they are even more scared of the Mughals than Achyuta is, even though their god is the same. I try to explain to him, god is not the thing. Being able to rule ourselves is the thing. Not being conquered and obliterated, but being powerful and free, this is the subject, for the sultans as well as for us. But he only says, *Kalyug, Kalyug,* the Dark Age is upon us, the demons are coming, and we must pray to Lord Vishnu, who comes to save us from the miseries of the Dark. We must pray for his strength against *them* and crush them all. It's like a four-year-old trying to understand the sacred books. 'Crush them all'? It would be stupid to try even if it was possible. 'Crush them all' is like asking, please come now and crush me. I'm talking to the sultans nicely, to avoid all this talk of crushing-vushing."

"What does he say about that? Your . . . 'talking-shalking'?"

"These days we don't say much to each other. That's also bad. So here's my idea. I have invited the Five Sultans to Bisnaga as our guests, to mediate between Achyuta and me."

"But, husband, excuse me, isn't that a terrible idea? It makes us look so weak, na?"

"It makes Achyuta look weak," Aliya replied, looking off into the distance and smiling an unamused smile. "Not necessarily the rest of us."

"But what if, thinking the king is weak, they attack and take some of our territory?"

"Why, then, dear wife, it will prove to all of Bisnaga that the king is not up to the job, and a change may be required."

"So this is your plan," Tirumalamba Devi said, shaking her head. "I don't know, husband. People already say about you that you're too sly. This will just prove it, no?"

"The people will accept *sly,*" Aliya said, quietly, "if it is accompanied by *capable.*"

Tirumalamba saw that there was no point in further discussion. "Have you told the king?" she asked.

"I'm going to tell him now."

"But he will never agree, isn't it? *So* stupid he isn't."

"The sultans are already on their way," Aliya said. "I have already given orders for a grand welcome, and a banquet. They arrive tomorrow."

Tirumalamba Devi stood up and prepared for her day with Pampa Kampana at the *mutt*. "*Sly* isn't a big enough word for you," she said as she left. "Maybe *sneaky* also. Also *calculating.* Maybe also a little *underhand.* It's not so much 'Yes and No.' It's more like, he says 'No,' and you say, 'Then watch out for your back.'"

"Thank you," Aliya Rama Raya said, and bowed slightly. "You can be a flatterer when you choose to be." And he smiled, again, his thin little enigmatic smile.

"I'll need an umbrella today," she said, "and I'll still get wet. You should get an umbrella too. The way you're behaving, not just the rain but the whole sky could fall on your head."

The state visit of the Five Sultans of the Deccan—rulers of Ahmadnagar, Berar, Bidar, Bijapur, and Golconda—didn't last long, but brought about great changes. Old Adil Shah of Bijapur, heavily defeated by Krishnadevaraya at Raichur, arrived with a small army, and wore battle-stained military clothes. Even older Qutb Shah of Golconda brought an even bigger force, and arrayed himself in dazzling diamonds. Both of them gave the impression of men who needed a show of armed force to make them appear strong, and therefore they both looked weak. Hussain Shah of Ahmadnagar and Darya of Berar were unwell, and looked like men who knew they wouldn't live long. Ali Barid of Bidar was the youngest, healthiest, and most confident of the five. He brought the smallest retinue, as if telling the rulers of Bisnaga, *you wouldn't dare.*

No sooner had they arrived than Achyuta Deva Raya, infuriated by Aliya Rama Raya's stratagem, told them their services weren't required. "Okay, so you're here, not my idea but that's the way it is," he told them in his uncouth fashion. "However, we don't need any advice from the likes of you. You've made the journey for nothing. Too bad. Stay a while, rest up, we'll eat tonight, and then you can all be on your way."

What he thought was: *Four sick old men and a kid. Nothing to fear here.* He also had a number of unpleasant thoughts about followers of *that* religion which it is unnecessary to repeat here. The Five Sultans no doubt entertained equally unpleasant thoughts about him.

That evening at dinner, Aliya Rama Raya spoke one by one to all Five Sultans. He soon learned that Hussain Shah of Ahmadnagar and Darya of Berar looked down on Ali Barid of Bidar and Adil Shah of Bijapur because their dynasties had been started by former slaves of foreign origin (their slave ancestors had come from Georgia). Qutb Shah of Golconda looked down on Hussain Shah and Darya because Hussain's family had originally been Brahmin Hindus, and the Berar sultanate descended from Hindu converts too. Qutb Shah was hated and feared by all four others because of the wealth and power of Golconda. All five seemed happier talking to Aliya than to one another. As for Achyuta, he sat some way away from his guests at the far end of the table, and drank. It was the only way, he reckoned, to get through this disaster of an evening.

Aliya Rama Raya thought: *How interesting that they really don't like one another. We need to keep it that way.*

Outside, the rain thundered down. The roof of the banqueting hall proved to be in need of repair and provided an imperfect defense against the downpour. Water came through in several places. Palace staff ran about with buckets and mops. It was necessary to hold umbrellas over the heads of the sultans of Bijapur and Golconda. This did nothing to improve the general mood.

Achyuta the king was right. The evening was a disaster. The Five Sultans left the next morning before dawn, all of them furious about their pointless journey.

Adil Shah of Bijapur thought: *Bisnaga is in terrible shape, divided against itself, run-down, leaky-roofed, confused. Time, perhaps, to make a decisive move.*

The banquet was notable for one other thing. It was the last function of state at which the now very old Nagala Devi was present, seated between her grim daughter ex-Queen Tirumala Devi and her reserved, though pleasant-faced, granddaughter Tirumalamba Devi. The three women sat upright, ate little, drank less, said nothing, and retired early. That night, Nagala Devi died.

The old lady slipped away quietly in the night lying in bed listening to the frogs croaking during a break in the rain. "It was the only thing she did quietly in her whole life," her granddaughter Tirumalamba said to Pampa Kampana at the *mutt,* before bursting into tears. "You can go on loving somebody even if you feel unloved by that person, isn't it," she wept. "Maybe it makes things worse. If you stopped loving them the pain would be less. When I was a little girl I sat at her feet and she told me stories and took me to see things. She was different then. Maybe she was happier. She told me about Tirumalaiah, the chief who built our great temple, or so she said, more than five hundred years ago. Then she took me to the temple and showed me everything, all the way inside, even the sanctum containing the god and the snake with seven heads. She also took me to the beautiful waterfall. Srirangapatna is an island inside the Kaveri river which divides when it reaches our home and then reunites beyond it. She is the one who told me that that place, the place where the two streams of the river rejoin, is the most auspicious place for the scattering of ashes. She took me to see it and pointed to the best place from which to do that work. So now we must take her there and scatter her on the water."

"Talk to your mother," Pampa Kampana said. "She has lost her mother and she needs her daughter by her side."

"You are my mother now," Tirumalamba Devi said. "I am your daughter."

"No," Pampa Kampana told her. "Not today."

Tirumalamba found her mother Tirumala Devi alone in her bedroom with a dry-eyed face as impenetrable as a locked door. "Your grandmother gave up her marriage to come and live here in Bisnaga with me. She loved your grandfather and he still loves her and yet they agreed she would come with me and make sure I was safe in this hellish place where everyone thought we were nothing but poisoners."

"We should take her back to her husband now," Tirumalamba said.

"I want to go back also," her mother told her. "You don't want or need me and I have no place here anymore. I want to spend the few years that remain at home, as my father's daughter once again, so that we may comfort each other for our loss."

"Ask the king," Tirumalamba told her. "I'm sure he will agree."

They did not embrace, or weep together. Some wounds are too deep to be healed.

Tirumala Devi asked for an audience with Achyuta. He received her formally, seated on the throne while she stood before him like a common supplicant. She ignored the insult and spoke courteously. "As my husband and mother have both left us," she said, "I ask that I be allowed to return to my father's house, my work here being complete."

"But it's not complete," Achyuta said, picking strands of fatty meat from his teeth. "You being in Bisnaga keeps your father honest. He will not dare to break our agreement or move against us in any way while we have you."

"I must scatter my mother's ashes in the Kaveri," Tirumala Devi said. "It would be her last wish and I must fulfill it."

"There are holy rivers here also," the king said dismissively. "Put her in the water of the Pampa or the Krishna. They will serve you just fine. No reason to make the long journey into the south."

"So I am your prisoner," Tirumala Devi said. "Or should I say, your hostage."

"You are a peace treaty in the form of a living person," Achyuta said. "Think of it that way. That should feel better, huh. Well, even if it doesn't."

The former senior queen returned to her rooms where her daughter found her, still with a face of iron.

"He refused, then," Tirumalamba Devi said. "I'll talk to Aliya. He will surely find a way."

But this turned out to be a rare instance when the two disputatious heads of Bisnaga spoke as one. "He's right," Aliya Rama Raya told his wife. "If we lose your mother, we lose Veera too. There are already rumors of his growing disloyalty. She will have to stay."

"You have me," she argued. "Isn't that enough?"

"No," Aliya told her, without trying to soften the blow. "It isn't. Not until I am really the king on the Lion Throne."

"You mean 'unless,' I suppose," the princess corrected him.

"If I had meant 'unless,'" he replied, "I would not have said 'until.'"

Tirumalamba left him and brought the bad news to Tirumala Devi. "He won't help," she said, and her mother made no attempt to hide her scorn. "So you are still a second-rater," Tirumala Devi told her only living child. "If my son had survived, I know my situation would have been very different."

Her daughter turned to go. "Don't worry about me," Tirumala Devi called after her. "I know how to get out of here without anybody's help." Then she turned her gaze to the window and watched the rain fall, the improbable, unyielding, interminable rain. The next morning they found her dead in her bed, holding a small bottle in her hand that had contained a poison so deadly that there was no known antidote for it. And so the prophecy of Krishnadevaraya came true. *The poisoner ends up drinking the poison.*

Aliya Rama Raya accompanied Tirumalamba Devi on her rain-sodden journey back to Srirangapatna with the ashes of her mother and grandmother, along with a heavily armed guard of honor. King Veera met them with an equally well-armed retinue of his own and escorted them to the confluence of the Kaveri. The rain stopped suddenly, the clouds clearing to reveal a bright sky, as if a curtain had been parted, as if the heavens were paying their last respects to the two queens. After the ashes had been scattered there were prayers and then a feast of remembrance and the next day the journey back to Bisnaga.

"I'm sorry to tell you that your grandpa Veera is definitely planning to break away from our alliance," Aliya told Tirumalamba once they were safely away from Srirangapatna. "Now that I've seen him face-to-face and looked into his traitorous eyes there's no doubt in my mind about it."

The *Jayaparajaya* tells us about the end of King Veerappodeya's story, in a manner one can only describe as terse. It's possible that Pampa Kampana kept it short so as not to distress his granddaughter unduly, or, alternatively, that Tirumalamba Devi abbreviated the account as she wrote it down. All we are told is this: that King Veera did indeed announce that his agreement with Bisnaga was at an end, and obliged the battalions of troops from Bisnaga stationed at Srirangapatna to withdraw. No sooner had this happened than the powerful neighboring ruler of Mysore, seeing that Srirangapatna no longer had the added strength of the Bisnaga army at its disposal, attacked in strength, overthrew King Veera, and absorbed Srirangapatna into the kingdom of Mysore. The text does not dwell on Veera's fate. If his head was severed, if it was stuffed with straw and displayed in Mysore as a trophy, we cannot say.

As a result of this tragic mishap, the southern frontier of the Bisnaga Empire was left vulnerable and exposed, and its enemies grew in confidence and strength.

Sad to relate, King Achyuta fell into bad habits as time went by. Pampa Kampana in her monastic room at Mandana listened to the whispers of the city and heard everything: how in the beginning Achyuta had been prevented by Madhava Acharya—whose opinions on widow-burning had been greatly reshaped by his growing friendship with Pampa Kampana—from throwing all of Krishnadevaraya's widows on his funeral pyre, and had therefore flung them all out of the palace to fend for themselves on the streets, even the high-ranking—and now relatively old—surrogates of the *gopis* of Krishna the god. After that he had acquired five hundred wives of his own, and spent most of his waking hours being pleasured by them. (They lived in cell-like rooms in cloisters adjacent to the palace, and when not involved in decadent acts with the king led lives more like celibate nuns.) He had also begun to insist that the court's senior noblemen should kiss his feet on a daily basis, which was not, let us say, an endearing requirement. Those who were willing to kiss the king's feet with genuine enthusiasm were given gifts of yak-tail fans, and it would not be exaggerating matters to say that those nobles who received such fans were also the ones who hated the king most deeply. He slept in a bed made of solid gold, refused to wear any garment more than once, and so great were the expenses of his lavish court that his ministers were obliged to increase taxes on the citizenry, after which the people hated him too. There were banquets at court almost every night, at which seventeen courses were eaten and much wine drunk, and while the king and his cronies were feasting on venison, partridges, and doves, the common people were reduced to dining on cats, lizards, and rats, all of which were sold in the city's markets, alive and kicking, so that people knew that they were at least getting fresh meat.

Pampa Kampana, too, was changing. When Tirumalamba Devi came to write down her verses, they were often little more than lamentations about her cursed gift of longevity, her obligation to go on living until the bitter end. "I can see it," she told Tirumalamba, "as if it had already happened. I can see the damage to the *gopuram* of the Vitthala

Temple, and the smashing of the Pampa statue and the Hanuman statue as well, and the burning of the Lotus Palace. But I must wait until time catches up with me before I set it down."

"Maybe it won't happen," Tirumalamba said, distressed by these images of destruction. "Maybe it was just a bad dream."

Pampa Kampana, kindly, did not argue. "Yes," she said. "Maybe so."

She was developing many of the attributes of great old age. The woman Tirumalamba saw before her, disfigured as her face was by the blinding, still looked like someone in, perhaps, her late thirties, but Pampa Kampana had given up caring what she looked like. The illusion of youth was of no import to her anymore. She no longer needed to bother about seeing her idiotically young reflection, so she was free to inhabit the old crone she felt herself to be. Her skin felt dry, so she scratched it. Her joints felt creaky, so she complained about them creaking. Her back hurt, and when she stood she needed a walking stick and was unable to straighten her body. "At my age things should be a whole lot worse," she told Tirumalamba. "But to hell with that. Things are bad enough."

She had also developed a sort of sleeping sickness. At times Tirumalamba would find her prone and unconscious and when the sickness first began Tirumalamba would panic and think the old lady had died, but then Pampa Kampana's heavy breathing would reassure her. Sometimes Pampa Kampana slept for several days at a time, and gradually these periods lengthened into weeks, or even months, and she would wake up with the appetite of a hungry elephant. The sleep did not seem natural to Tirumalamba, it felt as if it came from the divine sphere, perhaps as a gift to make it easier for Pampa Kampana to pass the time that needed to be passed before her final release from the goddess's spell.

It was during these long sleeps that Pampa Kampana dreamed the future. So they were not entirely restful.

By this time Tirumalamba herself was no longer young, and she, too, had various physical complaints, her bad teeth, her digestive tract, but she kept these to herself and allowed the old woman to fulminate. "Maybe if you just go on telling the story," she suggested gently, "that will make you feel a little better."

"I did have one dream," Pampa Kampana said. "I was visited by two *yalis,* not made of wood or stone but real, living creatures." She had dreamed of *yalis* before, and had been happy to be with those supernatural beings, half-lion and half-horse, and with elephant tusks, whom people thought of as protectors of gateways. "They came to reassure me. 'Don't worry,' they said. 'When the time comes we will appear at your side to take you across the threshold to the Eternal Realm.' That was comforting." The memory put an end to her bad mood. "Yes," she said. "Let's go on."

Then, to Tirumalamba's astonishment, she quoted Siddhartha Gautama, which is why the Buddha's Five Remembrances, or a version of them, can be found in the *Jayaparajaya,* which is otherwise not a Buddhist text.

> *I am of the nature to grow old. There is no way to escape it.*
> *I am of the nature to have ill health. There is no way to escape it.*
> *I am of the nature to die. There is no way to escape it.*
> *There is no way to escape being separated from everyone I love, and all that is dear to me.*
> *My actions are my only true belongings. My actions are the ground upon which I stand.*

Adil Shah of Bijapur had sworn an oath never to drink a drop of wine until he had recaptured Raichur. This was hard for him, as he was a man who loved good wine, and he was often tempted to break his oath, but did not. After the unpleasant gathering of the Five Sultans at Bisnaga, at which Achyuta and the other kings all drank copiously, Adil Shah, who had remained sober throughout that very long and awkward evening, decided it was time to act. He had never forgotten the humiliating message he had received from Krishnadevaraya, *Kiss my feet,* and resolved that Krishnadevaraya's degraded successor Achyuta, who was so enamored of foot-kissing that he obliged even his most senior courtiers to abase themselves, needed to be taught the lesson of good manners that Krishnadevaraya had never learned.

He gathered his forces and attacked Raichur. The Bijapur army's surprise arrival found the forces of Bisnaga unprepared for battle, and they were swiftly overrun. In the next few weeks the whole of the Raichur *doáb* region came under the control of Bijapur once again, and Adil Shah, standing beside the famous freshwater spring in the Raichur citadel, declared, "Today this spring will yield not water, but wine."

Things were going badly wrong for Achyuta Deva Raya. Not only had he lost Raichur, which Krishnadevaraya had thought of as the jewel in his crown, but the king of Mysore, having overwhelmed King Veera in the south, had further expansionist plans, and there was a new Portuguese viceroy in Goa, Dom Constantine de Braganza, who was not content with being a horse-trader, was eyeing the whole of the west coast, and developing imperialist ambitions of his own.

Achyuta did nothing, as if he was afraid to act. He was unpopular at court, in the streets, and among the armed forces, and his inaction proved to be fatal. Aliya Rama Raya seized the moment, dethroned him, and packed him off to Chandragiri to rot. He died there a short time later. And so the last ruler of Bisnaga came to the throne.

21

Now here is Aliya Rama Raya ascending to become a Lion on the Diamond Throne. Or a Diamond on the Lion Throne. Simultaneously with that event, Pampa Kampana in her telling of the history of Bisnaga, and Tirumalamba Devi in the writing down of it, have caught up with the present moment. The verses telling of the fall of Raichur, and the rise of the aggressive Portuguese viceroy to the west and the prince to the south have been firmly set down, and the coronation of the new king described at a moment contemporaneous with the event itself. (We can safely assume, and it looks to be so in the manuscript as we have it, that the verses revealing the death in exiled captivity of the unloved Achyuta, in the distant Raj Mahal of the Chandragiri fort, are inserted later, when that unmourned event occurs.)

With Aliya on the throne, there were inevitably substantial changes at court. Tirumalamba Devi was now queen of Bisnaga, so the five hundred wives of Achyuta were released from their duties and dismissed from their cloisters, and Aliya, by nature an austere man as well as a duplicitous one, chose not to take any wives but his queen, a departure from long-established practice, but a popular one, and if his duplicity caused him to find secret lovers, we are not told of them. Tirumalamba Devi, freed from the shadow of her mother and grandmother, the two notorious poison queens, was also well liked. Her work as Pampa Kampana's scribe had endeared her to many, and she set out to make her reign one in which both the literary and architectural arts might flourish. So it seemed as if Bisnaga might be entering a new age of glory.

(It is said, however, that terminally ill people suddenly rally in their penultimate hour, and give their loved ones joyful reason to believe that a miraculous recovery might be occurring; but then they fall back against their pillow, breathlessly dead and cold as the winter desert.)

Pampa Kampana moved back into the palace; Queen Tirumalamba Devi insisted on it, and insisted, too, that old Pampa take the suite of rooms reserved for the queen of Bisnaga. "We must show the whole of Bisnaga that love has triumphed over hate," she said, "that irrational anger cannot have the last word and rationality must answer it, and, yes, that reconciliation follows remonstrance. Additionally, I personally want to show that to you, because I am and will always be your scribe, sitting at your feet, and you are and will always be the true queen."

"I'll do it if you want," Pampa Kampana told her. "But I don't care about comfort, and I don't feel like the queen of anything anymore."

They didn't have much work to do. The book was up to date, and Aliya's reign was just beginning, so there wasn't a great deal to record. "I have dreamed the future," Pampa Kampana said to Tirumalamba. "But it would be improper to write it down before it happens." The queen begged her, "At least tell me, so that I am prepared for whatever comes." Pampa Kampana was reluctant for a long while. Then finally she said:

"Your husband, my dear, will make a fatal mistake. This mistake will take a long time to make. Sometimes it will look like it is not a mistake, but in the end it will destroy us. You can't stop it and neither can I, because the truth of the world is that people act according to their natures, and that is what will happen. Your husband will act according to his nature, which you yourself have called *sly, sneaky, calculating,* and *underhand,* and that will destroy us. We inhabit at present the moments before the calamity. Enjoy them while it lasts because maybe they will last for twenty years, and for those twenty years you will be queen of the greatest empire our world has ever seen. But underneath that surface the mistake will be happening, slowly. You will be an old lady when the world ends, and I am finally allowed to die."

Tirumalamba buried her face in her hands. "What a cruel thing you have told me," she sobbed. Pampa Kampana remained dry-eyed and stern. "You shouldn't have asked to hear it," she replied.

Aliya Rama Raya, observing the divisions between the Five Sultans at the unpleasant dinner with Achyuta Deva Raya, had calculated that the best way to safeguard the northern frontier of Bisnaga was to make sure those rifts were never healed. As long as those five were quarreling among themselves he could easily deal with any threats from Mysore to the south and the Portuguese viceroy on the west coast. He wrote to all five, holding out the hand of false friendship. "Now that the unfortunate Achyuta is out of the way," he said, "there is no reason for us to fight. We each have our kingdoms, and we all have more wealth than we need. It's time to be friends. Stability brings prosperity."

When he told Tirumalamba what he had done, her memory of Pampa Kampana's prophecy was still fresh, and she grew agitated. "Do you really mean what you're saying?" she asked. "I know you too well to believe that it is. So it must be the start of some terrible scheme."

"Scheme, yes," her husband answered. "Terrible, no. Please accept that, as your senior by thirty years, I am also the wiser half of this marriage. Kindly attend to poetry, dance, music, and build a temple if it pleases you, but leave matters of state to me."

This was a haughty, insulting, and belittling speech. There was little she could do about it but maintain her personal dignity. "Be careful," she told him as she left his presence. "Or your wisdom may ruin us all."

In the beginning Aliya wanted to be avenged for the loss of Raichur, so, pretending to be an ally who had information about Adil Shah's treacherous intents toward them, he persuaded the sultans of Ahmadnagar and Golconda to attack Bijapur.

Then he persuaded Ahmadnagar to change sides, to make peace with Bijapur so that they could jointly attack Golconda.

Later, when Qutb Shah of Golconda's younger brother Ibrahim fell out with his older sibling, Aliya arranged for him to take refuge in Ahmadnagar, which resulted in another war between that sultanate and Golconda.

When that ran out of steam, Aliya persuaded Adil Shah of Bijapur to demand two fortresses from Hussain Shah of Ahmadnagar, who refused contemptuously, as Aliya had known he would, and so conflict broke out between Bijapur and Ahmadnagar once again.

The whole region of the Five Sultanates was in turmoil, which was exactly what Aliya wanted. He incited lesser nobles within each sultanate to rise up against their sultan, so the sultanates had to fight civil wars as well as wars between one another.

And so the years went by. The Portuguese ravaged the Malabar coast, killing most of the inhabitants of Mangalore, but Aliya didn't interfere. He made a peace treaty with Viceroy Constantine de Braganza, elected to ignore the horrors being wrought upon Goa by the excesses of the Inquisition, and was pleased by the foreigners' destabilization of the west, which occupied much of the sultanates' attention.

Also, he persuaded Ahmadnagar and Bijapur to attack Golconda again, and then secretly negotiated an alliance between Bijapur and Golconda, which led to Ahmadnagar suffering a humiliating defeat.

And the years went by, and by.

Aliya's machinations continued, and, thanks to his plotting, the war between the sultanates, with their many dizzying, broken alliances, and changes of side, went on. And after each victory, each defeat, there were surrenders of land and fortresses and gold mines and elephants and tributes were paid in gold and precious stones, which made it easy for Aliya Rama Raya—who continued to profess friendship to all parties—to incite further conflicts whose purpose was to regain lost territory and wealth and honor.

The years passed. Everyone grew older. Tirumalamba Devi did not dare to ask Pampa Kampana any more questions about the coming catastrophe, but knew it must be close. Pampa Kampana composed perfunctory verses about the battles of the Five Sultanates, and Tirumalamba duly wrote them down, and placed the pages in the old satchel where the great book lived. And Aliya Rama Raya celebrated his ninetieth birthday, proud of having kept Bisnaga safe from the sultanates, who hated one another more than they hated him.

"It is a strategy," he told Tirumalamba Devi, "that I have named 'Divide and Rule.'"

One day in the year 1564, old Adil Shah of Bijapur experienced a moment of dazzling clarity. He summoned his family and closest advisers and spoke like a man to whom the gods—or in his case, his one god—had provided a moment of revelation. "How blind we have been!" he declared. "The reason we have been fighting one another like cats and dogs for the last two decades is one man, who has pretended to be our friend." He immediately sent a message to Ibrahim Qutb Shah at Golconda. "That old schemer has fooled us long enough," it read, in part. "We can't defeat him by ourselves, but if we come together, we can surely take him down." Adil Shah's greatest enemy was Hussain Shah of Ahmadnagar, but Qutb Shah acted as an intermediary between them, and two marriages were arranged, one between Hussain Shah's daughter Chand Bibi and Adil Shah's son

Ali, the other between Hussain Shah's son Murtaza and Adil Shah's sister. When Ali Barid of Bidar learned of this new grouping, he joined it too. And so the grand alliance of Four of the Five Sultans against the emperor of Bisnaga was born. Only the sultan of Berar, whose general Jahangir Khan had been executed by Hussain Shah of Ahmadnagar during the inter-sultanate wars, refused to join.

"Let nobody say," Adil Shah declared when the Four Sultans met at Bijapur to ratify the alliance, "that we come together today on behalf of our one true god against their many false ones. If this was about god versus gods, we five would not have been fighting one another, true god versus the same true god, for the last twenty years. Simply said, we go now to teach that conniving trickster bastard a lesson he will never forget."

January 1565. A cold dry winter. The immense armies of the alliance were on the march. Their agreed meeting place was the great plain near the little town of Talikota.

Talikota lay on the banks of the river Doni, one hundred miles due north of Bisnaga City. News of the gathering army traveled quickly, but nobody in Bisnaga was unduly concerned. These battles happened from time to time. Maybe the Four Sultans were about to fight one another again. At any rate, the seven walls of Bisnaga were impregnable. The giant army of Bisnaga was invincible. There was nothing to worry about. The business of the city continued as normal, and caravans of bullock-carts traveled to the western seaports without fear of interception. At length, however—a little late, a little hurriedly—Aliya Rama Raya mobilized his forces and headed north. The whole army of Bisnaga went with him, except for a group left behind to defend the walls, which nobody believed would need defending. He had six hundred thousand infantrymen, a cavalry force of one hundred thousand, mostly mounted on trained and armored battle elephants, as well as artillery—cannon, archers, javelin throwers. "If they are all coming for us," he told Tirumalamba Devi, "then they will find out how mighty the power of Bisnaga really is. Make sure everyone stays calm. There is no cause for concern."

There is no cause for concern was a sentence that struck fear into Tirumalamba's heart. However, she tried to put a brave face on things, and announced a great poetry recitation on a stage at the gates of the Royal Enclosure, to which all were invited. By this time the only two surviving Elephant poets were "Nosey" Thimmana and Allasani Peddana, and even though they were old and infirm she insisted that they come before the people and recite their masterpieces. This event, which was intended to show the enduring cultural richness and undefeatable magnificence of Bisnaga, in fact demonstrated the reverse. The two toothless, balding, emaciated old gentlemen, weak in memory, stumbled over their lines, until finally Tirumalamba brought the fiasco to a close ahead of the intended time. It was a bad omen. Concern, for which Aliya Rama Raya had insisted there was no cause, spread rapidly through the city. If the age of the Elephants Whose Genius Held Up The Sky had come to an end, was the sky about to fall?

Tirumalamba Devi went in some distress to visit Pampa Kampana and found the old lady waiting for her, standing up, holding paper, quills, and ink, with the satchel containing the manuscript of her life's work slung over one shoulder.

"It's time," she said. "Let's go up on the roof of the Elephant Stable." *More elephants,* Tirumalamba thought, but she didn't argue. They walked alone through the safety of the Royal Enclosure to the house of the eleven arches—Pampa Kampana stooped over with a walking stick, the queen upright—and they climbed the unadorned steps up to the roof, Pampa Kampana ascending very slowly, resting between steps, but refusing help.

"Look for nests," Pampa Kampana said when they reached the top. "The *cheels* like to nest here, next to the domes. Timmarasu's pigeons preferred the roof of the palace. They never came here because the *cheels* were here."

"It's winter," Tirumalamba said. "There are old nests, but they are empty."

"Are there feathers?" Pampa Kampana asked.

Tirumalamba looked. "Yes," she said. "There are some feathers."

"Take them," said Pampa Kampana. "Today's the day."

She sat down with her back against a pillar of the central dome, the largest one, like a small pavilion with a turreted upper story, and held out the writing materials for Tirumalamba to take.

"Write," she said. "The battle is about to begin."

"How do you know?"

"I know," Pampa Kampana said. "I've known for a long time. And now it's time to tell."

She turned her eyes to the north. A light breeze was blowing into her face. She sniffed at it, as if it bore tidings that confirmed what she already knew. Her blind eyes seemed to see every detail of what was happening a hundred miles away.

"Your sons are on the left and right flanks," she said. "Tirumala Raya is on the left, with the army of Bijapur before him, and Venkatadri is on the right, confronting Golconda and Bidar. Your husband, in spite of his great age, insists on taking command of the army in the field, and is riding his battle elephant in the center, leading the vanguard against Hussain Shah and Ahmadnagar. This is how it begins."

(It is worth noticing that this is the first point in the entire text at which the poet tells us that Queen Tirumalamba Devi and Aliya Rama Raya had two children, both boys, both by now adult and acting as their father's lieutenants at the Battle of Talikota. We may even say that this omission is a fault in the work. But after all these centuries, who among us can guess at Pampa Kampana's reasons? Perhaps she never met them? Perhaps she did not deem them worthy of her verses because they had done nothing of note before this day? Here they are, anyway, girding their loins for battle.)

. . .

"It begins!" Pampa Kampana screamed. She looked like a woman possessed.

"Oh, their guns, their guns! Oh, in the front their mighty cannon, and behind them the smaller, swiveling guns, that can shoot in all directions! And behind the guns, the archers! Foreigners from Turkmenistan, oh bowmen of deadly aim, better than our Portuguese mercenaries! Oh, their crossbows, so much deadlier than our bows! Oh, their Persian horses, so much faster to twist and turn than our poor, huge, slow, cumbersome elephants! Oh, their spears, longer than ours! Oh, here comes trouble! Trouble!

"The army of Bisnaga retreats! We are more numerous, but the attack is fearsome, their weaponry more modern, and back we go, back!"

"Is it over, then?" wept Tirumalamba. "Have we lost?"

"We fight against the tide!" Pampa Kampana shrieked. *"Ah, the tide turns! Our rocket batteries pound them! On the right, Venkatadri and his heavy guns! Oh, Bidar's soldiers are broken, running this way and that! Oh, Golconda is retreating! Bravo, bold Venkatadri! And on the left flank, Tirumala Raya is no less bold! He rallies! He attacks! Bijapur, where this conspiracy was born—Bijapur also retreats!"*

"Ah, ah," Tirumalamba exclaimed. "So are we winning now? Is the day ours?"

"Oh, the battle at the heart of the battle! Here is Hussain Shah of Ahmadnagar on his warhorse, galloping this way, that way. See how he inspires his troops! See how they fight!"

"And my husband?" Tirumalamba Devi cried. "What of the king?"

Pampa Kampana fell silent and put her hands up to her face.

"The king?" Tirumalamba Devi shouted. "Pampa Kampana, what news?"

"Alas, the king is old," Pampa Kampana wailed. *"He is old and the battle is long. He has been up on that elephant a long time."*

"What has happened?" Tirumalamba Devi cried. "Tell me at once!"

"Alas for us all, my queen," Pampa Kampana wept through sightless eyes. *"The king . . . the king . . . needed to piss."*

"To piss? Pampa Kampana, you speak of piss?"

"Oh, the king came down from his elephant to relieve himself. He was on the ground. And oh, here come the elephants of Ahmadnagar! The beasts of Hussain Shah! I see an elephant's trunk. It stretches out! It curls around your husband! It captures the king in the middle of his stream."

"He is taken? Oh, day of terror, day of doom!"

"Oh, my queen, my queen, I dare not say what there is to say. I cannot say the words and then ask you, 'write them down.'"

"Tell me," Tirumalamba Devi said, all of a sudden very quiet and still, with a blank look in her eye.

"They bring the king to Hussain Shah. Aliya does not ask for mercy, and receives none. Oh, my queen, my daughter. They have cut off his head."

Tirumalamba Devi showed no trace of emotion. She gave the impression of being completely focused on her work as Pampa Kampana's scribe.

"His head," she repeated, and wrote the words down.

"Oh, they have stuffed it with straw and put it up on a long pole and they are riding back and forth so all the army of Bisnaga can see it. Oh, sad discouragement of our men, and our women soldiers too. See, they cease the fight, they retreat, they turn, they run. Oh, Venkatadri is fallen, and Tirumala Raya flees the battlefield. He is coming back to Bisnaga. The army is finished. The battle is lost."

"The battle is lost," Tirumalamba Devi repeated, as she wrote. "The battle is lost."

Pampa Kampana emerged from her trancelike state of possession. "I'm so sorry, my daughter," she said. "And now you must go. The army of the alliance cannot find the queen of Bisnaga here when they come."

"Where could I go?" Tirumalamba Devi said in her insanely controlled voice. "How should I go anywhere? I am the daughter and granddaughter of the poison queens. I should leave the way my mother did, by drinking down my death."

"You said once that you wanted to become a foreigner," Pampa Kampana said. "That you envied their wandering lives as strangers, without attachments. Now you should do it. You should fly away and go, who knows where. Far from here, far from murder and fire. Put down the feather pen and pick up the other feather. What little remains to be written, I can write."

"Fly away," Tirumalamba Devi repeated.

"Will you do it?" Pampa Kampana demanded. "You must. They must not take you."

"What about you?"

"Nobody cares about an old dying blind woman," Pampa Kampana said. "My time here is finally over. Don't worry about me. Pick up the *cheel* feather and you can go."

"You can really do that?"

"This one last time," Pampa Kampana said.

Tirumalamba Devi stood up with the *cheel* feather in her hand.

"Goodbye, then, my mother," she said. "Do it. Send me away."

Nobody saw the moment when the last queen of Bisnaga rose into the sky and departed forever, to places we cannot guess at. Even she who gave Tirumalamba the last gift of transformation could not see what she had wrought. She sat down again by the turret dome on the roof of the Elephant Stable, and wrote down just a little more.

22

Madhava Acharya had died some years earlier, and there was a new young Acharya in charge of the Mandana religious complex, but as an act of respect Madhava's monastic cell had been left untouched, as if he had just walked out of the door for a minute and had not yet returned. It was a small and sparsely furnished room: a wooden cot, a wooden table, a wooden chair, and a shelf of books, Madhava Acharya's personal copies of the *Itihasa,* the collection of the most important sacred texts, including the *Mahabharata,* the *Ramayana,* and the eighteen major and eighteen minor *Puranas*—copies which, according to the lore of the *mutt,* had once belonged to Vidyasagar himself. When Pampa Kampana as a young girl had first come to seek refuge in Vidyasagar's cave he had taught her the traditions from these very same volumes in which, he said, all the knowledge necessary for a life in this world was contained. She had memorized many of the most important passages. It was to this room, to these volumes, that Pampa Kampana returned after the flight of the *cheel* who had been her friend, the queen. Hobbling with her stick through the rowdiness of the city, she made her way to the seminary with her satchel slung carefully over her shoulder. She knew she had entered the last days of her life and sought the comfort of the old books before the end, even though she could no longer read them. She longed to hold the *Garuda Purana* in her arms one last time, for she was thinking of Tirumalamba Devi's transformation into a bird as well as musing about her own impending death—death, which was the last metamorphosis of life—and she wanted to recite that book's account of the bird-god Garuda and his conversations with Vishnu, the most metamorphic of all the gods.

The young Acharya, named Ramanuja after the legendary eleventh-century saint, greeted her at the door to the residences. "The war is lost," she told him. "The victors are coming." He did not ask her how she knew. "Come inside," he said. "Maybe they will have the grace not to murder the monks or to desecrate this holy place."

"Maybe," Pampa Kampana replied. "But I do not think this will be a time of grace."

A runner arrived in the city, at death's door after running one hundred miles from the Talikota battlefield, and lived just long enough to give news of the defeat. After that the city was plunged into chaos. The army of the Four Sultanates was on its way and the army of Bisnaga had fled, hundreds of thousands of warriors dispersing pell-mell into the immensity of the countryside. Only the seven circles of walls remained to shield the city from the horde now descending upon them. But the soldiers on the walls had lost their nerve and they were fleeing too, and people understood for the first time that no wall would save them if there were not human beings upon it; that in the end the salvation of human beings came from other human beings and not from *things,* no matter how large and imposing—and even magical—those things might be.

As the news spread that the defenders on the walls had run away, the city surrendered entirely to panic. Crowds filled the streets, carrying possessions, loading carts, harnessing bullocks, stealing horses, seizing whatever was there to be seized, fleeing, fleeing. One million people, desperate to get away, anywhere, even though they knew that the empire was collapsing so there would be nowhere to hide. Men and women were weeping openly and children were screaming and even before the enemy had arrived the looting had begun, because greed exists, and can be an even more powerful driving force than fear.

One day after the calamity at Talikota, Aliya Rama Raya and Tirumalamba Devi's surviving son, Tirumala Raya, came back to Bisnaga, wounded in the arm and leg and with a bandaged head, but staying on his horse, and accompanied by the small force of two dozen loyal soldiers who had helped him get away from the bloody rout, a ferocious band of old-timers who had fought their way out of the killing field, led by the most ferocious old-timers of all, Thimma the Huge's almost-as-enormous descendant Thimma the Almost As Huge and Ulupi Junior's blood kin, Ulupi the Even More Junior. "All seven gates to the city stand open!" Tirumala Raya cried out in the midst of the great bazaar. "We need good men, and women too, to close the gates and defend the city! Who will come? Who is with me?" Nobody paid any attention, even though, now that his father and brother were dead, he was technically the king. His was a ridiculous voice from another age of the world, an age of confidence, courage, and honor. In this new dark age, the age that had begun one day earlier, it was every man for himself, yes, and every woman for herself as well. The new king on his horse might as well have been a phantom, or a statue made of stone. The citizenry swarmed around him and ignored him. He was not a hero returning from the war. He was just a beaten fool.

Tirumala Raya changed his plan. "We must go at once to the treasury," he said, "and we must collect all the gold we can. Then we must go south to Srirangapatna. That is my family's kingdom and the sultans will not dare to follow us there, so far from their own lands. We will be welcome there, and safe, and with the gold we will not be dependent on anyone, and we can rebuild an army, and begin to save the empire from these foes."

"Your Majesty," Thimma replied, "excuse us for saying this, but no."

"Our place is here," Ulupi said. "We will stand at the city gates and face the enemy and strike terror into his black heart."

"But the enemy is perhaps half a million strong," Tirumala Raya cried, "and heavily armed, and made bold by victory. And you are only two dozen. They will kill you immediately and you will have achieved nothing except your own deaths."

"Five hundred thousand of them against twenty-five or so of us," Ulupi said thoughtfully. "That sounds reasonable. Thimma, what do you say?"

"Very fair," Thimma replied. "I like those odds very well."

The young king was silent for a moment. Then he said, "You're absolutely right. The bastards have no chance. I will stay as well."

"And the treasury?" Ulupi asked.

"To hell with the treasury," Tirumala Raya replied. "Let's go to the gates."

On the third day after Talikota the army of the alliance reached the gates of Bisnaga. Pampa Kampana stood in Madhava Acharya's cell hugging the *Garuda Purana* to her chest like a shield. The noise of the descending marauders was like the baying of a thousand wolves, and the sounds of the despairing people of the city like the death-shrieks of helpless sheep. She heard voices crying out in disbelief, because the seven walls had collapsed, had crumbled away like dust, as if their magic could not survive the city's despair, as if their foundation had been its confidence and hope, and when those vanished, the illusion could not be maintained. After the dissolution of the walls the thunder of the assault filled the sky. Lost somewhere in the grand cacophony of death was the last stand of the two dozen, who fought their last fight, led by the last king, until the arrival of the angel of the end, Death himself, known in the ancient tales as *the Destroyer of Delights and the Severer of Societies, the Desolator of Dwelling Places and the Garnerer of Graveyards.* Death. The streets ran with blood and the air was full of vultures and the treasury was looted and everything that could be taken was taken, including human life. And there were flames, eating at the buildings of bricks and wood, until only their stone foundations remained. For what felt like forever, but might have been six months or six hours, or six days, there was the sound of smashing: the destruction of palaces and statues and all that had been beautiful. The giant statues of Lord Hanuman and of the goddess Pampa were broken into so many pieces that afterward it was impossible to believe that such statues had ever existed. The bazaar burned; the "foreigner's house" burned; almost all that had been the capital city of the empire of Bisnaga was reduced to rubble, blood, and ash. Even the oldest temple, the so-called Underground Temple because it had emerged fully formed from beneath the earth on the day of the scattering of the seeds when Bisnaga was born, was burned and utterly destroyed. The monkeys who lived there ran for their lives from the flames.

So the story of Bisnaga ended as it began: with a severed head and a fire.

A few things were spared. Some temples, and parts of the Mandana *mutt* remained standing, with only partial damage, and many of the *mutt*'s monks survived, except those who ran into the streets to help the dying and mourn the dead. The head of the *mutt*, young Ramanuja Acharya, was one of these, his body hidden in a mountain of the dead; and after the burning of the city, the bodies burned in the streets, and all of what had been Bisnaga became a funeral pyre. And vultures came down from the air, to finish off what remained.

Pampa Kampana survived. On one of the last pages of her book she wrote: "Nothing endures, but nothing is meaningless either. We rise, we fall, we rise again, and again we fall. We go on. I too have succeeded and I have also failed. Death is close now. In death do triumph and failure humbly meet. We learn far less from victory than from defeat."

The day came when the forces of the alliance departed, having done their work, and silence descended on the ruined city like a shroud. In the Mandana *mutt* Pampa Kampana wrote the last of all her pages. She went to the corner of her room and found the pot she had made to receive her work, and placed the manuscript inside. We must assume she had a helper after that, a surviving monk perhaps, but we cannot know for certain. We know only that she left the *mutt* and made her way to the rubble of the statue of Pampa with the sealed pot (who helped her seal it?) and a shovel (or shovels) to dig with. Then she, or her unknown helper, found a piece of earth that was not covered in broken stones. And she, or he, or they both began to dig.

When she had buried the *Jayaparajaya* she sat down, cross-legged, and called out, "I have finished telling it. Release me." Then she waited.

We know this because she wrote down what she was going to do on the final pages of her book. We may allow ourselves to imagine that her wish was granted, that the centuries swept over her at long last, her flesh withered and her bones crumbled, and after a few moments there were only her simple clothes on the ground, filled with dust, and a breeze sprang up and blew the dust away. Or we may believe, more fancifully, that the magical *yalis* of her dreams appeared and led her through the celestial gates into the Eternal Fields, where she was no longer blind, and eternity was not a curse.

She was two hundred and forty-seven years old. These were her last words.

I, Pampa Kampana, am the author of this book.
I have lived to see an empire rise and fall.
How are they remembered now, these kings, these queens?
They exist now only in words.

While they lived, they were victors, or vanquished, or both.
Now they are neither.
Words are the only victors.
What they did, or thought, or felt, no longer exists.
Only these words describing those things remain.
They will be remembered in the way I have chosen to remember them.
Their deeds will only be known in the way they have been set down.
They will mean what I wish them to mean.
I myself am nothing now. All that remains is this city of words.
Words are the only victors.

ACKNOWLEDGMENTS

These are some of the books I read before and during the writing of this novel. In addition there were many scholarly (and newspaper) articles, essays, and websites I consulted, which are too numerous to mention. My gratitude to them all. They were immensely helpful. Any faults in the text of the novel are my own.

Vijayanagar—City and Empire: New Currents of Research, Vol. I—Texts and *Vol. 2—Reference and Documentation,* edited by Anna Libera Dallapiccola in collaboration with Stephanie Zingel-Ave Lallemant

A Social History of the Deccan, 1300–1761, by Richard M. Eaton

India in the Persianate Age, 1000–1765, by Richard M. Eaton

Beyond Turk and Hindu, edited by David Gilmartin and Bruce B. Lawrence

The Travels of Ibn Battuta

From Indus to Independence—A Trek Through Indian History: Vol. VII, Named for Victory: The Vijayanagar Empire, by Dr. Sanu Kainikara

Toward a New Formation: South Indian Society Under Vijayanagar Rule, by Noboru Karashima

India: A Wounded Civilization, by V. S. Naipaul

A History of South India: From Prehistoric Times to the Fall of Vijayanagar, by Sastri K. A. Nilakanta and R. C. Champakalakshmi

Court Life Under the Vijayanagar Rulers, by Madhao P. Patil

Raya: Krishnadevaraya of Vijayanagara, by Srinivas Reddy

City of Victory, by Ratnakar Sadasyula

Hampi, by Subhadra Sen Gupta, with photographs by Clare Arni

A Forgotten Empire, by Robert Sewell, which also contains his translations of *The Narrative of Domingo Paes,* written c.1520–22, and *The Chronicle of Fernão Nuniz,* written c.1535–37

ABOUT THE AUTHOR

SALMAN RUSHDIE is the author of fourteen previous novels: *Grimus, Midnight's Children* (which was awarded the Booker Prize in 1981), *Shame, The Satanic Verses, Haroun and the Sea of Stories, The Moor's Last Sigh, The Ground Beneath Her Feet, Fury, Shalimar the Clown, The Enchantress of Florence, Luka and the Fire of Life, Two Years Eight Months and Twenty-Eight Nights, The Golden House,* and, most recently, *Quichotte,* which was shortlisted for the Booker Prize in 2019.

Rushdie is also the author of a book of stories, *East, West,* and five works of nonfiction: *Joseph Anton: A Memoir, Imaginary Homelands, The Jaguar Smile, Step Across This Line,* and *Languages of Truth.* He is the co-editor of *Mirrorwork,* an anthology of contemporary Indian writing, and of the 2008 *Best American Short Stories* anthology.

A fellow of the British Royal Society of Literature, Salman Rushdie has received, among other honors, the Whitbread Prize for Best Novel (twice), the Writers' Guild Award, the James Tait Black Prize, the European Union's Aristeion Prize for Literature, Author of the Year prizes in both Britain and Germany, the French Prix du Meilleur Livre Étranger, the Budapest Grand Prize for Literature, the Premio Grinzane Cavour in Italy, the Crossword Book Award in India, the Austrian State Prize for European Literature, the London International Writers' Award, the James Joyce Award of University College Dublin, the St. Louis Literary Prize, the Carl Sandburg Prize of the Chicago Public Library, and a U.S. National Arts Award. He holds honorary doctorates and fellowships at six European and six American universities, and is an Honorary Professor in the Humanities at MIT and University Distinguished Professor at Emory University. Currently, Rushdie is a Distinguished Writer in Residence at New York University.

He has received the Freedom of the City in Mexico City, Strasbourg, and El Paso, and the Edgerton Prize of the American Civil Liberties Union. He holds the rank of Commandeur in the Ordre des Arts et des Lettres—France's highest artistic honor. Between 2004 and 2006 he served as President of PEN American Center and for ten years served as the Chairman of the PEN World Voices International Literary Festival, which he helped to create. In June 2007 he received a knighthood in the Queen's Birthday Honors. In 2022 he was admitted to the prestigious Order of the Companions of Honor. In 2008 he became a member of the American Academy of Arts and Letters and was named a Library Lion of the New York Public Library. In addition, *Midnight's Children* was named the Best of the Booker—the best winner in the award's forty-year history—by a public vote. His books have been translated into over forty languages.

Midnight's Children has been adapted for the stage. It has been performed in London, Ann Arbor, and New York by the Royal Shakespeare Company. In 2004, an opera based upon *Haroun and the Sea of Stories* was premiered by the New York City Opera at Lincoln Center. In 2016, an opera based on *Shalimar the Clown* was premiered by the Opera Theatre of Saint Louis.

A film of *Midnight's Children*, directed by Deepa Mehta, was released in 2012.

The Ground Beneath Her Feet, in which the Orpheus myth winds through a story set in the world of rock music, was turned into a song by U2 with lyrics by Salman Rushdie.

salmanrushdie.com
Facebook.com/salmanrushdieauthor
Twitter: @SalmanRushdie

ABOUT THE TYPE

This book was set in Baskerville, a typeface designed by John Baskerville (1706–75), an amateur printer and typefounder, and cut for him by John Handy in 1750. The type became popular again when the Lanston Monotype Corporation of London revived the classic roman face in 1923. The Mergenthaler Linotype Company in England and the United States cut a version of Baskerville in 1931, making it one of the most widely used typefaces today.